I0745843

PREMEDITATED

REDEMPTION, BOOK IV

GIACOMO GIAMMATTEO

INFERNO PUBLISHING COMPANY

"© Copyright **2017** Giacomo Giammatteo

All rights reserved. No part of this book may be reproduced or transmitted in any form or by any means, electronic or mechanical, including photocopying, recording or by any information storage and retrieval system, without written permission from the author, except for the inclusion of brief quotations in a review.

This ebook is licensed for your personal enjoyment only. This ebook may not be re-sold or given away to other people. If you would like to share this book with another person, please purchase an additional copy for each reader. If you're reading this book and did not purchase it, or it was not purchased for your use only, then please return to

INFERNO PUBLISHING COMPANY, Houston, Texas.

For more information about this book, visit the website.

Cover design by Natasha Brown

Book design by Giacomo Giammatteo

This edition was prepared by Giacomo Giammatteo gg@giacomog.com

Print ISBN 978-1-940313-34-4

Electronic ISBN 978-1-940313-33-7

This book is a work of fiction. Names, characters, places, and events herein are either the product of the author's imagination or are used fictitiously. Any resemblance to actual persons, living or dead, is entirely coincidental."

ISBN: 978-1-940313-33-7

❀ Created with Vellum

CONTENTS

NOTE TO READERS

The first chapter was written in "neutral" first-person point of view (POV). I did this because, at this point in the story, we don't know who is speaking—by design.

The remainder of the story is written the way I always write, with Gino, the detective, in first-person POV—represented by the badge symbol at the beginning of the chapters—and the rest of the characters written in third-person POV—represented by the gun. (Whether they are good or bad)

Thanks for understanding,

Giacomo

Note: As always, the story is told in first- and third-person POV. A detective's shield image indicates that scene is being told from Gino's POV, in the first person. A gun image at the beginning indicates any and all others in third person.

Also to note, I started doing my own eBook formatting, which has allowed me to insert images, which I've selectively done. Let me know if you do, or don't, like that. I think it looks good, but that's just me.

PREFACE

The difference between love and hate is familiarity.

Gino Cataldi

INTRODUCTION

What happens after twenty-five years of marriage, when one spouse grows tired of the other? The easiest way out is divorce; another option is *murder*.

After being married for twenty-five years, I realized that I no longer wanted to be married. *What should I do?*

The simple answer was file for divorce, but life was seldom that simple, and mine certainly wasn't. There was the house to consider, two cars, the jewelry—and the safe deposit box. I considered the options and decided that murder was the best solution—not the easiest, but the best—and I knew *just* how to do it.

INTERNET CAFÉ

June 10, 2016, San Mateo, CA

I woke a little earlier than usual, perhaps due to the heat wave we'd been having, or perhaps because during the night I had decided to commit murder. The more I thought about, it the more convinced I was that thinking of murder was the real reason, so I had better do something about it. Besides, I was awake now, and I never have been the type who could go back to sleep once awakened.

I got up and dressed, ate and started the engine to the car. It was going to be a long drive for coffee this morning—thirty miles—and it was in a section of the city that did not embrace strangers. Not that this place had such good coffee, but they had internet access that was "invisible," guaranteed to be non-traceable according to the whispers I'd heard. I don't know how they guaranteed that, but I needed it.

I headed down to Highway 101 and took it north toward the magnificent city of San Francisco, fighting traffic as I passed the airport and even more traffic as I looked at poor old Candlestick Park, now abandoned like an early spouse. I cringed as I thought that; why had that particular thought come to mind today of all days.

Cursing the long trip, I realized I could have gone anywhere with WI-FI access and been fairly safe from prying eyes, but it would have been a hit-or-miss type of operation and I couldn't be certain of the information I'd get. I needed this to be right the first time—no second chances in this type of work.

From what I'd been told this place guaranteed not only the anonymity but the quality of the information. It was worth venturing into the seedy underbelly of San Francisco if it got me what I wanted.

When I got to where I needed to be, I parked and locked the car, but I knew that if someone wanted that car it wouldn't be there when I got back. Keeping eyes alert, I half-walked, half-jogged, across the street and around the corner, stepping onto the sidewalk near the middle of the block. A short trip to the corner and an abrupt right turn had me next to the Morning Sun Coffee Shop.

I looked at my notes before entering the café, making sure to do things in the proper order. Any messing up, and I'd get nothing, or so I'd been told. Placing the note in the palm of my hand, I went to the counter and asked for a double-grande, private-buzz coffee, no cream or sugar.

The man in the booth nodded. "That's our most expensive coffee, you know."

"I understand," I said, and reached for my money. "By the way, do you know anything about the movie *Double Indemnity?*"

The guy looked at me as he made the coffee. "Can't say that I do. Why don't you tell me about it."

My body twitched, and a shiver tingled the tops of my shoulders. "It's about a woman who kills her husband for the insurance money. I believe it stars Barbara Stanwyck and Fred MacMurray."

A creepy smile appeared on his face. "Oh yeah, I know the one you mean now." He handed me my coffee, punched in what looked to be far too many numbers on the cash register, then gave me the receipt and a small key—the kind that looked as if it might open a pirate's chest of gold.

"That's $4.65 for the coffee, and $50 for the use of the computer. You're number eighteen." He nodded toward the rear, where a sheer curtain and some hanging beads separated the room. It looked like a leftover from a movie set they used in the sixties. "If you like old movies, you should try this site," he said, and scribbled what appeared to be gibberish on a piece of paper.

"Type these letters and numbers into the browser *exactly* as you see them, then hit the space bar. That will trigger an expansion into an encrypted web address that will take you to where you want to go. But be warned, it only works once, and in ten minutes, it will no longer work, so be quick and be accurate."

I nodded, then I gave him sixty dollars, told him to keep the change, and headed toward the back of the room. There was no danger of spilling the coffee; it was barely half full.

Number eighteen was near the back. The booth boasted a red vinyl cover with white fluff peeking out from a few tears in the back. The corresponding booth was similar, and a table covered in light-brown laminate sat between them. It looked as if it had come out of a 1950s diner, but that was okay; I liked diners and always had.

An episode of *Happy Days* came to mind, and at any moment I expected to see the Fonz or Richie Cunningham sit at the booth next to me. I set the coffee to the left side and inserted the key the man at the counter had given me into a slot in the wall. A laptop slid out like meals do on those sci-fi shows set in space. I stared for a moment. *This* was not Richie Cunningham's diner.

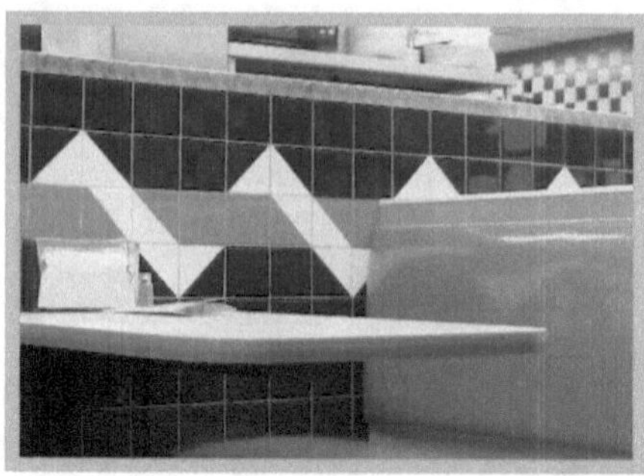

Diner booth

The laptop opened like any other. I don't know what I expected, but whatever wild thoughts had been lurking in my imagination were disappointed. I navigated to the site as directed and browsed through a listing of old movies from the thirties to present. The instructions had said to go to the *Double Indemnity* link and click, and then enter the password, which was the receipt number from my coffee purchase. I hesitated but finally got the nerve.

It loaded lightning-fast—even before I finished my sip of coffee. Something in my gut produced a shiver that raced through my body. I turned my head quickly—unobserved, I hoped—to see if anyone was watching.

Was anyone listening?

I stood and peeked above the booths, but all I got were antagonistic looks from others, who, like myself, were secreted into their own booths tucked into dark corners behind a wall of sheer curtains. *Paranoia.* I had heard the word used, and knew its meaning, but I had never experienced it before this morning.

Satisfied that Russia, Red China, or other countries with advanced technology weren't watching me, I continued, pulling the laptop closer to shield it from prying eyes. *Cameras!* The thought struck me like cold water on my face in the morning. I looked behind me, up, around, then checked the back of the booth.

Calm down. Truly, this *was* paranoia.

The site I navigated to sat before me waiting to be entered. It didn't flash red or have gates with pointed spears. No warnings or contracts I had to agree with. Just a black screen with a green button. I wanted it to frighten me, perhaps a warning that said "Abandon all hope, ye who enter here." Something. *Anything.*

But it was just a green button. At that point I almost gave up. Quit, and said the hell with it. But then I thought of the suffering for more than twenty long years...and I hit the return key.

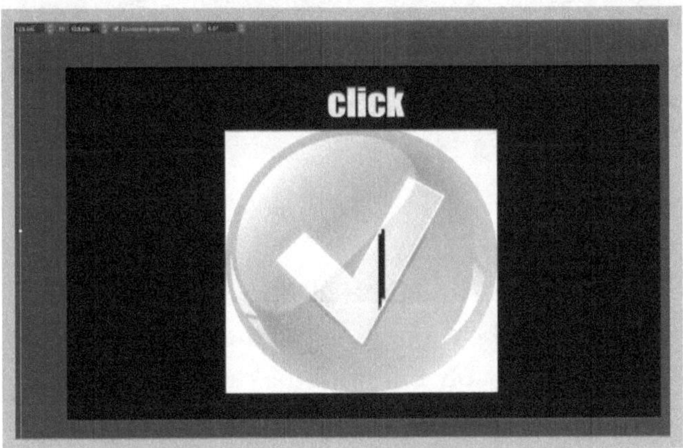

Blank screen

I closed my eyes for a second, but opened them again quickly in case I missed an instruction. It took an eternity for the site to load. At least it seemed as if it did. It couldn't have taken too long, because I held my breath the entire time, and I can't hold my breath for long.

I wrapped my arms around the computer and stared at the screen. The shiver that raced through my body earlier returned with a vengeance. It was now a gong pounding in my head. This was warning enough. The words jumped off the page and, though there was no sound, I felt certain everyone in the place knew what I was doing and could see the information I sought.

Welcome, Killer

Welcome Killer screenshot

Breath left me. I sat erect and inhaled. *There, it's done.* How it was done I don't know, but just the act of going to that site did it. I had no more worries. Not now. Probably not until the time came to do it. I plugged in my little USB flash drive and prepared to download material. To do this right would take a lot of planning and that required hard copies. When I was done with the research, I pushed the laptop back into the wall. It clicked into place, and then I dropped the key into a slot in the wall beside it.

I'm sure I looked as guilty as I felt when I left that place, but that is probably normal after you make plans to kill the person you've loved for more than twenty years.

A QUIET LUNCH

Susan parked the car, got the groceries from the back seat and headed into the house, careful when stepping into the marble entrance hall so she wouldn't slip. "Kev! I could use a hand with groceries."

Kevin pushed the *mute* button on the TV remote and got up. "There was a time when you could handle the groceries yourself."

"Yeah, and there was a time when your butt didn't sag to the back of your knees," she said, and set the bags on the kitchen table while catching her breath.

"Now get your ass out there and get the rest of the bags." Susan looked at the TV. "And what the hell is ESPN playing for? You don't watch sports."

"I thought I'd better catch up on the games, since we're going to Winston's party. You know Winston and his buddies talk about sports —and nothing else, I might add."

Susan shrugged. "Then I guess you better learn the lingo."

A minute later, she met Kevin at the door, took a handful of groceries from him while he went and got more, then she made her way to the kitchen and the bags on the island. As she put the milk and cheese away, Kevin came back in, arms full, and set the rest of the bags down.

"There were a few more bags in the front seat," Kevin said. "You must have forgotten about them. Old age does that to people."

Susan laughed and swung a cucumber at him. "Be careful. This amazing vegetable can function as a weapon or a sex toy. If I choose the latter, it means I no longer need you."

"That'll be the day," Kevin said. "By the way, where have you been all morning?"

"I had to do some grocery shopping—as you see—then pick up a few things at the hardware store." She grabbed the cheese from his hand—which he had obviously taken out of the fridge—and put it in the cheese drawer. "Speaking of which, I stopped home between trips, but your car was gone. Where were you?"

"Me? Just the normal errands. Nothing really."

"*Nothing* took you this long?" More than a little suspicion tainted her voice, and when she glanced over she thought she saw an embarrassed look on his face.

"I did stop by the bookstore to pick up some reading material."

Susan nodded, finished putting the groceries away, and watched as her dear spouse walked down the hall toward the bedroom.

Things were in motion. All that needed to be decided was where to do it.

Kevin slipped into his favorite pair of jeans and pulled a red shirt over his head, then tied the laces on his Nikes.

He stood, adjusting his clothes, when Susan walked in, fixing her earring. "You better hurry," she said. "We're supposed to be there at 4:00."

"Stop worrying. We've got plenty of time. Now do something worthwhile, like tell me how I look."

She never turned her head, but said, "Like you just threw a couple of touchdowns, or hit homers, or something. She bent to get a pair of nylons from one of the lower drawers on her dresser."

Kevin laughed. "Keep bending over in front of me, and maybe I will score a few goals."

She quickly straightened. "And maybe you won't."

As she went down the stairs, she called back. "I'll be in the car so don't be long."

"Be right there," Kevin said.

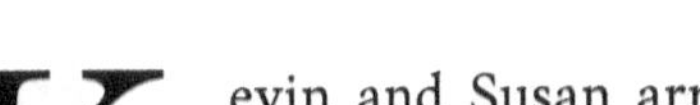

Kevin and Susan arrived at the Mulbert's house right on time, but from the number of cars parked in the driveway, and curbside, it looked as if they were an hour late. Susan rang the doorbell, leaning on her right leg to help support the deep-dish casserole she had slaved over earlier. Kevin stood behind her, holding a death grip on two bottles of a rare Pinot noir that a friend had located for him. The wine was bound to be a hit with this crowd. Winston Mulbert was a snob if nothing else, and not much got him more excited than a bottle of good wine or good Scotch.

Winston answered the door, Scotch glass in hand, and evidence of his imbibing on his breath. "Kevin, Susan. About time you got here."

Kevin glanced at his watch and said, "Weren't we supposed to be here at 4:00?"

Winston took a long swig, slapped Kevin on the shoulder, and said,

"Technically, yes, but nobody arrives on time. They're either early or late. Someday you'll learn that, buddy."

Susan laughed, and Kevin handed the bottles to Winston. "Here, take these before I drop them. They're you're responsibility now, *buddy*. And happy Giants' Day or whatever the hell it is."

Winston took the bottles, called for his maid to get them, then looked at Kevin and whispered. "I know you're not a big fan, Kevin, but the Giants aren't playing today."

"Oh well," Kevin said. "You can't blame a guy for trying."

"I *could*," Winston said. "And some folks in here *would*, but I won't. The way I see it is it's your prerogative. If you don't want to join the rest of the world, that's your issue."

"I'm glad you see it that way, because I don't want to join the huddled masses that stand around the coffee table or the water cooler on Monday and rehash the events of the weekend; there's always work to do."

Winston slapped him on the back and took another swig of his drink. "Come on in, you dinosaur. Glad you could make it. Now, give me a good stock tip and we'll call your visit worthwhile."

"You're an ass," Kevin said, then walked ahead to chat with a few others.

Winston waited for Susan, whispering in her ear when she got next to him. "All set for tonight," he said. "Are you ready?"

She smiled. "Ready as I'll ever be."

The party went on for several hours, then dinner was served—prime rib with baby carrots and garlic mashed potatoes.

It was standard fare for one of Winston's parties, nonetheless—it was excellent. After dinner, they tasted some wine that had been brought by Kathy—the next-door neighbor—then Winston's wife Simone served up more wine. Afterward, she rang a dinner bell. Everyone fell silent.

"And now a special toast," Winston said. He held up one of the bottles of the wine that Kevin had brought, and said, "To the man who doesn't know a damn thing about sports, but who does his best to pretend he does. Happy birthday!"

Winston surprised Kevin with that. Kevin didn't think that Winston even knew. He turned to Susan, who was smiling and leaned to whisper. "You damn sneak."

Susan smiled and said, "Enjoy the party. I'll give you my present tonight."

Kevin grinned like a kid on Christmas morning. "I'll be eagerly waiting."

He suffered through a few more hours of non-stop talking—about nothing—then he and Susan said goodnight.

"Have to give the birthday boy his present," she said, offering the excuse for leaving early.

Everyone laughed, wished Kevin a happy birthday again and said goodbye.

They pulled into the driveway, went into the house, then up to the bedroom. As they undressed, Susan said, "We should go to the summer house for a while."

"It's too damn hot this time of year."

"That's why it's called a summer house," Susan said.

"It's called a summer house so you can go *there* when it's winter *here*, and you can enjoy it. It's not to go to in the summer and be tortured by the heat and humidity."

Susan chuckled. "Shut-up and take your clothes off or risk losing your present."

Kevin kicked his pants to the corner. "On second thought, Houston is fine by me."

"Good," Susan said, "Besides, if I get too hot there's always skinny-dipping."

"I don't intend to miss that," Kevin said, "So I guess we're going to Houston." He laughed and pulled her onto the bed.

~

Ray Challock tried to ignore the continual buzzing from his computer, but it was annoying as hell—like an oven timer that wouldn't stop.

"Turn that goddamn noise off," Sean hollered from across the room. "It's loud enough to wake the dead."

"Which is exactly what you're going to be if you don't shut-up," Ray said.

"What's it for, anyway?" Melinda asked.

"I've got it set to trigger the alarm if anyone accesses a particular website," Ray said, while quickly typing on the keyboard. "And it looks as if someone just did."

Sean got out of his seat and walked over. He stood next to Ray. "Which website?"

"A site that provides information on how to commit murder. It used to get a lot of hits, but I think they were mostly curiosity seekers. Now it's down to only a few visitors, but the ones that go there seem legit."

"No shit?" Melinda asked, now joining the group.

Ray nodded, but he didn't turn around to look at her. "We caught two guys last year near Chicago and three already this year—one in Los Angeles, one in Portland, and one in Miami. Every one of them had plans to kill someone. In the Miami case we didn't get him in time. He did the deed."

"So what do we do now?" Melinda asked.

"We'll have San Francisco PD pull surveillance tapes from nearby. I know there's an ATM across the street. If we're lucky, we'll get a hit on someone."

"Not our worry anyway, is it?" Ray asked.

Sean stopped what he was doing and looked at Ray as if he were summing him up. "Somebody wants to kill someone, and we *might* be able to prevent it. So, to answer your question—no—it's not a Homeland Security issue, but it's sure as hell humane to try to do something. Where's your fucking heart?"

Sean turned to walk away. "It's in the same place it was the last time I checked—the upper-left side of the chest."

Ray shook his head. "You're a first-class dick," he said, then picked up the phone to dial SFPD.

"Who are you going to alert?" Melinda asked.

"Homicide," he said. "It hasn't happened yet, but if we don't stop this, someone is going to die. It'll be a homicide then."

❧

Detective Don Flaherty listened as Ray told him what he had. "You mean this is a site for getting information on how to kill someone?"

"You got it," Ray said. "And don't act surprised. There are sites for damn near everything if you know where to look. We've got one we're monitoring that instructs people on how to build bombs."

"Son of a bitch," Flaherty said. "Okay, we'll check it out. Give me the address again."

After much work—meaning long hours of scrutinizing video from ATMs and other surveillance, Flaherty narrowed it down to a few people based on the plates he was able to get. The best video came from the ATM across the street. Flaherty grabbed the files from the desk he was working on, stepped into his office, then picked up the phone and called the Houston Police Department (HPD).

A CALL FROM LEFT FIELD

Captain Gladys Cooper relaxed in her overstuffed recliner while she finished the last of her morning tea. She seldom performed many tasks before drinking her tea, and today was no exception.

Her eyes were closed, thinking of all she had to do, when the intercom sounded. Cindy's voice seemed to be a scream.

"A Detective Don Flaherty on the line for you, Captain. He's from the San Francisco Homicide Department."

SFPD? I wonder what the hell he wants? Tired as she was, Coop got out of the chair and reached for the phone. Curiosity made her.

"Cooper," she said.

"Captain Cooper, my name is Detective Don Flaherty. I'm with the Homicide Department of the San Francisco Police Department."

"Go on."

"This is a strange call, I know, and I'm sure you're wondering why I'm calling, so I'll try to be brief."

Cindy poked her head in the office, and Coop signaled her to bring more tea, by fake sipping from her empty cup.

"We received a call from Homeland Security. They had been monitoring a certain café in a seedy part of the Tenderloin District. This café is apparently a known spot for those who want to access the darker side of the Internet and to do it anonymously. Anyway, to make a long story short, *someone* accessed a site that HS had an alert on. It's a site on how to commit murder. We pulled surveillance from the surrounding area, and we've managed to narrow the suspects to a few people. One of them is a married couple who recently left on a flight bound for Houston."

Coop took a few breaths. "So you're saying that a married couple is coming to my city, and that one of them is planning to kill the other? Which one wants to do the killing? And what are their names?"

"Names are the easy part," Flaherty said. "Kevin and Susan Hemphill. The 'which one' is the difficult part. We don't know who used the computer. All we have is a license plate which *might*, and I say *might*, identify them as the suspects."

"And why do you say *might?*"

"Because all we could get were partial plates, but we got enough of the plate so that when it was combined with the make and model we were able to narrow the list down to just a few cars. We're checking out the local ones, but the Hemphills are on their way to Houston, hence the call."

Coop tried to digest all that Flaherty was saying. "Okay, Detective. Thanks for the warning. I'll put a pair of my detectives on this right away." Coop reached for the button to disconnect, then said, "Anything else you can tell me?"

"Not much. They're rich, that's about all I know. You should see the place where they live."

"Okay. Thanks."

After hanging up, Coop thought for a moment, then called Cindy. "Get Gino and Ribs down here. And tell them it's a priority."

Ten minutes later, Gino and Ribs walked into the office. "What's up, Captain?"

Coop gave Gino and Ribs the names, and explained the situation to them. "I got a call from SFPD. It seems like somebody went to a café that Homeland Security has under surveillance and they accessed a website that HS also has under surveillance, then—"

"Do they have *everything* under surveillance?" Ribs asked. "Do they know Gino watches porn?"

Gino shook his head. "You're getting as bad as Tip." Then he spun around to Coop and said, "Ignore him, and tell us about the site."

Coop filled them in on the rest of what Flaharty had told her, then said, "They should arrive at Bush in about forty-five minutes." Coop slid the glasses off the bridge of her nose and eyeballed them. "You know what this means?" She twisted her wrist and looked at her watch. "It means you're going to be late if you don't get your asses to the airport now. Head over there and find out what these people have on their minds. And make sure to tell them that we don't tolerate that shit in Texas. Make it damn clear."

"Yes, ma'am," Ribs said, then he grabbed Gino's elbow and steered him toward the door. "Let's go, cuz. We need to drive Tip-Denton speed if we hope to get there on time."

"Don't start on me," Gino said. "I vowed never to ride with that maniac again."

I sat in the seat next to Ribs. Assuming we had all of the information, the Hemphills would be landing and de-planing any minute. I grinned and looked at Ribs. "Let's make sure to give them a proper Texas greeting."

We sat for a few minutes before the announced arrival of UA 1589, from San Francisco, sounded over the loudspeaker. "That's the one we want," Ribs said.

I recognized who I thought were surely the Hemphills immediately. They were the second ones out of the chute. It was no surprise. The detective from California had said they were rich, so first-class seating would be standard.

The man walked far ahead of the woman, and it made me wonder if I had been correct in the assumption of who they were. He was wearing a pair of brown shorts with a light-green top, and he had a pair of sunglasses on.

I waited for him to step from the ramp, then introduced myself and Ribs. "I'm Detective Gino Cataldi, and this is my partner, Detective Hector Delgado. Are you Kevin Hemphill?"

He furrowed his brow, looking confused, then said, "I'm Kevin. What's this about?"

"We're looking for Mrs. Hemphill. Is she with you?"

"I don't know that my wife's whereabouts is any of your business. Perhaps if you tell me why you're asking—"

"Kev, wait up."

I looked behind Hemphill to a woman hurrying to catch up. "Is she your wife?"

"Again, not that it's any of your business, but yes."

Mrs. Hemphill was wheeling a small carry-on behind her. She stopped beside her husband, then stared at me and Ribs. "Do you want to tell me what's going on?"

"We'd like you to follow us down to the station and answer a few questions."

"What? You're nuts," Mr. Hemphill said.

I realized I'd said "follow us" so I corrected the statement. "I didn't mean *follow us*," I said. "I understand you don't have a vehicle here. If you want, I'll arrange to drive you wherever you're going afterward."

"You're still nuts," Mr. Hemphill said. "Suppose I said we were going to Florida. Would you arrange to have us driven there?"

Ribs stepped between us. "I think you know we wouldn't, sir."

"And I think you know we're not coming with you," he said. "We don't *have to,* you know. I understand my rights."

"You're right," I said. "You *don't* have to. It was simply a request."

Mrs. Hemphill placed her hand on her husband's arm, as if to calm him, like he required that from time to time. It made me wonder if he often needed calming.

"And what kind of questions did you have, Detective? Perhaps we can answer them here."

I looked at Ribs, but he was shaking his head. "Maybe another time," I said.

As we started to walk away, she said, "What are the questions, Detective? I'm curious."

I thought that maybe we could use her curiosity to an advantage. "We had a call from San Francisco, ma'am. It seems as if they were worried that one of you might want to harm the other."

"Don't be ridiculous," Mr. Hemphill said. Then he grabbed hold of his wife's arm, just above the elbow. "Let's go, Susan. I'm through with them."

She shook off his grip. "No, it's fine, Kev. Let's do it. It may help the detectives." She turned to face me. "We'll ride with you, Detective. Presuming that's all right?"

"Fine, ma'am. It won't take long."

INTERROGATION

*I*t didn't take us long to get back to the station. Ribs wasn't kidding when he said Tip-Denton speed. I don't think the odometer dropped below eighty once he hit the freeway.

HPD Headquarters

"You want some coffee or tea, or anything else?" I asked as we walked toward the interview room.

"Yes, a martini," Mr. Hemphill said. "I believe that would fall into the *anything else* category."

I wanted to smack him in the mouth, but I chuckled instead. "You're a riot, Mr. Hemphill. If I could get you a martini, I would."

I took a few steps toward the end of the hall, then said, "We're going to use separate rooms, if you don't mind. It will make it less confusing." I pointed to the door on the left. "Mr. Hemphill, in here please, if you don't object?"

Ribs took Mrs. Hemphill to the interview room on the right.

Mr. Hemphill settled into the seat at the end of the table, and I handed him a bottle of water, which was the compromise we agreed on since a martini was not included in the offer.

"So what do you want to know?" he said.

I sat in the chair next to him. "What are you in Houston for?"

"If you mean why did we choose such an inhospitable place, you'll have to ask my wife." His tone was full of sarcasm, bordering on bitterness.

"All kidding aside, why? As you've already mentioned, this is not the ideal place to visit in the summer—the heat makes it *inhospitable* as hell."

"An understatement, Detective, but the short answer is that we have a vacation home on the lake."

"Which lake?" I asked.

"Conroe. In Bentwater."

I whistled. "Nice place. You play golf?"

"Not really. I've got a set of clubs, but they haven't seen much use. I usually only venture out with clients."

"If you don't golf, why Bentwater?"

"My wife wanted someplace safe and secure, a place where she could have solitude to write. She's a mystery writer."

I perked up. "A mystery writer?"

"Sheila Wingate is her pseudonym. Ever hear of her?"

"Sheila Wingate? You're shitting me? I've read a few of her books. They were great."

Hemphill seemed to loosen up. "Yes, she is quite good. I'm proud of her."

"So what brought you to Houston now? Is she in the middle of writing something?"

Hemphill shrugged. "I'd like to say I knew definitively, but I don't. She's forever working on *something,* but unfortunately, I don't know what it is. She's a prolific writer."

"So what do you do while she's writing?" I asked. "It must be boring."

"Not really," Hemphill said. "Once in a blue moon, I play golf, as I said. I go to the Galleria to shop. I drive around. I work. And if all else fails, I go sailing. It makes it a natural choice with the lake right there."

"What kind of work do you do?"

"I'm a consultant in project management. Mostly for biotech companies."

"Travel much?"

Hemphill sighed. "Yes, I do, Detective, but I'm sure you didn't bring us here to inquire about my work, that is, unless you would like a recommendation for a pancreas transplant. Assuming that *is not* the case, what else would you like to know?"

I could see the slow approach wasn't going to get me anywhere, so I went right for the jugular. "Why do you want to kill your wife?"

Hemphill almost choked on his water. "Kill my wife? Are you crazy? I love her. Not to mention that she's the one who makes all of the money."

"What kind of money does she make?" I asked.

"The green kind," he said.

"You know what I mean. If you don't want to tell me, that's fine. I can find out from IRS records."

Hemphill set his bottle of water down hard. "She makes more than a million a year, if that's close enough to satisfy you."

He brushed against the bottle of water as he sat. "And if she were dead, I'd collect a nice insurance policy, but not nice enough to cover her earnings for more than a year or so."

"Define *nice*," I said.

"Nice is about $2.5 million. That's less than two years of income. So yes, I would be fixed well if she were to die, but no, it would not be enough to warrant me *wanting* her to die."

I nodded. He was right. Unless divorce was imminent, as in a few months away, he'd be better off hanging in there. "And what about the policy on you?"

"The same," he said. "They're policies to cover grievance, not income. If I were to die, I'd hope she would be upset enough that she couldn't write for a while, a short while anyway. The insurance would cover the loss of income while that transition took place. The same goes for me."

"So you're saying that you don't *need* the money?"

"Correct. We don't need it. Both houses are paid for, plus we have a small villa outside of Sienna, in Italy. We usually go there in the winter months."

"Must be nice," I said.

Hemphill leaned forward. "It *is* nice, Detective. And it has been nice for twenty-five years. I married Susan when we were eighteen. We love each other. We have a great sex life. There isn't a reason in the world for either one of us to want to kill the other." He leaned back and slugged another drink, then looked me in the eye. "Satisfied?"

"I know about the café," I said.

"Which café? The Café de Flore on the Boulevard Saint-Germain in Paris? Or the Antico Caffé Greco on the Via dei Condotti in Rome? My wife loves to haunt both of them."

"I'm talking about the one in San Francisco."

"I have no idea what you're talking about," Hemphill said. "And I think it's time to leave. I've had enough of your company. If you want to detain us, I'll call my lawyer. It's your decision."

Mrs. Hemphill sat in the seat near the center of the table. She had her hands wrapped around a cool glass of unsweetened iced tea.

Ribs placed his coffee on the table and then sat. "Mrs. Hemphill, in light of the reports we've had from San Francisco, do you have anything to say?"

"As of yet, I have nothing to say. You haven't asked me anything. And I know nothing of *reports* from San Francisco."

"Then tell me, why did you come here?"

She laughed. "Come on, Detective. You can do better than that. We have a house here. If you were any kind of detective, you *should* have known that; therefore, I could just say we were coming here to stay for a while."

Ribs shrugged. "I guess so. Why would you be coming here to stay?"

"Again, if your detective skills were up to snuff, you'd know that I am a writer and, as such, might want privacy to write."

"Guess it makes sense," Ribs said. "You write anything I might know. I read thrillers and suspense novels."

"I've written a lot, but *Death and Deception,* and *A Poisonous Illness* were two of my better-known ones."

"*Dios mío,* they were classics," Ribs said. "I read both of them. I loved how the killer selected his victims in *Death and Deception.*"

"Did you guess?" she asked, "Or were you surprised at the end?"

"Surprised, for sure. You had me guessing about everything. They were good reads. I finished them in two nights."

Mrs. Hemphill smiled. "I'm glad to hear that, Detective. It's always nice to hear good things from people who've read my books, especially professional detectives."

"You'll have to sign a book for me before you leave," he said. Then he took another sip of water, and looked over at her. "You're a writer, so tell me—if you were going to kill your husband, how would you go about it?"

She thought a moment, then said, "First, by not telling you."

They both laughed before she continued. "Seriously, though. You'd have to have a motive, a real one. Not something stupid like you read in so many books."

"Like what?"

"Well, money is always a motive, as is jealousy. You know, one spouse cheating on another—that kind of thing."

"Should I suspect something?" Ribs asked.

Hemphill laughed again. "Don't be silly, Detective. We've been married forever. And neither one of us needs the money. I'm afraid you're fresh out of motives."

"How about the café? Why did you go there?"

Hemphill looked confused, and it appeared to be a real reaction. "Café '? I don't know what you're talking about. The last café I was in, was during a trip to Italy, and that was too long ago."

Just then a knock sounded at the door. A few seconds afterward, it opened. Gino poked his head inside. "Mr. Hemphill said he's ready to leave. Or to get his lawyer. It's our choice."

Ribs pushed his coffee cup to the side. "I'm done anyway. She can go any time she wants."

Susan Hemphill stood, shook hands with Ribs, then smiled at Gino as she left. "It was a pleasure, Detectives."

"I've got somebody waiting at the front door to drive you to the rental service or home or wherever you want to go," Ribs said.

"Susan Hemphill waved and said, "Thank you, Detectives. It was fun."

Gino waited until she was down the hall, out of earshot, before saying, "You get anything?"

Ribs shook his head. "Nothing, unless you count realizing that I like what she writes. How about you?"

"Not even that much," Gino said. "He was an ass. I found out they have multimillion-dollar insurance policies on each other, but it doesn't make much difference. She makes so much money, he's better off with her alive, and she has *no* reason to kill him."

Ribs shrugged again. "I guess we let them go and see if one of them winds up dead."

"Guess so," Gino said. "Not much else we can do."

AN IDEA IS BREWING

Susan sat in an old rocking chair on the back porch, a glass of wine in her hand.

"I don't know how you sit in that thing," Kevin said. "It hurts my ass."

"I think someone warned you of a sagging ass a long time ago."

"I hear you," he said. "And just so you know, I saw a young woman today who actually *had* a nice ass. She must have taken care of hers, unlike some people I know."

Susan put her index finger to her chin. "You know, I was thinking that what we went through today could be interesting."

"What could be interesting?"

"The premise—a husband wanting to kill his wife, but she doesn't suspect anything. It could be a great book if it were done properly."

"Or a wife wanting to kill her husband," Kevin said.

"Yes. You're right, of course. And I like that even better."

Kevin laughed while he poured more wine. "I don't know if I like the fact that you like that."

Susan seemed not to hear or at least not to not be paying attention to him. "It could make a great plot for a book," she said. "I need a new angle."

Kevin shifted his weight to the right side of the chair. "What kind of an angle?"

"Suppose we carried through with this? Did, in theory anyway, what the cops were thinking."

"What are you talking about?"

Her eyes widened, and she focused intently on her husband. "I mean, suppose we faked my murder, but I gave you the perfect alibi? Then we could see how good the detectives really are. They would be like live beta readers. They'd be doing our work for us—finding the plot holes. If it works, I could use it for the plot of my new book."

"I think they might get a little pissed off," Kevin said.

"Bullshit. Name the characters after them and mention them in the acknowledgments, and they'll be as happy as a tick on a dog, as they say in this neck of the woods."

Kevin grinned. "Get up to speed, honey. They probably haven't used that saying in fifty years, but that aside, how are we going to develop the perfect alibi?"

She took a drink, set the glass down, then chewed on her fingernail. "That might take some doing. But I'm sure you can help."

"How?"

"By helping me figure it out. What *is* a perfect alibi? It's one that is a *real* alibi."

"You've lost me," Kevin said.

"Alibi is a Latin word meaning 'elsewhere', hence, when someone asks what's your alibi, what they're really asking is where you were. Were you elsewhere? Nowadays, alibi has weakened, and it's come to mean any excuse, no matter how lame. But the original is irrefutable. If you can prove you were somewhere else when the crime was committed, then you couldn't have committed the crime."

"Sounds simple but difficult at the same time. Just how are you going to provide me with this perfect alibi, and how am I going to kill you?"

Susan picked up her glass again and sipped. "I thought for the killing we'd do something simple, like a shooting. As to the alibi, we'd have to make it good. Maybe have you in another city when the deed happens."

Kevin nodded. "All well and good, except how do I commit the crime if I'm in the other city?"

She stopped rocking and leaned forward in the chair. "Exactly! I want them to think the same way. If they're focused on trying to prove you weren't in the other city, then we'll have to make sure that you were— or, at least, that they *think* you were."

Kevin sucked his beer dry and tossed the empty can in the trash. "I'm game. Tell me how."

"Let me think on it," she said. "Nothing comes to mind yet."

shield

Ribs and I spent the remainder of the day sitting in the car while we waited on witnesses to give us clues about a junkie's death. If we weren't doing that, we were walking the streets trying to get clues. Right now, we were in the "sitting" phase.

We weren't going to put much time into the investigation—only enough to carry us over until the next *real* body came up.

"Shouldn't be long," Ribs said, leaning against the headrest. "Not at the rate we've been getting bodies."

"I hate to sound crass, but I hope it's not too long. All we've got on this case are whores and drug dealers for witnesses, and we're not getting the truth out of them."

"If they even know the truth," Ribs said. "And I doubt if they do. What they *think* is the truth, and what *is* the truth are usually different."

"Ain't that the truth?" I said, and we both laughed.

"Speaking of the truth, how did poor little Marissa fare after telling you lies about where she was?"

"She's *faring* in her room," Ribs said. "She told us she was going to a friend's house and we found out that the 'friend' was actually the corner store. Next it will be the mall."

"Don't be too hard on her," I said. "She's a good girl."

"And I intend for her to remain a good girl," Ribs said. "A nice long stay in her room will help. Or a trip to a convent."

"Don't start your nun shit on me," I said. "I never did like them."

"I know. I know. According to you, half the troubles in the world are caused by nuns and the other half by priests. That's fine if you want to believe that—in your sick, warped way—but other people don't have to agree. Some people think nuns and priests do a good job."

"Yeah, the same people who foolishly give their hard-earned money to the church each week."

"Maybe it makes them feel good?" Ribs said.

"I don't mind a heartfelt donation making people feel good, but they should donate to someone who really needs it, like the homeless and poor."

Ribs sneered. "What good would it do? The homeless will buy booze or drugs, and the poor will buy lottery tickets."

"And you call *me* cynical," I said. "Did they teach you that philanthropist philosophy in Catholic school?"

Ribs looked at his watch and said, "Let's go. I'm ready to call it a day. Besides, Marissa has been bugging Rosalee to drive her to the mall. I need to get home and put my foot down. I don't know what these kids do at the mall, but she's too young to go."

"I guess we might as well call it a day," I said. "We don't have a single lead yet anyway."

"Let the other junkies figure this one out themselves," Ribs said. "I'm hungry."

I turned the key to start the engine, revved it up, and looked to my left to see when to pull out. "I'm sure the good citizens of Houston will sleep well tonight knowing you're on the job."

"Go to hell, cuz. Let them sleep well knowing I'm at home eating nachos."

I saw an opening in the traffic and pulled into the lane. "It'll sure make me comfortable," I said. "At least I'll know you're not in my kitchen, drinking my beer."

Ribs laughed. "It wouldn't take much to get me there tonight. And I could use a beer before talking to the little demon. I can tell you one thing, she's not going to the mall."

"Leave the girl alone, Ribs. She wants to go to the goddamn mall for Christ's sake, not a drug party."

"Mall, drug party. All the same if you ask me." Ribs rested his legs on the dash. "Just get me home so I can kick her ass and get this over with."

"You got it, *cuz*. Stay tough."

He grinned. "You never call me cuz. Is that a jab?"

"It's whatever you want it to be," I said. "It doesn't matter, because you know I don't agree with you."

"That's because you'd let Marissa do anything. You're a sucker. All she has to do is smile, and you'd do anything she wants. That's okay for you, though, because you're only there once in a while. I have to live with her."

I pulled alongside his car and unlocked the doors. "Time for the taskmaster to get out," I said.

"See you tomorrow," Ribs said. "If I don't kick my daughter's ass first."

"You'd never do anything remotely like that. First, Rosalee would kill you, and second, you'd feel guilty for a month."

Ribs laughed. "Okay, you might have a point. But it's a weak one."

~

I waited for Ribs to open his car door, then headed for home. It had been a long day, and I was ready for some relaxation. While driving, I called the sheriff in Conroe and filled him in, as the Hemphill's house was on the lake in Bentwater. If anything were to happen, I wanted him to let me know about it.

As I got closer to home, I thought about dinner, which reminded me I had to stop at the grocery store.

Fifteen minutes later, I was in the fruit aisle and doing my best to select good tomatoes—a near impossible task in Houston—when I heard someone call my name.

"Detective Cataldi, what a surprise. It's been a long time."

I looked around and saw a woman who seemed familiar, but I couldn't place her.

Then she said, "Did you ever get that watch back?"

And I knew immediately—she was Number Two, the kidnapper who had gotten away..

I'm sure my cheeks reddened. I shifted my stance and set the tomato down. "I *did* get it back. *Someone* sent it to me."

She picked up a tomato and smiled. "Must have been a nice person to have done that?"

She was taunting me and we both knew it. "Yes, it must have been."

"What are they for?" she asked.

"What?" I said, then realized she was referring to the tomatoes. "Red sauce. I'm planning to make spaghetti and meatballs."

"Am I invited?" she asked.

Her question took me off guard. "I, uh…I guess so."

"You guess so? Am I, or aren't I?"

I don't know how she did this to me, but I felt as if I'd fallen. "Yes, come on over. It will be tomorrow night."

She smiled. "I'm hungry already. I'll need the address," she said.

I looked at her with my eyes squinted. "You don't know where I live?"

"How would I? I've never been to your house."

"I guess not," I said, then wrote my address on a card and handed it to her.

She placed two tomatoes in her basket and said, "Great. See you tomorrow. What time?"

I thought for a moment, wondering what time I'd be home. "Make it around 7:00," I said. "But you better call first. The number is on the card."

"Sounds good. See you then."

With that, she headed off down the aisle, and I was left watching her ass.

THE PLOT

One week later

Susan had been working on the plot ever since the night she and Kevin had discussed it, and it was finally coming to fruition.

Kevin walked out on the porch and took a seat next to her. "What's up, Suz? Getting anywhere on that plot?"

"I think I've got it worked out. Or mostly worked out." She turned in her seat to face him. "You're going to kill me. But you're not, because you won't be here."

"Whatever ideas you have will need a lot more explaining than that. I have zero idea what you're talking about."

Susan grinned and handed him a yellow notepad. "Take notes," she said. "This might get complicated."

Kevin took the notepad from her hand and picked up a pen from the table. "Go slow," he said. "You know I don't write fast."

"Okay. Here we go. Let's assume you need to go to Atlanta on a business trip. Atlanta is perfect because it is a big city, and it's far enough away that they wouldn't necessarily count on you driving back as it's about an eleven-hour drive. Besides, we'll have it arranged so that it appears as if you'd been in Atlanta the entire time."

Kevin jotted the information down:

Atlanta, business trip, need to fake like stayed there.

"Go on."

"Okay. You go to Atlanta, but you really don't. You go to Dallas instead, then drive back here, but you do it using another car—not your rental. They'd be able to check mileage on your car."

"It doesn't work," Kevin said. "First, how do I go to Dallas, if I'm supposed to be in Atlanta? Second, assuming they figure out I'm in Dallas, won't they figure that I could drive back here? It's not that far —no more than four hours. You could do it in a lot less if you hurried."

"I've got that taken care of. Don't worry."

"Don't worry? It's my ass if this doesn't work. It *might* be my ass if it does. I'm sure there's some kind of law for *faking* a death. It might not be as bad as the real thing, but I'm sure it's not a slap on the wrist."

"Don't worry about that, either," Susan said. "Besides, as I said before, if I name the characters in the book after the detectives and make sure to mention them prominently in the acknowledgments, they'll be satisfied."

"As happy as ticks on a dog?" he asked.

Susan laughed. "Maybe not *that* happy, but satisfied."

"So how am I going to magically teleport from Atlanta to Dallas?"

The look on Susan's face resembled the infamous cat who had just eaten the bird. "Leave that to me."

She finished telling Kevin the plot, and, although he had questions, she had convinced him of the plan's viability to succeed—convinced him enough so that he agreed to go along with it.

Kevin finished taking notes, then handed her the notepad. "Here's your masterpiece," he said. "It better work for both of our sakes."

As Kevin neared the bottom of his glass of Chardonnay, a car pulled into the driveway, headlights blinding him as to who it was. "Who could that be?" Kevin said. "Are you expecting anybody?"

"I'm not expecting anybody, but it might be Chlorinda. She said she might come over."

The car door opened, and Chlorinda got out, locked it, and headed up the sidewalk.

Chlorinda was Susan's assistant. Her home was in the Houston area, so it worked out perfectly on the occasions when Susan traveled to Houston in order to write.

"Don't say anything," Susan said to Kevin. "We might as well start the ruse now. And nobody should know but us."

Chlorinda stepped onto the porch. "Whew. It's been a scorcher today."

"You've got that right," Kevin said. "The heat index was 107 degrees. I'll bet it was cooler than that in San Francisco." He shot a look to Susan, that said, "We shouldn't have come."

"What's up, Chlorinda? Anything new?"

"Other than the heat? We got your draft back from the editor." She handed a large envelope still in its FedEx package to Susan. "I thought you'd want to see it, so I brought it with me."

"Thanks for bringing it. Did you look at it? Were there many corrections?"

"Not as many as the last one. She even commented that this was good. If you want, I can work with you while you're here."

Susan got up out of the chair. "I'm getting more wine, Chlorinda. Want any?"

"Please? White, if you have it."

Susan returned a few moments later and handed a glass of wine to Chlorinda. She placed hers on the table. "You know, speaking of work, Kevin is going out of town next week, so it would be nice if you could come by a few evenings. I hate being by myself—unless I'm writing, of course."

"No problem," Chlorinda said. "Just tell me which nights."

"I don't know." She turned to the left. "Honey, which nights will you be gone?"

Kevin raised his eyebrows. "I don't know yet. I just found out I'd be going."

Susan faced Chlorinda again. "I can let you know. It won't be much anyway. Maybe a couple of hours."

"No problem," Chlorinda said. "I don't have anything else to do."

They chatted for a few more hours, enjoying the occasional breezes off the lake. Around midnight, Susan said, "I'm calling it a night. *Some of us still have to work.*"

"I need to go, too," Chlorinda said. "It's far later than I intended to stay, although with this view, I *could* stay forever."

She sighed. "I swear, Susan. I don't know how you go home and leave this. I could live here forever."

House on the lake

Kevin leaned over and pecked Susan on the cheek. "I guess that leaves me to finish up this wine. But don't worry, I won't be remiss in my duty regarding the vino. By morning, it will be gone."

Susan laughed. "I'm sure it will," she said. "Good night, all."

"Good night," Chlorinda said, and started toward her car.

"See you in the morning," Kevin said, just as Susan closed the door.

A TABOO ACQUAINTANCE

*I*t had been a week since I'd had Number Two over for dinner, and I couldn't get her off my mind.

What the hell was she doing? She had to know I knew who she was, and yet she continued to play the game.

Dinner had been a success and despite a predisposed opinion, I enjoyed her company. She was well-spoken, well-traveled, and her sense of humor was terrific.

Maybe it's been too long since I've been with a woman? Maybe I'm so desperate that I would be happy with anyone?

I didn't even want to be happy, at least, not with her. She was everything I *didn't* want. Even her name—Marissa—was wrong; that was Ribs' daughter's name. When I thought of *Marissa* I thought of her, a sweet little thing that did nothing more than fib about going to the mall. I didn't *want* to think of a hardened criminal, and that's what Number Two was.

She was the one that got away. Maybe that's what bothered me more than anything. Maybe thinking she had outsmarted me irked more than it should have.

Regardless of what I thought, I had invited her over for dinner again. I don't know why, but I had. Perhaps it was her amazing sex appeal. Combined with how long it had been since I'd been with *any* woman, and it created the perfect storm.

I pondered what to have for dinner, when an old gnocchi recipe came to mind. It was served in a tomato basil cream sauce. I decided to cook some asparagus—pencil thin, of course that was fried in olive oil with garlic and a little bit of lemon-honey. The lemon-honey gave it an almost-sweet flavor, enough to make the asparagus palatable. At the last minute, I changed my mind and decided to make *Bucatini All'Amatriciana*. I never knew anyone who didn't *love* that dish.

Bucatini All'Amatriciana

I stopped and picked up an inexpensive bottle of Chianti. There was no sense in trying to impress this woman, even though somewhere in the back of my mind I wanted to.

What I wanted to do was to charm her right out of her pants. What I was afraid of, is that I might succeed.

At 6:45 the doorbell rang. I quickly removed the apron I'd been wearing and went to answer it, straightening my hair as I crossed the dining room.

I opened the door and smiled. I knew I was in trouble the moment I saw her. She stood there, sun reflecting off her long hair, and her white teeth almost glowing against her tanned skin. *I forgot how gorgeous she was!*

"Come on in," I said.

She handed me a bottle of wine that I wasn't familiar with, but it was a Brunello, and that alone put it out of my reach as far as price goes.

"Thanks," I said. "I'll uncork this. Dinner is almost ready."

"I didn't tell you, but I had a good time last week." She sounded serious.

"Me too," I said. And I realized as I said it that I meant it. I *did* have a good time.

We were only a few bites into the meal, when she said, "Oh my God, this is fantastic. I can't believe you made this. Are you sure you didn't get takeout somewhere?"

"Not a chance," I said. "This is one of my old recipes. I used to cook this all the time for…"

"That's all right," she said. "I understand, and I'm honored that you cooked it for me." She reached across the table and patted the back of my hand. "Thank you," she whispered.

I nodded, then excused myself to go to the restroom. When I came back, her plate was almost empty. Her glass was.

I grabbed the wine bottle from the island. "More wine?" I said.

She held up her glass and said, "Please. And a little more bucatini, too, if you don't mind. It's delicious."

"I'm glad you like it," I said. "It's one of my favorites."

She held her gaze fixed on me as I scooped more bucatini onto her plate. "Tough day?" she asked. "You look tired."

I tensed. I didn't like her asking about my work, and I didn't want to tell her about it. Instead of answering, I said, "More garlic bread?"

"It's all right if you don't want to talk," she said. "But the question was genuine. I'm not here to pry information from you."

She was a person who got straight to the point. I liked that. "I didn't think you were trying to get information. It's just—"

"It's just that you don't trust me. Right?"

I almost lied, but reconsidered. She had been direct with me. "Yes. I guess so. I'd rather not discuss work."

"Thanks for being honest. I don't like dishonesty."

She must have noticed me twitch. "I guess you think that's an odd statement coming from me, but it's true. And don't be so surprised; doing one thing wrong doesn't mean you do everything wrong."

She got up and walked around the kitchen. "I wish we had met under different circumstances. There are things in my past that I'm not happy about—things I would have done differently. But unless you tell me you're perfect, I'm betting you have a thing or two of your own."

She took a sip from her wine glass. "I don't know about you, but I always try to look at the good side of people, not at what they've done wrong."

I thought about what she said. Then I thought about Rico, and what I'd done to his family. She was right. Who was I to judge?

"All right," I said. "I might have been looking at this wrong. Let's start fresh."

She set her glass on the table, walked over and gave me a deep kiss. "I'd like that," she said. "I'm ready for a fresh start."

During the next few days, Kevin and Susan set everything into motion, including the purchase of a round-trip ticket to Atlanta. "I didn't think we were doing it this soon," Kevin said.

"The ticket is not for you," Susan said. "It's for the decoy, so he can fly to Atlanta, then drive to Alabama and buy a gun and a silencer. They're easy enough to purchase, and this way it won't be in your name if they check. And that's assuming they find the gun, which they won't."

"How are we going to get it?"

"I'm going to meet him at the airport when he gets back. He'll fly to and from Atlanta using your name—consider it a test—then he'll fly back to Dallas using his. After he returns from Atlanta, he'll give me the gun."

"How is he going to fly with a gun? And why do we need a silencer?"

"I"m not sure yet about the silencer, but it's better that we get it while we can, in case we need it. And as far as the gun goes, he can check it in with luggage as long as it's unloaded and in a locked case, which it will be."

"So, what, you pick up his luggage from Atlanta, go outside, he gives you the gun, then he leaves?"

"You're getting good, dear. Pretty soon, you'll be good enough to help me plot."

"You think of everything, don't you?"

"I try, dear."

The decoy plan went off without a hitch, so Mrs. Hemphill made arrangements for the real trip.

Two weeks later, on the day the ruse was to happen, Kevin called a cab to take him to the airport. The cabbie dropped him off at the door, then Kevin progressed through security, showing all necessary documents.

About half an hour later, he went to the bathroom, but the stall he needed was occupied. He had to wait a couple of minutes for the stall to empty, then he went into the stall on the end and sat.

A few seconds later the person in the next stall said, "What's the weather like in Austin? I just came from Dallas, and it was fine."

"I don't know. But I hear it's all sunshine in Atlanta."

No sooner had Kevin responded than a bag slid under the space between the divider and the floor. The bag was packed with clothes and other things. Kevin undressed, and replaced the clothes he had worn with the items from the bag. In no time, he was wearing a pair of gray wool pants, black shoes, black socks, a pale-blue collared shirt, and a beard and sunglasses. A wooden cane filled out the disguise.

In the stall next to him, a man was dressing in Kevin's outfit and removing a fake beard. They exchanged briefcases, which were filled with mobile phones and tablets—oh, and the all-important IDs and plane tickets—then the man from the other stall walked out. Kevin was waiting. He leaned close and whispered, "Don't forget to act as if you're sick at the hotel. Order room service, watch some movies, do anything to show you stayed in the room."

"So don't go anywhere?"

"Nowhere. And when the detective calls, and I'm sure he will, sound like you'd been sleeping. And don't forget about the flights home. Give him the time for the second flight to Houston. I'll meet him earlier and say I took the first one."

"Okay," the decoy said. "Got it."

"One more thing," Kevin said. "If anybody asks, and I mean *anybody*, stick to the story of you were never in Atlanta. You flew to Houston on business, then flew back to Dallas a few hours later. Got it?"

"Got it," the man said.

Kevin went back into the stall and waited almost an hour before leaving again. If anyone had been watching real time—which he couldn't imagine—or if they watched the video later, he felt certain they would have gotten tired by this point in the video.

He was no longer Kevin Hemphill. He was now Roger Farnsworth, and he had to hurry or he'd miss his flight to Dallas. As he hustled down the corridor, he examined Roger's photo ID and was amazed at the resemblance. The photo looked just like him! Kevin wondered how Susan had arranged all of this and, for the first time since the plot began, he believed it might work. Now there was one more thing to do.

He found a quiet corner and dialed home. "Hello?" Susan said.

"Babe, it's me."

"Why are you calling? Is everything all right?"

"Fine. Well, maybe not. Sensor Design called. They really *do* need me to go to Atlanta. I tried getting out of it, but I couldn't. And they're my biggest client. There's not much I can do."

"Shit! All right. If you have to go, you have to go. We'll do this another time. Have a safe trip, and I'll see you when you get back."

Susan hung up the phone. Kevin heard the click and smiled. Now she would think he's not coming. And she'd be relaxed and unprepared. Things were working out perfectly, and the best part of it was that she had planned it all—the master plotter had plotted her own demise.

~

The decoy, now clean shaven, looking like Kevin, and dressed similar to him, boarded the flight to Atlanta using the ticket Kevin had purchased. He made his way back to seat 21A, got a pillow and a blanket, and leaned his head against the window.

When passengers were asked later—and they would be asked—they wouldn't be able to say it *wasn't* Kevin, because the man in seat 21A had been an everyday person doing an everyday thing. People wouldn't be able to identify him any more than they would the passengers occupying seats 32B or 9C or any other seat.

Kevin held the decoy's ticket which was the return flight to Dallas. The decoy—Roger Farnsworth—had flown in this morning and was scheduled to return at noon. The only difference was it would be Kevin, not the decoy, that took the flight.

He boarded at 12:30, took his window seat, and followed the same instructions, being as inconspicuous as possible. By 2:10, he was in Dallas. He got off the plane, then made his way to the Roger's car. He had told Kevin where to find it.

There was a brief moment in Houston, when Kevin had thought the plan was going to fall apart. The lady checking tickets had looked at the ID, then back to Kevin several times. But eventually, she sent him on his way.

When Kevin got to the garage where the car was, he located the aisle, found the car, started the engine, exited the parking lot, and began the long, slow drive to Houston. Once he was clear of the parking garage, he removed the damn itchy beard. He wanted to stop and take a shower. He should. He had plenty of time, as he didn't have to be in Houston for almost eight hours. "The hell with it," he said, and kept driving.

Kevin enjoyed driving—most of the time—but the trip from Dallas to Houston was boring, to say the least. He hadn't experienced many that would qualify for *most-boring drive*, but this was one of them. It consisted of 200 miles of flatland, ranches and farmland sprinkled with a few trees, and with nothing to break the monotony.

The drive was bad enough, but worst of all was the requirement that he drive the speed limit—or under. The farmland wasn't torturous when zipping by at eighty-five miles per hour, but at sixty-five it was painful.

He passed through Huntsville at about 6:30 and though tempted to refuel his car *and* stomach, he resisted the urge. He estimated that he had more than enough gas to make it to Houston, and as for his stomach, even though he was hungry, he wouldn't die.

Kevin drove south to Conroe. Thirty minutes later, he found a crowded coffee shop and stopped to waste time. It would be dangerous to be exposed, but as Susan always said he'd be one of the *invisible* ones—the people who nobody noticed, just one of the crowd. He'd be an everyday person doing an everyday thing and nobody would be able to describe him if asked—just like the decoy on the plane.

Shorty before 10:00 that night—as planned—Kevin sneaked through the woods off Highway 105. He followed a small animal trail—probably made by deer or wild pigs—and it led him to an almost-never-used cove where a boat had been stashed.

He put on a pair of latex gloves, started the engine on the boat and steered it across the lake to the shore close to their summer home, stopping the engine about one hundred yards out and rowing it in by hand so he wasn't heard.

Kevin tied the boat to a nearby tree, waded to dry land, and made his way to the house. If Susan had done her job right—and he was certain she had—the gun the decoy had purchased in Alabama a few weeks before would be lying on the kitchen counter, loaded with blanks. If she had put it away because she thought he wasn't coming, a quick search would reveal it. If not, he'd have to use his own, which he had brought with him.

He checked to ensure that no one was watching, at least conspicuously, and sneaked into the back door, using using all the trees for cover. He made his way to the kitchen where he found the gun. *So she didn't put it away.*

Everything was going according to plan, but here's where he was going to deviate from the plan. He removed the blanks and filled the gun with real bullets, then moved to the bedroom, where Susan was to supposed to be fake sleeping. He looked to confirm that she was there.

Perfect—she was sleeping, with her head facing the wall. He took a deep breath, then pulled the trigger three times. With the silencer, the noise was barely audible; he doubted that the neighbors could have heard.

He was tense, nervous, but it was finally over. "See ya in hell," he whispered. Then he took the gun, ransacked the house a little, and left the house the same way he entered. Before he left the house, he removed the silencer and fired three more shots out into the lake.

He felt sure that the neighbors would report the shots and that meant it wouldn't be long before the cops arrived. He remembered Susan telling him that the people next door—Bob and Cyd—*always* went to bed around this time, so there would be a possibility that they would see something through the blinds, but it was almost a certainty that they'd hear the shots. After all, it was quiet on the lake, and the windows were open in order to catch a breeze.

On the other hand, if they didn't hear or see anything, then the body would be found…whenever, and it would be left to the coroner to determine time of death. Either way, Kevin's alibi would show that he was in Atlanta. That's all he needed to know.

After he crept around the other side of the house, he got in the boat—careful not to rip his latex gloves so that no prints would be found. Then he returned to the cove, where he had tied the boat up, buried the gun, walked to his car, and drove to a spot near Huntsville where he wouldn't be seen.

He parked at a pre-determined spot, slept a little, then awoke and waited for the phone to ring.

SCENE OF THE CRIME

My phone rang, waking me out of a deep sleep, and it was a good sleep, too. I'd been dreaming of Number Two, and all of the magnificent things I'd like to do with her—or to her.

She'd forced me to open my eyes and look at her in a new light, and now that I'd taken that step, I liked what I saw.

I grabbed the phone. "Cataldi."

"We've got a body, and I thought you'd want to know about it." It was the night-duty desk sergeant.

"It's the middle of the goddamn night. I don't want to hear about *any* body unless she's naked and very much alive."

And she looks like Number Two.

"It's not the middle of the night; it's not even midnight. And besides, you'll want to hear about this one. The police up in Conroe called. I guess you had talked to them about some people of interest who had a summer house. Well, whoever that was regarding has now got a body in the bedroom."

"Shit. Okay. Tell them I'm on my way. I have to get dressed, but then it won't take me more than thirty minutes."

I called Ribs. There was no way I was going to let him sleep if I wasn't able to. When he answered, I told him what we had, and suggested he meet me at a nearby Starbucks. Not that I liked Starbucks, but they were still open, a plus when it was 11:30 at night.

Ribs ordered plain coffee—I don't know how he drank that stuff but he did—and I opted for a small latte.

On the drive to Bentwater, we discussed what we might find. "I'm guessing it's him," Ribs said. "I think she did him in."

"No way. He did her in, for sure. She's a decent lady. No way she'd kill him."

"The thing I can't figure out is why did he, *or* she, do it when they knew we were looking at them already?"

"She's a writer. Maybe he picked up a thing or two from her plots."

"I guess we'll find out in about fifteen minutes," Ribs said.

"So, what did you do about Marissa?" I asked.

"Screw you," he said. "We took her to the mall. But it's not fair. You knew Rosalee would give in."

"Oh, it was Rosalee, huh? I'll have to mention that to her the next time I come over. Damn softie."

"Screw you again."

"Where did you go after you dropped her off?" I asked.

Ribs laughed. "You're a real prick, cuz. Have I told you that?" Ribs finished his coffee and crunched the cup. "What the hell do these kids do at the mall anyway?"

I laughed. "Don't tell me you didn't follow her. You were probably sneaking through that place like a ninja. Besides, what they do is hang out, play games at the arcade, assuming the mall still has one, people watch, and plot to piss off their parents."

"You really *are* a prick," he said, and then he laughed like hell. "And for your information, Marissa and her two friends went to the pet center."

"And what vicious things did she do there—play with turtles?"

"Shut-up and keep driving."

~

We turned onto FM 1097, drove across the bridge, then left into Bentwater. It was a gated community, so we had to stop at the guard house and identify ourselves. Afterward, we followed the main road for about a quarter of a mile and turned left again. We could see the flashing lights from the main road. Conroe PD had come in numbers. I can't say that I blamed them. Conroe didn't get many murders, and I imagined Bentwater got even fewer. This might have been the first one.

Ribs opened the door as I put the car into *park*. He stepped out onto grass that was still wet from an earlier sprinkle.

The scene reflected the inexperience of the local police department. Not that they were doing anything wrong, simply that they were doing their best to appear *busy*. It was reminiscent of a bee hive.

I walked up and introduced us to the deputy standing by the door. "Detective Gino Cataldi," I said, reaching to shake. "And this is my partner, Detective Hector Delgado."

"Deputy Rawlins," he said. "Don Rawlins."

"We had notified the chief earlier that we were expecting possible trouble at this location. Unfortunately, it looks as if that came true."

The deputy nodded. "Dead female, about thirty-five. Three GSWs to the side of the head. Looks like she was sleeping when it happened."

"Son of a bitch. I *knew* that prick was gonna' do it."

"What are you talking about?" the deputy asked. "You know something?"

I filled Rawlins in on what we knew, including the phone call from San Francisco, and our questioning of the couple." I felt like punching myself in the face. I should have done something to try and prevent this.

"Take it easy, cuz," Ribs said. "I know that look. You've got no reason to blame yourself."

I nodded. "Yeah. I know. But it's easy to say don't blame yourself. It's more difficult to not do it."

"I guess I better call the grieving husband," I said, then I looked to Ribs. "Have you got his number?"

Ribs reached behind him for his wallet and pulled out a business card. "I saved it just in case. I guess 'just in case' happened."

I took the number, and called. Hemphill answered after a few rings. He sounded sleepy.

"Mr. Hemphill, this is Detective Cataldi, from Houston PD."

"What can I do for you?"

"Where are you, sir?

"I'm on a business trip in Atlanta. Why?" He coughed, then said, "I'm sorry, Detective, but I've come down with something."

Business trip? I wondered where, as his voice sounded crackly, like a bad connection. "Sir, I'm afraid there's been a break-in at your house. When will you be home?"

"Break-in? What? Is my wife all right? Is she okay?"

I thought how to answer, then opted for a version of the truth. "I haven't spoken to her yet. When are you returning?"

"I'm not supposed to be home for several days, but I'll reschedule. I'll take an early flight home. I think there's one that arrives in Houston at about 8:30."

"I'll be waiting at baggage, sir. Just get your things and go outside."

The decoy hung up and dialed the number of the phone the Hemphills had given him. Kevin answered immediately. "Yeah?"

"A detective called a few minutes ago. Said there'd been a break-in. What the hell is this all about, anyway? Are you sure it's like you said —that it's for a book. This guy sounded legitimate."

"I promise. No problem. Now do like we told you, and this will all be over with soon."

"Okay. See you in the morning."

"Wait," Kevin hollered. "Did you get sick? Keep your voice low?"

"All of the above. Now, I've got to go. I need sleep if you want me on that early flight."

"One more thing," Kevin said. "Instead of taking the flight you mentioned, take an earlier United flight. Use my credit card to pay for it. I think it gets into Houston at about 6:30. Meet me in the parking garage. We'll exchange everything there and get you paid."

"Shit, that's early, but okay, I'll see you then."

~

K evin rested his head on the back of the seat and tried to sleep. He'd have to be on his way to Houston in a few hours, and he wanted at least a little rest. It wasn't a far drive from Huntsville to the airport, but it was an hour at least.

H e waited for the decoy in the garage, parking in the same far corner which no one would use unless forced to, and he used the same disguise as before. When he saw Roger coming, he got out and made his way to the elevator. It would be much easier to change in the elevator than in a car.

He opened the door, waited a moment for Roger to get in, then said, "How did everything go in Atlanta?"

"Atlanta is having nice weather." He laughed after he said it. "Everything went fine. I got room service, watched two movies, and even called some local 'hot spots.'"

Kevin placed the decoy's briefcase on the floor of the elevator, and then picked up the one that the decoy put in its place. Inside were all of the essentials agreed upon during the planning stage: license, credit card, cell phone, plane ticket receipt, clothes, and for the decoy, a fake beard, car keys, and an envelope stuffed with $5,000, the remainder of his payment.

He heard the decoy shuffling through the items. "All there?" Kevin asked.

"Everything's good. It was a pleasure doing business with you."

"Same here," Kevin said. "I'm leaving now. Remember, wait about fifteen minutes minimum before you leave."

"For this kind of money, I'll stay here all day," the decoy said.

"That's fine, but don't forget you have to eventually get back to Dallas."

"I'll get there. Good luck."

Kevin opened the elevator door, wiped his hands on his pants, then exited. He proceeded to the entrance of the airport to meet Detective Cataldi, and he was using a fast walk.

He walked to the luggage claim, went outside, and waited. In the meantime, he decided to call Detective Cataldi.

shield

"Cataldi."

"Detective, this is Kevin Hemphill. I caught an earlier United flight, so I'm already in Houston. I'm outside of luggage now."

"Shit. Okay. I'll be there shortly."

It didn't take long for me to get to the airport, and it didn't take long to spot Hemphill. I beeped the horn and waved, and he wheeled his carry-on to the car. He got a funny look on his face when he saw me. "What is it, Detective? Is anything wrong?"

As Hemphill got into the car, I said, "I'm afraid so, Mr. Hemphill. There's been a murder at your house."

"A murder! What? Susan!"

"It looks as if it happened during the break-in. The house appears to have been ransacked."

His hands raised to cover his face. "Oh my God. Oh my God. How could this be? Susan!"

"Sir, that's the other thing, the body is not your wife."

"What? Who is it? Where's Susan?"

"I was hoping you'd be able to tell us that."

"I have no idea. I was out of town. How would I know?"

"I presumed you two must have spoken. That perhaps she mentioned where she was."

"As I said, I have no clue. Sometimes she goes to a hotel to write, but that's normally for privacy. With me gone there'd be no need."

Hemphill's face turned ash gray. "Oh my God! Oh my God! When she goes to write, Chlorinda usually comes over. If that's her…"

Hemphill looked at Gino. Panic was evident. "Detective, what did she look like? The body, I mean. Did she have blue eyes? Was there a mole on her right cheek?"

"I don't know, Mr. Hemphill, but we'll be there before long. Relax. We'll find out soon enough."

WHO'S DEAD

*H*emphill nearly jumped out of the car as I pulled up to his house. He ran for the door and flung it open.

"Where is she?"

I was twenty yards behind him and could still hear. It was a far cry from the sick guy I had struggled to hear last night when I called him in Atlanta. *Or was it Atlanta. I made a mental note to check on that.*

"Chlorinda! How did this..."

I walked into the bedroom to find Mr. Hemphill holding her in his arms, blood and all. It struck me as odd—more than odd. Most people shy away from a dead body, let alone a dead body covered in blood, and yet here we had Mr. Hemphill holding her to his chest. It didn't add up. Something was wrong.

I glanced at Ribs, who was focused on the same scene. *You see this? I* mouthed.

He nodded then stepped forward. "Mr. Hemphill, do you know your wife's whereabouts?

He shook his head. "No. I already told the other detective. But this is Chlorinda. She is, or *was*, my wife's assistant."

I joined Ribs, standing alongside the two of them. "Assistant?"

"Yes. She did all kinds of work for her: proofreading, answering her emails, responding to Twitter messages, all of it. She was invaluable."

"And what was she doing here last night?" Ribs asked.

He shook his head again. "I don't know. I guess we'll have to ask Susan —if she ever makes an appearance."

I made a note—*odd reaction*—then proceeded. "Do you know her social particulars—name, address, email address, etc.?"

He looked at me oddly.

"We're going to need to check her emails to see if there were any threats or things like that."

"Of course," he said. "Susan will have all of that. She'll get it for you."

Twenty minutes later, we were still standing in the bedroom, trying to understand the nuances of the relationship between Chlorinda and Susan. At that time, a commotion sounded at the front door.

Susan arrived, wearing fancy clothes, shades, and expensive shoes. It looked as if she had been on a shopping spree, not a weekend retreat.

I leaned toward Ribs. "Maybe this guy is having his chain yanked. Or even more. Maybe she's at the hotel for reasons other than writing. Let's check that out."

When I looked to the front, the deputy had hold of her arm. "I live here, for Christ's sake."

I walked to the front. "Let her in," I said. "That's Mrs. Hemphill."

She yanked free of the deputy and pushed through the door. "What is going on?"

"There's been a break-in," I said.

Her face registered shock. "A break-in?"

"And someone's been killed."

"Oh God!" She ran for the bedroom, knocking over the trash can in the kitchen.

"Chlorinda! Oh my God. What happened?" She knelt beside Chlorinda, occupying the space where Mr. Hemphill had just been.

Blood smeared on her white blouse and even on her cheeks.

"Where were *you*?" Hemphill asked. The tone was demanding.

Susan looked up at him and said, "I went to stay at a hotel so that I could have privacy to write. What difference does it make?"

"Privacy? You didn't have privacy here? I was in Atlanta, for Christ's sake."

Susan shook her head, as if to clear it. "Privacy might not have been the best choice of words. Comfort might have been better. The hotel has room service."

"Room service? Chlorinda's dead because of room service?"

"No," Susan said while she stood. "Chlorinda is dead because *someone* broke in and killed her. Would you rather it have been me?"

I waited for the fireworks to settle down, then approached. "How did you get here, Mrs. Hemphill?"

"I used Chlorinda's car," she said. "God, I can't believe she's gone. I can't believe someone did…*this*."

"Why were you using her car?" I asked.

"What?"

"I said, "Why were you using Chlorinda's car?"

"Something was wrong with mine. It stalled out every time I stopped —red lights, stop signs, even when I slowed down."

"And what was she doing here?"

"She had come over to do some work on my latest manuscript. It's horrible to say now, but her incessant talking was keeping me from writing so I went to the hotel and left her here. On second thought, I guess it's not nice to say *incessant*. I should have said, *continual*."

Susan took a moment to compose herself before continuing. "Chlorinda *was* a talker. Besides, I often go to the Marriott and spend the night, the weekend, or even the whole week, so I can write in privacy. You know, no neighbors, no phones, no husband—just room service and blank walls. Oh, and a glass or two of vino. And that magnificent waterway to walk along. Oh, God, there I go again, talking when I shouldn't be."

"What hotel were you staying at?" Ribs asked.

"As I said, the Marriott on the Waterway, in the Woodlands. It's where I always stay. Well, not *always*, but usually."

"What time did Chlorinda come over?" I asked.

"About dinner time, maybe sixish. We ate, chatted, did a little work, then I left. My God, I feel terrible. To think I was probably sitting in my hotel room drinking wine when poor Chlorinda was..."

"Speaking of time, what time did—"

"Did I check in? I should have known. I realize you're suspicious, Detective, based on the reception we received at the airport and that's all right. I like my detectives cynical. So to answer your question, I left the house around eight-thirty or so, and checked in about nine or nine-thirty. I had a glass of wine at the bar, went to my room, wrote, ordered room service, then slept."

"And you can prove this?"

"I'm sure that I can, but I didn't realize that I had to." She gestured to Kevin. "As far as my husband is concerned, as you are well aware, he was in Atlanta on a business trip. Surely, that will exonerate him."

Ribs leaned close to her. "Did your husband know that you'd be gone last night?"

Susan seemed to think for a moment, then said, "No, he didn't, but you can't think Kevin could do this. Good God, Detective, give it up. He couldn't hurt anyone." She glared at Ribs. "And besides, as I've already said, he was in Atlanta."

For the next couple of hours, we asked questions, mostly regarding the dynamics of the relationship between Chlorinda and the Hemphills. Sometime around 3:00, Mrs. Hemphill said she was too tired to continue and was retiring.

"I'll be here for a few more weeks if you need me, Detective. And besides, you have my cell phone, so call anytime." She grinned. "But not too early; I'm a late sleeper."

Ribs and I stopped at Denny's on the way home, much to his displeasure. I ordered coffee and the Grand Slam breakfast. He complained but he got the same, despite it being almost dinner time.

"What do you think, Ribs?"

"I think the bacon is greasy, the coffee is bad, and the home fries aren't cooked enough."

"You know what I mean, what do you think about the case?"

He considered the question for a moment, but only for a moment. "I think Chlorinda looks a lot like Mrs. Hemphill. It would be easy to mistake them in the dark."

I took a long sip of coffee, and said, "I was thinking the same thing."

WHAT WAS TAKEN?

We had to do our work by the numbers, so it was imperative that we looked at the possibility that this *was* a break-in, despite the way the whole case began—with the odd lead from San Francisco. To help with the situation, Conroe PD was already checking out the break-in angle.

Hemphill said there was about sixty thousand dollars in jewelry missing, not much according to him, but I saw it differently. There were more than enough meth heads who would cut out a person's tongue for half that much.

We got a brief description from the Hemphills—they had the jewelry insured—and began making contacts with the known fences. I also asked for the insurance company to send us a more detailed description of each piece. Hemphill had alerted them, so they'd be working it from that angle.

After being up most of the night, I felt terrible and needed sleep, but it looked like coffee would have to suffice. When we walked into the coffee room, I saw Tip sitting at the corner table with his partner,

Connie. "Yo, Tip. I need you to talk to some of your contacts, put the word out on some missing jewelry."

"What have you got?" he asked.

"A woman was killed up in Conroe. We like the husband, even though it looks like he was in Atlanta at the time. But there is missing jewelry, so to cover our asses, we have to search for it."

"Being in Atlanta doesn't mean he didn't have her killed," Connie said. "If he was in Atlanta, all that means is he didn't pull the trigger."

"Already thinking that," I said. "And unless I've got it all wrong, that's how this case is going to play out: husband hires hit man to bump off rich wife. That's my take for now, anyway."

"You think the husband killed the wife?" Tip said.

"Not technically. As I said, I think the husband *hired* someone to kill the wife, and by happenstance, he killed her assistant instead; she was there house-sitting."

"Sounds like you've got work to do," Tip said. "Anyway, get me a description of the jewelry, and I'll check around. We'll be here for an hour or so. If it's after that, call me on my cell."

An hour later, a fax came in from Hemphill's insurance company. I made a copy and gave it to Tip. He knew every criminal that was worth knowing when it came to gathering information, and most of them owed him favors.

"Don't forget to get the word out," I said. "This is a lot of money, so those jewels are going to be fenced somewhere."

After dropping off the fax, I stopped by to get Ribs, then we headed out. It was time to see the Hemphills. We needed to make heads or tails of the mess.

As we were driving up I-45, I said, "You think he killed her, Ribs?"

"I think he tried to kill his wife," Ribs said. "Or should I say he hired someone to kill his wife, and they fucked up—big time."

"So how do we prove it? He seems to have an airtight alibi."

"We find the guy he hired, or we bust his alibi. There aren't many options."

I nodded. "I guess you're right."

We drove in silence for a while, then I said. "Did I tell you I had Number Two over for dinner?"

Ribs spun his head around quicker than Linda Blair had in *The Exorcist*. "What? What did you say? Number Two? I thought she was dead?"

I smiled. "I might have exaggerated that part of the story. The truth is, she outsmarted us."

"Outsmarted us? I know that. She outsmarted us for the whole case. But you said she died in a fire at the warehouse."

"No two ways around this, Ribs. I lied. I figured she must have staged the whole scenario to make us think she died. The truth is, she got away with all of that money."

"And you had dinner with her?"

"How could I not? I bumped into her at the grocery store, and she invited herself."

"Invited herself? You could have said no."

I looked at Ribs. "Really? She was the thong-panties girl. Remember her? Remember that body?"

Delgado whistled. "Okay, you're forgiven. Now tell me what happened."

"Nothing happened. We had dinner and talked. We ended up talking until almost midnight."

"You talked? With a body like hers, and all you did was talk? You're a sick son of a bitch, you know that? I know you were married to my cousin, but damn. That's all I've got to say—damn."

"A woman is more than a naked body, Ribs."

"Don't tell Rosalee. I've been training her for twenty years to think otherwise."

"You mean she's been training you? I know the real story. Anyway, yes, Marissa—that's her name. Marissa and I just talked. And we had fun."

"Marissa? That's my baby's name."

"I know. At first it bothered me, but now I'm used to it. Don't worry. You'll get used to it too."

"Get used to it? So you plan on keeping her around for a while?"

I smiled. "It depends on her, but if she wants to continue, I guess I do, too. I kind of like her."

"Damn, cuz. You're stepping up in the world. Going from widower to player in one night, or should I say *could have* gone from widower to player in one night."

I laughed. "Shut the hell up, Delgado."

I drove across the lake, admiring the view and wondering how such tragedy could visit a serene place like this. Spots like this were meant for vacation homes, retirement villas, and golf courses. They certainly weren't meant for murder.

We turned into Bentwater, stopping at the guard house for entry. It made me wonder.

Bentwater entrance

I pulled out my badge and flashed it to the guard. "Do you log in all the cars that come and go?"

"Is this about the murder?"

"Yeah," I said. "So answer the question, do you?"

He nodded. "Every one. I'm positive no one came through. I know about half the people who live here, and if I don't know them by sight, I ask for ID, and log it in the book. I log in the regulars, too. It's all there for you to see."

He handed me the log book. "Stop by on your way out, and I'll have a copy for you." He pointed to the other guard. "Lazaro can run down to the clubhouse and copy it."

I handed him back the book. "Sounds good. Thanks."

e pulled up to the Hemphill's house, a sprawling yellow-stucco house that sat on a secluded cove of the lake.

"Jesus Christ," Ribs said. "The goddamn front doors probably cost as much as my whole downstairs."

"Probably more," I said. "But then again, you don't write mystery novels, you only solve murders—sometimes."

"You mean the way you solved that kidnapping?" Ribs said.

We both laughed as we got out of the car and approached the house. It looked different in the light, and without all of the black-and-whites parked in front.

Susan answered the door. "Detectives, come in. We were just finishing breakfast."

Instinctively, I glanced at my watch, the one Mary had given me.

Susan must have noticed. "Yes, I know. It's late for breakfast, but we haven't gotten much sleep with all that's been going on."

"I imagine," Ribs said.

I stepped slowly toward the kitchen table. "I spoke to the Conroe Chief of Police. He said he didn't have any next-of-kin information. Do you know who that would be?"

Susan looked down at her half-eaten bowl of cereal. "Chlorinda had no one. Her mother died last year, and she was an only child. Her father was never in her life. He might be alive, but I've never met him."

"How about her estate—a will, anything like that?" Ribs asked.

"I gave the police in Conroe all of that information," Susan said. "It's in a file cabinet in her bedroom. I know because we often spoke of it. I think it was all going to some animal shelter. She was fond of animals."

I pulled a chair out and looked at Susan. "May I?"

"Of course. Sit. You, too, Detective," she said to Ribs.

After I sat, I pulled out a notepad and pen. "I'm sure you've heard all of this before, but I have to ask. It's not to be cruel."

"I understand, Detective. I've been through this a dozen times before."

At seeing my questioning look, she said, "I write mystery novels, remember?"

I laughed. "Oh, yes. Forgive me. I forgot for a minute."

"First you, Mrs. Hemphill. You said you spent the night at the Marriott. Is that correct?"

"Yes, and I checked in a little after nine, if I remember correctly."

"Did anyone see you there?"

"If you mean, neighbors, no. If you mean anyone who could alibi for me, absolutely. The waiter at the restaurant, room service, more than likely the bartender. Perhaps more."

"And you never received a call from your husband telling you of the break-in?"

She straightened and paused. "Well, no. I guess I didn't." She then turned to her husband and said, "Kevin, why didn't you call when he told you there'd been a break-in?"

"I uh...I uh...I guess I got nervous. I figured you'd be upset or something, so I got on the first flight home."

"That still left you all night to call," Ribs said. "I'm sure you weren't sleeping the whole time."

"The truth of the matter is, when Detective Cataldi called, and when I heard it was him, I remembered he was with homicide, and I thought the worst."

"But you didn't ask?" I said. "I find that odd."

Kevin pushed his plate back and slid the knife and fork to the side. "Odd? I'll tell you what's odd. That my wife's dear friend and assistant is murdered, and you're busy berating me for not thinking to ask a question."

Ribs placed his hand on the back of Mr. Hemphill's. "We're sorry, Mr. Hemphill. That wasn't very thoughtful. Now, if you can tell me when you got to Atlanta and where you stayed, we can wrap this up."

Kevin sneered, then he stood and got some papers off a table near the doorway. He shoved them into Rib's hand. "Here. I knew you'd be asking, so I had them prepared. Canceled airline ticket, hotel receipt, taxi receipt, and a receipt for magazines at the Atlanta airport book store."

Ribs placed them into a folder he had open on the table. "Thanks, Mr. Hemphill. We appreciate that."

Ribs and I stayed for another half an hour, mostly asking questions about Chlorinda, her habits, lifestyle, the kind of work she did, etc. When we were satisfied we'd gotten all we were going to for the time being, I stood. "Guess it's time to go," I said. "We'll call if we have any more questions."

"One more thing before we leave," Ribs said. "You mentioned some jewelry that was stolen?"

"I'll have the insurance company send a report to you in the morning. Some of the items are unique, so they shouldn't be difficult to locate."

"Okay, great." I said. "See you."

We got in the car and slowly retraced our tracks to the entrance of Bentwater. On the way out, we stopped so I could pick up the log-in book. We had a lot of work to do, and this book should help.

"We've got a lot of alibi-busting to do," I said.

"No shit. Not the least of which is how do you kill someone in Houston when you're in Atlanta?"

"I think it's more like we said to begin with—he hired someone to do it. We just have to find out who he hired. My guess is financial forensics will break this case."

"I'm guessing you're right, cuz but, just in case, we need to be able to prove he was not in Atlanta when the murder took place."

"That does present a problem," I said. "So first, we need to check with the airlines and with security and make sure he *was* in Atlanta. It's not that far away that he couldn't have sneaked home, done the deed, then gone back."

"Should be easy enough to verify," Ribs said. "It's about impossible to take a flight nowadays without ID."

"We've got his seat numbers (to and from) on the ticket, and we can check with the hotel. Between the two of them we should find any holes. We also need to check with the phone company to get GPS on where that cell was when I called him from the scene. He said he was in Atlanta. If he really was, our case takes a major hit."

"We need to check her out, too," Ribs said. "Just because she says she was at the Marriott, doesn't mean she was."

"And I've already asked Tip to check out the jewelry. He has more criminal connections than half the department combined."

Kevin waited for the detectives to leave, then he turned to Susan.

"What happened? You were supposed to be here."

"Well, I wasn't. Are you disappointed? Would you rather it was me lying on that bed? I was at the hotel."

"How did this happen?" Kevin asked. "I was in Atlanta."

"Then it must have been an *actual* coincidence as hard as that is to believe. But how did it happen when I had blanks in the gun?"

"I don't know how," Kevin said.

"I should not have left the gun on the counter."

"Why *did* you? You knew I'd be in Atlanta."

"I forgot. I was in a hurry to get out of here," she said. "Besides, it couldn't have been that. Like I said, I had blanks in it."

"Somebody must have broken in, shot her and then stolen the gun," Kevin said. He paused to give his statement more thought.

"But why was your car was here? It was in the driveway when the detectives brought me here."

"I already explained that. It was acting up, so I used Chlorinda's car and left mine here. I was going to take mine to the mechanic in the morning."

Susan took her cereal bowl to the sink. "What happened to Sensor Design?"

Kevin looked over to her. "Obviously, I had to cancel when I got the call from Cataldi."

"And surveillance? Assuming the cops check."

"What about surveillance? I went to Atlanta, for God's sake, so it will show me going. The other guy—whatever his name was—went back to Dallas."

"Roger," Susan said. "His name is Roger."

"Whatever. The important thing is I was there to answer the call from Detective Cataldi, so it will show Atlanta when Cataldi checks, which I'm sure he'll do."

"Okay. Good," Susan said. "I'm verifying this data because I want your alibi to hold up once they start checking. It's more important now than before. Before, if things had gone wrong, it would have only been explaining a fake murder. We don't want them thinking you had anything to do with a *real* murder."

"Me? What about you?"

"I was at the Marriott. I have half a dozen people who can vouch for me, including the waiter at the restaurant and room service."

"Those detectives suspect something," Kevin said. "We need to make sure tracks are covered."

"No doubt about that," Susan said. "We have to figure a way to make this go away."

"We didn't kill her."

Susan turned to glare. *No. We didn't, but you did. And if these guys are half as good as I think, that Atlanta alibi won't hold up.* "We need to come up with something solid."

"I don't know why. I was in Atlanta. You can't get much more solid than that. And if you can prove you were at the Marriott, we're set."

Susan nodded. "I guess you're right. I just like to be certain."

WHERE ARE THE JEWELS?

Tip paid a visit to Johnny Long. Johnny was a known fence, and he was aware of what was for sale all over the city, even the goods he wasn't selling.

He walked in the door and, at first Johnny looked cautious, then he said, "Hello Tip, how are you?

Tip's scar twisted into a menacing smile. He knew that it had because he had practiced doing it while standing in front of the mirror. He'd gotten so good at it, that it was now second nature. He could do it on command, like a twitch.

He showed Johnny the picture of the jewelry collection they had gotten from the insurance company.

"Seen these?" Tip asked.

Johnny stroked his head. "Can't say that I have."

"Look again, it might jog your memory."

Johnny looked at the picture again, but he still shook his head. "No such luck. I would remember something that looked like that."

"That's good," Tip said, "because if I don't hear something about that jewelry within two days, I'll be coming back here often. Maybe every day. I've been thinking about getting one of those fancy high-rise apartments across the street anyway. The commute from where I live now is getting too much to bear."

Long looked around the shop, then leaned close to Tip and whispered. "I haven't seen them. If I had I'd have told you. If they do show up, I'll tell you. Now get off my case. I've got work to do."

"Work? Since when is brokering stolen goods considered work? You're a piece of shit, Johnny. And you better remember what I said. I'll be back in two days."

Around lunchtime, I caught up with Tip. He was at his desk with Connie. "What's up, Tip? Did you get anything?"

"I got the runaround, if that counts. Something's fishy though. As much as I think Johnny Long is a scum-sucking bag of dirt, I believed him when he said he hadn't seen the jewelry. And if that's the case, we've got a problem. Those jewels should have shown up somewhere. You don't steal jewelry for the sake of having the jewelry; you do it for the money, especially when it's that much money."

Connie reached over and tossed her coffee cup in the trash. "What about you, Gino?"

I sighed. "I looked at everything else before focusing on the husband. I interviewed the neighbors, checked for similar break-ins, so I'm with you—why haven't we seen the jewelry? Why hasn't it been sold?"

"Maybe the money was gotten through another kind of insurance," Ribs said.

"Exactly what I'm thinking," I said.

"Let's check it out. See how much insurance was on the wife?"

"He already told us he had two or three million."

"Whoa, you lost me," Connie said.

"Why check insurance on the wife?"

"Because if we presume that insurance was the motive, then the assistant was shot by accident.."

"Let's suppose for a minute that insurance was the motive. Imagine he thought he was killing his wife. Did you see when he came home? He thought it was his wife for a minute."

"Yeah, and I saw how upset he became when he realized it wasn't," Ribs said.

"He seemed more upset when he realized it was Chlorinda, than when he thought it was his wife."

"Yeah. Maybe there's a reason for that. Chlorinda is not bad looking. Or wasn't bad looking."

"Combine that with a nice insurance settlement and you're approaching motive for murder." I thought for a moment more, then said, "Tip, have you seen the wife? Do you think she's good looking?"

He snorted. "Who? That woman you had in here with her husband? Good looking? Hell, I've seen goats that looked better than her. Shit,

I've seen male goats that look better. Come to think of it, on a trip to Mexico, I've *eaten* goats that looked better than her."

Ribs said, "Tip's got a point, maybe we ought to broaden the suspect pool to include goats. At least female ones."

Connie shook her head. "Maybe I should partner up with Gino and let you two lunatics work together."

"If Gino keeps up his shit, he can partner with Tip and I'll take you up on that offer, Connie. But for now, I've got to call Rosalee and get her cousin to check on the Hemphill insurance."

"How's she going to do that?" Tip asked.

"She's got a cousin that works for the insurance company."

"How many cousins does she have?" I asked.

"Too many," Ribs said. "I have to feed them at get-togethers."

Ribs left and walked down the hall. He passed by Fat Charlie's desk, who had a picture on the screen that looked remarkably like him.

"What have you got, Charlie?"

His face flushed when he turned around. "Oh, Ribs. How are you doin'? I was just checking out this new program. It's sort of like celebrity match, but it's for normal people."

Ribs laughed. "Keep at it, Charlie. You'll make it in the movies yet."

Ribs finished checking on Susan's insurance, then went back to join the others. On the way, Miranda, Rosalee's cousin called.

"Hola. Cómo estás?"

"Bien. ¿Recibiste las fotos?"

"¿Cuándo las mandaste?"

"Have una hora."

"Está bien, gracias."

Tip shifted in his chair and leaned his elbows on the table. "Let's assume for a minute that there's an affair going on, and he likes his women to be more on the attractive side. If that's the case, when do they get together? Other than when he comes to Houston to visit."

I finally decided to sit, so I slid a chair to the side. "If I were fooling around with someone, I'd want to see them more than a couple of times a year."

"You got that shit right," Tip said. "I'd get checking on likely spots to meet. See if you can nail him."

Ribs walked in on the tail end of the conversation. "But nail him for what—adultery?"

"Use the affair to squeeze his ass and get him to lie," Tip said. "Catch somebody in one lie, and they'll likely start breaking."

"Well, how's this? Mr. Hemphill bought an additional three-million-dollar insurance policy on his wife three months ago, and, of course, he's the beneficiary. That brings the total up to almost six million."

"Now we're talking motive," Tip said. "I might kill somebody myself for that much money."

"The problem with that is he told me about it when I first met the guy. Maybe not the exact amount, but it was in the millions. She has a policy of an equal amount on him. I don't think it means anything anyway. She makes too much money."

I stood, and walked toward the door. "Let's go, Ribs. We need to have a chat with the Hemphills anyway—both of them."

A CHAT WITH THE HEMPHILLS

*S*usan answered the door right away, almost as if she'd been expecting us. "Mrs. Hemphill," I said, "We have a few more questions, if you don't mind."

She swung the door wide, in an inviting gesture. "Not at all. Come in and sit."

We sat on the sofa, and Ribs pulled out his notebook. We had agreed on the way up here that he would handle the questions while I observed. The questioning would likely come to nothing, but it had to be done.

"Mrs. Hemphill, how much life insurance do you have on you and your husband?" Ribs asked.

She laughed. "I'm sure you already know, but Kevin and I both have about two and a half million. Not enough to worry about."

Ribs raised his eyebrows. "Two and a half million? Is that all?"

"Yes, we haven't bothered to take the time to update our policies properly. I think we bought the original policies right after my first books were published—maybe twelve years ago."

Ribs flipped through his notes. "Did you know that three months ago your husband took out a policy in your name for an additional three million dollars?"

She laughed. "That's impossible. I would have known."

"You *should* have known. Did you have any medical tests about that time? A physical, a stress test?"

Susan thought for a moment then said, "I did have a cardiology exam with a stress test, and I had a general physical, but that was standard procedure."

"And did you sign any papers?"

"Hell, I don't know. I'm always signing papers. Anyway, I don't like where you're going with this. Let's clear it up." She walked toward the steps and shouted, "Kevin. Kevin, come down here, please."

Susan came back and took her seat in the chair. Kevin showed up a moment later.

"Mr. Hemphill," Ribs said, "did you purchase an insurance policy for your wife about three months ago?"

He scrunched his eyebrows and looked from Ribs to Susan. "Yes, and she knows it. I told her."

Ribs quickly glanced at Mrs. Hemphill, then back. "She claims to know nothing."

"Remember, dear. I told you about the insurance guy that I played golf with, and he suggested based on your income that we get you covered for more. It didn't much matter what mine was because I didn't make enough, but your income was substantial enough to warrant a new policy."

Susan placed her finger on her lips. "I don't remember."

"Sure you do. I sat right here and told you about it, then we set up your stress test and physical. Well, it wasn't *here*; it was at home in San Francisco."

"I recall having the stress test and the physical, but I thought they were routine medical exams. I didn't know they were for an insurance policy."

Kevin waved it off as if it were nothing. "Well, it doesn't much matter. We needed it, and now we have it."

I jumped into the conversation. "That's a big policy."

"Like hell. She makes half that in one year from her books."

I looked to Mrs. Hemphill, and she nodded. "It's true," she said. "I earned almost two million dollars last year. So get your mind out of the gutter and stop thinking Kevin had anything to do with this. Find the *real* killer."

We finished up a few questions, then excused ourselves. It was obvious from her attitude that we weren't going to get anything out of her anyway.

I stopped at the guard house on the way out. It was a different set of guards, but I felt sure they could answer the questions.

"Is there any way else to get in here besides this entrance?"

The guard shook his head. "None."

"So if I wanted to sneak in here, how would I do it?"

"You couldn't. Only way in here is through this guard gate or on the lake."

"Somebody might find a way through the woods," the other guard said. "But it would be damn difficult."

"No other roads, though?"

"None."

"Okay, thanks," I said, and drove off.

"What were you thinking?" Ribs asked.

"I'm thinking that if the only way in is through the guard gate, and they have no record of anyone coming in, how did the supposed burglar get in without being recorded?"

"That does present a dilemma," Ribs said.

"Maybe they were already inside the gates. If you're thinking it really is a break-in, I wouldn't put it past someone to come in and hide out for a few days until the time was right."

"So you're saying we should check the gate log for a few days before it happened?"

"And a few days afterward," Ribs said. "If they waited inside beforehand, they might have done the same after the fact."

I nodded. "We'll have to check the book."

"What about the insurance? What do you think?"

"I think it's damn odd that he took out a policy without her knowing, but she's also got a point; with her income, even three million in insurance isn't much. If she were dead, he'd lose more than that in two years."

"So how do you think we should go about this?"

"We'll check into the gate log. Make sure no one got in here. But I'm convinced it was him. I saw that look on his face when he realized it was Chlorinda. Something was going on. I say we dig into the financials. I mean deep. Not just improprieties, but cross-checking from Kevin's records to Chlorinda's to see if they were in the same place at the same time. I'm still convinced that something was going on, and I doubt if he'd wait five or six months to see her. And all of his so-called business travel would present the perfect opportunity for them to get together, especially since she was single."

"Good idea," Ribs said.

"And get his cell phone records too. I want to know who he's been talking to. He had to use somebody to set this up."

"Unless he did it himself," Ribs said.

"He was in Atlanta. Remember?"

"So he says."

"All right get everything about the trip too. Airline flight schedule, hotel security, airline security. I want to know if this son of a bitch was on that flight or not."

"You got it, cuz. By the time I'm done, you're gonna' know what color his piss was."

I turned to stare at Ribs. "You're a sick son of a bitch, you know that? Maybe you *should* partner with Tip. You deserve each other."

"Just an expression."

"Find another expression. That one's disgusting."

"So, like you've said before, you're thinking Mr. Hemphill tried killing Mrs. Hemphill, but things got mixed up and Chlorinda got killed instead?"

"You've got it. I'll still be thinking that when we throw his ass in prison."

"*If* you get enough to convict him. Remember, we haven't even gotten the jewelry yet. If you can't find that, how do you expect to get him?"

"That's another thing. If this was a real break-in, that jewelry would have shown up. A sophisticated burglar might hold onto it but, then again, a sophisticated burglar wouldn't kill someone. No, I'm convinced it was him. And I'm going to nail him."

"You're worked up on this one, cuz. I think you're still pissed off that

Number Two kicked your ass on the last one." Ribs smiled. "How's that going, by the way? You getting any yet?"

"You *definitely* should be partnered with Tip."

"I was partnered with Tip. Remember? On that *el Terrible* case? The one that brought me my lovely Marissa."

"Yeah, I remember. Lovely Marissa, the serial killer who haunts malls."

"Screw you," Ribs said. "I'm through talking."

"Good. And since you asked, my relationship with *my lovely Marissa* is going fine. I'm having dinner with her again tomorrow night. And it's going to be at her place."

"You know we're not supposed to be working this case, right? Just sayin'."

"I tell you that I'm having dinner with Marissa tomorrow night, and you respond with *that*? What kind of partner are you? Hell, what kind of *cousin* are you?"

"Oh, I'm you're cousin now? Usually you don't admit—"

The phone rang.

"Hello?"

"Cataldi, where are you?"

"Coop? Is that you?"

"You know damn right well who it is. Now tell me where you are."

"Ribs and I just left Bentwater, and before you say anything—"

"I'm saying you better hurry your ass up and solve this case. I know it's not your jurisdiction, but Conroe isn't about to solve it, and the heat is coming down."

I put it on speakerphone so Ribs could hear.

"Apparently, the mayor of San Francisco knows Rusty, and he's putting pressure on him, who in turn is putting pressure on Renkin. The West Coast papers are already running with a headline that reads like this:

I heard the shuffling of pages turning, then,

Local Bestseller's Assistant Brutally Murdered in Sleep While on Vacation in Houston.

"If you don't want us to look bad, and I know you don't because *I* don't, then get this case solved. Find out who killed the woman and why, and bring them to justice. *Legal* justice."

"Yes, ma'am. I'm on it."

"More importantly, *I'm* on it," Ribs hollered.

"Good. Between the two of you there might be enough brains to get it done."

I hung up the phone and set it on the seat beside me. "I've got enough brains to know you've got a fat ass," I said.

Just then, Ribs punched my arm. I turned to see a panicked look on his face. He was whispering, "Hang up the phone. Hang up the goddamn phone."

Now, he had me panicking. I grabbed the phone...but it was hung up.

Ribs laughed so hard, I thought he was crying. "You should have seen your face when you thought the phone was still on, you freaked out."

"You son of a bitch," I said. "You rotten son of a bitch."

"What, were you worried that Coop would kick your ass?"

"I'll get you back for this," I said. "I don't know when, but I'll get you back."

"Just drive," Ribs said. "We've got security footage to view at the airlines."

"We're not going there yet," I said. "We've got plenty of other things to do. Besides, that footage isn't going anywhere."

WHO FLEW WHERE

Two days later, and after no more leads, we were on our way to the airport. They said they had all of the tapes ready for viewing.

"I asked Miranda about the insurance stuff," Ribs said. "She said they *should* have told Mrs. Hemphill what the tests were for, but she couldn't swear that they would have. I'd be surprised if they didn't, still…"

"I'm not too big on the insurance angle anyway. But did you hear from Julie on the financials? Has she connected Mr. Hemphill with Chlorinda yet?"

"I spoke to her this morning, and no, she hasn't made a single connection, but she said she has a long way to go. I told her to ask Coop to let Joyce help her."

It didn't take long to get to the airport, but it did take a long time for TSA to produce the material, despite having given them several days notice that we needed it. Finally, an agent arrived and escorted us to a viewing room. "We can't let you have the tapes, but you can view them, and if any of them turn out to be evidence, I'm sure we can make you a copy."

"Sounds good," I said.

I took a seat in an uncomfortable chair supported by rolling wheels, the kind you might find in a cheap office building, and I mean cheap. Ribs sat next to me.

"My ass already hurts, and it's only been five minutes," he said.

"Wait until it's been five hours."

We had advised TSA before coming of which airline and which flight we were interested in. They had recordings for the main security line at times prior to departure, and we had footage that was taken at the departure gate for Delta Airlines for the flight to Atlanta.

After thirty minutes of viewing, we located Mr. Hemphill arriving. I watched him go through security, then we followed him to the restroom.

We lost view in the restroom, naturally, but it picked him up again about fifteen minutes later when he exited.

From there, it was a pretty boring trail. Not that it had been exciting as of yet, but this was no different. He stopped and got a cup of coffee and a bagel, sat at a table and ate it, then made his way to the book store where he purchased a crossword puzzle, a copy of the Wall Street Journal, and a magazine—Forbes, I believe.

He left the book store and went directly to the gate, took a seat, and sat there until it was time to board. All he did the whole time was read —first the paper, then the magazine.

After we watched him walk down the chute, I turned to Ribs and said, "Looks like that theory of a hit-man is looking better and better."

"Hang on," Ribs said. "The plane hasn't taken off yet."

We waited another twenty-five minutes but when the flight took off, and we still had no additional sign of Hemphill, we had to face the facts.

"He must have been on there," I said.

Ribs shook his head. "He must have been, but…I don't know. Let me think more on this."

"There's not much to think on. Even somebody as slow as you could see that he got on the plane and it took off for Atlanta."

"Let's check the airport and the hotel in Atlanta. I want to see him arrive."

"Waste of time, but we'll do it," I said.

"Good."

"Out of curiosity, what do you expect to find? Do you think he jumped out of the plane before it took off?"

"I don't know. But all of it is worth checking into. Including talking to the stewardesses," Ribs said.

"They're called flight attendants now."

"I don't give a shit what they're called. We need to talk to them. I want to talk to someone who *saw* him on the flight. That's better than a ticket."

"And you think they'll remember one nondescript person, when they fly hundreds of people per day?"

My cell rang. Caller ID showed it was Julie. "Hello?"

"Gino, I might have something."

"Hang on. I'm putting you on speaker so that Ribs can hear. Not that it will make any difference, mind you, but…"

"I cross-checked all of the charges for the credit cards. Hemphill and

Chlorinda both had charges at the Chicago Hilton, the Phoenix Marriott, and Shutters on the Beach in Santa Monica during the same weekends. And the charges were for not only the hotel but other items as well."

"Like what?"

"Some of those 'other items' were pretty personal, like a negligee in Phoenix and a couple of pair of silk pajamas in the other locations."

"Wouldn't you bring those with you if you were traveling?"

"Ordinarily, yes. But if it's a romantic afterthought, maybe not. Especially if you want it to be remembered as a special occasion. I know guys aren't necessarily like that, but women like to be able to say, 'I got that on a trip with so-and-so when we went to Santa Monica'. Stuff like that."

I shook my head, but looked over and saw Ribs nodding as if he agreed. "So you're saying she went to Phoenix, or wherever, got all worked up and decided to purchase evening wear just so she could remember going there?"

"I'm not saying *why* she did it, just that the charge-card records show that she did."

"Okay, thanks, Julie. This helps."

Ribs looked over, shaking his head. "I know you've been absent from a woman's company for a while—too long a while if you're judged by your actions with Number Two—but Julie's right about the buying of special items. Every time that we go somewhere special, Rosalee does the same thing, and she talks about it later in the same way Julie said. As far as I'm concerned, it sounds like Mr. Hemphill and his wife's assistant had more than a casual acquaintance."

"Come on, Ribs. It could have been coincidence that she *happened* to be in three cities on identical weekends as him, and she *happened* to stay at the same hotels."

"Yeah. And the Lone Ranger rode a black horse."

"You're a sick fuck, you know that?"

"Not me, kemosabe."

A QUIET DINNER

e were almost to I-45 when Ribs said, "Why don't you come for dinner tonight? Rosalee is making fajitas."

"You're hurting me, Ribs, but I have dinner plans already. With Marissa."

"Holy shit. Say no more. I wouldn't come to my place either. Not even if Rosalee's mother was cooking. Not with Number Two waiting at the table. Just promise me you'll do more than talk tonight. It drives me crazy thinking of Number Two going to waste like that."

I laughed. "You're so full of shit, Ribs. Did you forget that I know you? That your macho bullshit is just that?"

"Hey, you're talking to the Stud of the South here."

"You can stop that bullshit too. I happen to know that the only person to ever call you that was your little cousin, and you paid him to say it."

I dropped Ribs off to get his car, then hurried home to change. It was only five minutes to Marissa's house, but I didn't want to be late. "Being late" was almost as bad as a sin the nuns at school used to say, and the impression that made apparently stuck with me.

t 6:45 I showed up at her door, nervous as hell. I felt like a teenager on a first date, instead of a grown man calling on a criminal.

Damn. I felt like smacking myself in the head. I had to stop thinking like that.

Marissa answered the doorbell in a moment. She looked like a goddess—long flowing dark-brown hair, smooth-as-silk skin, deep-brown eyes, and a smile that disarmed me. And that wasn't the only thing disarming—I had forgotten what a big house she lived in. She was out of my league in more ways than one.

"Gino! So good to see you. I was afraid you wouldn't show."

And I shouldn't have, I thought, but I said, "Why is that? I told you I'd be here."

"I know, but you didn't seem…convinced."

"If I wasn't, the mention of bucatini in red sauce pushed me over the edge."

Marissa walked toward the kitchen, her ass pushing hard on the seams of her skirt. "Don't read too much into that. It's not like I know what I'm doing. I stole this recipe from a friend of mine."

"That's all right. I'll lie and say it's good even if it isn't."

She laughed. "You might very well have to do that. And I won't be offended. By the lie, I mean."

Now, I laughed. I liked her. I liked her sense of humor and I liked her laugh; it was contagious.

"Want some wine?" she said. "I picked it up at the grocery store. The manager said it's good, but I've never had it, so I can't vouch for that."

"Sure, I'll have a glass. What kind of wine is it, anyway?"

She held the bottle up and looked at the label. "A Chianti. Santa Cristina."

"Oh my God! I love it," I said. "It's what I drink all of the time."

"For real?"

"No shit. I love it."

"Then it looks as if the wine is a hit. If nothing else, we can drink dinner."

"Deal," I said. "I can do that. I've done it before."

"Haven't we all?" she said, and brought two glasses of wine and sat on the sofa next to me.

At first, I shied away. Her sitting so close made me uncomfortable and made me feel good at the same time. I wanted to grab her, forget dinner, and carry her upstairs. I also had the urge to grab my keys and run. Live the rest of my life as I had been, wishing I had Mary there to share it with me.

"Did you hear about that school shooting out by El Paso?"

"No. I've been busy all day."

"Working on that mystery-writer case?"

I pulled back. *How did she know?* "Yes. But how—"

"How did I know?"

She grinned. "I called for you to make sure you were coming, and they said you weren't there. I then asked for Detective Delgado. Then they said you were at the airport. I put two and two together and figured out you were on the mystery-writer case."

"Damn, they shouldn't have told you where I was."

"Yeah, I know, but don't be hard on them. Most people wouldn't have been able to figure it out. I knew from the news that the husband's alibi was a flight to Atlanta, and I know from experience that the husband would be a suspect even though the wife didn't get killed. I put it together from there."

"Pretty smart," I said. "But then again, I knew that."

We talked about a number of things, then fifteen minutes later, dinner was served. I sat next to her at a gorgeous mahogany table that seated eight.

"Do you entertain much?" I asked.

"Not really," she said. "I got the table to fill the room more than anything. I don't think I've ever had all of the chairs filled. It would be nice, but…"

She took a sip of wine, then said, "At one time in my life I dreamed of filling that many chairs with children."

"What happened?"

"Life."

"It's never too late," I said.

She sighed. "For some things it is."

I noticed a tone of regret in her voice. I wondered about that. It made me think about why she never had kids.

She got up and opened a second bottle, poured another glass of wine for both of us, then sat, and we started in on the bucatini. The bucatini was done just right but the red sauce was tart. No way I was going to say anything, though. The garlic bread, on the other hand, was delicious. Just right.

After another small helping for each of us, Marissa served a cup of coffee. A cup of perfect coffee, I might add.

"Is this…?"

"Martin Henry. Yes. It's the one good thing I got from Alexis' father. He had the sense to find good coffee."

"That was the only good thing about that case."

"The *only* thing?" she said.

I smiled. "Well, *almost* the only thing."

"What did you think of the bucatini?" she asked.

I almost lied, but stopped myself. "The next time try adding a pinch or two of sugar to the sauce. It makes it not so tart."

She laughed. "You're probably the only person who would have told me that. And I love it. Thank you for being honest."

She slugged the last of her coffee and set the cup on the table. "Want to go for a swim? The water is perfect."

I'm sure I blushed. "I'd love to, but I didn't bring a suit."

"Who says you need a suit?" she said, then laughed.

I wanted to take her up on the offer, but didn't. "No thanks," I said. "Maybe next time."

"How about a walk, instead? I love walking at this time of night."

A walk sounded great and it sounded safe. No commitment. "A walk sounds good," I said. "Where do you want to go?"

"I've got a route mapped out. You can follow me, as long as you're not staring at my butt."

"I can't promise that. It's too nice not to look at."

"Ooh. I'd hate to think that was a compliment from the rigid detective?"

"It might be. It depends on how you take it."

"In that case, I'll take it as a compliment." She curled her finger, as if to beckon me on, then said, "So come along, stay close, and follow the jiggling butt. I'll make sure you don't get in trouble."

We walked for almost two miles, taking a course that took us around the duck pond and through the woods, where we spotted a few deer. It was an enjoyable end to a wonderful evening.

When we got back to her house, she invited me for a nightcap, but I told her I had to go. She leaned forward and gave me a warm kiss, the kind that held promise. I kissed her back, and we held the kiss for a long time.

We finally broke off. I looked into her eyes and said, "Marissa, this has been a wonderful evening."

"Even though the sauce was tart?"

"That's not all that was tart," I said. "And some things are better when they're tart."

She smiled and kissed me again. "Next time, forget your suit again, and we'll go swimming anyway. Then it *will* be a perfect evening."

"You've got a deal," I said, and walked down the sidewalk toward the car.

MEDICAL EXAMINER

J was in the coffee room when Ribs got into work. He walked in, sat down, and said, "Well?"

"Well, what?"

"Fess up. Tell me what happened."

"Nothing happened."

"Oh my God, don't tell me that."

"You just said to tell you what happened."

"I meant what *really* happened. Not some boring shit about talking."

"Forget about it, Ribs. Let's discuss what matters. Did you get the phone logs yet?"

"No phone logs, but Ben called with preliminaries."

"Good. Let's see what we've got."

We read the report then called Ben for a few follow-up questions. "So you're saying three GSWs to the side of the head. Any signs of struggle?"

"None. But the drug screen shows that she had a lot of clonazepam in her. I mean a *lot.*"

"How much is a lot, and how does that compare to a normal dosage?"

"I estimate she had about eight milligrams in her. According to her prescription, she was prescribed one milligram."

"So, she had a prescription?"

"For one milligram, yes. But the amount she had in her would knock her on her ass. Combined with the wine, I would almost guarantee she was asleep."

"What caliber were the bullets?"

"Like you suspected, .38s. They were fired close enough to leave gunshot residue on her head. And the noise would have been pretty damn loud. If the windows were open—and they were—the neighbors would likely have heard the shots."

"They did hear the shots, Ben. They reported hearing them. But if she was drugged, and presumably asleep, it makes me wonder why she was killed, and who did the killing. A random burglar wouldn't kill her if she presented no problem."

"Was there evidence of a break-in? Locks broken? Windows open?"

"Windows were open," I said. "Other than that, no signs at all. But getting back to the drugs. Would it be out of the question for someone like her to take so much?"

"I didn't know the woman, so I can't say. But for a normal person, no, not out of the question, although it's a lot to swallow, so to speak. She'd have had to *want* to get buzzed. Especially since she had alcohol in her system also. With all of that said, I don't think she took it on her own."

"What do you mean?"

"There were traces of clonazepam in the wine bottle. When we found alcohol in her system combined with that much clonazepam, I had my people do a thorough search. They found the wine bottle out back in the garbage."

"What?"

"Yeah. The wine bottle. To me, it's obvious, someone wanted her out cold."

"Or they wanted someone else out cold," Ribs said.

I nodded. "If Mr. Hemphill didn't know Chlorinda would be there, he might have thought his wife would drink the wine."

"And be sleeping like a baby when he, or whoever he hired, came home. Then the shooter could kill the woman, dump the wine bottle and leave." Ben paused. "That *is* what you thing, isn't it?"

"Absolutely, Ben. Now, what else can you tell us?"

"Not much. TOD is like I estimated—9:00 to 11:00. And cause of death is as initially reported, multiple GSWs to the head. Other than that, nothing new."

"What about prints?"

"We're still checking, but nothing yet."

"Okay. Thanks, Ben. See ya later."

I hung up, then I looked at Ribs. "And the crime scene unit has nothing else?"

"Nothing more than the original. No gun found. No obvious evidence of a break-in."

"And where was the wine bottle found?"

"Like Ben said—according to our crew, his guys found it in the garbage can, out back."

I thought for a moment, then said, "Don't you find that odd? That someone would drink the drugged wine, then have the wherewithal to throw the empty bottle away? And to throw it away out back, not in the trash under the sink."

"Not unless someone else threw it out, and they knew it had drugs in it."

"Exactly," I said.

"But then again, why not take the bottle with you?" Ribs asked. "Why put it in the trash at all. They had to know that we'd find it there."

I thought about that and nodded. "You've got a point, Ribs. A damn good point."

I went back to the phone and called Ben. "Are you sure about the TOD? Could it have been later?"

"It might have been a little later, but based on blood pooling, body temperature, and other things, I'll stand by the original estimate of between nine and eleven. Why?"

"Nothing. Just wondering."

"Don't go trying to get a medical degree on me," Ben said. "I already have to deal with Denton and all of his wild-ass theories."

"God bless you for that," I said. "You've heard the expression, 'Once is not enough.' Well, partnering with Denton is the exception to that—once *is* enough."

"I'll raise a glass of Scotch and sing a rousing amen to that," Ben said. "And I might even throw in a hallelujah for good measure."

WHO CALLED WHOM?

"*D*id the phone logs come in?"

"I talked to the phone company this morning. They said we'd have a report by this afternoon."

"We haven't followed up on the information from Julie yet. Remember? The three-city rendezvous?"

"Then let's get on that topic. I want to know what was going on between the two of them."

We drove up to Bentwater, discussing how to approach the topic the whole way. When we got there, Susan greeted us at the door.

"How can I help you, Detectives?"

"We have a few questions for Mr. Hemphill," Ribs said. "Is he here?"

"Certainly. Come in." She walked briskly through the living room to the back door and slid it open. "Kevin! The detectives are here. They have a few questions for you."

Kevin came in and sat. "What do you want?"

"You can tell us about your relationship with Chlorinda," I said.

He furled his eyebrows. "Relationship? She was my wife's assistant. What else is there to tell?"

"There is an explanation needed for why you and Chlorinda stayed at the same hotels in Phoenix, Santa Monica, and Chicago on the same weekends last year. Do you have an answer?"

Mrs. Hemphill looked at him incredulously, then at us. "Is this right?" she asked me. Then she shot a look back at her husband. "Kevin, is this right? Were you having an affair with Chlorinda?"

"That's ridiculous. I'm not going to honor that with an answer."

"Like hell you won't. I want to know, and I want to know now. Were you having an affair with Chlorinda or were you not?"

Hemphill bit his lower lip and twitched. "There were a few times…but it's over."

"You son of a bitch! You rotten son of a bitch! How could you? After all of this time, how could you do this to me?"

"Excuse me," Ribs said. "But you said it was over. Since when?"

"Last year. It only happened a few times. And it wasn't planned."

"That's easy to say now," Susan said. "She's dead and can't deny it. I'd have loved to hear your answer prior to this."

She walked to the sink and got a drink of water, then returned. "How did this start? *When* did this start?"

Susan sat at the table with her fists curled into a ball. "And that son of a bitch worked alongside me acting as if she were my friend. I'm glad she's dead. I'm glad. She got what she deserved."

Ribs cleared his throat. "Why do you think someone wanted to kill her, Mr. Hemphill?"

"Don't be ridiculous," Susan said. "Kevin might be a cheating, dirty bastard, but he's no killer. Besides, he was in Atlanta. You already know that. Find the person who broke in here, and you'll have the killer."

"And how about you, Mrs. Hemphill? Do you know anyone who would want to hurt her?"

"Now you're really stretching. I had nothing to do with this and I have an airtight alibi. Ask any number of people at the Marriott, and they'll tell you. Besides, I had no motive. Until a few moments ago, I didn't know there was an affair, and even if I had known I would have filed for divorce, not killed her."

She shot Kevin a look that could kill. "You heard that right—divorce—as in you are through living off my money."

Mr. Hemphill glared at Ribs. "You *bastard,*" he said, and then got up and left the table.

"I guess that concludes this talk," I said, then I gave a slight bow to Mrs. Hemphill. "I'm sorry we had to bring this up, but we need to get to the bottom of this."

"You're not fooling me, Detective. I'm sure you're not the least bit sorry, and furthermore, I'm sure you had it figured that in one way or another this would turn me against Kevin. Well, that worked in one sense; I'll file for divorce when we get home. But I still stand by my opinion that he *did not* kill Chlorinda. He was in Atlanta for God's sake."

"Yes, ma'am. Thank you," I said. Then, "Come on, Ribs. Let's go."

We drove out of Bentwater slowly, pondering the situation. "What do you think, Ribs?"

"I think he just screwed himself out of a lot of money. Two million dollars a year is nothing to sneeze at."

"I meant, do you think he killed her?"

"Motive-wise I still like our theory that he tried killing his wife and got Chlorinda by mistake. But the wife makes a good point that we've already talked about—he was in Atlanta. So unless we find the hitman he hired, we're screwed."

We didn't get back to the station until 2:00. Ribs checked with Julie, but nothing had come in on her watch. "Phone logs aren't here yet," he said.

"If you're looking for the phone records, I have them," Coop said, from down the hall. "Get to my office, and we'll review them together."

We followed Coop down the hallway, her square block stature moving methodically in front of us. I elbowed Ribs and said, "Fat ass."

He laughed. "I dare you to say it louder."

"Not a chance," I said. "I like living."

Once in Coop's office, I relaxed in one of the chairs. Coop handed us copies of the phone logs. "These are all of the calls from Mr. Hemphill's phone for two week prior to the murder, and it continues until the present. It shows both incoming and outgoing calls. And the other sheets are the outgoing and incoming calls of the numbers we couldn't identify based on Hemphill's records."

I scanned through Hemphill's calls. Most of them were innocent enough: his wife, a pizza delivery service, Delta airlines, the Hyatt hotel in Atlanta. Then I got to the day of the murder, and I located the time I called his phone. Atlanta.

So, he *was* in Atlanta.

But the next call stuck out. Not two minutes after my call to him on the night of the murder, there was a call from his phone to a phone in Houston. It was highlighted orange, which Coop had done to signify a burner or unidentifiable phone number.

"What's this?" I asked.

"What?" Ribs said.

I pointed to the line where it was listed. "Look, a call to an unidentified number not two minutes after I told him of the break-in. By his own admission, he pieced together it must have been a homicide, since I was calling. So the question is, who did he call?"

"And why?" Ribs said.

"And why indeed," Coop said. "You don't order Chinese food after being told there's been a murder at your house."

I flipped a few pages until I found the one that listed other calls by and to that number. "Nothing," I said. "Not shit. And there is no previous record. It's a new phone."

"It's the hit-man," Ribs said. "As Tip would say, I'd bet my—"

"We all know what Tip would say, Ribs. No need to repeat it. But you're right, I'd bet it *is* the hit-man."

"Who else would it be?" Coop asked.

I scanned through the records again. "He didn't even call his wife's phone. That right there is suspicious as hell."

"No shit," Ribs said. "Gino still picks up the phone to call Mary, and she's been dead for two years." He then turned to me and said, "No offense, cuz. Just sayin'."

"None taken, Ribs. Thanks."

"I think what Ribs is saying is that any normal man, upon hearing of a break-in—let alone a potential murder at their house—is going to call their wife. Instead this guy calls a third party."

"Agreed," Coop said. "We need to find out who was on the other end of that phone and what was said."

"Got it," I said.

"Don't tell me you've 'got it', go *get it*."

Ribs snapped a salute. "Yes, ma'am."

Coop grinned. "Get him out of here, Cataldi. Pretty soon, I'm going to categorize him in the unwelcome category, like Denton."

We were halfway to the door when Coop said, "And find out who that goddamn phone belongs to."

WHO OWNS THE PHONE

"Coop sounded like she wants this done," Ribs said.

"We knew that going in," I said. "Remember, she called when we were on our way back from Bentwater. Rusty is putting pressure on her.

"By the way, did you ever hear back from the hotel in Atlanta?"

"Not yet," Ribs said. "I expect to today. They said they'd call. I do have a question, though. Hemphill said he was sick."

"Yeah, he said he got sick after dinner."

"Right, but when you look through his receipts, there is a taxi receipt but no rental-car receipt."

"So he took a taxi instead of getting a rental, so what?"

"'So what'? Look at his records—he *always* takes a rental. And if we go on that assumption, supported by receipts, why did he take a taxi this time?"

"Because he was sick."

"He got the taxi on the way *to* the hotel. So how did he know he was going to be sick?"

I thought about that for a moment, then said, "You're right, Ribs. Ordinarily, he would have gotten a rental as soon as he landed. So why didn't he this time?"

"Because he knew he wouldn't be staying, that's why. He knew he'd have to leave in a hurry."

The phone rang, and Ribs answered. "Delgado."

"This is Jean Louis from the Hyatt."

"Yes, thanks for calling back. I called because I had a few questions regarding Mr. Kevin Hemphill's recent stay. And if it's all right with you, I'm going to put this on speaker so that my partner can listen in."

"That's fine. What can I do for you?"

"As you know from the message I left, I called regarding Mr. Hemphill. Do you know when Mr. Hemphill arrived?"

"On the seventh, about 1:00 P.M. He checked out the next morning."

"Was he there the whole time?"

"Apparently he became ill after dinner. He called and asked for medicine to be sent up, then he called late that night for room service. In the meantime, according to the bill, he watched two movies. Oh, and he accessed several items from the mini-fridge during the evening."

"Did you see him yourself?"

"No, but several of the busboys did—the one who brought Pepcid to the room, and the person who delivered room service. Plus, Mr. Hemphill asked for extra pillows at about ten o'clock, and the maid saw him when she delivered the pillows. I know all of this because I asked before calling you."

"Does Mr. Hemphill stay with you often?"

"Not often, but he has stayed here before."

"Do you have security footage? Or would your people be able to iden-tify him if we sent over a picture?"

"Certainly," he said. "Let me give you my email address: jeanlouis@hyatt.com."

I hung up and called Julie. "Send a picture of Hemphill over to this address: jeanlouis@hyatt.com."

"Now we need to take a trip back to the airport to watch the security tape of that flight from Atlanta."

TSA got us set up quickly this time. No unnecessary wait and no delays. In no time, we were watching the video of passengers deplaning from the flight that had departed Atlanta the morning after the murder. "Remember, Ribs, he took an earlier flight, so it should be the first one we see."

Hemphill exited the chute after first-class got off. He seemed in a hurry. "There he is," Ribs said. "Just like he said."

"So it had to be a hit-man," I said. "Must have been the person he called from Atlanta."

"Let's find out," Ribs said.

"Okay. Why not?"

We headed up to Bentwater and drove up to the house. Mr. Hemphill answered right away, although he didn't seem pleased to ask us in.

"What do you want?" he asked.

Ribs smiled as we followed him to the kitchen. "What, we get you into trouble last time?"

A noise sounded from the dining room, and he turned to see Susan entering the kitchen. "Screw you," he whispered.

"Good afternoon, Mrs. Hemphill," I said. "Sorry to bother you again, but I had a question for your husband."

"Soon to be ex-husband," she said.

"Yes, well, sir, I was curious as to who you called in Houston the night of the murder?"

"I have no idea."

"Really? You made the call a few moments after I informed you of the break-in, and you told us yourself that based on me calling you, and me being in homicide, that you presumed there had been a homicide."

He nodded. "Yes."

"So after learning of that, who was it that was so important for you to call *before* you called your wife? And by the way, there is no record of you calling her."

"I don't remember."

"Don't remember? Let me help. It was a burner phone, and it was a Dallas number, but it was answered in Houston."

"Maybe it was a wrong number?"

"Really? That's the best you can come up with is that it was a wrong number? Well, that won't work. The call was far too long for it to have been a wrong number. Wrong numbers last five or six seconds. This was almost two minutes. Try again."

I waited but he said nothing—offered no more excuses or explanations. I reached for his phone. "If you don't mind, Mr. Hemphill, I'm going to call that number to see who answers, or if anyone answers."

"You can't do that," he said.

"File a complaint," Ribs said. "We're doing it."

I dialed the number on the sheet, then handed the phone to Ribs. "You do it."

It rang about three times then was answered, but no one said anything. After a moment of silence, Ribs said,

"*¿Hola? ¿Quien es?*"

Nothing.

"*¿Quien es?*"

"Who is this?" a voice asked.

"*Ricardo. ¿Quienes?*"

"Who? Ricardo? I don't know any Ricardo."

Ribs sat silent for a moment, occasionally tapping the speaker or making other sounds to mimic a bad connection. When he felt he'd waited long enough, he continued.

"*¿Quien es?*"

He got no answer, so he asked again.

"*¿Quien es?*"

With no response, Ribs hung up. "There was somebody there," he said, "Whoever it was just wasn't talking."

I looked at Hemphill and said, "What about it, Hemphill? Are you going to tell us who that was?"

"I have no idea."

I reached over and patted the back of Mrs. Hemphill's hand. She had moved closer and was now sitting alongside me. "I hate to do this, ma'am, but being a mystery writer, you'll understand." Then, I turned to Mr. Hemphill and said, "I'll tell you what I think. I think this is probably the guy you hired to kill your wife, but he screwed up and killed Chlorinda instead. I think that, and I'm going to prove that."

Hemphill sneered. "You're nuts."

"Nuts or not, I'm going to prove it. That guy answered because he recognized your number. He didn't say anything because he didn't hear your voice. But it doesn't matter. We've got him now. You screwed up. You should have tossed the phone."

"I don't know what you're talking about."

"Maybe not, but you soon will. I'll let you know just before I slap the cuffs on you."

Hemphill stood and pointed toward the front door. "You can leave now."

Mrs. Hemphill looked over at me. "Detective, I might be angry with Kevin, and you know I am, but I'm convinced he had nothing to do with killing Chlorinda or plotting to kill me. I think you're on the wrong track. Besides, he never was good at plotting."

Ribs and I left and drove back to the station slowly. "Ribs, we need to locate that cell phone. Get the phone company on the horn as soon as we get back. I want to know where that person was."

"It's odd that the person answered," Ribs said. "You'd think they would have thrown the cell away after they used it. I mean it's not much money."

"People are odd like that, Ribs. I'll tell you what I find odd, though. I find it odd that she keeps protecting him. If it were me in her shoes, I don't know if I'd defend him even if I believed he was innocent. If a guy cheated on me after all those years and especially with my assistant…"

"Not everybody's like you, cuz. People have affairs. It's a fact of life. And some people actually engage in sex after their wives die. Remember that the next time you have dinner with Number Two."

I stomped on the gas, accelerating quickly. "Just for that, I'm going to drive like Tip all the way back."

When the speedometer hit eighty, Ribs said, "Woo hoo. Now we're walking in the tall grass and pissing with the big dogs."

I let off the gas and laughed. "That does it. I'm asking Coop for a new partner. I hadn't realized how much Tip had ruined you until that last statement. That sounded just like one of his sayings; in fact, it may have *been* one of his sayings."

WHERE DID THE CALL GO?

Ribs walked up to my desk holding a folded paper.

"Dallas," he said. "That's where they say the cell call went. Somewhere on the northwest side of town. From the map, it looks to be a few miles west of the Galleria."

Julie walked in while Ribs was talking. "Here's something interesting," Julie said. "I just got this from another bank account that was set up in Mr. Hemphill's name only. We have withdrawals of more than $15,000 in the past twelve months."

Ribs whistled, long and slow. "That's a lot of money, cuz."

"I wonder where it went," I said. "Or what it went for."

"I'd bet a big portion of that money went to the owner of the cell number we traced to Dallas."

"I won't take that bet, Ribs. I'm guessing you're right on that, but I *am* curious to hear what Mr. Hemphill has to say about where the money went."

"No doubt he'll have some lame-ass excuse, without receipts to back it up."

"That's fine. We can use that to our advantage. We might even nudge Mrs. Hemphill to the right side of the fence, make it so that she sees things our way."

"Speaking of fences," Ribs said, "did you ever hear from Tip on the jewelry? Didn't he talk to a few connections?"

"No, I haven't heard. Let's see if he's in." I got up and headed to Tip's office. He was sitting at the desk when Ribs and I walked in. "Tip, did you ever hear anything from your guys on the jewelry?"

"I talked to Johnny Long today. He's the one I was counting on for help, but he said there's been nothing. I mean nothing. He said he asked everybody he knew and no one has seen any signs or even heard anything about the jewelry."

"Shit."

"More than shit," Tip said. "If that jewelry was worth as much as you said, it should have shown up. If they took the items to another city, I'll buy it, but why do that? Most guys I know would simply dump it as fast as they could and wipe their hands clean. Fences would do the same. That jewelry would be in New York or even London by the end of the week."

"I'm betting it was the husband who did it to make it look like a burglary," Ribs said. "He doesn't need the money, so he could ditch the jewelry anywhere without having to worry about it."

"What have you got so far?" Tip asked.

I pulled out my notes. Not like I needed them, but I wanted to get it right or close to right. "The wife's assistant was murdered while she was sleeping—in the wife's bed, I might add. She was shot three times in the head. Neighbors reported hearing the shots shortly after ten.

"The assistant appears to have been drugged with a prescription that both she and the wife were on. It was in the wine, and the empty bottle was later found outside in the trash. I might add here that the assistant was unexpectedly on the scene. Originally, it was only going to be the wife."

"So the wine might have been for the wife?" Tip said. He got up and started toward the door. "I need a cup of tea. Follow me."

Ribs and I walked with him, toward the coffee room.

"And where was the husband when all of this took place?" he asked.

"In Atlanta on a business trip."

"You sure?"

"You can never be sure of anything, but he had a ticket; the cameras from airline security show him checking in; and the hotel in Atlanta has him registered. So unless we can break what seems to be a damn tight alibi, yes, I'm sure."

I flipped through a few pages of my notes, then added, "Oh, and he apparently answered a phone call I placed to his cell the night of the murder. The phone company confirms the cell was in Atlanta."

"That doesn't mean much," Tip said. "There are technologies that can make calls appear to be answered in one place when it's really some-where else."

I nodded. "I know, but he's not savvy enough to do it."

"From the sound of it, he's rich enough to pay someone to get it done."

"Speaking of pay someone. That brings up our theory. But first, some more details. We met these two to begin with because San Francisco PD called and said they had a tip that one of them wanted to kill the other. Or kill someone. Add to that the fact that a life-insurance policy in the amount of three million dollars was taken out by the husband on the wife, and she didn't know about it. And this happened three months ago."

"How did—"

"In a minute, Tip," I said. "Add to that the fact that on the night of the murder, while the husband was in Atlanta and his wife was supposedly home alone, I called and told him there had been a break-in. By his own admission, he put the facts together, knowing who I was, and assumed there had been a homicide. But did he call his wife's cell? No. Two minutes later, he called a number in Dallas. A burner phone.

"More still, but compounding the issue is that when he saw the body on the scene and realized it *was not* his wife, but the assistant, he flipped out. I think he was more upset when he realized it was *not* the wife. I might add to that part of the story that Ribs and I have determined the assistant was having a fling with him."

Ribs cleared his throat. "And the wife has an airtight alibi."

"So what's the problem, Tip said. "Lock his ass up."

"I'd love to. It would be oh-so nice but there's no hard evidence. We've got nothing solid to convict him on—nothing but speculation, hunches."

"Any past associations with known criminals?" Tip asked.

I shook my head. "None. And I can't figure out opportunity either. Bentwater logs in all the cars. You know that. You've played golf there. They've got no record of Mr. Hemphill or his wife between the time they said they left—him for the airport, and her for the hotel—and the time they returned to the crime scene.

"And there were no suspicious vehicles for several days before or after. It could have been a resident, but I doubt it. The one couple who was having financial troubles were out of town that whole week. And I mean out of town as in, visiting relatives in Idaho, not having fun in Austin.

"The rest of the cars belonged to residents who seemed to be fairly solid citizens."

"And there's no other way in there," Ribs said. "Unless we can figure this out, we're stuck."

Tip kicked his feet up on the empty chair next to him. "Should be easy enough to figure out. Someone could come in through the front gate and be logged in, or they could sneak in across the lake if they had it planned well. I guess they could make their way through the woods from FM 1097, but I can't see a smart person doing that, and from what you've told me so far, whoever did this is smarter than average."

I perked up. "What do you mean about the lake?"

"I mean there are a million little coves bordering the shores of that lake. Not quite a million, but you know what I mean. Someone could have taken a small boat across the lake, cut off the engine when they got up close, and then paddled it in so no one heard. Then, if they did the same going out, no one would be the wiser. They could have parked it back in the cove where they started from and trekked through the woods where they left a waiting car. It doesn't much matter if your killer was a hit-man or a burglar, either one could have done it."

"How the hell did you think of that so quickly?" Ribs said.

"When I was with the county, an almost identical thing happened in Walden a few years ago. We caught the sons of bitches because they used flashlights to see in the dark and someone reported them. But... if someone did this and didn't use flashlights, then...well, I'm betting no one would see them."

"What do you think is the best way to proceed?"

"Back then, they put out flyers, and even did radio spots requesting residents who were home that night to report anything unusual— anything. That's how we got the flashlight lead. I'm guessing the same thing might work here. Ask the locals if they saw anyone on the lake that night or anything else out of the ordinary."

I made notes. "I'm guessing that Conroe PD would be better equipped to handle this."

"They'd be better equipped to handle the flyers, as it's their territory, but Coop could do the radio spots easier. And she's got more juice with the news. She might even get a TV spot." Tip laughed. "You could be a star, Gino."

"Marissa would like that," Ribs said.

"Whoa! Marissa? Who's Marissa? I guess I missed something."

"Missed something? More than something," Ribs said. "You remember the kidnapping case?"

"Of course I remember," Tip said. "You wouldn't have solved it if not for me."

Ribs shook his head. "Anyway, old cuz here is dating Number Two."

Tip shot up straight. "What? Number Two? I thought she was dead."

"That's what good old cuz wanted us to think. He wanted her all for himself."

"Son of a bitch! Gino, you're pissing with the big dogs now."

I raised my head toward the ceiling. "God save me."

"It won't happen," Connie said, as she walked in. "If you're asking to be saved from my lunatic partner, it's not going to work. He must have some arrangement with God—I think he's part of the cross-on-earth that we all have to bear."

"So fill me in on Number Two," Tip said. "What's going on?"

"Nothing's going on. I had a couple of dinners with her. That's all there is to it."

"A couple of dinners is going to lead elsewhere. As sure as shit stinks, it will."

I knew I was in for it now. *Damn that Ribs. I'd get even for this.* "Tip, do all of your sayings have to do with shit or dicks?"

Tip seemed to give it a lot of thought, then he said, "Well shit, I don't know, but you can bet your last dick that I'll find out." Then he laughed so hard, he bent over. In fact, he laughed so hard, he got me laughing, then Ribs and Connie, too.

Coop walked in while we were all in hysterics, and said, "I'm glad something's so funny. Want to share it."

Tip stopped laughing long enough to say, "Shit no. Not me, but ask Gino, he's in a good mood today; in fact, he's as happy as a dog with two dicks." When he finished, it brought on another round of uproarious laughter. I laughed so hard that I started coughing and had trouble catching my breath.

"All right. All right," Coop said. "Just remember that while you're in here drinking coffee and laughing, there's a killer out there who should be in prison."

Ribs snapped a salute, then said, "Yes, sir, Captain. No need to worry. Detective Delgado is on the job."

Coop shook her head while she poured a cup of tea, then left.

"I've about had it for the day," I said. "Anybody want to stop by for a beer?"

"I'm game for another night, but tonight I have to be somewhere," Connie said. "And if we're doing this tomorrow, I'll need directions. I'm not riding with Tip if I don't have to."

Ribs looked at his watch. "I've got an hour or so tonight. But like Connie said, tomorrow would be better."

"Count me in for tomorrow," Tip said. "Elena is visiting her sister. Damn woman won't stay home."

"Maybe it has something to do with who she'd be keeping company with."

"Oh, shut-up," Tip said. Then he turned to Gino. "And by the way, how's Ron? I've been meaning to ask you. I talked to Tony last week, and he said he thinks Ron's adjusting well."

Tip mentioning Ron's name reminded me I hadn't called him yet today. I tried to call at least once a day to let him know I cared. "He seems to be doing great," I said. "I went down last week, and he was looking good, and he seemed to have made quite a few friends."

"That's great," Tip said. "He's a good boy. He'll do fine."

Tip must have noticed the same confused look on Connie's face that I did. "Gino's son had a drug problem. He's getting help and doing great."

"Fantastic," Connie said. "Good luck with that."

"Thanks, Connie," I said. Then I turned to Ribs and said, "You picking up the beer? If you and Tip are both stopping by, I won't have enough."

"I got it cuz. No worries. See you in a little bit."

Tip sat up straighter in the chair. "Well shit, I didn't know we were doing this both nights, but I'm game. I'll be there in a little while."

A LITTLE BIT OF LOGIC AND A LOT OF LUCK

Ribs got to the house quickly, and we started right in on the beer. The way I figured it, Tip wouldn't arrive for another hour, so we had plenty of time to chat and maybe even work something out.

"Why? Why did Hemphill call that number?"

"I think you know why," Ribs said. "You had just called and told Hemphill that the house was broken into. It's as plain as day to me. He wouldn't call a burner phone in Houston that was registered and bought in Dallas unless he had something to do with it. And because he *did* call a burner in Dallas, as far as I'm concerned, the owner of that phone had something to do with it too."

I thought a moment, then said, "I hear what you're saying, but we have to think this through logically. So what other answer *could* it be? If we assume for one minute that Hemphill had nothing to do with the crime, who would he have called after hearing that news?"

"There are a lot of answers to that question, cuz. If we didn't know better, we might say he could have called a sibling—but he didn't. He might have called one of *her* siblings—but he didn't. He might have called the insurance company if he was a coldhearted son of a bitch—but he didn't. He might have picked a random number out of the Dallas phone book, but we know he didn't do that either. Face it, cuz, he's the one who tried to kill her, and the person he hired to do the job owns that phone."

"That puts it in perspective, Ribs."

"It's fine to be in perspective, but how do we find out who owns the phone?"

"Dallas."

"What?"

"It has to have something to do with Dallas," I said.

"No shit. He probably lives there," Ribs said. "It *is* a Dallas number. And whoever answered the phone when I called was in Dallas."

"I'll grant you that he lives there, but Dallas has to have something else to do with it."

"Like what?"

"I don't know yet. But let's assume for a minute that you're right and the killer lives in Dallas, how would he get here? Would he fly? Or drive?"

"What difference does it make. If he drove, we'd never know. And if he flew we'd never know."

"If he drove, I'll agree with you. But if he flew, we might find some anomaly in the airline passenger list. Early morning Dallas to Houston fliers typically fly on a regular basis. There are plenty of business people who fly that route five times a week. Hell, it's only a forty-minute flight. That's shorter than some commute times. So what we look for is the exception. The guy who takes it only once and maybe it's been the only time this year, who knows."

"Cuz, do you know how many flights go back and forth between Houston and Dallas?"

"Exactly. You just hit on another angle. Whoever did this would have probably flown in the day of the murder and back out again the next morning. They wouldn't be hanging around the city after having killed someone. So all we need is a list of passengers who flew in from Dallas on *that* day, are Dallas residents, and flew back to Dallas the following day. I think we can also eliminate women and men under twenty-five or over sixty. We can probably use ethnicity and other factors to narrow it down further. Before long, we'll have a fairly short list."

Ribs lifted his head, as if thinking. "You might have something, cuz. Some of my intelligence must be wearing off on you, but I still have a problem. Even if we find this guy, what then? We can't convict him of flying to Houston, although some people would swear that's a crime. We can't convict him of anything. All he did was fly from Dallas to Houston and answer a phone call from Hemphill. He might look guilty to us, but anyone sitting on a jury would laugh us out of court."

I nodded. "I know that. But just knowing who he is will allow us to put pressure on him. Maybe make him crack."

"All right," Ribs said. "I don't buy it, but all right."

"First thing in the morning, we'll head over to the airport and talk to some stewardesses. I want to check on Hemphill's flight to Atlanta, anyway."

"What, you want to make sure he didn't jump off that plane after it took off with him on it? And by the way, cuz, stewardesses are called flight attendants now."

I laughed. "You *did* spend too much time with Tip."

The glare of headlights turning into the driveway made me turn my head. "Must be Tip," I said.

Tip got out of his car and took his time walking up the sidewalk. As he was making his way to the porch, the phone rang. It was Ron.

"Hey, Ron. What's up?" For the first time in a while I didn't get nervous when I knew it was him calling.

"Not much. Got three new people in today. Tony said if I continue making progress, he'll make me a house manager in a couple of weeks."

"Fantastic."

"Yeah. It really is fantastic, because then I'll be able to help people. I mean *help*."

"And is that what you want to do?"

"Absolutely. Most of these people *want* help. They crave help. They're a lot like I was. I didn't want to be on drugs; I just didn't know how to get off. These guys can help with that, and I want to be a part of it."

"Sounds good to me. I'm proud of you."

"I'm sorry for all of the trouble I caused you, Dad. I didn't mean it."

I felt like crying. I wasn't good with these kind of emotions. "I know you didn't mean it, and nothing makes me happier than to hear you say you're sorry." I made up my mind right then to make sure things never got out of hand again. "I'll be down on Saturday around noon," I said. "We'll hang out, shoot the shit, then run out and eat dinner, if that's all right with you?"

Ron laughed. It was so good to hear him give a genuine laugh. "It's more than all right. I'm dying for something good to eat. The food's all right here, but it doesn't compare to your cooking."

"Great. See you on Saturday. Oh, and I forgot to tell you. I met a woman."

"What? Forgot to tell me?"

"It's nothing serious. At least not yet. We've had dinner a few times is all."

"What did you cook?" Ron asked.

"The first time it was my *Bucatini All'Amatriciana*. The last time, it was gnocchi in tomato basil cream sauce. After that, we ate at her house and had bucatini in red sauce."

"Nothing serious, my ass. If you cooked bucatini *and* gnocchi, she's as good as got your name. You sly old shit."

I laughed. "We'll see."

"Who is she?"

"Nobody you'd know."

"Who?"

"A lady named Marissa," I said.

"A lady named Number Two, Ron," Tip hollered.

Ron obviously heard, and it was no surprise, as loud as Tip was. "Number Two? Wasn't that one of the kidnappers on that other case you did?"

"Yes. But I don't know if it's the same woman. I—"

"Don't know my ass," Tip said. "You don't mistake a fine body like that."

"So she's got a fine body, huh?"

"Pay no mind to Tip Denton. You know how he is."

"Yeah, I know how he is, and these guys talk about him all of the time. Tell him I said hi, and tell him I said thanks. This place is great."

"Okay. I better go now. Tip and Ribs are here causing trouble, so it will be impossible to talk."

"Dad. Before you go. Remember, don't be hard on the lady."

"I'm trying, Ron. But it's difficult. A kid was killed on that case I worked where Number Two was involved. She—"

"Did she do it?" Ron asked.

"No, but—"

"Maybe she's trying to change. I see it every day. People who did wrong things and are now trying to make it right. She might be like that. Just like me. One year ago, I wouldn't have given a nickel for my life, now I feel as if I have a purpose. She could be the same way."

What he said touched me. And he was right. I was holding what she *had done* against her. I needed to look at what she'd become since then. She wasn't the same woman. "Thanks, Ron. That helps."

"Good. See you on Saturday," he said.

"Yeah, see ya."

"Ron giving you love advice?" Ribs asked.

"Ribs, I'm not inviting you and Tip over here again if you keep this up."

"I know why, too," Tip said. "You're chasing Connie's ass, aren't you? Wait till I tell her."

I shook my head. "Denton, you're as incorrigible as ever."

He crushed an empty beer can in his hand and tossed it toward a trash can on the other side of the porch. It missed. "Son of a bitch," he said. "I should have made that shot."

"What you shouldn't have done is tried," I said. "Now, you can pick it up."

"Isn't that what maids are for?"

I looked to the side, grabbed my grilling apron and tossed it to him. "Pick it up, Helga."

Ribs laughed hard, hard enough to snort with beer in his mouth.

"I can't wait until tomorrow," Tip said. "With Connie here, we're going to nail your ass to the cross." Tip picked up the empty and fake-dunked it into the trash can.

"Don't go talking about crosses; Gino's paranoid about crosses."

"Okay, I think that signals it's time to call it a night," I said. "It's going to be a long day tomorrow, and apparently an even longer night."

Ribs got up to leave. "See you tomorrow, cuz."

CHECK THE FLIGHTS

 got to the station early—or at least what I thought was early—but Ribs was already there, drinking coffee and chatting with Hernandez.

"About time you got here, cuz. I thought I was going to have to solve this case by myself, or with this sweet chiquita."

"That does it for me," Hernandez said. "When Delgado starts in with his bullshit, it's time for me to leave."

"So you know it, too?" I asked.

"Since day one," she said, and smacked Ribs on the back of the head. "See you later, big boy." She laughed then, and continued laughing all the way down the hall.

"Looks like it's time to get to the airport," Ribs said.

"Then let's go."

"Where do we need to go?" I asked.

"Delta. Terminal A. I asked Carolyn Meechum to meet us at the entrance. Also another ste…I mean, flight attendant by the name of Kristan Karber. They should be there by the time we arrive."

Carolyn was polite but not so helpful. We showed her Hemphill's picture, and she didn't remember anything. "You've got to realize, detectives, that we fly several fights a day and most of the flights are full or nearly full. That amounts to hundreds of passengers, so unless one stands out—like giving us trouble—we're not going to remember him, or her."

After a few more questions, we let Carolyn go and focused on Kristan. She nodded as soon as I showed her the picture. "Yeah, I remember him."

Flabbergasted, I grabbed the picture and pointed at Hemphill again, hoping she was wrong, wanting her to be mistaken. "You remember *him*? You're sure?"

"Sure, I'm sure. I remember because he looked just like a guy on my morning flight from Dallas."

Hearing her mention that got me excited again. "What do you mean your morning flight?"

She sighed. "It was a minor pain, but my best friend was supposed to do the Dallas to Houston run for United. She got sick, so I filled in for her. It was a pain in the ass because she flies United, and I fly Delta—different airlines, different terminals—but they let us cover for each other when we have to. Anyway, it was a nothing flight, forty minutes maybe, so it was no big deal. If I'd have had to cover for a Coast flight that would have been different."

"Tell me about the guy," I said.

"Not much to tell." She pointed her finger at the picture. "He looked just like this guy. That's the only reason I remember him, because I got off the hop from Dallas, changed uniforms and immediately went to Terminal 'A', where I got on the Delta flight to Atlanta. And there he was, or so I thought."

"What do you mean?"

"It wasn't him. At least he said it wasn't him, but it looked like him. He even had on similar clothes—similar but different—still, he said it wasn't him. I think he was lying, but I can't swear to it."

"How can you be sure?"

"Because I know people, and he acted the same and talked using the same cadence. When I first saw him, I thought it was the same guy, so I said, "Hey, fancy seeing you here."

"And what was his reaction?"

"He just looked at me as if I were nuts, and said, "'Do I know you?' Then he asked if I could get him water, then he went and sat."

"From what you said, it sounds as if he *didn't* know you. So how can you say it was the same guy?"

"Nah. It was him trying to cover for something. You know, like when you bump into somebody who is somewhere they shouldn't be, and they pretend not to know you. It was *that* kind of reaction. One more thing. I realized after he said that that he didn't have his beard. He had a beard on his way from Dallas, so he must have shaved it off in the meantime."

"And you're sure his reaction wasn't genuine?" Ribs asked.

She raised her eyebrows. "I guess it could have been, but if you ask my opinion, no. In my opinion, it was the same guy, but he was trying to pretend it wasn't."

I fidgeted. This was tremendous. We had nothing yet to prove

Hemphill wasn't on that flight, but this was leading me to conclusions."

I finished writing notes, then asked her, "Could it have been a different guy? Suppose he just didn't want to be bothered and was brushing you off? Could it have been that?"

She thought for a long time, then nodded. "Like I said, I guess it *could have been a different guy*, but I don't think it was. If you ask me, I'd say it was the same guy. I don't know that I'd swear to it in court, but I *think* it was."

Ribs stepped up until he was almost touching her. "Is there any way for us to check when the guy on the Dallas flight returned?"

"I'm sure there is, why?"

"I'd be curious," Ribs said. "Actually more than curious. See if you can find out—call me." He handed Kristan his card.

We asked a few more questions, then let her go.

On the way back to the station, Ribs and I discussed what we learned. "If it was the same guy on both flights—in other words, the guy from Dallas—then that means our friend, Hemphill was *not* on his flight to Atlanta. And if Hemphill *was* on the flight to Atlanta, then we have a guy who looks almost identical to him roaming around Houston."

"Either way, Hemphill or his look-alike, are in the city when the murder happens."

"And I'm betting anything that one of them pulled the trigger."

Ribs didn't say anything for a moment, then he became animated. "Lookalikes."

"What?"

"Lookalikes," he said. "It's got to be more than coincidence that we've got two guys who look so much alike. And neither one of us holds much faith in coincidence."

"What are you talking about?" I asked.

Ribs pulled out his phone and dialed. "Charlie, this is Ribs. I need some information, and you're the guy I need it from. We'll be there in half an hour. Yeah. See you then."

"Half an hour? I hope he's at a coffee shop halfway to the station, because I'm not getting to the station in half an hour."

"Pussy," Ribs said. "Tip would have done it."

"And that's why you should partner with him. You two can live fast, die young, and have good-looking corpses, as John Derek so famously said. Meanwhile, Connie and I will live to a ripe old age."

"There you go quoting those old fucking movies again. I wasn't even born when they were released."

"You weren't born when Mozart's music was released either. But it doesn't mean you shouldn't listen to it."

"Hurry-up and drive."

We got to the station in forty-five minutes. Not the thirty Ribs predicted, but Charlie was at his desk, waiting. "What's up, Ribs? What can I do for you?"

"Remember the other day when you were looking at that picture of Jessica Alba?"

"Come on, Ribs, don't bust my chops for that."

"No. I'm not busting your chops. I want to know how you found that picture. In other words, if I wanted to find someone who looked like me, is there a way to do it?"

Charlie's face lit up. "You betcha. There's a new program out. I think it started as a spin off of the celebrity match program, but this one is for ordinary people."

"What the hell are you two talking about?" I asked.

"How does it work?"

"It's easy," Charlie said. "You go to the website, use your computer or iPad, or iPhone's camera—the site says it will support Android soon—and snap a pic of yourself. Then the site uses proprietary technology that was developed by a company in China, and it makes use of deals it struck with Facebook, Apple, Google, and others, to match you to someone.

"It uses their databases. And it's not stealing information. People agreed to allow them to use it, probably during one of the too-many updates to the terms of service. The people who took the time to read the terms of service—almost none—were excluded, but it was such a small percentage it had no visible effect on the program's ability to locate a match. The software also uses it's own facial recognition technology."

I was still confused, but then again, technology did that to me. Ron was always making fun of my inability to adapt. "So if I wanted to find a person who looked like me, how would I?"

Charlie laughed. "Gino, you kill me. Like I said, you'd take a picture of yourself, put it in front of the computer, and the computer would then run a match on your image against the millions it has on file. When it finds a match, or matches, it displays them for you to choose."

"How good are the matches?"

"That depends," Charlie said.

"Matches are rated percentage-wise based on accuracy, and they are presented that way by default. You can alter the way you search or display results also. You can search by location—such as find only matches in Houston or only matches in Texas, etc.

"You can even search and find the best matches in other nationalities. For example, if you wanted to find someone who looked like you but was Oriental, you'd check that box and then it would find only Oriental matches."

"How would you know where the person is?" Ribs said.

"You wouldn't know specifically. As close as they let you get is a big city. If you did a big-city search, they would say five matches found in Houston, or some such nonsense, but it wouldn't say North Houston or anything. Same with Dallas, or Philadelphia or any other big city. In New York, it breaks it down by borough, like Brooklyn, or the Bronx, things like that.

"If you're looking at smaller populations, it will display differently. For an example, it might tell you a seventy-five percent match was found in New Hampshire, but not the town, and never the person's name."

"How do you get the person's name? Or make contact?" Ribs asked.

"If you want to get access to a match you have to join and pay a fee of one hundred dollars. One fourth of that goes to the other person, the rest to the company. So, you find a match, approve it, request a connection, then wait. The company contacts the other person, tells them there is a request for contact, and see if they get approval. If they do, initial contact is made."

"It sounds like a lawsuit waiting to happen," I said.

"I don't know, Gino. They put all the decisions in your hands. If you don't want your city or even your state listed, you don't have to. Nothing you don't want listed is displayed. It's all up to you."

"In other words, if your face is out there, you okayed it?" Ribs asked.

"You got it," Charlie said.

"Let's try it out," I said.

"You can get a generic hit," Charlie said, but if you want the real thing you'll have to join and ask for contact, remember?"

"If I do this generically, will the other person know I'm searching if they are displayed?"

Charlie shook his head. "Only if you ask for contact to be made. Otherwise, it's no different than if a person searched for your name using Google."

"What do I need to get started?"

"If you're talking just a search, all you need is a picture of who you want to search for. But it's going to have to be a high resolution picture."

I looked to Ribs.

"Don't worry, cuz. We'll get it. The picture we have now won't cut it, but I can take one with the camera on my phone. It'll work fine."

Charlie nodded. "If it's a good shot, that'll do."

"Then we need to go to the Hemphill's house and get a picture. Besides, I want to question him about the look-alike."

"Not yet," Ribs said. "I'd wait until we know more. Ask him about the cash withdrawals instead. He needs to answer that anyway."

"Okay, you've got a deal. Meet me at Denny's in the morning, and we'll drive up there."

"Denny's? Goddamn," Ribs said. "You know I hate Denny's."

Denny's the Woodlands

"Which Denny's are ya'll meeting at?"

"Too far from your place, Charlie. This one is far north of the city."

"Oh, okay. Shoot, I was gonna' join ya'll for breakfast."

"You're welcome to if you want, but it's pretty far out of your way—all the way up in the Woodlands."

"Name the time, and I'll be there," Charlie said. "I love breakfast."

"Be there at eight o'clock, right by Shenandoah," I said. "Don't be late."

"I'll be there," he said. "Now, I've gotta' run to the restroom."

"We still on for tonight?" I asked Ribs.

"I haven't spoken to Tip or Connie, but I assume so. I'll be there right after work. And, yes, I'll pick up the beer."

A GATHERING OF DETECTIVES

*J*hung up from my nightly call with Ron just as Ribs pulled up. He got out of the car, carrying three six-packs. I walked to greet him and took one from his hands.

"These feel nice and cold," I said.

"Goddamn freezing," Ribs said. "They had them on ice. I think the corner store does one hell of an after-work business."

We put the beers on into the cooler—on more ice—then took a seat in one of the lounge chairs. "How do you want to work this tomorrow?" I asked.

"You're the boss," Ribs said, "but I'd say go straight at him. Just ask where the damn money went."

I thought, then nodded. "You're probably right. No sense in beating around the bush. He already knows we suspect him."

"Shit. That ain't the half of it. I'm all for Tip's suggestion. Snap a pair of cuffs on him, throw him off the bridge into the lake, and tell him we'll fish him out when he talks."

"I guess we'd save some time that way."

"No guessing about it. It wouldn't take him long to talk. I figure about as long as he can hold his breath."

"We'll sleep on it, maybe ask Charlie what he thinks in the morning."

"Charlie?" Ribs said. "He'll just say to parade Jessica Alba in front of Hemphill while she's wearing a thong, and have her promise to take it off if he talks."

"That's not a bad idea, Ribs. It might work quicker than the cuffs."

Ribs seemed to give it consideration, then said, "On second thought, it just *might* work better. It would for me."

A car turned into the driveway. I leaned forward, squinting. "That's Tip," I said. Then another car pulled in right behind him. Ribs said, "And that's Connie. Looks like the gang's all here."

Tip walked up the sidewalk, already slugging a cold bottle of beer.

"*Buenos noches, mi amigos. ¿Como estás?*"

"*Muy bien. ¿Y tu?*" Ribs smiled. "I see someone's been practicing his Spanish."

"Just keeping you on your toes," Tip said.

"I have to put up with this all of the time," Connie said. "He learns half a dozen words in Italian, then he tries speaking it—and the emphasis is on *tries*—to repeat the words in some kind of understandable manner, but he fails miserably."

"Speaking of failing miserably, have you guys caught a case yet?"

"Looks like we just got one. Some wacko is grabbing little kids *and* their dogs and doing God knows what with them."

"How many?" Ribs asked.

"Two so far," Tip said. "But we've got no clue as to why he's doing it, or what he's doing with them."

"Maybe you'll get lucky," Ribs said.

"Speaking of lucky, Ribs and I caught a break today. One of the flight attendants happened to see what we figure *had* to be out Dallas burner guy on a flight to Houston. Then she saw him again, right afterward, on a flight to Atlanta. And it just so happens it's the flight our guy was supposed to be on."

"That's it?" Connie asked.

I smiled. "And the guy looked identical to Hemphill."

Then Ribs explained the whole match software thing and told them how it works.

"We're going to test it out tomorrow and see what it comes up with. I'm using a picture of Hemphill to prompt the search."

After about two more beers, I noticed a car come down the street, then slowly turn into the driveway. My heart sank when I thought I recognized it, then *she* got out of the car.

Marissa walked up the sidewalk like she walked everywhere, as if she owned it, as if she were the only one in the world using it, or that the rest of the world didn't matter.

She got up to the porch, smile on her face. I fumbled with my manners, but then nodded to each person in turn. "Connie, this is Marissa. And Ribs and Tip, you may or may not remember her, but in case you don't, or in case the name was different, this is Marissa."

She smiled at them. I know it had to melt their hearts, because it melted mine.

"Would you like a beer or a glass of wine?" I said.

"Beer is fine," she said. "It seems to be the drink of choice tonight, so I'll join the crowd."

I handed her a cold beer from the cooler and got a kiss in return. "Good evening, handsome. You didn't tell me you were having company."

"I didn't know," I said. "And I didn't know you were coming over either."

"Should I leave?" she asked, and I could tell she was sincere, not just being polite.

"Not a chance. Stay right where you are."

"You're not embarrassed?" she asked.

"No—"

I started to answer a typical 'no way', but thought better. Marissa and I had a good thing going on with the truth, so instead, I said, "I was embarrassed at first, but then I caught myself almost acting like an ass. Now I'm fine with it. Besides, I learned something from my son. He told me that you might be just like him, on the road to change."

I was still whispering, but I was sure Ribs and Connie could hear. Maybe Tip, too. But the truth was, I didn't care.

"Ron sounds like a smart boy," she said. "I like him already." When she said that, she stood on her tiptoes and kissed me again. "In fact, I like it more that you told him about me."

"Give me time, and I'll tell the world about you," I said.

She laughed. "Deal. You have two weeks."

Connie reached over and grabbed Marissa by the arm. "Come on. I'm sure you know where Gino hides the snack material. Let's fix something up."

I started to protest, but Marissa smiled and went inside with Connie, blowing me a kiss as she stepped through the door.

"What do you want to fix?" Marissa asked.

"I don't know. Maybe nachos and cheese. I haven't met a guy yet who doesn't crave nachos and cheese with beer."

"Easy enough," Marissa said. "I know just where he keeps everything for it. I saw it the other night when I was here." She opened the pantry and took out a bag of tortilla chips and a can of Rotel, which was canned diced tomatoes & chopped green chilies. "There are a few jalapeños on the counter," Marissa said. "Grab them and we'll chop them up."

"I would say put extra jalapeños in Tip's, but he'd probably enjoy it."

"Seems like you know Tip's habits. You and him?"

Connie laughed. "God no. He's got a dream girlfriend, and even if he didn't…well, let's say he's not the best match."

"Who is the right match? A woman as good looking as you, there must be someone."

"Thanks, Marissa. There is one guy back in New York, but he's…well, he's not on my side of the law. I could probably get along with him, maybe even grow to love him, but…how could I?"

Then Connie must have realized what she said, stopped, and looked to Marissa. She was embarrassed.

Marissa smiled. "It's okay. You didn't offend me. It's the truth, right? I was on the other side of the law for a while, but I'm not now. Gino and I have a thing about the truth. We don't lie so we don't have to remember to lie. It makes life easier. He knows what I've done in my life, and I think I know what he's done."

Marissa put her hand on Connie's shoulder. "Just remember. What's not right at the present, is just that—not right at the present. All of it could change in a moment. There are plenty of people who started out life doing not-so-good things, then they changed for the better."

"I don't think there's much hope for him; he works for my uncle."

Marissa got a questioning look on her face, then Connie said. "My uncle is a Mafia boss. Actually, he's not my uncle, but he helped raise me and I call him Uncle Dominic."

Marissa was surprised that Connie opened up so much, but it made her feel good that she did. Perhaps Connie knowing of Marissa's past helped.

"It looks like I'm not the only one with a tainted past," Marissa said. "Well, don't worry. Remember, it was Lucky Luciano who helped the government during WWII. And it was the government who screwed *him* afterward."

Marissa cleaned the spoon she was using for the Rotel, then stood next to Connie. "I'm sure you see the good in your uncle, right?"

Connie nodded.

"Then look for that same good in your other friend. It's there. It might not be as obvious, but it's there."

Connie smiled. "Thank you. That's good advice." She went back to slicing the jalapeños, then said, "Did you know that Ribs has a daughter named Marissa? He adopted her after a case they did last year. She's adorable. And smart as can be."

"Yes. Gino told me. I thought what Ribs and his wife did was sweet. I even talked to Gino about that possibility—adopting, I mean. How about you? Do you have kids?"

Connie shook her head.

"Why not?"

"Well for one thing because I'm not married."

"And the other thing?" Marissa asked. "I'm sorry, but it sounded as if there was more to your answer. Don't you want kids? I'm not prying, just trying to find answers."

Connie stopped slicing for a moment, and said, "I always thought I did, but… I don't know. Something happened on the job. Now, I'm not sure if I want kids."

"What happened?"

"Nothing."

"That's fine. I understand if you don't want to talk about it, but talking to someone often helps. Not always, but often."

Connie put the knife on the counter, leaned on the island and looked at Marissa. "I was raped."

Marissa stopped, walked to her and hugged. "Oh my God. I'm sorry, Connie. I didn't mean to press."

"No. It's okay. It was the first case I was on in Houston. The guy would have killed me if not for Tip. Tip saved my life. I just haven't talked about it much. Not to anybody."

"And that's all right. I didn't know. If you ever decide you want to talk, let me know. If you don't, I'll never bring the subject up again."

"No. I know I *should* talk about it. I just don't. It would probably do me good." Connie almost cried, then she did. Tears rolled down her cheeks. "Not to change the subject, but what about you? Do you plan on having kids?"

"I want to. I love kids. I guess it depends on who I end up with. If it's

Gino, or someone like him, yes, I definitely want kids. I think he'd be a good role model and a good father."

"Gino needs someone like you. He needs a good, strong woman to help him through. He lost his first wife to cancer, you know."

"I know. And I'd like to fill that void. I think I could."

"Go for it. He's ready," Connie said. "Or at least Tip thinks so."

Marissa smiled at Connie, who scraped the sliced jalapeños into the Rotel, mixed it with the cheese, then put it all in the microwave. "Be ready in one and a half minutes."

"I think I'll take your advice," Marissa said. "I'm going for it."

Connie slapped her a high-five. "Go, girl. I'm right with you."

"By the way," Marissa said. "I'm going to need your help on this. I need to learn how to cook a few good Italian dishes. Gino loves to eat, and I'm assuming you know how to cook some dishes he might like."

"In my family, Uncle Dominic wouldn't let any of the kids grow up without learning to cook or make espresso—and that included his brother's kids—so yes, I know a few dishes, and yes, I'll be happy to teach you." She reached into her pocket and pulled out a card. "Take this. It has my home and cell numbers on it. Anytime you want, just call me and we'll make it a night. I'd love the company."

"Deal," Marissa said. "Thank you."

They ended up having to go two and a half minutes on the microwave, but it was finally done. Marissa grabbed the bowl with the cooking mitts. "Connie, would you please bring the chips. I'm sure they're foaming at the mouth by now."

I got up and held the door open allowing Marissa and Connie to step through.

"Damn, that smells good," Ribs said. "And I'm hungry enough to eat more than my share."

Connie passed paper plates around, placed the chips on the table, then took a seat. "Marissa did most of the work," she said. "Blame her if something is wrong."

Marissa finished swallowing, then laughed. "Me? Connie's a traitor! She's the one who prepared it all. If it's not up to par, blame it on her."

"No need to worry," Tip said. "It's good. Not as good as mine, mind you, but good."

"Marissa, you'll have to get used to talk like that," Connie said. "According to Tip, you'll never find barbecue or nachos as good as his —again, that's according to him."

"I only said it because it is the truth," Tip said.

"Tip, you haven't uttered the truth since that day you told me not to believe anything you say."

Marissa looked around for an empty seat, but when she didn't see one, she sat on Gino's lap, bringing a surprised look to his face.

"Am I too heavy?" Marissa cooed.

"Go ahead, answer that one with anything but a negative reply. I dare you," Connie said.

Tip patted his thighs with the palms of his hands. "Come on over here, darlin'. There's plenty of room on Tip's lap."

Marissa smiled. "No thanks, darlin'. I've got my own man, right here." Then she wrapped her arms around Gino's neck and kissed his cheek. "Besides, don't you have a girlfriend?"

"Shit. Does everyone know?"

Connie used one of the few remaining chips to scoop the last of the cheese and popped it in her mouth. After she finished chewing, she said, "I don't know about the rest of you spoilsports, but I'm heading home and leaving Gino and Marissa to themselves. Looks like things are heating up."

Tip stood. "I can take a subtle hint. Well, I usually can't, but Connie isn't known for subtlety." He started off down the sidewalk. "See ya'll tomorrow. Marissa, I'll see you whenever."

Ribs tossed the empties in the trash then took the chip bag and the empty bowl inside. When he came back out, he tapped Gino on the shoulder, and said, "See you tomorrow, cuz."

Connie leaned over and kissed Marissa on the cheek and said, "Thanks for listening. And don't forget to call." Then she said, "Good night, Gino."

I watched Connie go down the sidewalk, and when she was getting into her car, I said, "What was that about? The call, I mean."

"Connie and I were talking. She's nice. Anyway, I asked her to teach me how to cook a few Italian dishes and she agreed."

"I could teach you."

"I know. But this way, I'll be showing you something."

I smiled. "Maybe I like that."

"If you let me show you other things, you'll *love* it."

"Then maybe I'll let you," I said, and kissed her.

We met Charlie for breakfast, and once we all ordered, Charlie looked at us and asked, "So what's up?"

I explained the cash withdrawal to him and waited to see what he'd say. Charlie wasn't the brightest bulb in the closet, but he had come up with a few ideas before, notably on the kidnapping case.

Charlie took a bite of his toast, seemed to be thinking while chewing, then said, "I'm with you, Gino. I'd go straight at him and document where he says he spent the money. I'd make sure he was specific. Then I'd check."

"But if it's cash, there won't be a record."

"There aren't many businesses that even accept large cash payments, and if they do, they almost always record them, even if it's to say, 'cash payment' of…" Charlie took a sip of his horrible coffee. "So if he says he spent X amount at a particular store, and you check and their books don't show any cash payments that day…chances are, there weren't any."

"But if the cash payment does show up?"

"Then you've got pretty good proof that what he said was true."

"So a cash payment isn't as foolproof as people think?" Ribs said.

"Not even close," Charlie said. "A merchant will get hundreds of credit card sales on a typical day, and they won't remember who bought what, unless it's a big-ticket item. But if you pay for something with a large amount of cash, trust me, they'll remember. And they'll more than likely be able to pick you out of a lineup too."

"Okay, that's good info, Charlie. I think I'm going to be able to use that to help break this guy."

"Really? No shit?"

"No shit, Charlie. I take what you tell me seriously. You helped bust the last case, and with the information on the lookalikes, we've got somewhere to go on this one. Good job."

Charlie smiled so wide I thought his cheeks might crack. "Thanks, Gino. I'm glad it helped. Any time you need something, come and get me or give me a call."

"I will. And thanks again."

We finished eating, then got in separate cars and made our way back to the station.

Ribs had a shit-eating grin on his face when I walked in. "So tell me all about it."

"There's nothing to tell."

"I'm beginning to think you're lying, cuz. Nobody, and I mean nobody, spends that much time with a fox as hot as her and has nothing to tell."

"Shut-up, Ribs, or I'll tell Rosalee you're having wet dreams about women other than her. As Tip says, you'll be eating duck shit soup from then on."

"Goddamn, you're a prick, cuz."

"I guess you'll have to learn to live with it. Now, let's talk about the case. What's do we need to do?"

"You said you wanted to go back to the airport and look at security again. I already called this morning and asked if they could have the tapes ready that show the flight from Dallas to Houston that the other guy was on."

"Okay. What are we waiting for? Let's go."

T raffic was light, so we made it to the airport in a little more than thirty minutes. And much to my surprise, and delight, TSA had the tapes ready and available for us to view. They even had it fast forwarded to the spot we were looking for.

Ribs and I got as comfortable as possible, then they started the tape. Within seconds, the guy exited the chute. I almost fell out of my chair. "Jesus Christ, that looks *just* like Hemphill. He could pass for him with ease."

"I think he *did* pass for him," Ribs said. "We'll see, but I'm betting this guy gets on Hemphill's flight to Atlanta."

"If he does, that would leave Hemphill free to stay here and do the dirty deed."

"It makes more sense," Ribs said. "It's not easy hiring a hit-man, but obviously, with that new software Charlie showed us, it's a hell of a lot easier to hire a look alike."

We followed the guy, who—thanks to Kristan—we now knew as Roger Farnsworth—through the airport to the underground tram. Kristan had remembered he was in either twelve "A" or thirteen "A." Then she tracked him down on the flight's passenger manifest.

He took a tram to Terminal "A" and went directly to the men's room.

Cameras couldn't follow him in there, so we waited until he exited. About fifteen minutes later, when I was beginning to wonder if he'd fallen asleep, he came out, but he had no beard, and his clothes were different.

"Is that the same guy?" I said.

"It's him," Ribs said. "He's just trying to look different. Look at the way he walks. See how he favors the right side. I'm betting that somewhere in the past, he had an injury on that side which makes him lean that way."

I hit the fast-forward, and Ribs halted me.

"Hold up. Wait a while. I know it's been a few minutes but bear with me. I was on surveillance one time where the guy did this exact thing. He waited me out in the bathroom, sending out a decoy dressed like him beforehand."

I waited for what seemed like forever, playing solitaire and checking email messages on my phone, while frequently glancing at the screen. Finally, Ribs' diligence paid off. A guy exited the bathroom who looked just like Roger Farnsworth, but it wasn't him. Now that I knew what to look for it was obvious."

"No way that's him," Ribs said. "You see the walk? He's not favoring the right side. I'm telling you, he was the other guy, the first one out of the rest room, and this is Hemphill."

"Then let's see where Hemphill goes," I said.

We followed who we believed to be Hemphill, tracking his movements all the way back to the Dallas flight around 1:00. He took an occasional stop at the coffee shop and the bookstore, but other than that, nothing spectacular.

Then I went back to the original tape they prepared and we picked up on who we believed to be the decoy, from the restroom on. He went to the bookshop, then straight to the Delta gate leaving for Atlanta.

I paused for a minute and asked them to bring Kristan in. She arrived a few minutes later. "Is this him?" I asked. "Is this the guy who flew to Atlanta?"

She leaned closer to the screen then said, "That's him. No doubt about it."

I then switched to the other tape showing who we believed to be Hemphill, and I asked the same question. "This guy looks more like the one who flew down with you from Dallas."

She stared, got real close and watched him, then said, "Yes, he does look like him, especially with the beard, but he doesn't walk like him. The other gentleman walked and leaned to the right. Not quite a limp, but he *favored* the right leg."

"Okay, you can leave," I said. "That's all we need."

After she left, I turned to Ribs. "If we're right on this, why did Hemphill fly back to Dallas?"

"To get to the other side of the state," Ribs said, then laughed like hell.

"You really do need to be partnered with Tip. You're even picking up his sick sense of humor."

"Okay. All kidding aside, let's wrap this up and go back to the station. Once we're there, we can figure out why he went to Dallas."

"All right, but I want to take one more look at him getting on that plane."

We watched Hemphill get on the flight to Dallas, and we kept watching until it took off.

"He's on it," Ribs said. "Now let's figure out why."

We thanked the TSA employees for their cooperation and headed back to the station.

"Let's assume for argument's sake that we're correct about who is on which flight—that Roger, the decoy, is on his way to Atlanta, and Hemphill took the flight back to Dallas."

"Okay, I'm assuming."

"It's logical to assume that Hemphill is the one who shot Chlorinda, because it's about an 11-hour drive from Atlanta to Houston, and we already know Roger didn't fly back."

"Okay."

"So that leaves Hemphill as the one who needs to be in Houston. Suppose he drives back, using a rental or the other guy's car, then gives Roger the car back the next day when he returns from Atlanta."

"Fine, but why go back to Dallas?" I asked. "He could have stayed here and let Roger fly back the next day."

Ribs thought for a moment, then said, "I don't know. I'll have to think on that."

All the way back to the station, we discussed it, and talked about options, but none of them proved satisfactory. When we got in, we talked it over with Coop and Tip, and even Charlie, but nobody had a solution.

"You don't need to know *why* he did it," Tip said, "just that he did."

"Call Roger's number again," I said to Ribs. Let's see if he picks up."

Ribs dialed the phone and it rang, but no answer. "He's on to us by now," Ribs said. "I'm guessing this phone is in a dumpster somewhere in the south end of Dallas."

"Or worse," Tip said.

"What's the last location we have on this phone?" I asked.

Ribs opened his notebook. "Got it right here. It was just off the North Loop in Dallas, west of the Galleria."

"I say we see if Santos will help us out. Maybe stake a ten or twelve-block radius out, and see if he spots him."

Tip shrugged. "Doesn't hurt to ask."

Suddenly, it struck me. "I thought you and Connie just caught a case?"

Tip said, "Hell, that was yesterday. I got that solved already."

He had me going for a minute, then I said, Denton, you're the same ass you always were."

He smiled. "Connie had a doctor's appointment, then she was doing something, I think with Marissa. So I'm hanging out here."

"With Marissa? What are they doing?"

"I have no idea. I don't mess around asking questions I shouldn't."

"Okay. Well, I've got to get going," I said.

On the way home, I wondered what Connie and Marissa could be doing, even though Marissa had told me they might cook together. On the one hand I was tickled to death that they seemed to be getting along. On the other, I was scared to death that they seemed to be getting along. I guessed it was okay to have Marissa to myself, but it felt intrusive to have her be friends with my friends.

I banged myself in the side of the head. *What the hell was I thinking of.* It was like Ron said, people can change. *Hell, people* do *change.*

I turned onto the street leading to my house and looked at my watch as I did. It had taken me more than an hour to get home. Not ideal, but not horrendous.

Besides, during the drive I got to do a lot of thinking. Thinking about my current situation with Marissa and where it might lead, if anywhere. In the past, I had always used the memory of Mary to keep people away, and it worked, but I vowed that I wasn't going to do that anymore. It wasn't fair to Mary. It wasn't fair to Ron. And it wasn't fair to me.

Mary would not have wanted me to live a life of solitude. She'd have been the first one to encourage me to move on, find someone else. Hell, even her relatives were pushing me. I thought about it again, and nodded. No doubt about it, Mary would have wanted what was best for me. She always did.

As I thought that, I realized that in many ways, Marissa was like that, too. She never demanded anything. Never asked for anything. Always gave. *Always* did. She was a good person.

I pulled into the driveway and realized that Marissa's car was there. *What the hell?*

I got out of the car and quickly walked to the house and opened the door. The magnificent aroma of freshly cooked meatballs, red sauce, and garlic assaulted my olfactory senses. I grew hungry immediately.

"Hello? Marissa?"

"In here," she yelled.

I stepped into the kitchen and witnessed a sight I had only dreamed of. Marissa was at the stove, with apron on, cooking several pounds of meatballs while a pot of sauce boiled in the background.

I laughed. "What the hell is going on?"

"Connie gave me her recipe for spaghetti and meatballs. I know it's nothing fancy, but you have to start somewhere."

"Nothing fancy, my ass." I walked over, grabbed her shoulders, pulled her toward me and kissed her lips. "Marissa, I think I love you."

She was holding a wooden spoon covered in red sauce. She set in on the island. "What? What did you say?"

I didn't know whether she was looking for clarification or confirmation, so I squeezed her shoulders tightly, kissed her lips again and said, "I love you, Marissa."

She wrapped her arms around my neck and hugged me. I could feel her tears on my neck. "No one has ever told me that," she said. "Not since before my mother died."

"From now on, you're going to hear it every day," I said. Then I unwrapped her arms and stared into her eyes and said, "And every night."

Marissa looked at me and said, "Gino, you have no idea what this means to me."

"I hope it means a lot," I said. "Because it means a lot to me."

"More than you know," she said, then, "Now, we better get this food on the table. I want to make sure you have enough energy for other things."

I lowered my head. "As far as the *other things*, I haven't had much experience since Mary died."

She smiled. "Good. I haven't had much experience either. I might act like it, but I don't. Now, let's eat."

We ate nonstop until the meal was finished. I don't want to say we didn't speak, but it would be close to the truth. And it was good. Even better than what I used to make.

"Damn, this is good. I wonder where she learned to make her sauce."

"She said she learned from her Uncle Dominic. He's a Mafia boss. Did you know that?"

"A what?"

"A Mafia boss. In New York."

I shook my head. "I had no idea. She told you this?"

Marissa nodded. "Maybe I shouldn't have said anything."

"I'm sure she wouldn't have told you if she was worried. Besides, that was up North. Now she's down here."

"I guess," Marissa said. "Besides, people can change, right?"

I laughed and squeezed her hand. "They sure can."

She grabbed my plate and set it on top of hers, then stacked the silverware on it. "Leave that," I said. "I'll get it later."

"And by then the sauce will be stuck hard on the plates. I need to get this done so I can call Connie."

"Call Connie? For what?"

"To tell her how the dinner came out, and to tell her how the dinner really came out."

"What the hell do you mean?"

Marissa laughed. "To tell her how the food tasted, and to tell her what you said."

"Tell her what I said?" Marissa stunned me with that one. *Did I want people to know yet?*

She lost her smile. "I won't tell her if you don't want. I just—"

I put my finger to her lips. "Tell anyone you want. Because if you don't, I will."

"Really?" she said, and her smile returned. "If you're serious, I'm calling Connie. It's been so long since I've had someone to share good news with."

I took the dishes from her and walked toward the sink. "Go. Call her. I've got this."

"Are you sure?" she said.

"I'm positive. God forbid I come between a woman and her gossip—I mean news sharing."

Marissa laughed and reached up for a kiss. "Thanks," she said, and walked out back with her phone.

After I was done the dishes, and much later, after Marissa and Connie finished chatting, we sat in the living room to talk.

She snuggled next to me on the couch. "You look like something's on your mind?"

"Only you," I said. "But that's a whole lot better than anything else I can think of."

She giggled, and kissed me again. "I feel like a teenager," she said.

"You *look* like a teenager. You're far too young for me. Not that I'm complaining, but…"

Marissa rested her head on my shoulder. "Just hold me tightly. I don't want this night to end."

"Me neither, though it will end, because I've got a case to solve."

"What's going on with that? Not that I'm prying," she quickly added.

I stroked her hair. "I'm not worried about things like that anymore. I used to be, but not now."

I thought about where we were on the case and then had an idea. "Maybe you can help," I said. "Ribs and I are stuck trying to figure out why Hemphill would do something. See if you have any ideas."

She sat up. "I'd be happy to; in fact, I'd be honored."

I shifted to the side and faced her. "I'm giving you the short version. Hemphill hired a decoy to take his flight to Atlanta, then he took the decoy's return flight to Dallas. In the long run, it doesn't matter, but why would he go to Dallas instead of staying here?"

Marissa sat erect, sipped her wine, then thought some more. After a few minutes, she said, "If it were me, I wouldn't want to be seen leaving the Houston airport when I was supposed to be on a flight to Atlanta."

I furrowed my brows. "What?"

"Think about it," she said. "This was going to be a murder investigation, so he had to know you'd verify his alibi, *including* looking at security footage of who exited the airport."

"Yeah?"

"So—as I said—he wouldn't want to be caught on film leaving the Houston airport when he was supposed to be in Atlanta. It would spur a deep line of questioning. The easy way around that—assuming you have to be in Houston that night—is to fly to a nearby airport and drive back. But, and this is a big but, you don't want to have to rent a car which would be recorded in your name. That rules out logical possibilities, like Austin or Hobby. If the decoy lived in Dallas, he'd have a car already there, so it would be easy enough to fly to Dallas, take the decoy's car and drive back to Houston. Then, the next day, when the decoy flies home, he takes his car and drives back to Dallas on his own."

I sat silently while I digested what she said, then, when it all hit me, I said, "Goddamn. Goddamn, you might have it. I think that's it."

"One more thing," Marissa said. "If Hemphill had't gone to Dallas and drove back, then the decoy would have had to fly back because he'd have no car. That would mean another ticket (and a one-way ticket at that, which are always suspect) and another chance he'd be recognized on security tapes.

I almost leapt from the couch. "Holy shit, Marissa. You've got it. That's it."

"If I'd have known what it took to get you excited, I'd have done it long ago." she said.

I leaned against the back of the couch and pulled her close to me. "All it takes to get me excited is you."

Marissa unbuttoned the top of my shirt and let her finger trace across my chest. "And I'm going to make sure it stays that way," she said.

I think she was succeeding, because further thoughts of work vanished from my mind.

EXPLAIN YOURSELF, MR. HEMPHILL

I called Hemphill to let him know we were coming up. He wanted to know what for, so I told him we had more questions regarding his trip to Atlanta. I didn't want him to prepare answers for the cash withdrawal questions, and I didn't want him to know we needed a picture for the look-alike program. The picture I had wasn't good enough.

About thirty minutes into the drive, Ribs said. "What were you doing last night? I tried calling but nobody answered."

"I was with Marissa."

"At 11:00?"

"And at 1:00 and 3:00 and 5:00."

"What? Son of a bitch! She spent the night?"

I nodded. "She did, Ribs, and if you tell anybody, I'll kill you."

"You don't have to worry about me," he said. "Just give me the scoop. What happened?"

"We had a quiet dinner, drank some wine, talked business, then—"

"Wait. Talked business? Cuz, what the hell is the matter with you? Didn't I teach you anything? You don't talk business when someone like Marissa is with you."

"You'll be singing a different tune when I tell you that she solved the airport dilemma."

"What do you mean?"

"I mean, she figured out why Hemphill flew to Dallas, and I have to agree with her."

"Bullshit. Tell me about it."

I filled Ribs in on what she said, then waited.

"Son of a bitch," he said. "I think she might have something. And she's right, we would have checked the security for people leaving, wouldn't we?"

I nodded. "We would have, Ribs. At least, I would have."

"What the hell is wrong with us for not thinking of this ourselves? Goddamn. Marissa is sexy *and* smart. Don't let that one go, cuz. No matter what you do, don't let her go."

"Don't worry about that," I said. "Last night sealed the deal. I found out she could cook too."

"*Dios mío!* If only I could live my life again."

"You're so full of it. You'd do everything the same. If not for Rosalee, all of those kids wouldn't be there, and then where would you be?"

Ribs laughed. "I know, cuz. But it's nice to dream."

About fifteen minutes later, we turned left into Bentwater. We slowed as we approached the guard house. "Good morning, detectives," the guard said. "Still working that case?"

"Still on it," I said. "This one's a tough nut to bust."

"Good luck on it," he said, and patted the side of my car, as if it were a horse or something.

We made our way to the Hemphill house and pulled into the driveway. Susan answered the door and showed us in. We took a seat in the living room, me on the sofa, Ribs in a chair opposite it.

"We're here to see Mr. Hemphill," I said. "We called on the way up and told him we were coming."

"Then I'm sure he's expecting you," she said. "I'll let him know you're here."

She returned a couple of minutes later with Mr. Hemphill trailing a few steps behind. "What do you want, now?" he asked.

Ribs smiled. "I respect that you want to get right to the point, Mr. Hemphill, so I will too. A routine investigation of your financial accounts revealed several large cash withdrawals. Would you care to explain them?"

"No."

"No? That's your answer?" Ribs said. "I'm trying to be polite."

"Then don't ask me such questions."

"We need answers whether you want to provide them or not," I said.

"People don't always get what they need," Hemphill said.

"Then I guess the jury will hear our version of how you paid for things with cash so they wouldn't be recorded. Things that covered up your plan to murder your wife."

"You're nuts."

"But that plan backfired, didn't it? You killed Chlorinda instead of Susan. Not quite what you wanted."

"Get out of my house."

"It's not *your* house," Susan said. "And I think I want to hear what the detectives have to say. So answer the questions, or you won't have my money to support the legal bills, which sound imminent."

"Now that that matter is settled, let's get at it," Ribs said. "First, I need a good facial picture." He pulled out his iPhone and snapped a high resolution photo.

"As far as the questions, we show withdrawals of more than fifteen thousand dollars in cash in the past year. What did you use that money for?"

"I don't know."

"I don't know won't cut it," Ribs said. "We need specifics."

"I don't know. Things. Miscellaneous items. Wine. An iPhone. Cigars."

"Bullshit," Susan said. "All of those items were purchased with credit cards, and I have the receipts to prove it. It may take a while to locate them, but I have them."

Kevin shot her a wicked glare. "Don't look at me like that," she said. "I'll defend you with my last breath, but I'm not going to lie for you."

Hemphill reached toward the coffee table, opened a cigar box and pulled one out to light. He leaned against the cushion on the sofa as he exhaled the puff of smoke. "I'd ask you if you minded that I smoke, but I don't give a shit," he said, and smiled.

"As to the money, I didn't want to tell you because I spent it on a special necklace for Susan—one she fell in love with when we were here last time."

"And you can prove this?"

"Absolutely."

"Why didn't you tell us about this before?" I asked.

"Because I didn't want Susan to know about it. It was supposed to be a surprise."

"I didn't see it on the list of items taken," Ribs said.

"That's because it wasn't on the list. I didn't have it insured yet, and I didn't want her to know about it, as I said. In the turmoil, I guess I forgot to mention all of that."

"We'll need the receipt," I said.

"Of course. Check with Donoho's in The Woodlands. That's where I got it."

Susan raised her hands to her mouth, pressing the palms against her lips. She sighed. "You mean that necklace I loved. The one—"

Kevin smiled. "Yes, dear, the one you drooled over the last time. I was planning on giving it to you for your birthday or Christmas."

"Oh my God, dear, that's so sweet. I don't know what to say."

I smiled, but inside I was sick. *This sick fuck was planning to buy her a necklace*—with her money—*and she was excited about it."*

"You know, they'll have a record of the transaction even though it was cash," Ribs said.

Hemphill furrowed his brows. "I would hope so, Detective. I'm counting on it."

That took the wind out of our sails. "Okay, Mr. Hemphill. We'll check on it."

Ribs and I left then, and he probably felt as confused as I did. "You think he's telling the truth?"

"He sure seemed to be," Ribs said. "Anyway, it won't take much to find out. I'm sure the jewelry store will have it recorded."

We called Donoho's on the way, hoping they'd have the financial records available by the time we go there.

The owner's niece greeted us, and when I showed my badge, she smiled and said, "Of course, Detective. I was the one you spoke with. Come this way."

She then led us to a back room, where a guy who looked like anything but an accountant waited. "What is the problem with this order?"

"No problem," I said. "We simply need to verify purchase."

"Oh, I see. Well, yes, I can verify that Mr. Hemphill purchased the Eternal Necklace on the date specified. And that he paid cash. I found it odd that he'd do so, considering his other purchases had been on account, but he insisted."

"Why wouldn't he want it on account?" Ribs asked. "Are interest fees high?"

The man laughed. "On the contrary. For good customers like Mr. Hemphill, we have no interest fees, simply a monthly payment. I reminded him of that, but he refused."

I shook my head. "That's odd."

"Not as odd as one might think."

"What do you mean?"

The guy shuffled his feet and looked the other way then back. "The lady who accompanied *Mr. Hemphill* was not *Mrs. Hemphill*."

"Are you sure?" Ribs asked.

"Positive," he said. "I've seen her enough times to know. I even read her books."

"Can you get us a description of the necklace so we can put it in our report?"

"Of course, Detective. That's no problem. Give me your card, and I'll have it faxed to you. Or better yet, I'll email you a photo."

"Okay, thanks," I said, and Ribs and I left.

On the way to the car, I said, "Why would Hemphill tell us about a cash purchase that would further incriminate him in an affair? He had to know we'd find out."

"Beyond me," Ribs said. "You'd think he would do anything to keep that hidden."

"Unless he *is* guilty and desperate for an alibi."

"Have to be pretty damn desperate."

"If he wanted us to stop looking into the cash withdrawals, he might be willing to take the heat for the affair."

"Maybe he was afraid we'd find the real money," Ribs said. "Maybe this was a decoy also, like the guy from Dallas."

While driving, I called Mrs. Hemphill. I had her on my favorites list now, so I could dial her quickly.

"Hello?"

"Mrs. Hemphill. This is Detective Cataldi." I put the phone on speaker so Ribs could hear.

"I was wondering if there has been anything of value missing during the past year? I'm talking monetary value, in the neighborhood of ten or fifteen thousand dollars."

"Goodness, no. Nothing has been— Well, wait a minute. About eleven months ago, Kevin did lose his watch. It was a Rolex. He never found it either."

"And how much was the watch worth?"

"I don't know. Maybe twenty or twenty-five thousand on the open market. New, it would be much more."

Ribs whistled, then he leaned toward the phone and hollered. "For a goddamn watch?"

Susan chuckled. "A 'goddamn watch' as you call it, can cost in the hundreds of thousands, depending on what you want. The brand Kevin owned was far less."

"Did you report it missing?" I asked.

"No reason to," she said. "If you ask the insurance company to pay for it, they raise your rates, so in the long run, you're paying for it anyway. Besides, it wasn't that much."

You know you're rich when you can say twenty thousand dollars is "not that much." "If someone were to come across an item like that, where would they go to sell it?"

"You mean, if Kevin wanted to get money from it, how would he go about it?"

I laughed. "I guess so, yes."

"Assuming a person would want to—which Kevin wouldn't—I would suggest he go to Craigslist or a not-so-reputable jeweler…any number of avenues."

"Okay, thanks," I said. "That helps." I hung up the phone and shot Ribs a look. "What do you think?"

"I think Mr. Hemphill sold that watch somewhere, pocketed the money for a rainy day, and bought the necklace for the Chiquita on the side so he'd have an excuse for secrecy."

"Pretty complex for him."

"Pretty complex for anyone, but it can't be too complex if we're onto it. We're not that good."

I laughed. "I can't argue with that logic, Ribs. Let's stop and get some coffee."

"I'm game, as long as it isn't with Charlie and as long as it isn't at Denny's."

"How about Starbucks by ourselves."

"I'll go for that. Hurry up. I'm thirsty."

Starbucks, the Woodlands

We sat in a corner booth, away from nearby listeners.

"What's up next?" Ribs asked. "And why didn't we sit outside?"

"It's too damn hot," I said. "Besides, we still have to do discuss the look-alike thing and that may take a while."

"All we need to do is run Hemphill's picture through and see what we get. I'm betting that Roger comes up as the number-one hit or at least the number-one local hit."

"That's a sucker bet, and you've got no takers here. If Roger's not the number-one match, he's in the top three. Those sons of bitches look like they're related."

"Speaking of related," I said. "Marissa and I were thinking of visiting next week. Maybe spend some time with the kids, play games, then grab something to eat. Is that all right?"

Ribs lit up. "Are you shitting me? Of course it's all right. Name the time. I'll make sure that the girls have their homework done."

"Don't you need to check with Rosalee first?"

"Hell no. She's been bugging me to have ya'll over ever since I told her you might have a girl. You know Rosalee. She loves matchmaking."

"Shall we bring food?"

"No way. Rosalee would have a heart attack. She'll cook something and love it. Just come hungry. You know how she love to cook. And tell Marissa she better be prepared to talk, because Rosalee loves that almost as much."

"Okay. Count on it. We'll plan on Wednesday. Around seven?"

"Wednesday at seven it is," Ribs said. "Don't forget to tell Marissa to come prepared to talk and she needs to be prepared for mega rounds of makeup. The girls love to have someone to put makeup on."

"You got it," I said. "Now, let's get back to work."

LOOK-ALIKES

We returned to the station and went straight to Charlie' desk. "We need to look at that software program," Ribs said.

"Have you got a decent picture?" Charlie asked.

Ribs gestured to me. "Gino took one. It should be good, although he is notoriously bad at taking pictures." Ribs laughed like hell, then said, "Just joking, Charlie. It'll be a good picture—in other words, one I took."

Charlie sat at his desk and brought up the site. "Sit down, Gino. You're going to need to fill out a lot of forms to set up an account. They don't make it easy."

A half hour later, when the account was set up, I entered Hemphill's picture as my own. It took a few minutes to process, then it displayed a message that said it was ready.

"Are we ready to go?"

"Ready as you'll ever be, "Charlie said. "Put in the search parameters like we discussed, and you'll have results within minutes."

"What parameters?"

"Remember? Location, ethnicity, match percentage, all of it."

I opted for the Southeastern and Southwestern United States only, Caucasian, and fifty-five percent or more for a match. Then I hit search.

"This might take a few minutes," Charlie said. "If you want coffee, now is the time to get it."

Ribs jumped at the suggestion, and I hollered to get me one also. Ten minutes later, the program produced matches. The best match—as we knew—was in Houston, a ninety-nine percenter. That was followed by a ninety percent match in Dallas, which we also knew, and an eighty-three percent match in New Orleans. There was a seventy-one percent match in Memphis and a fifty-nine percent match in Atlanta. We had to keep in mind that the cities listed were only the metropolitan area. The New Orleans match might, in fact, be Baton Rouge, and the Atlanta match might be as far away as Clemson, South Carolina.

"Well, that does it," Ribs said upon his return. He handed me my coffee. "Now we know how he did it."

"I want to be sure," I said. "How do we get their names or addresses?"

Charlie looked over at me. "Like I said before, if you want specific information, you need to pay. Otherwise, all you get are anonymous pictures and location results by metropolitan area."

"Then we pay," I said. "I'm sure Coop would approve it."

"We've still got a problem," Charlie said. "If you pay, it's going to have to be with your card, and the machine is going to match up your account information with your credit card information. If they don't match, it won't work."

"Shit," I said. "He might recognize my name. Can he see my name?"

"Yeah. Once you request contact, whoever you asked to contact can see your whole profile. I mean not your financial info, but your name, address, age, ethnicity, etc. They can also see who else you requested contact from—not the person's name, but their general location and what percentage match it is. It's a good negotiating point. If they are a ninety percent match and they can see that the only other people you requested contact from are less than sixty percent or are really far away, then they know they can squeeze you, if you really need a close look-alike."

"Sounds like a hell of an operation."

"You don't know the half of it. I know a guy over in Austin who make almost two grand a month on this."

"What does he do?"

"A little bit of everything and most of it not legal. He poses for fake ID'S, waits in line for TDLs for those who don't want to give their fingerprint, things like that. Imagine having a driver's license with your picture, but somebody else's fingerprint? Or passports. Being so close to Mexico, all of that is valuable."

"Okay, so what do we do? I can't do it under my name. We can't use you, Charlie, because you're already a member. We've got the same problem with Ribs. He might recognize the name from our investigation."

"Tip," Ribs said. "Roger would have no reason to recognize Tip."

I ran down the hall and got Tip. On the way back, I explained what we needed.

"I'm up for it," Tip said, "but it won't work. You're not going to find anyone as pretty as me."

Ribs shook his head. "It doesn't work that way. We're just using you for a name and address and credit card. We're going to use Hemphill's photo."

"I'm not sure if I like this," Tip said. "You're just using me for my money. I feel like a whore."

"I was chatting with Coop, while Ribs explained to Tip how things worked.

She okayed the funds. "But we'll have to reimburse you. The funds will have to show coming from one of your credit cards or your bank account."

When I told Tip, he shrugged. "Okay. What have I got to lose except a hundred bucks?"

"You're not going to lose anything," I said. "Stop being paranoid."

"How long will this take?" I asked Charlie.

"It might take a little while, but it shouldn't take long. The request would have been sent immediately, and if they have the cell-phone app, which most people do, it's sent there, too. All the people have to do is hit 'yes' or 'no.'"

An hour later, we still hadn't heard anything. By this time, Ribs and Tip and I had retired to the coffee room. About fifteen minutes later, Tip's phone buzzed indicating he had a message.

He pulled out his phone and looked.

'Message from Anonymous in Houston.'

"Who the hell is anonymous, and why does it say Houston?"

"Better ask Charlie."

We headed back to Charlie's desk and met him on the way. "I saw the message," he said. "Don't answer it. It looks like it's from your guy in Conroe."

"How did he know about us?" I said. "I thought this was anonymous."

"It's supposed to be," Charlie said. "I'm guessing that your guy in

Dallas told him about it, and he's querying you to see what he can find out."

"Does that mean he's already seen the picture we used?" I asked.

Charlie nodded. "It sure does."

"We're fucked," Ribs said.

"That's one way to put it," Tip said.

"What's the other way?" I asked.

"We're fucked," Ribs said again.

I banged my fist on the desk. "Okay, Charlie, leave the connection request open. Don't respond. And don't answer Hemphill's request. Let's wait and see what happens. We might get lucky and have Roger respond."

"And it might snow tomorrow, too," Tip said. "Even though it's supposed to be ninety."

"Okay, so it's not the best idea, and I'm pretty sure it won't work, but does anyone have a better plan? If you do, say so."

"I've got a better plan," Tip said. "Go look for the boat."

"Why do you say that? Ribs asked.

"Because if you think Hemphill did this, and if the guard gate doesn't have him logged in, then he got to the house some other way. And like I said earlier, there are only two other ways—through the woods, which I highly doubt, or across the lake. That means that somewhere out there is a boat that was used in the commission of a felony. It might be floating around the lake. It might have been secreted away by an accomplice. Or, it might be stashed in a cove somewhere, probably on the south side of the lake."

Tip had my interest this time. "How would it work?"

"Easy enough. If we assume he came in from the south side, he could have pulled off any number of roads branching off of Highway 105. In fact, there's a golf course I used to play that sits just north of 105. It would be perfect, and there's about zero chance he'd be seen."

I turned to Charlie. "See about getting some men to volunteer to search that area. Also, ask Conroe PD if they'll help. We aren't officially on this investigation, so we can't assign anyone. Nonetheless, Charlie, I'm putting you in charge. See that it gets done."

"Yes, sir," he said. "I'll be on it first thing in the morning."

"Why do you think he wouldn't go through the woods?"

Tip smiled. "You obviously don't know that place too well. Montgomery County patrols FM 1097 pretty frequently—and erratically, too. If someone were going to the trouble of planning a complicated murder, they wouldn't leave their car on 1097 in case a patrol found it."

"But you could sneak in by way of the lake?"

"Sure as shit stinks. It'd be easy, too, as long as no one heard you. But there are plenty of places to land where it's isolated. From there, you could walk."

"This is sounding more and more as if someone took a hell of a long time planning this."

"I'd bet my last d—"

"You'd bet your last what, Denton?" Coop said as she entered.

"I'd bet my last doughnut," Tip said. "If I had only one doughnut, I'd be willing to bet it. Now that's strong, Coop."

"Well somebody better be willing to bet a lot more than a doughnut, because I need this case solved. And I need it solved quickly. I don't have budget for crap like this."

"You got it," I said, as Coop poured her coffee.

"I don't have it yet, Cataldi, but I intend to get it. Close this case. Do you understand?"

"Yes, sir."

Ribs was grinning as Coop was walking out the door. "And that goes for you, too, Delgado. Wipe that shit-eating grin off your face and get to work."

"Yes, ma'am," he said. His smile was now gone.

LET'S FIND ROGER

Kristan's boss got back to me early in the morning—too early if truth be known; I was still sleeping. I was glad he called though. He gave us an address in Fort Worth that Roger used with his credit card when he booked his flights from Dallas.

I got out of bed, made my way to the kitchen, and started boiling a pot of water for coffee. I was not the type to drink drip coffee, or coffee that had been warming on a hot plate for hours. I now only drank whole bean coffee from Martin Henry Roasters, and I ground it myself every morning, then used a French press to make the coffee. The coffee sat exactly four minutes in the boiling water, then I strained it into a Bormioli glass cup. It was a perfect cup of coffee.

At eight o'clock I called the Fort Worth Police and gave them the address the airline had given me. I asked them if they would mind picking Roger up. After I explained the situation, they said they'd be more than happy to oblige.

I got a good-morning call from Marissa—which pleased me to no end —called Ron to see how he was doing, then headed out to meet Ribs. We had gotten into the habit of meeting for breakfast to discuss things before we started the day. It was a tradition started when I worked with Tip.

Ribs was already seated in a corner booth at the Pork N Fork, one of the places we frequented. I wasn't fond of their coffee, but their eggs and their bacon were fantastic.

"What'll it be?" Ribs asked.

"We're waiting on Fort Worth right now," I said. "I called them this morning. And we'll have to see if Charlie and his team have any luck with the boat."

"What about the gun?" Ribs said. "Where do you think the gun could be?"

"Who knows? You know how people are about guns; most of them won't get rid of them. The killer might still have it, or it might be sitting at the bottom of the lake."

"My money is on the lake," Ribs said. "Whoever did this, thought it out. And if it was Hemphill, like we think, the price of a gun wouldn't mean much."

"It might after the divorce," I said. "She seemed serious about that."

"Yeah, that's another thing that gets me. She got mad enough to divorce him, but she's still defending him for murder when she *has* to see he was trying to kill her."

I thought about what Ribs said, and he was right. She was defending her husband as if it were blind love, but they were long past blind love. *So what was going on?*

"Getting back to the gun," Ribs said. "Where do you think he put it?"

"If he had driven back to Bentwater, I'd say in the lake under the bridge at FM 1097, but if we think he used a boat, it could be anywhere, although I'd bet on somewhere near the center of the lake on whatever route he took, which we won't know until we find the boat."

"Okay, so we have to find the boat and we have to find Roger. Charlie's looking for the boat, so let's you and I find Roger."

"I'm way ahead of you on that. I already spoke to the Fort Worth Police, and they're supposed to be picking Roger up now. All we have to do is kick back and wait for it to happen."

Ribs and I strategized on what to do next while we filled up on bad coffee. We paid the check and left, then went back to the station.

A bout two hours later, while loafing in the coffee room, Fort Worth called.

"Sorry to have to tell you this, but he's gone."

"What do you mean—gone?"

"I mean we went by the apartment but it was cleaned out. Closets cleared, drawers emptied, and the food in the fridge was spoiled. The milk was sour, and even the meat smelled bad. It had to have been in there more than a week."

"Goddamn. Son of a bitch." I reached over and slapped the side of the fridge. "All right. Thanks for checking," I said. "I'll call if I need anything else."

I sat at the table again, and lifted my hands up to massage my eyes.

"And by the way, the fridge apologizes for whatever it did wrong," Ribs said.

It was enough to make me laugh. "In case you didn't catch the conversation, that was FWPD on the phone, and they went to Roger's pad but it was cleaned out—which means we're back to square one."

"Not necessarily," Ribs said. "You worked with a detective in Dallas on that case with Tip, didn't you?"

"Yeah."

"Well, we've got the original ping we did on Roger's phone. Give the location to the cop, send him a picture of Hemphill, and ask him to stake out a radius from the location's center. You never know. He might spot him."

"It's a long shot. But it just might work."

I called Santos and told him what I had in mind. "Do you think your boss would approve it?"

"Hell no. He wouldn't approve a candy bar, but I could work it in after hours. Hell, I might even be able to convince my partner to help. He's usually up for stuff like this."

"Man, I'd owe you if you could," I said.

"Forget about owing me, just send up the picture to this number: 214-555-5544. And remind me of the location."

"Hang on," I said, then I turned to Delgado. "Ribs, where did the phone company show that ping was?"

Ribs shuffled through a few papers, then said, "About half a mile west of the Galleria, about three blocks north of the loop. I'll get the actual address in a minute."

"Got it," Santos said. "Send me the address and we'll stake out a ten or twelve block radius. If he lives around there, he has to show his face now and then."

"Santos, remember. We don't know if he lives there. That ping could have been him sitting in a car smoking a joint. This is a long shot."

"I know. I've bet on a long-shot now and then."

"Just so that you know," I said. "And thanks again. This helps a lot."

Santos sat in his car near the intersection of Alpha and Midway. The ping from the phone company had shown this to be the center, which put it a lot farther than Delgado's estimation of half a mile from the Galleria. In fact, it was a lot closer to two miles. Nonetheless, Santos said he'd hang out a while and see if anything happened.

Santos' partner, whom Santos had convinced to help, was situated on the west side of Alpha. If the guy lived in this area, or even frequented this area for whatever reason, Santos would nail him.

Roger Farnsworth pulled the curtains aside and peeked out the corner. The silver Ford had been parked in the same spot for hours now, and the guy behind the wheel was still reading the paper or pretending to be.

Am I being watched? Roger wondered. Or, *Am I being paranoid?* Neither option was good, but for now, if he had to choose, he'd go for the paranoia.

Ever since he had read about that murder in Houston he had started thinking this way, and it was no wonder. The guy who hired him to be a decoy was the husband of the murdered lady's boss. That was no coincidence; there had to be a connection.

Now, here he was, stuck in an apartment in Dallas with someone watching him. He didn't know if the guy was a cop or a hit-man, and judging from what he knew of this situation so far, he could be either one, and neither was good for Roger.

Roger decided on a plan of action, and pulled a chair to the window so he could wait in comfort, or at least some degree of comfort. It took nearly three hours, but the silver car finally left, and Roger didn't see any vehicle take its place. He waited another thirty minutes and when he still saw nothing, he left, rushing to his car by the curb outside.

He drove to Interstate 635, headed east, then north toward Plano. In a few miles, he made an abrupt turn and watched his rearview mirror to see if anyone was following. No one was. Now he felt safe. He didn't know if he was, but he felt that way. All that was left was to get the means to get the hell out of Dallas. He was ready to leave anyway.

Once he got to the south side of the city, he purchased a burner phone and called Hemphill.

"Hello?"

"We need to meet," Roger said.

I NEED A FEW BUCKS

Hemphill looked around, checking to ensure that he was alone. "What do you mean 'need to meet'? Our business dealings are over. They've been over."

"Maybe for you they're over, but not me. I had a cop sitting on my apartment half the damn night. And if it wasn't a cop, it was worse. I managed to ditch him, but I don't intend to live the rest of my life this way."

"You're imagining things. We didn't do anything wrong."

"What do you think I am, stupid? I read the papers, you know. I read about the murder of your wife's assistant. Is that what this is all about? Did you kill that woman? Did you involve me in a murder?"

"You're off your rocker. I didn't do anything but play a gag on someone."

"Yeah, well how's this for a gag? I need fifty thousand dollars to get out of the city and start a new life. Give me that, and you won't hear from me again. If you don't…well, maybe the police *will* find me. And maybe I'll be forced to tell them of our little deception."

"Fifty thousand dollars? I don't have that kind of money."

"Don't try giving me that line. I read the papers, as I've stated. I know what you and your wife are worth."

Roger sat through a long minute of silence. Finally, he said, "Hemphill, you still there?"

"I'm here. I was just thinking of how we could work this."

"Think quickly. I don't have a lot of time."

"Listen, I can't get my hands on fifty thousand dollars; however, even if Susan divorces me, she'll be paying alimony, so I could give you some now, then guarantee you a monthly payment of several thousand for however long it takes. Don't worry. You'll get your money."

"All of that sounds good," Roger said, "but how do I know you'll keep your end of the deal? I want it in writing."

"In writing? What am I supposed to use, the standard blackmail template?"

"I don't care what you use or how you phrase it, I want something in writing or it's no deal. Got it?"

"I got it. What choice do I have? You hold all of the cards."

Roger didn't know if Hemphill believed what he was saying, but it did give Roger a thought. "You're right about me holding the cards," he said. "In case you don't know it, I bought the gun on a trip to Atlanta. And I bought it using your name. I'm sure the serial numbers have been scratched off, but I'm just as sure that the dealer in Alabama, where I bought it, will remember seeing you. After all we *do* look alike. And it's probably not often they sell a silencer. When that dealer is presented with a picture of you and a few other gentlemen, guess who he'll pick out?"

Shit. "Okay, you've made your point. I'll have something drawn up to ensure that you get your money. It might take a few days, though."

"It needs to contain a clause to ensure I get paid even if you die."

"It will."

"And what about the down payment? When should I expect that?"

"I thought I told you, but in case you forgot, I could get you a few thousand today. Maybe five thousand. Just tell me where to meet. And in case you suspect trouble, I don't mind if you make it a public place."

"No need for that," Roger said. "There's a Best Western motel on the north end of Huntsville. It's on the west side of I-45, just north of Highway 30."

"I don't know it, but I'm sure I can find it."

"Meet me there in three hours. I'm south of Dallas now. I'll call you again when I get a room."

"See you then."

Susan stepped away quietly before Kevin saw her.

Two and a half hours later, Hemphill left the house and drove toward Huntsville. It was only about a thirty-mile drive, but he afforded himself enough time for errors. He already had the cash, so he didn't need to stop to get that. About thirty–five minutes later, he arrived at the Best Western, pulled to the back of the lot and waited. He didn't have to wait long before the phone rang.

"Hello?"

"Hemphill, I'm in room #112. Knock twice, wait, then twice more."

"No need to be so secretive," Hemphill said. "I came alone, and I doubt anyone else knows you're here.".

"Doesn't hurt to be cautious."

Hemphill pulled around to room #112, then walked up and knocked as instructed. Roger answered a moment later. He poked his head out the door and looked around, then went back inside.

"A little paranoid?" Hemphill said.

"They're not after you. If they were, maybe you'd be. paranoid too."

"I doubt it, but I guess that's not the point."

"Did you bring the money? And the contract?"

"I brought the money," Hemphill said. "The contract will have to wait a while longer. I told you that I needed to have it drawn up by an attorney, and for obvious reasons, it must be an attorney other than my wife's."

"Okay, I'll give you one week. If you don't have it by then, I'll go to the cops and tell them everything. Bank on that, because I'm not doing time for anyone."

"No problem. I'll have the papers before the week is up. Just stay calm, and call me if you have any troubles. And when this business of ours is finished, I want you to get rid of that phone. You should have already done that."

"Deal," Roger said.

Hemphill insisted that Roger count the five thousand while standing in front of him, then he headed toward the door, promising the contract to be delivered within days.

"One thing before you go," Roger said. "Why'd you kill her? Were you two screwing, and she wanted to tell your wife?"

Hemphill slowly shut the door, which he had already opened. He turned and glared. "You're not too smart, Roger. If I was the one who killed her, I just might kill you."

"You won't kill me because you don't know where I have information stashed or even what kind of information. So tell me. Why'd you do it?"

"Hemphill grabbed hold of Farnsworth's collar, shook him, then shoved him backward. "*I didn't.* Subject closed."

"Then what are you paying me for?"

"Because it would *look* like I did something wrong, even though I didn't. Satisfied? If you have no more questions, I'm leaving." Hemphill started to leave, then turned back. "One question I have before leaving. Why'd you buy the gun, and why in my name?"

"Because your wife told me to."

"What?"

"Yeah. She said you needed a gun to carry out the plot, and that me buying it would be a good test to see how well the ID stood up." Farnsworth smiled. "Guess it worked."

"Okay," Hemphill said. "Just wanted to know."

When Hemphill left, Roger went in to take a shower. He spent the first few minutes pondering what to do with the money. The down payment wasn't much. It would barely pay for his move. But the monthly stipend would come in more than handy. It would be the first time he had extra money to spend, and he had a lot he could spend it on.

Fifteen minutes later, while he was drying off, a knock sounded at the door. It was loud; he heard it even over the music he had playing. He cursed, finished drying, wrapped a towel around himself, then went to answer the door. He yanked it open. "What now?"

The next sound was a popping noise from a silencer, followed by two more of the same. The three shots hit Roger in the chest, forming a tight circle around his heart. He collapsed to the ground without being able to utter a word.

A BODY IN HUNTSVILLE

I sent Marissa home shortly after supper and retired early. Not long after midnight, the phone rang. "Hello?"

"Detective Cataldi, this is the Deputy Skelton up at Huntsville. We've got a body I think you'll be interested in."

"Not to sound callous, but why would I be interested in a body in Huntsville?"

"It's the guy you sent out flyers on, the one from Dallas—Roger Farnsworth."

As soon as Skelton said the name I recognized who it was. It hit hard. I had wanted this guy alive so that we might have gotten information out of him. "Okay, Skelton. I'll get my partner, and we'll be right up. It'll probably take us an hour and a half from where we are."

"We'll be here," he said. "And I know the body isn't going anywhere."

"Okay, thanks," I said. I dialed Ribs and told him to get his ass out of bed and meet me, then when I hung up, I thought about what Deputy Skelton had said. A lot of cops tried using humor to cover up the disgusting nature of the work. If that's what he needed, fine. Use anything that works was my theory.

As I dressed to go, I had to remind myself to keep an open mind. I had already convicted Hemphill of the crime and I knew nothing about it. I had to admit, it seemed fishy, with Roger being found in a motel near Houston, but it was by no means evidence.

I put a thin pair of socks on, then my comfortable shoes; this was going to be a lot of standing and with little chance to sit down. I had half a mind to call Ben, the medical examiner, but decided I'd give their ME a try first. If I wasn't satisfied, then I'd call Ben.

Twenty minutes later, I met Ribs at our favorite meeting spot—Denny's. It wasn't a favorite because of the quality of the food; Ribs despised it, and I wasn't fond of it, but it was open twenty-four hours a day, and that made it convenient if nothing else.

I felt sure that somewhere, someone was sitting in a booth eagerly awaiting their order and salivating over the thought of it. On the other hand, Ribs and I would be dreading the delivery of our meal, and wondering what it would taste like.

We suffered through the meal, drank half our coffee, then started off for Huntsville. Ribs left his car in the parking lot so he could ride with me.

"You see Marissa again?"

"Last night," I said. "But she went home early."

"Went home early? Are you crazy? That's like saying there was a Megan Fox movie on and you didn't watch it."

"I never watch Megan Fox movies. Besides, I thought you were a Jessica Alba fan."

"I *am* a Jessica Alba fan, but I've given up on her. Anyway, Rosalee was catching on to my obsession."

I laughed. "So you've given up on Alba, but you're still hanging on to the illusion that Fox might be interested in you?"

Ribs flushed, and appeared to be embarrassed. "Maybe."

"Maybe my ass. Just get your mind off Megan Fox's butt and think about this case. We've got a dead body."

"I hear you," Ribs said. "Now, leave me alone for a few minutes and let me dream."

For the next forty minutes, I drove while Ribs dreamed. Soon after that, we pulled off I-45 and into the parking lot of Best Western.

Ribs reached to unbuckle his seatbelt. "Damn, I wish he'd been killed in Dallas. I could have slept longer."

We walked across the parking lot and were stopped by a Walker County deputy. "Can't go there," he said. "Police scene."

I pulled out my badge and showed him. "I'm Detective Gino Cataldi, and this is my partner," I said, while gesturing to Ribs. "Are you Skelton?"

He nodded. "Are you the one I spoke to on the phone?"

"That's me," I said, "Though I might sound different because I'm awake now."

He laughed. "No shit. You'd think people would have the decency to be killed at a respectable time of day."

"Fat chance of that," Ribs said. "I think I can count on one hand the number of body-calls we've gotten during working hours. Excuse me, I meant to say 'regular working hours.'"

"What have you got?" I asked.

"I don't know. I'm just a lowly deputy. The ME's team is over there now. I suspect they'll be able to tell you more when they get done."

"Thanks," I said, then headed toward the motel room.

Inside the room was a buzz of activity. Crime-scene personnel were walking about carefully snapping pictures and taking measurements. They appeared to be doing things professionally, and that was good to see. I had worried that Walker County might not be as thorough as Harris County.

Deputy Skelton had followed us over. He now stood beside me. "There he is," Skelton said.

"I see. Pisses me off. I was hoping to find him alive."

"Not gonna' happen now," Skelton said. "He's deader than duck shit."

When Skelton said duck shit, I perked up. Maybe this guy was related to Tip. Or maybe Texans just had a thing for duck shit. Either way, Farnsworth was dead, and he wouldn't be providing us any information."

I saw a guy kneeling on the floor next to the body, but before I could say anything, the similarity between the dead body and Hemphill hit me. "Holy shit!" I said. "Ribs, you see that. He looks just like Hemphill."

Ribs whistled. "More so than in the pictures. I can't believe it."

"You know this guy?" the man asked.

"We don't know him, but he looks almost identical to a suspect we have in a murder case down in Houston."

"Any connection?"

"That's what we're here to determine," I said. "There's definitely a connection, but we don't understand the extent of it. We're hoping you'll be able to help with that. Got anything?"

"Nothing yet on the gun, but I can tell you that it appears as if he was shot when he opened the door, probably as soon as he opened the door. The position of the body and the blood pooling support that."

"So, he answered the door and someone plugged him?" Ribs asked.

"That's what it looks like."

"How did they find the body?" I asked.

"From what they told me, the lady in the next room complained to the manager about loud music. It was too late for music to be that loud, she said." The guy shrugged and looked at me. "Anyway, the manager said he got no answer when he knocked, so he opened the door and found him here, just like this."

"What about caliber of the gun?"

"I can't swear to anything until I get back to the office, but it looks as if he was shot with a .38."

"Sounds about right," Ribs said. "When can we get ballistics? I want to see if it matches our murder."

"I'll put a rush on it. You should have it by tomorrow late in the day."

I pulled a card and handed it to his assistant. "Here's my card. Call me as soon as you get it. And if you can, fax the ballistic report to that number. As my partner said, we're eager to see if it matches."

"No problem."

"What about TOD?" Ribs asked.

"If I had to guess, I'd say about noon or one. Not long after."

I made some notes, especially about TOD, and jotted down that we'd have to ask Hemphill about his whereabouts.

"I wonder why he was shot," Ribs asked. "What do you think, cuz?"

"I think he knew too much," I said. "But what I really want to know is if he was the killer or the decoy."

"I guess we won't have long to wait," Ribs said. "I'm betting that ballistics will show us who did it. If it's the same killer, my guess is, he used the same gun."

"On the way back to Denny's," Ribs said, "I'm betting it was Hemphill. We were getting too close to Roger, and somehow Hemphill knew."

"Maybe," I said, "but how did he know?"

"I'll tell you how he knew," Ribs said, "you alerted him with that bullshit phone call you had me make. Having me speak Spanish to him. What the hell, cuz? It was Hemphill's phone and Hemphill's number. I'm sure Roger had talked to him before, and that means he knew Hemphill didn't speak Spanish. So when he gets a call from Hemphill's number and whoever is on the other line is speaking Spanish…you figure it out. He might not immediately make you for a cop, but it won't take him long, and he sure as hell ain't gonna' think it's Hemphill."

"So what? He gets a call from someone he thinks is a cop?"

"So what? Are you an idiot? If Roger thinks the cops are onto him, he tells Hemphill. Then Hemphill gets nervous and takes him out. As far as I'm concerned, it's as simple as that."

"I guess I fucked up."

"I guess you did. And you went and got Roger killed."

"So what do we do now?" I asked.

"We find out if Hemphill left Bentwater around the time Roger was killed, and we find that fucking gun."

WHERE WERE YOU?

First thing in the morning we checked with the guards who had manned the gate at Bentwater. I parked the car, got out, and walked over to them. They had Hemphill recorded as going out at approximately 10:45.

I looked to Ribs and smiled. "If Hemphill left at 10:45, that would give him plenty of time to get to Huntsville, do whatever he had to do—include killing Farnsworth—and still fit the TOD estimation that the ME gave to us."

"No doubt," Ribs said. "It's only about thirty-five miles from here."

"Another thing, Detective—if you're interested—Mrs. Hemphill went out about thirty minutes after he did."

"What time did she return?" Ribs asked.

The guard scanned the list, then said, "She came back around 3:00. And he returned around 1:30."

"That would be pushing it for him," Ribs said, "but not by much. It wouldn't be too hard to drive thirty-five miles or so, shoot somebody, and then drive back in two and a half hours."

"It would be plenty of time for her," I said. "But she has no reason to kill Roger, and we have no evidence to suggest she even knew he was alive."

"True," Ribs said, "but to be safe, I'd like to check her alibi. See where she was, or if she knew where her husband was."

"I'm more interested in that angle," I said. "Let's go have a talk with both of them."

I knocked on the Hemphill's door, and we were invited in. We took a seat at the kitchen table and accepted Mrs. Hemphill's offer of coffee.

"What do you need?" Mr. Hemphill asked. His attitude seemed brusque.

"We need to verify where you were yesterday from about 10 a.m. to 2:00 p.m." I said. "The log at the gate shows you leaving here around 10:45."

"I'm sure it does," Hemphill said, "And if you need to know, I took a piss ten minutes before that and again when I returned."

"What a coincidence," Ribs said. "I did, too."

Hemphill shot him a glare. "What's this all about?" he asked.

"There's been a murder in Huntsville," I said.

"And you think I had something to do with it?" Hemphill said. "What the hell? Am I going to be a suspect in all murders now?"

"Not all of them," Ribs said, "But if you had a close relationship, yes. You can bet your ass we're going to look into it."

"What are you talking about?"

"Roger Farnsworth. He was murdered yesterday at the Best Western in Huntsville."

"Roger Farnsworth? Who's he?" Hemphill asked.

"Don't act like you don't know, Hemphill. We're past that stage. The guy looked just like you—I mean *just* like you—and we think you used him as a decoy to take your flight to Atlanta, while you stayed here and killed Chlorinda, thinking, of course, that she was your wife."

"I don't care what he looked like. As for where I was, I went for a drive out by Nacogdoches," Hemphill said.

"So you think we're off track?" Ribs asked. "What would you do, Mr. Hemphill? How would you look at the case?"

Hemphill stood and paced. I noticed he did that whenever he got nervous. "You're nuts. You're fucking nuts. I didn't kill this... Farnsworth guy, and I didn't kill Chlorinda."

"We'll see when ballistics come in," Ribs said. Then he turned to Mrs. Hemphill, who had joined us late. "In the meantime, Mrs. Hemphill, I'm sorry, but we have to ask, 'Where were you yesterday morning and early afternoon?'"

She laughed. "No apology is required, Detective. I understand about alibis and the need to verify them. I was shopping at the outlet mall. I believe it's on League Line Road. I have receipts of a few items that I purchased in my purse, and I'm sure that the sales clerk will recall seeing me, as we chatted for a long time. She reads my mysteries."

"How did she know who you were? Don't you write under a pseudonym?"

"Yes, but she recognized me from the picture at the back of the book, despite me having put on years *and* pounds since then. It was fun. She was a good conversationalist."

Susan reached for her purse, then said, "Would you mind handing that to me?" She shuffled through her purse, and shortly afterward she produced receipts from the Dressbarn and Nike. "The lady I spoke to for so long was at the Dressbarn. I believe her name was Miranda. I remember, because I told her I liked the name, and asked if she would mind if I used it in a future book."

"Thanks," Ribs said, putting the receipts in his shirt pocket. "Did you go anywhere else, I mean after you left the mall?"

"Nowhere after the mall, but plenty of places after the Dressbarn, although I didn't make purchases in all of them."

We asked a few more questions to both of them, then left and made a stop at the outlet mall. "Let's go to the Dressbarn first," Ribs said.

After confirming with the cashier—whose name was Miranda—that it was Mrs. Hemphill that she was talking with, we moved on to the Nike store, where the cashier also remembered seeing her. A few of the other stores did not recall seeing her, although she didn't buy anything there, so that was understandable."

"Looks like Mrs. Hemphill was where she said," Ribs noted as we got into the car.

"Yeah, but we have no idea about Mr. Hemphill. He says he didn't even stop for gas. Do you buy that?"

"It's not hard to buy, cuz. If he had a full tank, or even close to a full tank, three to three and a half hours of driving at country-road speed could be easily accounted for on one tank."

We were driving back to the station slowly when the phone rang. "See who that is," I said to Ribs.

He grabbed my phone from the drink holder, and said, "It's Huntsville."

"What? Well get it for Christ's sake."

"Hello?"

"No, it's not Cataldi. This is Detective Delgado, his partner. But hang on a minute. I'll put it on speaker. He's here. He's just driving."

"This is Deputy Skelton. We met last night."

"I remember."

"Well, the ME's office called. They have the ballistics."

"Shit. That's fast."

"You said you wanted it fast, so they expedited it. The faxed report should be waiting for you."

"Okay, great. Tell them thanks."

"In case you didn't hear, that was Huntsville. They faxed us the ballistics."

"I heard."

"So what are you driving so damn slow about? Get a move on it."

It took us almost forty minutes to get to the station, but only five more to get inside and locate Julie who had the fax.

"I'll bet you're looking for this," she said, waving the fax in front of us.

Ribs snatched it from her hand. "Don't worry," she said. "I've already sent it to our guys for comparison. I told them you'd want it rushed. They're looking at it now."

We retired to our offices, both speculating on why Farnsworth was killed. About two hours later, forensics called.

I answered the call immediately. "Cataldi."

"It's Finn. I've got your ballistics," he said.

"Don't keep me waiting."

"They're the same," he said. "Same gun, fired the same bullets. Striations match. There's no doubt about it."

"Son of a bitch," I said. "It's what I expected, but that's good to know for a fact."

Ribs was staring at me when I hung up. "In case you didn't grasp that, they're a match. Same gun killed both people," I said.

"Now all we have to do is nail him for owning the gun."

"Which means we have to *find* the gun," I said. "And that might not be so easy."

"I know. Maybe we'll talk about it tonight."

Tonight? Then I remembered I had told Ribs that Marissa and I would stop by. "Maybe," I said.

WHO DOESN'T LIKE ICE CREAM?

I dropped Ribs off then immediately called Marissa. Fortunately, she answered right away.

"Hello?"

Her voice sounded so good I almost forgot why I was calling. "Marissa, it's Gino."

"Well hello and what a pleasant surprise."

"I hope you still think so when I'm done talking."

"Why? What's the matter?"

"Nothing is the matter, but I promised Ribs that we'd come over tonight, and I forgot to ask you if that was okay."

She laughed, and it made me feel good. "Who cares if you forgot. I'm honored that you'd ask me. I thought you were still embarrassed of me."

Inside I smiled. "Baby, if I was ever embarrassed of you, it was my fault, and I never will be again."

"You're sweet, Gino."

"Does that mean you'll go?"

"Of course, I'll go. What time? And what should I wear, and do I need to bring anything?"

I'll pick you up at 6:30. Wear anything you want." *Or nothing.* "And no, there's no need to bring anything."

"Okay," she said. "I'll be ready. If I don't need to dress special, I'm ready now."

"One thing to note, Ribs has a lot of kids, and they love playing makeup with strangers."

"No problem here," she said. "See you in an hour."

I picked Marissa up at about 6:25. When she kissed me "hello," I felt like staying home instead of going to Ribs'. "My God, you look great," I said. "Smell great, too."

"That's what happens when you bathe," she said. "I bet if someone tried, they'd find out I tasted great, too."

"Don't get me started," I said. "I might turn the car around and go back to my house."

"I won't stop you," she said, and squeezed the top of my thigh as I turned the corner.

I laughed. "You're an evil son of a bitch. You know that?"

"I was hoping you'd notice," she said. "Now, tell me the names of the kids so I don't get it messed up."

"One of them is easy. Her name is Marissa, the same as you. She's the youngest, and she's adopted."

"That shouldn't be too difficult, even for me."

"Clarita is the oldest. She is named after Rosalee's mother. Then Thomas, Hector, Sheila, Mary, and Savannah."

"Was Mary named after your wife?"

I gulped. It was embarrassing, but it shouldn't have been. "She was," I said. "Mary and Ribs grew up together. They were cousins."

It took twenty minutes to get to Ribs' house. When we went inside, the kids were ready and wired up.

"Let me introduce you," I said to the kids, and when I did, they lined up from oldest to youngest, standing at attention like we used to do when I attended Catholic school.

"Kids, this is my friend, Marissa."

"Nice to meet you, Marissa," they said in unison.

Then I turned to Marissa and led her closer. "Marissa, this is —"

"Let me see if I can get it right," she said, then, starting at the right side, Marissa said, "I bet you're Clarita."

Clarita giggled. "How did you know?"

"Because you're as pretty as your name," Marissa said, and smiled. Then she moved on to Thomas.

She looked at him sideways, held her hand up to her eyes, as if measuring, then said, "And you must be Thomas. I'll bet you like to play with Legos."

Thomas's eyes opened wide, and he looked left and right. "Did you tell?" he asked Clarita.

"No, Clarita didn't tell," Marissa said. "You know how I knew that? Because your name means master builder, so I figured you must like Legos."

Marissa took another step and stood in front of Hector. "Do you know where your name comes from? In mythology, Hector was one of the greatest warriors. He was a prince of Troy."

"Really?" Hector said. He beamed, then he threw a lighthearted punch at Thomas. "Did you hear that?"

Sheila was smiling when Marissa walked to her. "Did you know that Sheila is the old Irish name for Cecilia. I love that name. When I was growing up it was one of my favorites."

"Did you know anybody named Sheila?" she asked.

"You bet I did. One of my sister's best friends was named Sheila."

"What about me? What about me?" Mary asked, while jumping up and down.

"Let's see…Mary. With a name like Mary, I bet you like to talk, and I'm guessing you're always happy. People with the name Mary usually are."

"She likes to talk all right," Clarita said. "You can't shut her up."

Savannah was the next in line. "Do you know that your name came from a famous city in Georgia?"

Savannah shook her head.

"Well, it did. And I think the city got its name from the Savannah River, which runs close by. It's a beautiful old name."

Marissa took a step and knelt in front of Little Marissa. She pinched her cheeks and smiled. "Marissa. You have a special name. Not that all names aren't special, but yours is special, *because* it's the same as mine. Some people say Marissa is another way to say Mary, but my mother told me it means 'Star of the Sea'. And I believed her." Then she leaned forward and kissed Little Marissa on the cheek.

"Okay, go outside and play now. Hurry up," Ribs said. "Mom will call you when dinner is ready."

Clarita ran over and grabbed Marissa by the hand. "You want to go out and play?" she asked.

"Leave Aunt Marissa alone," Ribs said. "She's company."

Marissa smiled and turned to Ribs. "I'm fine. I'd love to play with them."

As she skipped down the hall with Clarita, Ribs turned to Gino. "Did you teach her all of that?"

"Me? Hell no. I don't even know all of that. I just told her their names on the way over here."

"Goddamn, that's pretty good," Ribs said. "Maybe she looked it up on her cell or something."

"That's pretty sweet is what it is," Rosalee said. "Did you see the look on their faces? It was priceless."

Half an hour later, Ribs leaned out the window and called, "Time to eat."

Not three minutes after that, the back door opened and they all came running in, the two Marissas leading the way.

"Wash up," Ribs said. "And that means you too." He pointed at Marissa when he said it.

"Count on that," she said. "They wore me out."

"You shouldn't have gone out there," Rosalee said.

"Nonsense. I loved it. They're fantastic kids, and I needed the exercise."

"Oh my God, listen to that. You could sit around for a year and still have a gorgeous figure. I would kill for your body," Rosalee said, then she looked to Ribs and pointed her finger. "And don't you say a word."

Clarita and Thomas set the table, then we ate. It was noisy, but full of fun and laughter. Rosalee had cooked her specialty—beef and chicken fajitas—and, as usual, it was delicious. As we neared the end of the meal, Marissa leaned over and whispered something to Rosalee.

"Are you sure?" Rosalee said.

Marissa nodded. "Of course. I just wanted to see if it was all right with you."

"Go ahead. They'll love it."

Marissa tapped a spoon on the side of her plate. "All right, whoever ate a good dinner gets to go to Marble Slab, if they want to."

"Yeah!" came a rousing cheer. Mary quickly gobbled up the rest of her food, while the others began clearing the table.

"Can we, Mom? Can we go?" Clarita asked.

Rosalee smiled. "Since you all ate a good meal, I don't see why not. But you need to promise to be good."

"We will," they all said.

"Then get dressed to go," Ribs said. "They're not open all night."

We took two cars to the ice cream shop and, presuming Ribs's car sounded like mine, it was as loud as a school bus the night before a holiday.

It was only a fifteen-minute ride to the shop, but Marissa played games and sang songs all the way. The kids had a ball.

As soon as I parked, the doors flew open and the kids raced for the store, all except for Little Marissa, who waited with her hand extended for Marissa to walk her in.

"Looks like you've found a friend," I said.

Marissa smiled. "And I couldn't be happier."

All the kids got their cones, then we pushed two tables together and sat outside to eat, the kids jammed into chairs at one table, and us at the other.

We chatted about everything for a few minutes, then Rosalee said, "And what is it that's keeping my husband working so late?"

"Working late? We haven't been working late."

Ribs looked to me, panicked, then laughed. "Don't believe him. He's trying to get me back. Ask Marissa if you don't believe me."

Marissa raised her eyebrows. "Late? I don't know what you mean. I've been with Gino almost every night."

Rosalee shot Ribs a look to kill. "If you haven't been working, where have you been?"

Ribs appeared concerned. "I swear. I've been working. Gino's lying, and now he's gotten Marissa to lie as well."

Rosalee laughed so hard she almost lost her ice cream. "I know, *cariño*. Gino was just teasing you."

Ribs looked over, made sure his kids weren't watching, then whispered, "You son of a bitch."

I laughed. "That's payback for the Cooper bit. You got me on that one, so I had to think of something."

Everyone laughed then we returned to chatting about everything, and nothing. We eventually got around to the case, as we always did, and I told the ladies about our dilemma with the gun.

"I know we could bust this case if we could find the gun," I said.

"Ask Marissa," Ribs said. "Maybe she's got an idea."

I cringed at Ribs's implication, but I didn't say anything for a moment, then, as I was about to respond, Little Marissa leaned in her chair and faced us "I bet he threw the gun in the water."

"What?" Ribs said.

"The guy you're talking about, the killer. I bet he threw the gun in the water. That's where I would throw it."

Ribs tousled her hair, then said, "Why would you say that honey?"

"Because it would be a good place to hide it. I bet nobody would find it."

"Why did you tell Gino to ask Marissa? Rosalee said.

Ribs flushed. I think he knew he was in deep shit now. "No reason," he said.

Marissa chuckled. "I think it's because he knows us women are smarter than them. But I agree with Little Marissa. I think he threw it in the water, too. She's a smarty."

Little Marissa turned her head and smiled. Obviously the adult conversation was what she was listening to, despite the chatter coming from her table.

"It's about time to call it a night," I said. "I'm going to try to get in early."

"Don't expect me until nine," Ribs said. "I'm sleeping in."

We drove the kids back to the house, then headed home. "Want to stop for a drink?" I asked.

"What? Trying to get me drunk?" Marissa said.

"Yeah, that's it. I need an easy mark."

"Sure," she said. "Go someplace where we can get a private table."

We ended up going to a restaurant in The Woodlands called The Grotto. It had a nice bar area, and we sat and enjoyed a few drinks while we chatted.

"I had a great time tonight," Marissa said.

"I'm glad. I was worried that so many kids would bother you, but you were fantastic with them. I couldn't believe the name stuff you pulled out."

Marissa laughed. "That's what happens with smart phones. They make it too easy to get information, no matter where you are."

I reached over and touched the back of her hand. "Look, I'm sorry about what Ribs said. He's—"

"Think nothing of it. He meant no harm, and I'm flattered that he thought I might be able to help."

Marissa turned sideways and faced me. "Now, let's talk seriously. You have several friends who know something of my past. This kind of slip-up is going to happen. Is it going to bother you?"

I smiled. "Not if it doesn't bother you," I said.

"Then, we're good, because it doesn't bother me. Now, get me another drink so that my inhibitions will be low."

"If that's all it takes, I'll get you a *few* more drinks."

Marissa gulped the rest of her drink, and said, "I know I've already said this, but thanks for taking me. I felt like a normal person tonight for the first time in years."

I leaned and kissed her lips. "You *are* a normal person."

"I'm trying to be," she said. "But for a long time, I wasn't."

She looked at me intently and said, " It was you who did it you know?"

"What do you mean?"

"Seeing you in Alexis's house, the passion you had, the concern you displayed. It had an effect on me. It was refreshing. You showed me that ordinary people *can* care. And it made me want to do good."

I smiled. "That's the sweetest thing anyone has ever said to me. And I love you even more for it."

She set her glass on the bar and whispered, "Then take me home and show me how much you love me."

I slugged the last of my drink, threw two twenties on the bar, and said, "Let's go."

WHERE'S THE GUN?

I was going over case files at my desk when Ribs got in. "About time," I said. "I've been here for hours."

"I can't help it if you don't sleep. I do."

"By the way, that comment last night about Marissa was inappropriate."

Ribs sat down across from me. "I know, cuz. Goddamn, I'm sorry. It just slipped out. Was she upset?"

"No. It didn't bother her at all. But it did make me uncomfortable. What did you tell Rosalee? Did she ask?"

"You know Rosalee. She wants to know *everything* about *anything*. So of course she asked. And I told her the truth."

"What did she say?"

"She said, 'more power to her.'"

"What?"

"Yeah, that's what I thought, too. I imagined she'd be worked up about it when I told her, but she was fine with the whole thing. I think it had a lot to do with the way Marissa was with the kids. They loved her. Clarita and Little Marissa talked about your Marissa all night.

"And Hector is ready to go slay some Greeks now that he knows where his name came from."

"Did you tell him the name came from you?"

"I tried, but it didn't seem to matter. I'm just a lowly cop; Hector was a Trojan prince and a great warrior. How am I going to compete with that?"

"Don't even try," I said. "Just go with it."

"So let's talk about the gun. I got to thinking about what Little Marissa said, about tossing it in the water. I know we've talked about it and speculated, but maybe we should try to find it. We might be able to bust this case open if we find the gun."

"I'm sure it's in the lake," I said. "But it's a damn big lake. Where do we look?"

"I say we talk to Coop and see if she'll support this, because we're going to need money. No matter where we look in the lake, if it's not close to shore, it's going to be expensive."

I put some papers away in my desk drawer and stood. "There's no time like the present. Let's go see her."

We walked down the hallway leading to Coop's office. At times like this—when I was going to beg for money—this walk felt like I imagined the walk down death row must feel. We were going to have to present a strong case if we had any chance of getting funding for our search efforts.

"What are we going to say?" Ribs asked.

"I don't know yet. I guess we'll wait until we see how her mood is."

Cindy was sitting at her desk when we turned the corner. "Ask Coop if she's got a minute?" I hollered.

She shook her head and reached for the intercom. "You should have called for an appointment."

"And I should have taken a piss before I came here," Ribs said. "But I didn't do either, so we'll have to see what happens."

"Delgado, you're getting as bad as Tip. If you don't watch out, that attitude will develop into a bad reputation," Cindy said.

"It will only get that bad if I start using his sayings, and I don't intend to do that, darlin'."

Cindy laughed. "Coop said to go on in."

Her desk was covered side to side with papers, which in turn were covered with sticky notes, Coops's handwriting scribbled on all of them.

"Looks like you've been hard at work?"

Coop looked at us from over the rim of her glasses. "I'm hard at work trying to run this damn city's homicide department. And I sure as hell could use some help."

"We're here to do just that," I said.

"I don't like the sounds of it," Coop said. "Tell me what you need. You wouldn't be here if you didn't need something."

"That's a cynical attitude, Coop. But we could use a little help."

"What kind of help. And don't beat around the bush. Just spit it out."

"All right. Here it is. You know that case up in Conroe? The mystery-writer case?"

"How can I forget? I have people calling every day about it."

"Well, one of the suspects—who is now a victim—has been found dead in Huntsville. And he was shot with the same caliber gun as the one that shot the first victim, Chlorinda."

"Gino is understating things, Coop. Evidence is a hell of a lot stronger than that. It's the same damn gun according to Finn."

"And the body was found in Huntsville?"

"Yeah. And we have reason to believe that Mr. Hemphill might have been in Huntsville about the time the killing occurred." It was a stretch to say that, but I didn't mind, and I'm sure Farnsworth wouldn't mind, and it might go a long way in convincing Coop to get us help.

"So what do you need me to do?"

"Since this is the same gun, and since we suspect Mr. Hemphill might be involved, we figure that the gun might be at the bottom of the lake."

"The bottom of the lake? That's a damn big lake."

"We could find it. We've got an idea where it might be, but we'll need a team of divers to look. Maybe underwater metal detectors too."

"You think you know? Are you using ESP to figure this out?"

"I know it sounds crazy, Coop, but hear us out. If we assume Hemphill killed the assistant, and we assume he also killed Farnsworth—which would make sense since both killings were done with the same gun— then there is only one logical place to dump the gun—in the lake where FM 1097 crosses it."

"Why there?"

"Because he didn't have much time to drive to Huntsville, shoot Farnsworth, and get back. If he wanted to ditch the gun after killing him, the most logical place would be there—center of the bridge is my guess."

Coop leaned back in her chair. "And what would you need to do a search? Do you know how deep the lake is there?"

"I don't know how deep, but it's deep enough that we'd need a team of divers, a boat, and an underwater metal detector."

"Jesus Christ, Cataldi, that will cost a fortune."

"I know what it will cost, but you said Rusty wanted this done, and without that gun I don't see us getting it done. Not anytime soon."

Coop lifted her head toward the ceiling. "I'll ask, but I doubt it will get done. I can't see Rusty spending money on this when he's pissing and moaning about every penny we spend."

"All right. See what you can do," I said. "Let me know when you hear something."

By the time we got back to my office, Coop had us an answer—no. And it wasn't just a no, but a hell no. Rusty said he'd love to find out who did it, but not that much. He didn't even like the mayor of San Francisco.

"What do we do now, cuz?"

"We go back to see Hemphill. See if a little bluffing will work."

"What are you talking about?"

"If he *thinks* we know where the gun is, and he thinks we're going to look for it, maybe it will force his hand."

"We've got other evidence to shake him a little. And we can make some up."

"Now we're talking, amigo. I like it when you're thinking like this."

We rode up to Bentwater without much talking, which was fine with me, as it gave me time to ponder where my life was going. A lot had changed in a few short weeks, and a lot more was bound to, especially with Marissa, and it was a change I was looking forward to. I hadn't felt this way about anyone since Mary had died, and I had to admit, I liked it.

Marissa was smart, a fantastic conversationalist, and had a marvelous sense of humor. It didn't hurt that she was sexy as hell, not to mention beautiful. She was a dream and I wondered what I had done to deserve her.

"There's the bridge," Ribs said. "Now that I see it again, I see how easy it would be to toss a gun out while you drove."

Bridge at FM 1097

"Yeah, a person wouldn't even have to stop. Just roll the window down and throw it out."

A few minutes later, the guards waved us through the gate at Bentwater, having recognized us from the frequent visits. Moments after that, we parked in front of the Hemphill's house, then went up and rang the doorbell.

Mr. Hemphill answered a few seconds later. "Detectives, what on earth are you doing here again? I thought we were done with you."

"I bet that's a nice thought, Mr. Hemphill, and I bet you go to bed dreaming of that, but you won't be done with us until we slap the cuffs on you for murder. And that won't be long."

Hemphill swung the door open. "I presume you want to come inside."

"That would be nice," I said. "Thanks."

We had no sooner placed our butts on the seats, than I started in. "We got the ballistics report. It's a match. The same gun that killed Chlorinda, killed Farnsworth."

"That's impossible," Hemphill said.

"What's impossible?" Mrs. Hemphill asked while walking in from the other room.

"Why would you say that it's impossible, Mr. Hemphill? Do you know something that I don't?"

Hemphill turned his head from side to side, as if the answer was hidden somewhere. "I don't know. I mean it, uh…just seems like a, uh…God-awful coincidence."

"Is something wrong, Mr. Hemphill? You seem to be stuttering."

"No. There's nothing wrong. It's just that I, uh…couldn't think of what to say. This whole mess has me in a state of confusion."

I figured now was the best time to try something. "Did you see anything when you were there, Mr. Hemphill? I mean at the Best Western?"

"What are you talking about? I wasn't at the Best Western."

"Really? We have witnesses who will testify that they saw your car there about the time Mr. Farnsworth was murdered."

"That can't be. Unless…" Hemphill lit up. "Where is the Best Western?"

"Near Highway 30, off I-45, in Huntsville."

"That explains it. I drove up I-45 and went west on 30. Remember? I told you I drove out to Nacogdoches."

"That's fine," Ribs said. "It would explain your car being seen on I-45 or even on Highway 30 but not the motel parking lot."

Hemphill shook his head. "Somebody's mistaken. I wasn't there."

"You *were* there, and we've got a witness willing to testify. That's going to be hard to beat."

"I'm not trying to defend my cheating husband," Mrs. Hemphill said, "but where is this person going to testify? There is no trial, and I don't think you have enough evidence to do anything but speculate. I'm not a lawyer, but if Kevin needs legal representation, I'm sure Houston has a few good attorneys that we could speak to."

Ribs kicked my leg. I assumed he was sending a signal to back off so that we didn't push Hemphill into lawyering up. I was for, and against, that approach. On one hand, I wanted to back off. On the other, I wanted to push harder. I hated all of this lawyering-up bullshit. I opted for a compromise.

"I apologize. I didn't mean to imply that we had evidence yet. But once we have the gun analyzed we will. It's amazing what they can tell from a simple gun."

"So you've found the murder weapon?" Mrs. Hemphill asked.

I cleared my throat. "Not yet. But we're pretty sure we know where to look for it."

"And where might that be?"

"At the bottom of the lake, near the center of the FM 1097 bridge."

"If you know that much, why not look for it. I want to get this mess over with so we can get back to a normal life. I still have a divorce to file."

I smiled. "That is what we intend to do, ma'am, but we need approval from our superiors. There are budgets to consider."

"What's involved with looking? I presume you need divers. What else?"

"An underwater metal detector and a team of divers who are trained to look for such things. It's not as easy as it sounds. The bottom of a lake can be pretty murky, especially if it's deep or the waters are turbulent."

"No problem. Get the job done."

Ribs sat up straight and shot me a look. "What?"

"Tell your superiors that I will pay for the process. I want to get this resolved once and for all. Despite being furious with Kevin for his… indiscretions, I *have been* married to him for more than twenty years. The least I can do is help him clear his name, not to mention my reputation."

"Ma'am, I appreciate the gesture, but this could cost a lot of money. It may take them days, if not more, and they don't work cheaply."

"Detective, last year I made almost $2 million. Whatever it costs won't be enough to concern me. Please tell your boss, or whoever you need to get approval from, to call me and I will set up the arrangements."

I stood, my heart racing. "You've got a deal," I said. "We'll get right on it. Expect a call from Captain Gladys Cooper. I'll give her your number."

Ribs and I exited with smiles on our faces.

When the front door closed, Kevin grabbed Susan by the arm. "Why did you do that?"

"Do what?"

"You know what. Agree to fund the search. Suppose they find the gun?"

"How are they going to find the gun? You didn't kill Farnsworth. Whoever killed Farnsworth had to have used a different gun. Coincidence or not, there's no way in hell that whoever broke into our house and shot Chlorinda also happened to shoot Farnsworth. It's next to impossible, and the sooner we get this over with the better."

"But they said the ballistics match?"

Susan shrugged. "Cops say anything when they're trying to solve a crime. I have my characters say things like that all the time."

"But what if they find the gun?"

"Are you crazy? Listen to yourself. First off, they'd have to be right about where to look. Then they'd have to find the gun. Then the ballistics would have to *really* match. So unless you killed Farnsworth, it's not happening. And for the ballistics to match, it would mean you would have had to kill Chlorinda also. And you were in Atlanta, remember? So stop being an idiot."

"I don't like it," Kevin said. "It's too risky."

She laughed. "Don't be ridiculous. Think of what you're saying. What are the chances of a the same burglar who shot Chlorinda also shooting Farnsworth? Ask yourself *why* he'd do it to begin with. And how he'd even know him."

"I hear you, but I still don't like it. It's my ass on the line. They think I did this."

"I know. And that's why I'm providing the money, which is the last you're getting from me, by the way."

Susan went to the kitchen to boil water for tea. "Maybe we should just tell them?"

"Tell them what?"

"About the plot. About how we planned on tricking the cops in order to develop a plot for the book."

"No way," Kevin said.

"Why not? What can they do? You were in Atlanta and I was at the hotel. What are they going to charge us with, plotting a book?"

"If they find the gun, they'll know I bought it."

"What? You didn't buy the gun."

"I know that, Roger told me that you had him buy the gun. That means the gun dealer will think it was me. Which brings up a question —you had Farnsworth buy the gun using my name—why?"

"To run a test. I figured if he could purchase a gun using your license, then he could board a plane and fool them."

Susan took a drink of her tea and said, "Wait a minute. When did he tell you he bought the gun? You met with him, didn't you? That *was* you in the motel parking lot."

She stood and paced. "Oh my God! Did you kill him? Are the cops right? Did you kill Chlorinda? Were you trying to kill me? Was this you all along?"

She grabbed her keys and ran for the door. "I'm leaving. Don't try to follow, or I'll call the police."

LOOK HARD

Coop was on the phone with the Conroe Diving Club when I walked in.

"Do what you have to do, but I'm going to have Detective Gino Cataldi get in touch with you. He'll show you where to look and explain what you're looking for.

"It will be today. Probably in an hour or so. And don't be concerned about payment. You can submit an invoice to him when you meet."

She hung up the phone and shook her head. "Everyone wants to be paid before they even do the damn work."

"Obviously you found someone."

"A guy at the Conroe Diving Club. He has two other guys who work with him and they do this as side work. They did that recovery for Shell last year in the Gulf. That's probably why they're so damn expensive."

"I heard you tell him I'd be calling. Who do I ask for?"

Coop scribbled something on a scrap of paper and handed it to me. "Here's the name—Marty Sheppler. He should remember yours."

"I'll get Ribs and be on our way."

I heard Ribs running his mouth long before I turned the corner in the hall. "Get ready, Ribs. We're leaving in five minutes."

"Where are we going?" he asked when I got to the office.

"Coop found a diver; in fact, she found a whole team of them, so let's go. I don't want to keep them waiting."

On the way up to Conroe, I called Susan and told her we'd be starting. "He's expensive," I said. "It's going to cost you for this."

"It doesn't matter what it costs, Detective. At least not at this point. Just get it done. And by the way, I'll be staying at the hotel for a few days. The Marriott in The Woodlands."

"Is anything wrong? Do you need me—"

"Nothing to concern yourself with. I just wanted you to know where to reach me."

"Yes, ma'am. I'll keep you posted." I hung up the line and turned toward Ribs. "Did you hear that?"

"No. What?"

"Mrs. Hemphill is staying at the Marriott for a few days."

Ribs whistled. "Whoa. What the hell is that all about?"

"Maybe some of what we've been telling her is sinking in."

"Why do you think she's doing this?" Ribs asked. "She's got to think there's at least a chance we'll find something. Do you think she's hoping for that?"

"Maybe that's exactly what she's hoping for. Maybe after all of our conversations, she's convinced that he *was* trying to kill her."

"So you think she's trying to find the gun to burn him?"

"Or to help her alimony cause. Either way, I don't care. I just want the gun."

We met Marty at Starbucks in Conroe, as planned. We discussed the details, then he got his guys and followed us to the lake.

"I say search near the center of the bridge first, then widen the area. Assume the killer tossed it out his car window about halfway across."

Marty stood in front of Ribs and me. "You know this could take a while. It's not as easy as you think. A gun might seem big when you hold it in your hand, but when it's sitting at the bottom of a twenty-thousand-acre lake, it's another story."

Lake where FM 1097 crosses over

I had the feeling he was playing it up to sound like a bigger job than it was. Ribs must have felt the same.

"But we're not searching a twenty-thousand-acre lake," Ribs said. "We're looking in a half acre area at most."

"A half an acre is still a big area," Marty said. "Especially when the bottom might be nothing but mud. A gun blends in nicely with that background. I know. I've done this a few times`-."

"Do it again, and we'll all be happy," I said. "Now, let's get busy."

We stayed and watched until the first divers went in, making sure they were in the right location, then Ribs and I left. We had other work to do. We'd caught another case on the west side of the city, and we had to get out there before they wrapped up the crime scene.

The crime scene was a small ranch house in an older neighborhood off of Highway 6, north of I-10 and west of Highway 290. Ben was still at the scene when we arrived.

"What have you got Ben?" I asked.

"Just what you see," he said. "I doubt if you're going to find much different."

A male, probably forty years old, was sprawled on the floor with a pool of blood underneath him. A woman was sitting on the sofa not ten feet away, crying.

"Wife?" I asked Ben.

He nodded. "And unless I'm an idiot, she's the one who killed him. She was still babbling about it when we got here."

A uniformed officer stood about six feet away. "Officer," I said. "Can you step outside a minute?"

We went out the patio door, closed it, then stood under a porch roof. "Detective Cataldi," I said. 'Were you the first on the scene?"

"Yes, sir," he said. "I'm Officer Maloney. My partner is Officer Hernandez. We received a call about shots fired and got here right away. It couldn't have been more than ten minutes."

"And what did you find?"

"A Caucasian male—the one you see—about—"

"You can skip the normal police bullshit. Just tell me what you found."

"The guy was on the floor, already dead. The wife was on the couch like she is now, crying. When I asked her what happened, she said she had shot him."

"She said that? That she shot him?"

"Plain as day, sir. I asked her why, and she said he shouldn't have lied to her. Shouldn't have cheated on her."

"Were those the exact words?"

Maloney took out his notepad, flipped a few pages, then read. "Yes, sir. Those were her words. Exactly. I guess I remember because this is my first murder scene. She speaks with a Spanish accent but she seems to understand English. Speaks it well too."

I patted him on the shoulder. "That's great, Maloney. You did good."

"Don't tell me we've got an easy one," Ribs said.

"Every once in a while there's bound to be an easy one. Let's just hope this holds up."

We went in and questioned the wife, who was Latino, advising her of her rights. Ribs told her in Spanish that he understood, and spoke, the language, so if she felt more comfortable, she could speak that. She said she didn't need or want an attorney or an interpreter, and admitted that she had shot her husband.

"It was the third time he cheated on me," she said. "I warned him before. I guess he didn't believe me when I said I'd kill him."

We finished our chat, asked Officer Maloney to escort her to the station, wrapped up our talk with Ben, then we headed out.

"That might have been the easiest case I ever worked on," Ribs said.

"I wish they were all that easy. Hell, I'd settle for the Hemphill case being half that easy."

"Maybe it will be after we find that gun," Ribs said.

"That reminds me, I need to check in with Marty and see if they've found anything."

"I think he'd have called if they found it," Ribs said.

"Still. I'll call."

"Marty, it's Detective Cataldi. You find anything?"

"Nothing yet, Detective. But I didn't expect anything. I'll call the moment we find it."

"Are you sure you *are* going to find it?"

"No, I'm not sure. You don't even know that it's down there. But if it's there, then given time, I'll find it."

"You had all day. What's the problem?"

"Detective, put a blindfold on, take a penny, and and toss it into a field. Then try to find it. Now, imagine doing that under water in a much bigger area."

I thought for a moment, then said, "Okay, point made. I won't bug you again."

"I don't mind you bugging me, just don't expect the impossible."

I hung up and saw that Ribs was on the phone. "Yeah, okay," he said.

"That was Coop. The lady who shot her husband has a lawyer who is insisting that the confession was coerced."

"Bullshit."

"Should have known it wouldn't be so easy."

"Don't worry. It's his job to try, but that's all it's going to be. Tests will show she had gunshot residue on her hands, and we've got a confession to Maloney *and* us. She's not getting out of this one."

"What did the diver have to say?" Ribs asked.

"Found nothing. Not a damn thing."

"That's not good," Ribs said. "Mrs. Hemphill won't put up with that for long."

"She's got plenty of money," I said.

"I don't care how much she's got. She won't continue to spend it on nothing."

Two more days went by with nothing to show from Marty and his team. I was beginning to get nervous. Maybe we'd called this wrong. "Is this typical?" I asked.

"Nothing is ever typical," Marty said. "It is what it is. We've got a large area to search and we haven't found it yet. Remember, we've got to search *both* sides of the bridge. He could have thrown the gun out of either window."

I thought about what he said. "Okay. Keep at it."

"Think of it this way, Detective. Remember when that airplane from Malaysia went down? And remember how long it took to locate wreckage?"

I nodded.

"I'm not saying this is the ocean, or comparing the size of the area we have to search, but a gun isn't as big as a plane either."

When he put it like that, it hit home. "Okay, got it."

We were on our way back to the station when the phone rang. "Hello?"

"Detective Cataldi, this is Susan Hemphill. What have you got to report?"

I knew this was coming, but I wasn't prepared for it. "Nothing yet, ma'am. We're working on it, though."

"Working on it? I can't continue this forever. Do you know how much this is costing?"

"Yes, ma'am. It's quite a lot."

"That's putting it mildly, and it's been three days. How long do they think it will take?"

"He doesn't know. To be honest, ma'am, we don't even know if the gun is at that spot. It's pure speculation."

There was a pause, then, "Detective, I can't throw money down the drain forever. I'm going to have to pull the plug."

"But, ma'am—"

"I'm sorry, Detective. But as disgusted as I am with Kevin, it was obvious to me before that he didn't do it, and though you and your partner have made a few interesting observations, it is obvious now that the gun isn't at the bottom of the lake, or at least not in that specific part of the lake. You've wasted everyone's time and my money. I think you should get busy and find the real killer."

"But, ma'am. It might happen tomorrow. They might find it."

"And they might not. Which is more likely based on what I've seen. And just so that you know, I'm leaving soon to go back to San Francisco."

"Back to San Francisco?"

"Yes, Detective. That *is* where I live."

"What about your husband?"

"I don't know, and I don't care. Even though I don't believe he killed Chlorinda, I want no part of him. He can manage his own way back; he's already got the round-trip ticket we used to fly in with."

There wasn't much else to say. "Okay, ma'am. Thank you. If we find out anything, we'll let you know."

"I won't sit up waiting for your call," she said, then hung up.

"Son of a bitch," I said, and punched the seat next to me.

"What's up, cuz? Was that Hemphill?"

"Yeah it was her, and she's pulling back on funding the search, just like you warned. Now we're screwed."

"Like I said earlier, it was bound to happen. And you're right, we're screwed."

"Not yet." I grabbed my phone and dialed the office. Cindy answered pretty quickly. "Cindy, this is Gino. I need a cell number for Cybil Johnson.

"Yeah, the mayor's wife. And I need it quickly if you don't mind. And I prefer if you don't ask Coop before you give it to me."

"I don't know, Gino. I wouldn't be doing this if I were you," Cindy said.

"Yeah, I know. And you probably shouldn't have slipped under the bleachers with Mr. Wonderful back in high school, but you did. Now, please get me that number."

"All right. Hang on."

Twenty seconds later, although it felt like twenty minutes, Cindy gave me the number. "I'll swear I had nothing to do with it if I'm asked."

"I hope so."

"What the hell was that all about?" Ribs asked.

"Calling in favors."

I dialed the number and waited.

"Hello?"

"Mrs. Johnson, this is Detective Cataldi. I—"

"I know who you are Detective. You are the onetime partner of that Neanderthal, right?"

"Yes, ma'am. That would be me."

"What can I do for you?"

"I need a favor. I need a budget approved for a team of divers to search Lake Conroe for a murder weapon."

"I've already told the captain that I couldn't help with that. Despite my husband's reckless spending, unless a request involves golf or strip clubs, I'm afraid it doesn't pass the budget considerations."

"Come on, Mrs. Johnson. You owe me one."

"Owe you what?"

"It was me who got you out of a jam during the RB Ingle investigation."

A long bit of silence followed. "It was you?"

"Yes, ma'am. And all I'm asking for, is for you to put in a good word with Rusty…I mean the mayor."

Cybil laughed. "Call him anything you want. And since I don't like owing anyone favors, even though I don't remember what that favor was, I'll make sure this gets done."

"If you could try, ma'am, that will help."

"I'll do more than try. All I have to do is whisper in Rusty's big floppy ear and it's done. Count on it."

"Yes, ma'am," I said. "Thank you."

"Two days, Detective. That's all you have. Find the weapon or solve the crime some other way."

"We'll find it," I said. "And thanks again."

I hung up and smiled, turning to Ribs. "We've got him, Ribs. We've got the son of a bitch."

"We don't have shit yet, cuz. All we've got is two more days of making Marty and his team wealthier. We better do something on our own if we're going to make this work."

"All right. Let's do it, then. We'll go back to the motel first thing and question everybody. We'll call Santos up in Dallas and have him question everybody, and we'll talk to the people at the airport again if we have to."

"Now you're talking," Ribs said. "First thing in the morning we'll get started on all of it. For now, I have to get home and take the kids to the Marble Slab."

"Marble Slab?"

"Yeah. Thanks to Marissa. She got them hooked."

THE GUN

I called Marty first thing in the morning.

"No, we don't have anything yet," he said when he answered.

"That's not what I'm calling about. The money plug's been yanked. I managed to scrape up enough money for two more days, but that's it. I *need* that gun. You've got two days to find it. It's not going to look good on your references if you failed a search like this after so long."

He sighed. "I understand. We'll do what we can. If we find the gun, great. All is good. If we don't, we'll have to suffer a bad review."

"Okay. Just wanted you to know where things stood. See you tomorrow. I have to give you a new place to send the invoice for the last two days."

I met Ribs at the coffee shop instead of the station, as it was a lot closer to the direction we were headed. We had our morning shot in the arm, then headed out toward the Best Western in Huntsville again. On the way, I called Santos.

"Santos, this is Cataldi. I need another favor."

"What?"

"Remember that guy's place you staked out? He's dead."

"*Dios mío!*"

"Yeah, and we think the person who killed him is our murder suspect from another case."

"What can I do?"

"I need you to go through his apartment. Find anything that mentions the name Kevin Hemphill. It might be on his computer, an extra cell phone, a tablet, hell anything. It might be scribbled on a torn piece of paper. But if it's there, I want it. I need to connect these two."

"I'm on it," Santos said. "Knowing he's dead, I feel worse that I lost him that night. I still don't know how he got out. I only left for a few minutes."

"Don't beat yourself up over it. We've all been there before. Just let me know if you find anything."

"Will do, Cataldi. See ya."

We arrived at the motel twenty-five minutes later. "Let's start with the manager," I said. "I'm sure he'll swear he knows nothing, but we'll see if we can bluff something out of him."

Ribs walked in ahead of me and showed his badge. "We're here about the murder in room #112," he said, sounding as official as can be.

"I've already told the other police everything," he said.

"Maybe you *think* you have, but we'll see. What time did you start work that day?"

"Six a.m. Like always."

"When did you notice the light-colored Audi in the parking lot?"

"I never saw one. I don't even know what an Audi is."

"Good. Then when did you notice a strange car in the parking lot?"

"Listen. I'm not a car person. Maybe if it was a Ferrari or a Lamborghini or something like that, I'd notice. Otherwise, a car is a car."

Ribs sighed. "Okay. Let's move on to something easier. Are there any guests still here that were here that day?"

Ramesh—that was his name—flipped through the sign-in book. "No one. They've all checked out. Most of them that night."

"Then we'll need names and addresses," I said. "Anyone and everyone who was here that day."

"I can't do that," Ramesh said. "I have privacy to think of."

"How private will your information stay when we stake out this parking lot and bust every under-age kid who comes here to rent a room? I'll bet the local papers will have a field day with that."

"You can't do that."

Ribs pulled out his cell phone. "Lieutenant, this is Detective Hector Delgado. We need an emergency twenty-four hour stakeout team assigned to the Best Western in Huntsville."

Ribs waited a moment, then said, "That's right, the one near I-45 and Highway 30. Yes, the lobby. And make sure that everyone who checks in is at least 18 years of age. All right. Thanks."

"This is not right. This is America. You can't do this."

"Ramesh, we can do anything we want to. Now, give us what we want and you won't hear from us again. And nobody will know that the information came from you."

"The people will know. When you talk to them, they'll wonder how you got their name."

"We'll tell them a security camera captured their license plate numbers, and we used that to run a DMV check, which provided us with an address."

Ramesh thought for a minute, but only a minute, then he gave us the information. We ended up with sixteen people who were in sight of the room and the parking lot that would have been used that day."

"Okay, thanks, Ramesh," Ribs said.

"Don't forget to cancel the surveillance," Ramesh said.

Ribs smiled. "Nothing to cancel. Go back to work."

We thanked Ramesh again for his help, then set about locating the guests. Most of them were local, but the rest seemed to be either parents or loved ones of the kids attending college at Sam Houston State. A few were there to visit someone at the prison.

"Let's start with the locals," Ribs said.

The first person was a woman who went to the motel to "get away for the night," or so she said. I wondered who she got away with, but that was beside the point. She swore that she neither saw nor heard anything.

The second person we talked to said he thought he saw an Audi, but he couldn't be sure. "It's not something I could testify to. I'm nowhere near that certain."

But on the third, we hit gold. This was a couple who had gone out for the night and decided to rent a room and make a "night of it."

The wife recalled seeing the Audi the morning they checked out, a little before noon. She was cleaning up while the Audi was pulling in. She remembered because she had always wanted an Audi. She even gave us a partial plate, and when we checked, it matched Hemphill's. Best of all, the woman seemed credible. She said the car was white.

We spoke to six more people that day—the only ones we could get hold of—but no one recalled seeing Hemphill, his car, or Farnsworth.

Still, it had been worth it. We had a heck of a lot more than we started with, and it was enough to burn Hemphill as far as I was concerned.

Near the end of the day, Santos called. "Got Hemphill's number on a scratch pad," he said. "Wasn't on the top, but the impression of his number was underneath. The guys at the lab were able to make it out."

"Fantastic! Is there any way you can send that down to us? It would help."

"It's already on the way. Plus, I emailed a photo of it in the meantime."

"Santos, you're the best. Thanks. I owe you twice now."

"You're welcome. And don't worry. I'll collect some day."

Ribs and I were heading south on I-45, on our way back to Houston, when the phone rang. "Grab that, will you, Ribs? And put it on speaker. I want to hear."

Ribs answered as if he were me, "Cataldi."

"This is Marty. Nothing. I made it known to them what was at stake and they all agreed to start early tomorrow. We'll see. I'll keep you up to date."

This news was not unexpected and considering the day, it didn't dampen my spirits. "Okay, Marty. See what you get tomorrow."

The next day we finished questioning the people, but we got no more hits. Nobody remembered the car or the people. Not an observant bunch.

"I think they had more on their minds than who was driving what," Ribs said. "I know I would."

"People should pay more attention to things around them," I said.

Ribs laughed. "Like you would. If you checked into a place with

Marissa, the last thing you'd be worried about is a car. And don't deny it."

I laughed. "Okay. Maybe you have a point."

"I *know* I've got a point," Ribs said. "I'm just surprised you admitted it."

"It's only two o'clock," I said. "What do you want to do?"

"Make sweet passionate love to Jessica Alba."

"Ribs, you're so full of shit you make me laugh. If by some stroke of God, Jessica Alba disrobed in front of you, you'd run home to Rosalee like a whipped puppy."

He laughed. "Maybe, but you better not tell anybody or you'll ruin my image."

"You can forget that. You have no image, Ribs."

As we were crossing over F.M. 1960, the phone rang. "Hello?"

"Cataldi, this is Mattson, from the computer forensics department."

"Yeah?"

"We've been working on that dead woman's drive and we found something we thought you'd be interested in. It's a letter or draft of a letter that had been deleted. And in light of what happened, it appears to be incriminating for Mr. Hemphill."

"Did you find an email?"

"No, but she could have written the letter in any app, then sent it using an email from a phone, the library, a coffee shop. Damn near anywhere. The best bet would be to get his computer and let us have a look, see if we find it there."

"Good job, Mattson. Can you send me a copy of what you have as soon as possible? I'd like to look at it."

"You'll have it in ten minutes," he said. "And if you can get Hemphill's computer, let me know."

Ribs and I had planned on returning to the office, but after hearing about the letter, we decided to stop and look at that.

"Where you want to go," I said.

"There's a Dunkin Donuts on 1960 by Red Oak. That'll do nicely."

I exited on Ritchie Road, made a U-turn, and then a left under the freeway. In five minutes we were sipping hot coffee and munching on cinnamon rolls.

Dunkin Donuts on FM 1960

I checked my email and got the letter from Mattson. "Let's see what we've got," I said.

It's been a long time and still nothing has developed. I expected more than this. A lot more. You promised it would be done in less than three months and it has been more than nine. When is it going to happen? How long do I have to wait?

I'll tell you this much, if you don't do something soon, I will. You have until the end of the month, and if something doesn't happen, I'm telling Susan. She won't like it. I'm sure she'll be angry, but we all have to deal with things we don't like, right?

I hope you can handle this your way, but if not, I'll handle it my way.

Love forever,

Chlorinda

"Holy shit," Ribs said. "Does this burn his ass or what?"

"If we find it on his computer it does. If not, it does nothing."

"So let's get his computer."

"He's not going to just give it to us, Ribs. But with this letter and the evidence we have of an affair and everything else, we can surely get a judge to issue a warrant. Then, it's up to Mattson."

We left the donut shop and walked to the car. Before opening the door, the phone rang again. "Busy today, Ribs," I said.

"Hello?"

"Detective Cataldi, this is Marty from the dive team."

"Yeah?"

"We got it."

"What?"

"We've got it, sir. We found the gun."

I realized I didn't have the speaker on, so I turned to Ribs and shouted. "They found the gun, Ribs. They found the goddamn gun."

I returned to the call. "Marty, we'll be right up. Don't move. It'll take me maybe fifteen to twenty minutes."

"I'll be here," Marty said.

Marty and his team were waiting when we got there. They looked as if they wanted a few pats on the back, which I happily granted. "Thanks for all of the hard work and dedication," I said. "This is going to help us catch a murderer. You should be proud."

The smiles on their faces displayed their appreciation for the kudos, and when Marty handed me the gun, I'm sure my smile matched theirs. "I've been waiting for this," I said.

Ribs handed Marty a note. "In case Gino didn't give it to you, this is the name and address of our captain. She'll get the invoice signed and released right away. And thanks. Ya'll did a great job."

"Thanks," Marty said. "When we didn't find anything after three days, I was worried. I'm just glad it worked out." He laughed. "I hope it's the right gun."

Ribs turned it one way then another, then he put it in a plastic evidence bag. "I'm sure it is. Looks like the right caliber, and it has a suppressor. Not many guns have that. And besides, you don't find many guns at the bottom of a lake."

Once again, Ribs and I headed toward the station, but this time we had no interruptions. It took us almost an hour to get there, but it proved to be worth it. We went to Coop's office and told her, and she was ecstatic about the news.

"So, your little seek-and-find operation paid off?"

"Sure did," I said. "Tell Cybil I owe her one."

Coop laughed. "You don't have to worry about that. She'll remind you. Trust me."

Cindy walked in with a cup of tea for Coop, who always seemed to need it, like a person on life support needs a glucose drip. "Want anything? Coffee, tea, water?"

"No thanks," I said. "We just had coffee."

Coop cleaned a spot on her desktop and set her cup of tea down. "What now? What's the plan?"

"I told her about the letter that Mattson had recovered, and I placed the gun on her desk."

"It looks like the serial number has been scratched off, but I've got a friend at the FBI who can probably help with that. Also, if we can get a judge to issue a warrant for Hemphill's computer based on this letter, that would be great."

Coop nodded. "I'll get to work on the warrant while you work on the gun. Let's get this moving."

"You got it, Coop. I'll call him first thing."

THE AUTOPSY

*R*ibs was already in the office drinking coffee when I got in. "Early, aren't you?"

"I've got three kids home sick. I wasn't about to stay at home longer than I had to."

"Pour me a cup of coffee while I call this guy," I said. "He's in DC, so he should be in by now."

"How do you know him?" Ribs asked.

"I used to work with him in Philly. We went through the academy together."

"Go get 'em, cuz. I'll cover the coffee end."

I looked up the number and called. A pleasant and youthful-sounding lady answered. "Federal Bureau of Investigation."

"Vince Canale please."

"May I ask who's calling?"

"Tell him it's Gino from Philadelphia. He knows me."

"Yes, sir. One moment please."

I listened to music while waiting on hold. Finally, Vince answered. "Gino! You son of a bitch. How have you been?"

"Better than I should be. How about you? It's been a long time."

"I've been great. How's Mary? You two still together?"

I paused for a moment, feeling as if I'd been hit in the gut. "Vince, I guess you didn't know. Mary died a couple of years ago."

"What? Jesus Christ! I didn't know. How? What happened?"

"Cancer. She was suffering for a long time. It was a good thing that it happened when it did."

"I'm so sorry, Gino. Goddamn. I wish I were closer so I could do something."

"I wish you were closer, too, Vince. Mary always enjoyed having you and Celie over. But you might be able to help on another matter."

"Anything. Name it."

"I'm working a murder case, and we've got a gun with the serial number scraped off. I was—"

"Say no more. Send it up and I'll have my guys at the lab look at it. They can recover damn near anything. Give me your email, and I'll send you the address."

"Your guys? What, did you get a promotion?"

"I'm an assistant director now. It's more of a title than anything, but it does carry some juice."

"Okay. Great. Here's my address: gcataldi@hpd.com. Shoot me your address, and I'll have the gun FedExed overnight."

"Super. I'll get it right back to you. It's going to take a few days.

There's a new method my guys use, and though it's great at recovery, it takes a while."

"No problem. I'd rather have you do it."

"Okay. And sorry again about Mary. Celie and I didn't know. We'd have come down if we did."

"Thanks, Vince. For everything. Tell Celie I said hi."

Ribs was standing next to me when I hung up. "Coffee's cold by now. I was beginning to wonder if you were going to talk all day."

I grabbed the coffee, took a sip, and shivered. "You weren't shitting about it getting cold."

"I know," Ribs said. "And if there's anything worse than cold coffee, it's *bad* coffee that's cold. But, hey, that's what happens when you spend half an hour talking."

"He was a guy I worked with in Philly. He didn't know about Mary, and when he asked about her…"

Ribs lost his smile. He patted me on the shoulder. "Don't worry, cuz. If he didn't know, he didn't know. Besides, you've got a new path now, and it's a good one."

I fought back a flood of tears. No way I was crying in front of Ribs. "Thanks," I said. "I appreciate that."

About noon, we got a call from Coop. "I found a judge to issue the warrant," she said. "Judge Arthur Heinrich. I suggest you get the man's computer before he does something with it. I wouldn't put it past someone that rich to just toss the thing."

"You don't have to ask twice," I said. "We're on our way."

When Kevin Hemphill answered the door, it was with a smile. I was glad. It would be nice to see it disappear when I told him of the load of shit I was about to dump on him.

"What could you possibly want now, Detectives?"

I handed him the papers for the warrant. "Your computer, cell phone, and tablet, if you have one. What you're holding in your hand is warrant."

"For what?"

"I just told you for what. As to why, it was issued in response to a letter found on Chlorinda's hard drive."

"That stupid son of a bitch!"

"Don't be too harsh on the girl. After all, she *is* dead. And—in her defense—she had deleted it, but we found it. Just like we're going to find the one you deleted."

"Goddamn."

"Yeah, and guess what? Your day is about to get worse, because we found the gun. It was right where I thought it would be."

"Impossible."

"No. Not impossible. We found it. And right now, it's going to the FBI to have the serial number raised. Once we get that number and trace it, your ass is seriously fried."

He led us to an iMac sitting on top of a desk in the study. Ribs woke it from sleep state, then said. "I don't think this is his, Gino. It has a lot of files that appear to be associated with Mrs. Hemphill's books."

"Is it?" I asked.

"That's my computer," he said.

"All it will take is a call to your wife. I'm sure she'll be eager enough to help us identify the correct one." I waited for him to respond. When he didn't, I said, "Is that what you want me to do? Should I call her?"

He started to walk away. "Over here," he said. And he led us to a small desk in the corner of the family room. There was a laptop on it. "It's right here," he said. "Password is Jackrabbit313, with a capital 'J'."

"Good of you to cooperate," I said.

"I presumed it wouldn't make much difference," he said. "If you wanted into the machine, a simple password wouldn't stop you."

"Correct. I'm glad you realized that."

Ribs grabbed the computer, and we made our way to the front door. "As they say in the movies, Mr. Hemphill, 'Don't try to leave town.' We'll be seeing you soon."

"No worries, Detective. I'm not going anywhere."

We got in the car and started back. "Ribs, put out an alert to the airlines to watch out for Hemphill. Give them the particulars and send a photo over. We don't want him escaping."

We took the computer back to Mattson, and he made it a priority, swearing he'd be done by the end of lunch tomorrow. That was encouraging. Ribs and I reported the results of the warrant to Coop, and we filled her in on what the FBI was doing.

Two hours later, while catching up on paperwork, Ribs received a call from airport security. Hemphill was trying to take a flight to Rome, which was only a few minutes from Vatican City, which had no extradition treaty with the United States. I felt positive that was not by coincidence.

Ribs asked security to hold him until we could get there and pick him up. He then called Rosalee and told her he'd be late. Afterward, he turned to me. "And after we so politely asked him not to leave."

"Some people show no gratitude," I said. "Shall we pick up our guest?"

We went to security and showed our badges. Even though they knew us by now, we had to follow rules.

"Kevin," I yelled, as if I were excited to see him. "I didn't know you were heading out or, I'd have invited you for dinner. Now, I guess you'll have to spend the night."

I turned him around and cuffed his hands behind his back.

"You can't do this to me. What are the charges?"

"I've got a bunch of them, but let's start with murder in the first degree, and you can add to that, second degree murder, conspiracy to commit murder, insurance fraud. If that's not enough, I'm sure we can think of more."

"You're out of your mind. You can't arrest me."

"I just did," I said, then I read him his Miranda rights.

"Don't you wish you hadn't tried to kill your wife? If you hadn't, you'd be rich *and* free."

The phone rang and Ribs picked it up. "Hello?"

"Detective Cataldi, this is Deputy Rawlins. We met up at that killin' in Bentwater."

"I remember. This is Delgado, but you're good to talk. Gino is right here. I'm putting the phone on speaker so he can hear. He's driving."

"I'm calling because we thought you'd want to know. We found a boat in a cove on the south side of the lake. Actually, we found two boats, but the other one was adrift and was found by a fisherman near the north shore."

"Anything on ownership or why they'd have been there?"

"Nothing. They're both just little jon boats, but it's not something you'd just leave out on the water. Probably cost eight hundred dollars or more."

"Excuse my ignorance, but is this a usual occurrence? How often does it happen? And what the hell *is* a jon boat?"

"No problem on the ignorance. I imagine down in the city, I'd be the same way. As to what a jon boat is—it's just a simple flat-bottom boat. Lots of people use it for huntin' or fishin'. You can put a motor on it or leave it be. Works either way. And no, unless you got more money than ol' Jasper, who owns the feed store, you wouldn't go leavin' it out on the lake."

"Okay, thanks, Rawlins. And by the way, it's probably a lost cause, but keep people away from the boats so we can look for DNA."

"I'll lock 'em up tighter than a duck's ass," Rawlins said. "You comin' to pick them up?"

I restrained a chuckle about the *duck's ass* comment, and said, "Yeah, I'll send somebody by tomorrow."

"Son of a bitch," I said, turning to Hemphill. "What do you think about that? We've got your boat. But why'd you have two out on the lake?"

When Hemphill didn't say anything, Ribs turned halfway around in his seat. "I guess he's taking his right to remain silent seriously." He looked Hemphill in the eyes. "If I tell Gino to pull over and beat your fucking brains out, I bet you'd talk."

"Easy, Ribs. No sense in getting excited."

Ribs smiled. "You lucked out this time, Hemphill. But Gino won't always be here to protect you."

"So tell me," I said. "I assume you had a boat stashed in a cove. You used the boat to go to your house and shoot who you thought was your wife, then you took it back and left it in the cove. What I can't figure out is what was the other boat for? Why did you need two?"

He's not talking, amigo. Pull over and I'll fix that."

"Ribs, just let the man suffer in peace. Soon enough, he'll be locked up with guys interested in exploring all of his bodily cavities." Gino slowed down due to traffic. "By the way, Hemphill, why did you kill Farnsworth? Was he trying to blackmail you? Did you promise him a big chunk of money, thinking there would be an insurance payoff from your wife's death?"

"He's still not talking," Ribs said.

"Hey, Hemphill, while you're sitting there, being silent and sweating your balls off, I'm enjoying myself. I'm having so much fun, I don't know if I'll even sleep tonight."

"If Marissa is with you, you'll sleep," Ribs said. Then he cocked his head sideways and said, "Or maybe you won't."

"Enjoy yourselves while you can, boys. My lawyer will have me out in hours."

"Not with what we've got on you. I don't know about California, but we take murder seriously down here in Texas; in fact, if I'm not mistaken," Ribs said, "we typically execute five times more people than the next state on the list."

"You people are sick."

"You mean me and Gino, or the wonderful people of the great state of Texas?"

"Just get me to the police station. I'm bored with your company."

"Don't worry. We're on our way. Pretty soon you'll be nice and comfortable in your cell. By the way, do you want me to call Susan for you?"

"Screw you."

"I guess you're right. That's probably what she'd say."

Ten minutes later, we pulled into a near-empty parking lot and ushered Hemphill into the station. After completing the paperwork, we turned him over to the night shift for further processing.

"Make sure he's tucked in nicely," I said.

"The night-shift sergeant, Dugan, laughed. "Don't worry about that. I've got a special place reserved for guys who murder women."

As Dugan led him away, I said, "See you tomorrow, Hemphill."

YOU HAVE THE RIGHT TO REMAIN SILENT

The phone rang as I made the turn onto my street. At first, I was hesitant to answer; I didn't want any bad news, and if it was good news, I'd rather save it for tomorrow and start the day off right. God knows, enough days didn't.

I glanced at the caller ID, and noticed Marissa's name, so I picked up. "Hello?"

"Gino. I was beginning to think you wouldn't answer."

"If I'd have known it was you, I would have answered on the first ring."

She laughed. "I don't know whether to say you're sweet or full of shit."

"I prefer sweet. What's up?"

"I called to see if you wanted to eat dinner together."

"Sure. Where?"

"I was thinking your house since I don't have any food."

"God, what a user," I said, and laughed. "No, that will be fantastic.

Bring wine, though. I don't think I have any, and I've already passed the store."

"You got it. I'll be there in forty minutes."

I parked the car, took a quick shower, changed clothes, and got ready for dinner. I was attempting to decide on a meal when Marissa showed up.

She walked in, came to the kitchen and must have seen me standing in front of the open pantry, dilemma written all over my face.

"So you're telling me we should have met at the grocery store instead?"

I laughed. "I think so, unless you're up for something from the frozen-foods department."

"How about we go out to eat?"

"Where?"

"How clogged are your arteries? I was thinking that new place on Gosling. They are supposed to have a chicken-fried steak to die for."

"Sounds good, but I'm insulted. What makes you think my arteries are clogged?"

"Because of the way you eat and more importantly, the way you don't exercise."

"Okay," I said. "We'll make a deal. Chicken-fried steak tonight. Exercise tomorrow."

She pulled me close and kissed. "Deal." Then she grabbed my keys off the counter and spun around, saying, "I'll drive."

"Unless you stop at an ATM, you'll pay too. I'm fresh out of cash."

"No worries. Just get in the car."

"What's the name of this place, anyway?"

"Republic Grill. It's in the Panther Creek Center at Gosling and Woodlands Parkway."

We were seated right away. Marissa got the chicken-fried steak but I went for the chicken-fried chicken, and I opted for a side of tomato-basil soup. When the meal arrived, I gasped—the servings were huge. I was hungry, but not that hungry.

As it turns out, neither one of us was disappointed in our meal, and despite the first impressions of how big the portion was, I ate it all. The meat was delicious and the gravy fantastic, and the soup was some of the best I'd had. It was thick and creamy and had plenty of real basil in it.

"This place is a keeper," I said. "We'll be back."

"I'm encouraged to hear you say *we'll* be back."

I squeezed her hand. "You know I wouldn't have it any other way."

"Me neither," she said. "But it's still nice to hear." Marissa finished her last bite of food, then said. "We should bring Connie here. She'd love it."

"You think? I don't know if she goes for Texas food. I pegged her for strictly Italian."

"No way. She cooks Italian, but she eats anything that's good. She had barbecue today. I think she's been partnered with Tip for too long."

"You saw her today?"

"We had lunch together at the Galleria. Why?"

"No reason. Actually, I'm thrilled. I'm glad you found a friend. I think that's great."

Marissa smiled. It was a warm, sweet smile. "Thanks, Gino. It feels good, too. I like Connie."

"Yeah. She's a tough bird," I said. "But she makes a good partner for Tip. Keeps him in line."

I chugged the last of my water, then reached for the wine. "As I savored the meal, I said, "This is a perfect way to end a great day."

"What was so great about it?" she said.

"I told her about my call with Vince, leaving out the part about Mary, then I told her of the computer forensics with the dead assistant, how we arrested Hemphill, and of the boats found on the lake.

"There were two boats?"

"Yeah. Why?"

'That's my question—why? Why would two boats be adrift, or tied up, or otherwise abandoned?"

"I don't know."

"You might not know now, but you *need* to know. There must be a reason two boats were on the lake and you need to find out why. Think about it. Boats don't wander off on their own."

"What difference does it make?"

Marissa took a long slow sip from her wine glass. "I don't know yet. But you better find out, because as sure as money is green, there's a reason."

"What could the reason be?" I asked.

"I don't know, but he didn't use two boats to make his way across the lake. If you believe in coincidence, fine. But in case you don't, you better do your homework."

"What do you mean, homework?"

"Homework for the trial. As soon as you mention that he used a boat to get across the lake—which you'll have to do since he wasn't logged in at the Bentwater guard gate—his lawyer will bring up the fact that a second boat was found, and he will present that as evidence of a possible second murderer establishing reasonable doubt."

"Damn, pretty good for a career criminal."

"I wasn't always a criminal, you know."

"No, I don't know. What were you beforehand?"

She laughed. "None of your business. Maybe someday I'll tell you. In the meantime, find other emails from the dead woman to Hemphill and compare them. See if the language matches up. If it does, great. If it doesn't, you're screwed, assuming he has a good lawyer, which I'm sure he will."

I was busy taking notes. "I might have to hire you as a consultant," I said.

"I work cheaply. A few dinners and a couple of nights alone is all I charge."

"Deal," I said. "Count this as one of the dinners, and we'll go back to my place and count that as a night alone."

Marissa leaned all the way across the table and kissed me. "You might work out yet, Detective Cataldi."

Now it was my turn. I leaned across the table and kissed her. "And you might, too, Marissa…" I paused and looked at her. "Holy shit. I just realized I don't know your last name. I'm so embarrassed I can't stand it. I'm sorry."

"Maldonado," she said. "And don't worry. You're the first person I've told that to since grade school. So now you have my name. Marissa Maldonado."

"Maldonado? Is that Italian?"

"I don't even know. It is what it is."

"It doesn't matter. I love you anyway," I said.

"Me too," she said. "And that's the first time I've told anyone that since I told my mom."

"Now, I'm even more happy," I said, then signaled the waitress. "Check please?"

Marissa grabbed the check when the waitress arrived. "I'm paying, remember?"

I laughed. "That's good because I have no cash and it's questionable if my card has enough funds to pay it."

Marissa paid the check, then we left. She drove my car home, and when we got there, she got out of the car and started to get into hers.

"Hey, wait a minute," I said. "I thought you were coming in."

She closed her car door, walked over and kissed me. "I want this to be comfortable for you. I want you to take things at your own pace."

I took hold of her bare shoulders and pulled her close. "Trust me, this is as slow as I can go right now. I need you with me."

She smiled. "In that case, let's crack a bottle of vino and chat."

I smiled back. "I think you brought just the right bottle of vino."

She slipped her arm through mine and walked briskly toward the house. "I'm so glad you caught that case where we met."

"Me too," I said. "I can't imagine life any other way."

"And you'll never have to," she said, and flung the door open. Then she laughed. "I mean *we'll* never have to."

NOW WHAT?

$\mathcal{I}$ woke up beside the most beautiful woman in the world. I squeezed her abs, which were embarrassingly solid, then kissed her neck.

"Good morning, you she devil."

She slowly rolled my way and gave me a warm wonderful kiss. "If you don't mind morning breath, good morning to you," she said.

Mind morning breath. How could I mind anything about you?

"*Buon giorno,* beautiful." I said, then we kissed again. "I'm not going into work today."

She laughed. "Oh, yes you are. You're going in, and you're going to solve that case. One of us has to work. If for nothing else, to maintain appearances."

I ran my fingernails up her side. "Maybe I can just be a little late?"

She got out of bed, slipped on one of my t-shirts, then headed for the door. "I'll make coffee while you get dressed."

"What about being late?" I asked.

"You can be late another time. Get up."

I slowly got out of bed, wiping sleep from my eyes as I made my way to the bathroom so I could splash cold water on my face. I never seemed to be able to fully wake without it.

"Coffee's almost ready," Marissa yelled from the kitchen.

God it felt good to hear her voice in the morning. It gave me something to look forward to. At first, I had felt guilty because of Mary, but that feeling passed. Now, I just felt alive. Alive and in love. Yes, that's what it was. I *was* in love. Something I thought would never happen again.

"Be right down. I've got to brush my teeth first." I grabbed the automatic toothbrush, then the Waterpik. A shower would have to wait. When I was finished, I slipped on a pair of shorts and ran down the steps. I felt as if I were in the orphanage again.

"About time," Marissa said, while pouring my coffee.

I snapped a salute. "Gino Cataldi reporting for duty, ma'am."

"That's better," she said and took the seat next to mine. "What have you got planned for today?"

"Try to get Mattson to get us the recovered email, check for DNA on the boats, and make sure my friend in DC got the gun. Other than that, not a damn thing. How about you?"

"I thought I'd give Rosalee a call and see if she wants to do something. I didn't get to talk to her much the night we went over. The kids kept me busy."

"That they did. Ribs said they're still talking about it. They had fun. Of course, Marble Slab didn't hurt."

"Whatever it takes."

Marissa sipped her coffee, letting the steam rise from the glass. "What would you think about having the kids spend the night some time?"

"All of them?"

"Of course. We could go to a movie, then come home and play games. It would be fun."

"Are you serious?"

She laughed. "Yes, I'm serious. I think it would be a blast."

"If you want to, I'm game. And I know Ribs would love it. He'd kill for a night alone."

"Great. I'll check with Rosalee as to when would be good."

On the way to work, I thought about how lucky I was. I had been more than happily married for twenty plus years, and now I had found someone else. I decided to call Ron and see how he was doing and to tell him about Marissa.

He sounded wide awake when he answered, a welcome relief. "What's up, Ron? How are things at the center?"

"Great, Dad. Couldn't be better. We've got a full facility, people waiting to get in, and I'm learning a lot every day from the clinical side."

"How about you? Anything new?"

"That's part of why I called. I told you I met someone a few weeks ago. Well, it's moving along quickly. I really like her, and we get along great."

"Dad, that's fantastic. I couldn't be happier."

"Do you mean it? It doesn't bother you?"

"Bother me? Hell no. Nobody deserves it more than you. I'm super excited for you. When can I meet her?"

This was a great feeling. Ron was making my day. I had been worried about calling him, but he was making it easy. "I'll talk to Marissa. Maybe we'll come down for dinner on the weekend."

"Sounds good. I'll give you a quick tour while you're here. Marissa, too."

"Okay. Listen, I've got to go. I just wanted to call."

"You don't have to tell me, Dad. You've probably been worried sick over telling me."

I laughed. "Shut-up and go to work. You're too smart for your own good."

I hung up the phone and smiled to myself. A year ago, I had been ready to leap off a bridge or shove a gun barrel down my throat. Now, I felt as if life couldn't be better.

Ribs was in the office when I got there. "Morning, cuz. How's it going?"

"Couldn't be better, Ribs. Marissa spent the night, and—"

"Whoa! You can't jump straight to an 'and' after saying something like *Marissa spent the night.*"

"I was going to say, *and* she suggested we watch your kids for the night next week."

"What? All of them?"

"You heard it first right here."

"Hold on, partner. I've got to call Rosalee. She's going to die."

I grabbed his phone. "Let Marissa ask her. She was going to call her today."

"No shit? Fine by me. In fact, both things are fine by me. You watching the kids and her asking Rosalee."

We sat, drinking coffee while I filled him in on my night with Marissa.

Partway through the story, my phone rang. It was the Walker County Medical Examiner.

"Cataldi."

"Detective, this is Randy from Walker County."

"What's up?"

"We found some interesting evidence at the crime scene and we thought you'd want to know about it. Several strands of hair were on the victim, and surrounding the victim, that did not belong to him."

He had me excited now. "Can you send it over?"

"Consider it on the way. You should have it shortly."

As I didn't have the phone on speaker, I had to relate to Ribs what was said.

"We might just nail this sucker yet," Ribs said. "The evidence keeps mounting up."

"Speaking of evidence," I said. "Marissa brought up a good point last night. She asked why there were two boats."

"Getting help from the other side now, huh?"

I laughed. "I'll take it anywhere I can get it. We need it on this case."

"Speaking of evidence, as you said, did you check with your buddy to make sure he received the package?"

"I didn't yet, but it's on my list."

"It could be a big day," Ribs said. "DNA might tell us something, and Mattson is supposed to have the computer's email recovered."

"Let's hope it's all good," I said.

About 10:00 my phone rang. It was a guy with a pretty strong Texas accent. "Detective, I don't want to say who this is, but I was at that hotel in Huntsville when that man was killed."

"Why don't you want to say who it is?"

"I, uh. I wasn't supposed to be there is why. If my wife finds out, she'll have my balls, and I ain't exaggerating. She will."

I looked at the phone screen. Caller ID showed it to be a call from a Preston Fickel. He probably didn't know it showed. I thought I recognized the voice, but I couldn't place it. Now that I saw his name, I remembered. If I wasn't mistaken, he was one of the guys we interviewed from the Best Western list..

"What did you see?"

"Not much. But about 1:00 or 2:00 I saw someone at the door to his room."

"Can you be more specific on the time? Was it closer to one or closer to two?"

"Heck, I don't know. I remember it was about that time because I was gettin' hungry. Other than that I don't know."

"And you're sure it was his room?"

"No doubt about it. I was in the room about three doors down, and when I went out to get ice, the person was there."

"Can you describe him?"

"Not even a little. The person was wearing a long raincoat and a hat. Hell, I couldn't even tell you if they were six feet tall or five feet, or if they were a man or a woman. I know what I'm tellin' you ain't much. I just wanted to tell you what I did know. But I ain't gonna' testify. I can't do that."

"Okay. Thanks for calling. I appreciate it."

"Who was that?" Ribs asked.

"Remember that good ol' boy we interviewed from the motel?"

"Yeah."

"I'm pretty sure it was him. He didn't want his wife to know he was there but he wanted to do his civic duty. Damn fool left caller ID engaged. We've got him if we need him."

"He have anything?"

"He said he saw someone at Farnsworth's room about 1:00 or 2:00. That's a little later than we figured—well, at least the two is—although if he saw the person closer to one, it fits the general timeline."

"Did he remember him at all? See him before? Cross paths at the ice machine, anything?"

"He said he couldn't recognize who it was, so I doubt if he'd be much help. Either way, if it comes down to it, we know who he is."

We were going through the files, preparing our case for the D.A., when Mattson called. "Yeah, Mattson. Tell me something good."

"How about I tell you something better than good? We've got it."

"Goddamn. Fantastic."

"Time. Date. Everything."

I was so excited I almost forgot what Marissa had said. "Mattson, do me a favor. See if you can find other emails from her to him. The longer and more wordy the better. I want to establish a language pattern, you know, words she repeatedly used, sentence structure, that kind of thing."

"No problem. I'm on it."

I told Ribs what Mattson said, and he high-fived me.

"What was all that shit you said at the end?"

"Oh, nothing. Just an idea Marissa had to firm up the case."

"Marissa again. Maybe you should partner up with her."

I laughed. "Aw. Do I detect a soft shell? Are your feelings hurt?"

"Shut-up," Ribs said. "We've got work to do."

WE FOUND THE GUN

The next afternoon we received more ammunition. The DNA evidence from the strands of hair that Walker County had sent over proved to be a dead match—they were Hemphill's. They had been found on Farnsworth's chest as well as in his motel room.

There were other, unidentifiable hairs, but they didn't matter. What mattered was that the hairs we did have belonged to Hemphill. It would be hard as hell for him to get out of this one, especially since he swore he had never been at the Best Western.

When you added DNA evidence to the statement from a witness that his car was seen that very day, it damn near locked the case up, at least as far as I was concerned.

I finished reading the report, skimming through the section detailing the unidentifiable semen samples found on the mattress and the urine samples on the bathroom floor, then I called Ribs. "Let's go. We've got to pick up Hemphill."

"Pick him up? I thought we already had him."

"We did, but his scumbag lawyer got him out on bail. He's at his house in Bentwater. But not for long."

Ribs laughed. "Sometimes I love this job. Days like this make it all seem worthwhile."

We drove to Hemphill's house, told him what we had, then read him his rights—again. He smiled as Ribs put the cuffs on him.

"I'll be out in hours."

"Not this time," I said. "It's tough to beat DNA evidence. You screwed up Hemphill. You know that old saying, *Don't shit where you eat?* Well, I've got a new one for you. 'Don't leave hairs where you plan to kill someone.'"

"I didn't leave any hairs."

"Oh, so you're telling me you *were* there? The last time, you denied that."

"No. I meant. I didn't leave any hairs because I wasn't there."

"Good try, Hemphill, but I'm not buying it. You might not *think* you left any hair, but it happens easier than you would imagine. But regardless of how it happened, happen it did. And your ass is now ours. And will soon belong to your prison inmates, who I'm certain will make frequent use of it."

"Yeah, so pucker up that asshole, amigo, because it's going to become a well-traveled road."

Hemphill didn't say much on the way in; in fact, he didn't say anything. Ribs, on the other hand, did more talking than anyone had a right to. He talked about the weather, going fishing, shopping at the mall with Little Marissa, Thomas's schoolwork. You name it and he talked about it.

Within an hour, we had Hemphill back in the system. If we were lucky, maybe he'd stay.

After we dropped him off, Ribs said, "What now? Do we just hang around and wait for him to fry?"

"With the lawyers he's got, I doubt if he'll fry, but we can always hope. As to what to do now, have you forgotten we are scheduled to be deposed by the attorney for that woman out in Bear Creek?"

"Oh, shit. Yes, I did forget. What are we being deposed about anyway? She confessed on the scene."

"I'm sure some hotshot attorney got hold of her case and decided he could do something with it. Let's show him that he can't."

The lawyer's office was on the tenth floor of a building on Milam Street. We parked in the garage and went in, running into Maloney and his partner on the way out of the elevator.

"What are you doing here?" Maloney asked.

"Same as you, I imagine. Giving a deposition."

"What for? I mean, she confessed. You heard her. He's just trying to get her off."

"I know. But that's what attorneys do. Don't worry about it."

We went into the conference room. The lady's lawyer was there along with someone to record the proceedings.

The lawyer reached out his hand to shake. "I'm Glenn Demarco," he said. "Have a seat."

"We'll try to make this painless, Detectives. By the way, would you like anything to drink before we start?"

"Nothing for me," I said.

"Me neither," Ribs said.

"In that case, let's get started. Why don't you tell me in your own words what happened."

I clasped my hands together and set them on the table. "We received a call of shots fired at the suspect's address and proceeded to drive there. When we arrived, a male—approximately forty years of age was lying on his back in a pool of blood. He was in the kitchen, where it opened to the living room. It was obvious he had been shot. The medical examiner was already on the scene and was examining the body when we arrived. The suspect was sitting on the couch, crying."

I cleared my throat and sipped some water, which they had brought despite my refusal. "Officer Maloney and his partner were standing in the living room. I asked him to step outside and tell us what had transpired.

"Officer Maloney said he had arrived at the scene to find the victim already dead and the suspect on the sofa crying. She said—of her own volition—that she had shot him."

"Had she been read her Miranda rights?" the lawyer asked.

"I assume so, as it is standard procedure, but I have no way of knowing. I can tell you that my partner and I read her Miranda rights before we spoke to her."

"I see."

"See all you want, counselor. But she told us the same thing she told Officer Maloney—that she shot her husband because he cheated on her."

I took another sip of water. "I'm not here to judge right or wrong. I'm just telling you what she said, and that was that she shot him. I'll let a jury decide if she had reasonable cause to do so."

"Did you read her rights to her in English or—"

"Don't even try it, counselor. My partner speaks Spanish as his native tongue, and we advised her of that at the scene. we told her that he understood and spoke Spanish and that if she felt more comfortable with that it was fine by us. She opted to continue in English by herself, and, she declined her right to have an attorney present."

Ribs looked at the attorney. "If I were you, I'd find another angle. We did everything by the books, and it sounds as if Officer Maloney and his partner did as well. This is a dead end. Trust me."

"Okay, thank you, gentlemen," the attorney said, and he got up from the table, a cue to us that the session was over.

"That wasn't hard," Ribs said, as we got in the elevator to go down to the lobby.

"Thank God. Sometimes they have a lawyer who knows their stuff. This one seemed as if law school was just behind him."

"Probably was," Ribs said. "But we've all got to start somewhere, and poor people get the shaft on the legal help."

"Speaking of which, we need to get that weapon report from Vince. The more ammunition we have to go at this guy the better. Because you can bet he's not going to have a legal-aid attorney in his corner."

"No shit about that," Ribs said. "I want to nail this guy."

"We're going to. Don't worry about that."

WHO BOUGHT IT?

I hadn't been in for ten minutes when Vince called. He had gotten the report back from his guys and they were able to raise the serial numbers.

"Hot damn, Vince. I owe you one for this."

"Make it two," he said. "They also traced it to a gun dealer in Alabama, who sold it to a guy named Kevin Hemphill. Ring a bell?"

"You bet your ass it does. He's our number one suspect—now our only suspect."

"Good. Some days things work out."

"Does it look solid?"

"As solid as can be. I spoke to the dealer myself, and he said this guy… Hemphill, paid for the gun and a suppressor with cash, but Hemphill did show him a license, a California license. He mentioned he was in Atlanta on business and wanted protection."

"And what was the silencer for?"

"Exactly," Vince said. "I faxed the report to you this morning and I mailed the gun back via FedEx. You should have it tomorrow."

"Vince, you're the best. Thanks. This should cement the case."

I hung up from Vince, told Ribs the news, then he and I went to get the report. Afterward, we headed to Coop's office. Cindy let us in immediately.

"Good news," I said, waving the faxed papers. The report came in from my FBI friend. Hemphill bought the gun and the suppressor. We've got him, Coop. We've got the son of a bitch."

"All we need to do now is send a picture of Hemphill and have the gun dealer confirm that's who he saw, and we're set."

Coop shook her head. "I don't want any chance of some lawyer saying things weren't handled properly. Call the local police department... better yet, find out the closest city to the gun dealer, and we'll see if we can get them to cooperate. We'll put a picture of Hemphill in a photo array and send it over, then get them to hand-carry it to the gun dealer for identification. That way there won't be any question about procedure."

"You got it, Captain. I'll let you know when we get it done."

We checked and Birmingham, Alabama, was the closest big city, so we called the chief over there and explained our situation. He asked for volunteers to make the seventy-mile drive, and surprisingly, he got numerous officers who were willing to help. I got his email and told him we'd have the specifics sent over later in the day.

Ribs and I put together what was needed and had Julie send it off in an email by 3:00 pm. Now all we had to do was wait.

I went home early, happy with the day's events and cooked dinner for Marissa. Afterward, we sat on the porch to chat, then took a long walk by the duck pond. We had brought popcorn for the ducks, and

Marissa spent a lot of time feeding them, then we sat on a bench and watched.

"I think they swim better than you," she said.

"How do you know how I swim?"

"Just guessing. Do you deny it?"

I laughed. "Okay, maybe they *do* swim better than me. A *little* better."

Marissa put a handful of popcorn in her mouth and chewed. "This would have been better with butter."

"I didn't want to make the ducks fat," I said.

"You should worry so much about your own health. All of that bread and pasta aren't very good for your arteries."

"The ducks need more help," I said. "Just eat your popcorn, and I'll worry about my arteries."

"All right. I might have to make sure you get exercise. At least at nights."

"I'm all for that," I said. "We should go home and start right now."

"You have to earn your right to exercise. I'll make a set of goals," she said, then got up and started walking down the path around the duck pond.

"Where are you going?"

"Taking the long way home. I love to walk."

"I'm right behind you."

"Good. That's where I like you," she said, and laughed like hell.

I caught up to her, put my arm around her shoulder, and we walked home slowly, enjoying the night.

When we got home I opened a bottle of wine and poured a few glasses.

"How was your day?" She asked.

"It was actually a great day. We got the FBI report back and they connected the gun to Hemphill. I've got a photo array going out to the guy who sold him the weapon. If the guy recognizes Hemphill, he's toast."

"And if he doesn't recognize Hemphill?"

"He will. I'm sure of it."

"I hope so. In the meantime, you better keep looking for more evidence. This isn't over yet. Remember, he's bound to have a good lawyer."

Officer Willie McKenzie printed out the photo array that Gino had sent, then he started the drive toward the eastern side of Oxford, near the Georgia border.

He got to the store about six o'clock. Fortunately, he had called ahead and told the owner he might be late, so the owner of the shop was waiting.

He walked inside and showed his badge. "I'm Officer McKenzie. I called earlier."

The guy reached to shake. "Arnie Milford," he said. "I'm the one you spoke to."

McKenzie pulled a sheet of paper from a folder he was carrying and set it on the top of the glass counter. "If you don't mind, take a look at these photos and tell me if you recognize anyone."

Arnie picked the sheet up and looked. Then he reached for his glasses, sitting in a case next to the cash register. "Might need these," he said. After a moment of staring, he pointed to the one in the bottom-left corner. "Him," he said. "I'm pretty sure it was him. I sold him a gun, a .38, I believe, and a suppressor. I probably wouldn't remember except for that suppressor. Don't sell many of them. And he paid cash—full price—which was damn nice. Don't get enough of them either."

"And you're sure this was the guy?"

"If you're telling me it was one of them guys in the picture, then, yeah, it was him. Something about the eyes."

McKenzie then showed him a picture of the gun and suppressor. "And was this the weapon?"

"Hard to tell based on a picture, but it looks like it. Bring me the real thing and I'll tell you for sure. But if it had my serial number on it, then it was mine."

"Okay, thanks," McKenzie said. "That'll probably do. At least for now."

McKenzie called the number Gino had sent over with the pictures. He answered right away.

"Cataldi."

"This is Officer McKenzie over in Birmingham. I just left the dealer in Oxford, that's a little town near the border. Owner picked Hemphill out of the photo array. Didn't need no prompting or arm-twisting either. Looks like you got your man."

"Okay, thanks, McKenzie. I really appreciate it. I owe you one."

"That's nice, but I ain't driving that far to collect. You'll just have to owe me."

"Okay, consider yourself owed. Thanks again."

LET'S GO TO TRIAL

lmost a month passed before the trial date. It had been short by some standards, but it felt like a lifetime to me. I'm sure it felt longer to Hemphill, who was stuck without bail thanks to a favorable judge.

The prosecutor was Monica Sanchez, a hotshot up-and-comer who had one of the city's best conviction records. She had told us before the trial began that she thought we had a good case. Hemphill had a team of three professionals, led by Houston's famous defense attorney Randy Cusper, notorious for getting guilty people off.

Both sides did their normal dance during opening arguments, then it was Sanchez's turn to present evidence. I didn't have time to attend the trial, but Marissa said she'd go when possible and fill me in.

Monica Sanchez opened with a bang. She walked to the front of the courtroom, stood in front of the jury box, and said, "Ladies and gentlemen of the jury. My name is Monica Sanchez, and I'm the prosecutor for the state of Texas. You're going to be seeing a lot of me in the next few weeks, much to the dismay of the defendant, I'm sure. I feel certain that if it were up to him, you wouldn't see me at all."

"Objection."

"Sustained," said the judge, who then turned to the prosecutor. "Ms. Sanchez. You know better."

Sanchez smiled at the jury and said, "Sorry, Your Honor."

Sanchez was an attractive woman, with long, muscular legs and a skirt so tight it looked as if it might split at any minute, and the male members of the jury, and the rest of the courtroom, were surely eagerly awaiting that moment.

She placed her hands on the railing separating the jury box from the courtroom. "Suppose I were to tell you that on the day in question, the day Chlorinda Barker was brutally murdered, Mr. Hemphill was *supposed* to be on a business trip to Atlanta. At least that's what he told his wife. That's what he told the police also. How could he commit a murder in Houston if he were in Atlanta?"

Sanchez slowly walked down the jury box, letting her hand trace along the railing. "He couldn't. No way. Why am I telling you this? Because Mr. Hemphill *wasn't* in Atlanta like he claimed. In fact, the state will show that he conspired with another man—the second victim—to plan an elaborate scheme to deceive everyone about his whereabouts. He claimed to have been in Atlanta, but we will show he was actually in Houston, not thirty minutes away from the scene of the crime."

Sanchez walked to her desk, looked at her notepad, then said, "Another thing. There was supposedly a break-in at the Hemphill house on the night of the murder, an imaginary thief who stole sixty thousand dollars in jewelry after he killed Ms. Barker. *If* this happened, and I emphasize the word *if*, where is the jewelry? Why hasn't it shown up?"

Sanchez went back to her desk and picked up the notepad again. "There are plenty of other things to discuss, which we will go into at length, such as the DNA evidence that ties Mr. Hemphill to the second victim, the mysterious phone call placed by him to a throw-away phone on the night of the murder, two boats that were found adrift on Lake Conroe, large cash withdrawals leading up to the murder, missing drugs—the same kind found in Ms. Barker's system during an autopsy. And a gun and silencer, later found to have been purchased by Mr. Hemphill, which matched the ballistics reports from Ms. Barker's murder *and* the second victim. And let's not forget the three million dollars worth of additional life insurance taken out by the defendant on his wife just three months prior to this, and listing him as the beneficiary. Keep in mind this was an *additional* three million. He already had a policy worth almost that much on her."

Sanchez paced while she sipped a glass of water. "Why is the life insurance important, you might ask. Because it's our contention, that Mr. Hemphill intended to kill his wife. That all along, this whole scheme was for him to collect the insurance and rid himself of his spouse so he could be with his mistress full time. Yes, Ms. Barker was his mistress, and we have evidence to show that. So how did she get killed instead of his wife? That's a question for you to decide, but it all points to the premeditated murder planned by Mr. Hemphill. Planned and meticulously carried out, except for one detail—he got the wrong person."

Sanchez started for her desk, then turned around and said, "Oh, and we're going to prove all of this to you beyond a shadow of a doubt."

Randy Cusper was a man of medium height, slightly balding, and he owned a rich baritone voice with a deep Texas drawl. He was dressed in an impeccable dark-blue suit, a white shirt, and red tie. He walked to the jury box, stared at them one-at-a-time, then said, "I'm sure ya'll would rather ogle over Ms. Sanchez than you would look at a beat-up old lawyer like me. I know I would. But the way the law works, you have to give me equal time. That means for every minute you salivate over her more-than-delicious body, you must spend a minute paying attention to me. So now that you're paying attention, let me tell you the truth, because sure as rain is wet, Ms. Sanchez didn't.

"She said she would prove beyond the shadow of a doubt that Mr. Hemphill did all of these terrible things. I'm here to tell you that not only *didn't* he do them, but because of all of these accusations, my client has suffered irreparable harm, emotionally and financially. But I'm not here to seek reparations; I'm just here to clear his name."

Cusper started walking back, then turned to face the jury. "Just one more thing. I don't know what shadows Ms. Sanchez plays in, but doubt is hiding in all of them, and I intend to prove it."

For her first witness, Sanchez called the life-insurance agent, who testified that it was Mr. Hemphill who had ordered the increase in the policy amount. "And would Mrs. Hemphill have been required to have had medical tests conducted before the policy was issued?"

"Yes, of course, for that amount she would."

"But would she have necessarily known what the tests were for. Is it possible that she thought they were routine medical exams?"

"It's unlikely, but it *is* possible."

Sanchez asked a few more routine questions, then left him for Cusper to cross-examine.

Randy Cusper approached the witness stand. He was holding a pencil which he drummed against his other hand.

"Mr. Nathan, what was the amount of the policy that Mr. Hemphill took out?"

"As I mentioned, it was three million."

Cusper looked at him. "Dollars, right? Three million dollars?"

The man nodded, then must have thought better and said, "Yes."

Cusper whistled. "Three million dollars. That's a *lot* of money. What is the normal amount a person might take out on their spouse? Let me re-phrase that. Suppose a person made fifty thousand dollars per year. What would be the typical amount of insurance that person would be insured for?"

"Fifty thousand? I don't know. Anywhere from two-hundred to four-hundred thousand dollars."

"So, approximately four to eight times the annual salary?"

"Eight would be a lot but not unheard of. Four to five is not unusual."

"And how much money does Mrs. Hemphill earn?"

Nathan turned sideways to look at the judge, as if asking permission to answer.

"Answer the question," the judge said.

"Almost two million dollars per year."

"What? Wow. Two million per year. So, the policy amount was only about one and a half times her income. According to the figures you cited, that's actually low. Even when combined with the previous policy, it is only about three times her income. Isn't that low?"

Nathan seemed to blush. "It is a little low."

"So it would not be unusual for Mr. Hemphill to take out a policy of that amount on his wife considering her income?"

"No. Not at all."

"Okay. Thank you, Mr. Nathan. That will be all."

Ms. Sanchez stood. "For the next witness, the state calls Ms. Kristan Karber to the stand.

Once Karber had taken her seat on the stand, Sanchez approached. "You're a flight attendant for Delta Airlines, isn't that correct?"

"Yes, ma'am."

"On the morning in question, were you working on the early-morning flight from Dallas to Houston Intercontinental?"

"Yes, it was a United flight from DFW to Bush Intercontinental. I was covering for a friend who flies for United."

"And did you subsequently have reason to be on the Delta flight from Houston to Atlanta later that morning?"

"Yes. The Houston to Atlanta flight was my regular flight. As I mentioned, the early-morning flight was me covering for my friend. It's something we do, and the airlines okayed the arrangement. She covers for me if I need it, and I cover for her if she needs it."

"But you live in Houston?" Sanchez asked.

"That's right. I took an earlier flight up to Dallas so I could cover her flight. It's no big deal."

"So you flew from Dallas to Houston then to Atlanta. Was there anything unusual about the flight to Atlanta?"

"Not the flight, no. But one of the passengers appeared to have been the same passenger who was on my morning flight from Dallas. At first, I thought that was weird. Why would someone fly to Houston and then to Atlanta when they could have taken a flight from DFW to Atlanta directly?"

"Was it the same person?"

"At first, I thought that it might be. I even said hello to him. He didn't have his beard, and he pretended not to know me, but I still thought it was him."

"Ms. Karber, I'm going to show you a video of a security clip. Would you be so kind as to identify the man who was on your flight from DFW?"

Sanchez turned the video on, then a man approached the restroom. "Ms. Karber, is that the man who was on the flight from DFW to IAH?"

"That's him," she said. "No doubt about it."

Sanchez fast forwarded the video then stopped and a moment later, someone who looked like the man exited the restroom, but he didn't have a beard. "Ms. Karber, is this the man who was on the flight to Atlanta?"

"Absolutely. And although he doesn't have a beard in this picture, I think it's the same man."

"Thank you, Ms. Karber," Sanchez said, then to Cusper, "Your witness."

Cusper walked quickly to the witness stand. "Thank you, Ms. Karber. I'm so glad you appeared today. A quick question before we start. How many people do you see in a day?"

Cusper turned and smiled at the jury. "Let me rephrase that. I don't mean how many you *see*, but how many people fly on the same planes as you? Would it be safe to say on the days you are active, it might be as many as four hundred?"

Karber nodded. "Probably. Yes."

Cusper displayed a disbelieving expression. "Do you remember *all* of them?"

"No. Not at all."

"What was so special about this person that you remembered? Was it because the police questioned you about him?"

"Objection."

"Overruled. You may continue, Mr. Cusper."

"No. It was because he showed up on the next flight to Atlanta. That doesn't happen often. Besides that, it was a different airline, which is unusual, and he had shaved his beard."

Cusper placed his finger to his lips, as if thinking. "Interesting." He read from a notepad he held, then said, "You told the court you *think* it was the same man on both flights even though he did not have a beard on the flight to Atlanta. How certain are you? There's a difference between *think* and *certain.* According to the dictionary, think means:

> *to have an opinion about someone or something*

And certain

> *not having any doubt about something : convinced or sure*

"I'm not a linguist, but even to a country boy like me, that seems like a big difference. Wouldn't you say?"

Karber nodded.

"Please speak up, ma'am?"

She leaned forward. "Yes. It is a big difference."

"Thank you," Cusper said. "To further make my point, I'd like to give you an example: I might *think* that the winning number in tonight's lottery will be 2,7, 11, 24, 33, and 41. But I'm *certain* that last week's winning numbers were 4, 9, 12, 40, 44, and 51" Cusper laughed. "There is a heck of a difference; in fact, in this case it amounts to about twenty-one million dollars difference."

Cusper walked from the witness stand to the jury box, where he rested on his hand. "How sure are you, Ms. Karber?

"Let me rephrase that question. How sure are you, Ms. Karber that the man who flew from Dallas to Houston was the same man who flew from Houston to Atlanta?"

"Pretty sure."

"Pretty sure? But pretty sure does *not* mean certain. So does that mean that you are sixty percent sure? Or seventy percent or eighty, ninety, ninety-five percent?"

"Probably ninety percent."

Cusper grinned from ear to ear, and glanced at Sanchez who was shaking her head.

"Thank you again, Ms. Karber. So, you are ninety percent sure it was *not* Hemphill. That means that in your mind, there is a ten percent chance that it was. So, a one in ten chance that the person on that plane was Mr. Hemphill. Is that something you'd be willing to bet your life on? A one in ten chance, I mean?"

"No. Of course not."

"Of course not. I don't blame you." Cusper started to walk away, but turned back. "Then why are you willing to bet Mr. Hemphill's life on that chance?"

Karber stuttered and hesitated answering. Cusper walked past her and said, "There's no need to answer, Ms. Karber. You can step down."

Mumbling and whispering could be heard coming from the jury box. Cusper had scored major points.

"We'll recess until tomorrow morning," the judge said.

I parked the car and walked up the sidewalk to the house. Marissa was in the kitchen, cooking.

"Hey, babe," she said. "How was your day?"

"As good as it could be. How about yours? Did you go to the trial?"

"I did. And Sanchez got her ass kicked. Cusper managed to raise doubt about everything she brought up."

"Shit. Let's hope she does better tomorrow."

"She *needs* to do better or Hemphill is going to walk. I guarantee you."

"Then I'm going to have to find more evidence."

"You better start looking," Marissa said. "I have a feeling Cusper is going to show her up at every turn."

"He can't argue with DNA, but you're right. I need something else. I better call Ribs."

Marissa took me by the shoulders and pushed me gently into a chair. "For right now, sit. You and Ribs can get busy on it in the morning. Learn to relax, or let me teach you."

"I smiled. "Deal," I said, then, "Thanks, Marissa. I need this support."

"I know you do," she said, and kissed me on the lips.

THE TRIAL CONTINUES

The prosecutor first established that the guards logged in every car that came in or out of Bentwater, and that no one suspicious had entered or left for days before or after the murder.

Sanchez called the owner of one of the marinas on Lake Conroe. He testified that two boats had been found adrift on the lake in the weeks following the murder. "It's unusual for something like that to happen," he said. "Especially when no one steps up to claim them."

He said that one boat had been found tied up in a hidden cove on the southern side of the lake and the other boat had been adrift.

"And what is your theory as to why the boat was tied up in the cove?" Sanchez asked.

"Somebody must have been hiding something or doing something that they didn't want other people to see. It was a perfectly good boat, so there was no reason to leave it there."

"So if someone wanted to use a boat to sneak into Bentwater without being recorded by the guards at the gate, then a boat would be the way to go?"

"I've owned that marina for more than ten years," he said, "And that'd be the only way I know to get in and not be recorded, unless they sneaked for miles through the woods."

"Thank you, Mr. Fletcher. That will be all."

As Sanchez returned to her seat, wondering why Cusper hadn't objected to her questioning, the lawyer walked slowly to the stand, possibly allowing time for the witness to grow flustered. It was a well-known tactic of his.

Cusper looked at a notepad he held in his hand, then started in on the witness. "Mr. Fletcher. It is Fletcher, isn't it?"

The witness started to nod, then leaned forward and spoke into the mic. "Yes. Fletcher."

"You told the jury that 'it's unusual' for something like that to happen, meaning you don't often find boats adrift on the water.

"Yep."

"Let me ask you, is it 'usual' for a boat to come loose during a violent storm?"

"If it's a bad storm, yeah, no question."

"Mr. Fletcher, when I noticed your name on the witness list, I had my people do some legwork. We checked with the National Weather Service for the week after the murder of Ms. Barker. Would it surprise you to know that there was a horrific thunderstorm on two of those nights? The storm was so bad one night that there was a weather advisory issued. Did you know that?"

Fletcher leaned forward again. "Yes, sir. I remember. They were doosies."

"I bet they were. It raises a question though. How difficult is it for a boat to be blown away during a storm like that?"

"Not at all," Fletcher said. "Especially with the number of teenagers on the lake. A lot of them have the tendency to be in a hurry. I ought to know. Got two that way myself. Anyway, when they get in a hurry, they might not dock the boat properly—you know, tie it up right. Add that to a storm like we had and that boat is gone with the first big gust of wind."

Fletcher leaned back. He seemed relaxed. "Hell, I've seen waves on the lake that got as high as four feet. Blowing a boat away wouldn't be squat in a storm like the ones we had."

"Let me clarify, if I might." Cusper turned to look at the jury. "We had two nights of some of the worst storms the lake has experienced, and all you found in the weeks following that were two boats, one of them secured to a tree in a cove on the southern side of the lake."

"That's correct."

"I see. One more question, Mr. Fletcher. Isn't Wedgewood Golf course on the southern side of the lake?"

"Yes. I believe it is. At least for a while. Word is it will be closing soon."

"Do you play golf, Mr. Fletcher?"

He nodded. "I've been known to hit a few, yeah."

"Have you ever played Wedgewood?"

"Objection, Your Honor. Are we playing golf or conducting a trial?"

"Mr. Cusper..."

He held up his pointer finger. "One moment, Your Honor. This all ties together."

"All right, but be quick about it."

"No. I've never played Wedgewood," Fletcher said.

"All right, but picture this. The hole directly above that cove is a long par-five with a dogleg right. If someone were to overshoot or hook left, the ball would end up down the hill, in that cove by the lake. If you were to hit a shot like that, and found a boat adrift when you went to retrieve your errant shot, what would you do?"

Fletcher smiled. "Considering the guys I play with are impatient as all get out, I'd tie the boat up and go back and take my next shot."

Cusper smiled. "Thank you, Mr. Fletcher. You've been a very big help."

Sanchez next called Mrs. Shirley Albus.

"Mrs. Albus, did you have occasion to stay at the Best Western Motel on the night before Mr. Farnsworth was killed?"

"I did. Me and my husband, or I should say, my husband and I stayed there to have a little fun, if you know what I mean."

"And what can you tell me about the next morning?"

"I can tell you I was cleaning up the room just before noon when I spotted an Audi pulling into a parking space not far from room #112."

"And how did you know it was an Audi?"

"Because I've always wanted an Audi, a white one, and this fit both bills. I didn't think anything of it until those police came and told me about the murder."

"Okay. Thank you, Mrs. Albus. That will be all."

Cusper approached the stand, a concerned look on his face. "An Audi? Can you tell me what an Audi even looks like. I don't know."

"It's a…big, nice…well, it's an expensive car."

"So, sort of like a Cadillac?"

"Kind of, but different."

"Different? Sort of like a Mercedes?"

"More like that, yeah."

"And you say it was white?"

"Yes, sir. White as Uncle Ben's rice."

"White." Cusper had his assistants bring out two big-screen TVs. They hooked up a computer and displayed a picture of two cars on them, both Audis. Look at the pictures, Mrs. Albus. Was the car like the picture on the left or the one on the right?"

The woman never hesitated. The one on the left," she said. "It was white."

"Darn, that was quick. You're pretty observant, Mrs. Albus. By the way, was it a four-door or a two-door?"

She seemed to think for a moment, then said. "Four door."

"Good. Do you remember if it had an antennae or was it hidden in the windshield?"

"It had an antennae," she said.

"What kind of hubcaps did it have?"

"Hubcaps? I don't know. I wasn't looking at hubcaps."

"Okay, Mrs. Albus. You've been of great help. By the way," Cusper said, raising his voice. "Mr. Hemphill's car is a two-door, with no antennae—at least not on the hood— and it sports a set of A8 Chrome Wheel Rim Quattros which run more than fifteen hundred dollars. It was a one-of-a-kind rental."

"Oh. I guess I didn't notice," she said.

"For someone so observant, I would have thought that you would. But perhaps Mr. Hemphill's car wasn't there."

Cusper started walking back to his seat, then said, "You're excused. And by the way, Mrs. Albus, those pictures on the TV—the one on the right is the white one. It's as white as Uncle Ben's rice."

The jury chuckled at that, and although the judge settled them down quickly, Cusper had made his point. In fact, by the time he was finished questioning Mrs. Albus about her car expertise, it was doubtful if she could tell a Volkswagen from a Cadillac. When Cusper finally did finish, he thanked Mrs. Albus, then went back to his desk.

The jurors looked at one another and chatted. They had to be told to quiet down again by the judge. No matter how you looked at it, this witness was another mark in the win column for Cusper. Things were not going well for Sanchez.

Sanchez called Martin Sheppler to the witness stand. Once he was sworn in and seated, she began. "Mr. Sheppler, you are the owner of a dive team search operation, aren't you?"

"Yes, ma'am. For the past fifteen years."

"And you specialize in finding things that are lost or have been purposefully discarded in hard-to-find places?"

"Yes, ma'am."

"Could you tell us about your recent job that took place in Lake Conroe?"

"Sure. A detective from Houston engaged us to search the lake for a missing gun. He suggested it might be under the bridge on FM 1097. It took us a while, but after about a week, we found it. It was just where he said it'd be."

Sanchez held up a plastic evidence bag containing the weapon. She dangled it in front of him. "Is this the gun, Mr. Sheppler?"

Sheppler looked at the bag and said. "Sure is."

Sanchez placed the bag back on the evidence table and said, "Let the records show that Mr. Sheppler identified the weapon in the bag as the weapon belonging to Mr. Kevin Hemphill."

"Objection. Stating evidence not in the record."

"Sustained."

Sanchez turned to address the jury. "My apologies. Let the records show that Mr. Sheppler identified the weapon in the bag as the weapon that the state intends to prove belongs to Mr. Kevin Hemphill."

Cusper walked to the witness stand. "Mr. Sheppler, you said you've been doing this for fifteen years?"

"That's correct."

"I imagine in all of that time, you've come to form opinions as to how things got where you found them?"

Sheppler scrunched his eyebrows together. "I guess."

"How do you think this gun ended up where it did?"

"The most likely explanation is that someone threw it off the bridge. They could have done it while driving by."

"And Mr. Hemphill lives in Bentwater, doesn't he?"

"Yes. I believe that's what the detective said."

"And if you lived in Bentwater and wanted to drive to Huntsville, the most logical route to take would be to cross over the bridge on FM 1097, wouldn't it?"

Sheppler looked confused. "Yes, that would be the shortest route by far."

"Mr. Sheppler, do you know how many people cross that bridge every day?"

He shook his head. "No. I can't say that I do."

"Well, I do. I checked with the state of Texas Public Safety Department and State Highway Department. According to a study done way back in 2012, approximately fifteen thousand people cross that bridge every day. Excuse me, I misspoke. Approximately fifteen thousand *vehicles* cross that bridge every day. I don't know how many people are in each one. Regardless, though, I doubt that Mr. Hemphill is the only one strong enough to toss a gun out of his car window. I'm sure that someone in one of those other fifteen thousand cars could throw it out of the window."

Cusper looked at the jury, then around the courtroom, then back at Sheppler. "Isn't it possible that anyone riding in one of those fifteen thousand cars could have tossed the gun into the water?"

Sheppler shrugged. "I guess so."

"Yes. So do I," Cusper said. "That will be all."

Sanchez got up from her seat and walked toward the jury box. "The state calls Arnie Milford to the stand."

Arnie had been seated near the back of the courtroom. He stood and squeezed his way out to the aisle, then meandered to the stand. He placed his hand on the bible, then they instructed him to:

"State your name and occupation, please."

"Arnold Milford of Oxford, Alabama. I own a gun shop."

"How long have you owned the shop?" Sanchez asked.

"Goin' on about twenty years now. Long time."

"I imagine there are some rules and regulations you must follow when selling firearms."

"Alabama is about the easiest state there is to get a gun, but regardless, I check each person's license and photo, and record everything, along with the serial number."

"Last month, did Officer McKenzie from the Birmingham Police Department come to your store with a photo array of six individuals? And did he ask you if any of them was the person who purchased the weapon in question?"

"He sure did. He showed me the pictures, and it didn't take me but a minute to point out the guy who bought it."

Sanchez handed a few papers to Milford. "Do you recognize these?" she asked.

"They're the pages of a fax from the FBI showing the results of a ballistics test as well as the serial number, which they managed to recover from the gun. It's my understanding that the serial number had been scratched off."

"And do these papers identify the weapon as the one you sold to the man you identified as Mr. Kevin Hemphill?"

"Sure do. One and the same."

"And to your knowledge is there any way to change the serial number of a gun once it has been purchased?"

"No, ma'am. People try to scratch them off, but the FBI can usually raise the numbers. Them boys is good."

"Thank you, Mr. Milford."

Cusper took his time walking to the stand. He stopped on his way and picked up the evidence bag that contained the murder weapon. He rotated the bag left, then right, looking at it from several angles.

"Them boys sure is good. I can make out the doggone numbers from here."

Cusper walked back and placed the gun on the evidence table. "Mr. Milford, I have a lot of faith in the FBI, and if they say *that* is the weapon that fired the shots that killed Ms. Barker and Mr. Farnsworth, then I feel confident that it is."

"Me too."

Cusper reached over and took the copy of the photo array from where it lay in front of Milford. "What I'm less confident of is someone's ability to select the real person who bought the gun from a 'real' photo array."

Milford looked confused. "I don't know what you mean."

Cusper went back to the defense table and retrieved a new sheet of paper. "Your Honor, Ms. Sanchez, I'd like to enter this into evidence."

"Objection," Sanchez said. "We haven't even seen this…whatever it is."

"It's nothing more than a photo array, Your Honor. One that depicts pictures of people who look more similar to the defendant. It had come to our attention that the photo array that was used did not contain any such photos."

The judge examined the sheet, then nodded. "So granted. You may proceed."

Cusper walked to Milford and handed him the sheet of paper. "Mr. Milford, I'd like you to look at this and tell me which person was the one who bought the gun."

Milford stared for a moment, then he reached into his jacket pocket and withdrew his glasses. After he put them on, he stared again. "I'm not sure. A lot of them look the same."

"Indeed they do," Cusper said. "That's the point of a lineup whether it be a real one or a photo array."

Milford studied the pictures a moment longer, then he pointed to the one at the top right. "It's this one. He's the guy who bought the gun."

"Are you sure?" Cusper asked.

"Sure as rain," Milford said. "That's him."

Cusper peeled off the photo. Underneath, typed in red was the name: Roger Farnsworth. "This man is dead, Mr. Milford."

"I could've sworn," Milford mumbled.

"You did swear," Cusper said. "And you were wrong."

Cusper started back to his table, turned, and said, "By the way, Mr. Milford, flight records show that Mr. Farnsworth was in Atlanta that day. Atlanta isn't a far drive from Oxford, is it?"

DNA DOESN'T LIE

Sanchez stood, looked at her folder, then said, "For the next witness, the state calls Chester Marsom."

A man got out of his seat near the back of the courtroom and made his way to the stand. After taking a seat, Sanchez asked him, "State your name and occupation for the record, please."

"Chester Marsom, forensic scientist for the state of Texas, currently on loan to the Harris County Medical Examiner's office."

"It's my understanding that you examined the evidence supplied by the Walker County Medical Examiner's office regarding the murder of Mr. Roger Farnsworth in the Best Western motel in Huntsville, Texas."

"That's true."

"And would you share your findings with the court, please?"

"Of course. There were strands of hair found on, and around, the body. When compared against DNA records we had on file, it was found that they matched the records of Mr. Kevin Hemphill."

"And what are the chances of DNA being wrong?"

"You might hear anything, but it is millions to one, minimum. Possibly even a billion to one."

Sanchez looked at the jury and raised her eyebrows. "Those are high odds. And you're sure the DNA belonged to Mr. Hemphill?"

"Absolutely. We tested it twice to make sure."

"And how could Mr. Hemphill's DNA get onto Mr. Farnsworth's body?"

"Easy enough. In cases dealing with violent crime, the normal method is a struggle. During the course of an argument, a physical one, hair, and other things are transferred. It could be almost anything. Even a simple brush against someone would do it."

"I see," Sanchez said. "But there does have to be some kind of physical contact—or at the very least, for someone to have been in proximity of the other person?"

"Absolutely," Marsom said.

"Okay, thank you," Sanchez said, then she looked to Cusper and said, "Your witness, counselor."

Cusper got up slowly and approached the witness stand. "Wow. A billion to one sounds like a lot. Even millions to one sounds as if it were a lot. Is it possible the odds are less?"

"I guess they could be," Marsom said. "It depends a lot on what markers you're trying to match. What you're matching them against. And human error is always a factor."

"I'm glad that you mentioned human error," Cusper said, then turned to the jury box and chuckled. "It kept me from having to mention it."

A collective sound of laughter came from the jury box, putting a frown on Sanchez's face.

"Are you familiar with the case involving Josiah Sutton, the lad in Houston who served four and a half years in prison, only to be proven innocent?"

"If that's the one involving the forensics technician who compiled data wrong, yes."

"Yes, I was quite sure you'd be familiar with it. If someone were ruining the reputation of my profession, I'd be familiar with it, too."

"Objection."

"Sustained," the judge said. Then, "Mr. Cusper."

Cusper nodded to the judge, and said, "I'm going to go over a few facts in the case, in the event the jury isn't as familiar with it as you are.

"If I recall, the victim claimed to have been abducted then raped repeatedly by a black male, approximately five feet seven inches tall, and approximately one hundred and thirty five pounds. She claimed this happened in the back seat of a truck.

"After processing by the Houston PD Crime Lab, the DNA of Josiah Sutton was shown to be a match. His DNA had been in the system from a previous arrest.

"Josiah was arrested, and later convicted, based on this DNA evidence, even though he is six feet tall, and approximately two hundred pounds, a far cry from the victim's description."

Mr. Marsom leaned forward. "I might interject that victim's, especially rape victims, often provide bad descriptions."

"Thank you for reminding us, Mr. Marsom. And you're right—rape victims often do provide bad descriptions. But they often provide excellent descriptions, as evidenced in the case of Sheila Jones, who was able to give the police a good enough description that the sketch artist's rendering was used to apprehend the rapist two days later. Or the case of Margaret Stitcher, who described her attacker so well, that after his arrest, her description was shown to be within half an inch in height and three pounds in weight."

"Pretty remarkable," Marsom said.

"Yes, it is," Cusper said. "Wasn't there also a question as to whether the entire lab, or at least a good portion of the Harris County lab, was producing results that proved to be false positives?"

"I don't remember specifics, but yes, I do recall it being more widespread than just one technician."

"And are you familiar with the case in Massachusetts, in which they discovered the forensics technician lying about having conducted tests, so that he could cover up his backlog and relieve some of the pressure he was under?"

"That was an unusual—"

"Yes or no, Mr. Marsom. Are you familiar with it or not?"

Marsom lowered his head, and said, "Yes. I'm familiar with it."

"And how about the famous case in Arizona where the technician found that the FBI's statistics had been cited erroneously?"

"That's not entirely—"

"Yes or no, Mr. Marsom. Are you familiar with the case?"

"Yes."

"So, is it safe to say that while DNA statistics themselves might be close to infallible, the entire process is far from it?"

"I don't know—"

"Mr. Marsom, remember, I have evidence. I can provide many more instances if need be."

"I guess so," Marsom said.

"One more thing," Cusper said. "Who performed the tests on this DNA?"

"Harris County."

"The same county where those other tests were performed?"

"Yes, but that facility—"

"Was reprimanded, I know. I'm sure they would never do wrong again."

Cusper spun on his heels and went back to his table.

Sanchez stood. "Redirect, Your Honor?"

The judge nodded. "Go ahead."

Sanchez hurried to the stand. "Mr. Marsom, didn't the city of Houston put that lab under investigation and subsequently shut it down?"

Marsom fidgeted in his seat. "I know they put it under investigation, but I'm not sure if they shut it down; however, they were aware of the mistakes, and I'm sure they took care of them."

"Thank you, Mr. Marsom."

Cusper stood. "Your Honor, a few questions?"

The judge sighed. "Go ahead."

"You said that the city put the lab under investigation. Do you know what the result of that was?"

"No."

"Did the technician who made the mistakes get fired?"

"Not to my knowledge."

"Not to your knowledge? You *know* she didn't, Mr. Marsom. You were called to testify against that person at their hearing years later when they made an almost identical 'mistake', weren't you?"

Marsom again acted as if he were trying to hide from a camera. "Yes."

"And to your knowledge was this person fired from the job?"

"To my knowledge, no."

"If that person worked for you, would you have fired them?"

"Objection."

"I'll allow it."

Marsom looked at the judge, who nodded, then he said, "Yes, if they worked for me I would have fired them the first time. There wouldn't have been a second time."

Cusper smiled. "Thank you, Mr. Marsom. You may step down."

THE FINAL WITNESSES

I got into the station way earlier than usual. Ribs was already there sipping on his morning coffee. "Damn, you're in early," I said. "I expected you to sleep in."

"I was up with the crows," Ribs said.

"Up with the crows? What the hell does that mean?"

"It means I was up early. If you're up with the crows, you're up pretty damn early."

"How early?" I asked.

"By dawn at least. I know that. Crows aren't ones to sleep in. Not like some *people* I know."

I grinned, but generally ignored him. "Marissa said Sanchez got her ass kicked again."

"That's what I heard, too," Ribs said. "I hope she's got something else in the bag, because we don't have much to contribute, not beyond speculation."

"Yeah, and juries aren't big on speculation. We need to find something real. Something Hemphill's attorney can't rip apart."

"Let me know when you get an idea," Ribs said. "I'm fresh out."

During the next few days, Sanchez told the jury about Hemphill's affair with Barker, about the jewelry never showing up in any pawn shops, and about the damning phone call the night of the murder, the one Hemphill had made to the burner cell that was later proven to belong to Farnsworth.

The affair was nothing damaging. Juries seldom blamed anyone for affairs anymore, and besides Cusper made short work of motive as a result of the affair.

The jewelry wasn't a problem either. The bottom line was—'so what' if the jewelry hadn't showed up? It didn't mean Hemphill had anything to do with the missing jewelry just because it wasn't sold yet.

"In fact," Cusper said, "Isn't that ransom money from the plane hijack back in the 60s or 70s still missing? Do you think Mr. Hemphill had something to do with that?"

The only damning piece of evidence was the phone call. No matter the explanation, a call to a burner phone—especially one that ended up belonging to the next victim—did not look good. Particularly when that call took place within moments of Hemphill learning of his house being broken into.

Sanchez closed with the manager from Donoho's Jewelers testifying that the woman Hemphill was with when he purchased the necklace was not Mrs. Hemphill, leading to speculation that Hemphill had purchased the necklace for Ms. Barker and not his wife.

Sanchez excused the manager, telling Cusper that he was free to cross examine, but Cusper said he had no questions. "In that case, the state rests, Your Honor."

The judge called a recess until the next morning, when the defense would begin its phase of the trial. Sanchez packed her briefcase and left the court.

~

When I got home, I got out of the car and almost had to drag myself up the sidewalk. It had been an exhausting day, and not even the knowledge that Marissa was waiting cheered me up.

I slowly opened the back door and trudged in. "You look tired, babe," Marissa said from a spot on the sofa.

"I am tired. And I'll probably be ready for bed after a glass or two of wine."

"Don't get too comfortable," she said. "In case you forgot, tonight is the night we promised Ribs and Rosalee we'd take the kids again. So a trip to Marble Slab is in order, then games. And remember how tired you were after the last time?"

"Oh shit. I did forget. Let me take a quick shower. Maybe that will freshen me up."

Marissa laughed. "You better do something. I spoke with Rosalee a little while ago, and I could hear them in the background. Those kids were ready. They were excited."

"Christ's sake. Better make that a long shower instead of a quick one." I started pulling off my shirt as I headed toward the bathroom.

It only took about fifteen minutes to shower, but by the time I got out and got dressed, the kids were there. I could hear them from the bedroom. There was something about young girls' squeals that were ear-piercing. It was a sound that penetrated the thickest of walls.

And as sweet as little Marissa was, she had a scream that could deafen you.

By the time I got to the living room, they had quieted down a tiny bit, and they were all involved in a game called Twister, where the object was to contort your body into a variety of shapes while attempting to touch different colors.

"Okay, gang. More of this when we return. Uncle Gino is here, and that means Marble Slab time."

A rousing cheer went up and they all headed for the door, racing to see who would be first. "Don't forget seat belts," I said, wondering how all of them intended to fit into the car.

"Should we take both cars?" I asked Marissa.

"We probably should, but it would ruin their fun. I'm sure we can make it work with just the one."

It took another ten minutes, but finally we managed to squeeze seven kids, plus me and Marissa into one car. Little Marissa ended up sitting on Big Marissa's lap. From the look on her face, I felt certain that nothing short of riding on the roof would have made her happier.

There wasn't a quiet moment on the way over, and that trend continued throughout the selection process and the eating. Afterward, we walked by the duck pond, then Marissa played *King of the Mountain* with them on a small hill, then she finished off the night playing hide and seek just as the sun was setting. The kids loved it, and the woods served as the "hunting grounds" where everyone had to hide.

It was dark by the time we left. Mary and Sheila were asleep before we got home. I expected Little Marissa to be also, but I think her stubbornness kept her awake. She talked Big Marissa's ear off the whole ride home.

After two more games of Twister, everybody except Clarita was either asleep or ready for bed. I didn't have enough bedrooms, but they managed to squeeze into two. Girls in one and boys the other. They loved it.

Clarita sat up talking to Marissa after the others were out for the night. "Are you going to have kids?" she asked.

"Clarita," I said. "You don't ask questions like that."

"I'm sorry."

Marissa laughed it off. "No problem. She didn't do anything wrong." Marissa turned to face her and said, "I might. I think I want to, but it's up to Gino."

I gulped, astonished. "What?"

She smiled and looked at me. "You heard me, Detective. It's up to you."

Clarita beamed. "Are you, Gino? Are you gonna have kids? How many? Mom said you would."

I had to laugh. That was just like Rosalee to be speculating already. "We'll see," I said. "Aunt Marissa and I have to discuss it."

Marissa leaned close and sneakily pinched my butt. "Aunt Marissa, huh?"

"I smiled back. "That's right. Aunt Marissa. Get used to it."

Clarita went to bed about half hour later, then Marissa and I shared quiet time on the couch.

She leaned over and kissed me. "Feel better?"

"Absolutely," I said. "You were magnificent with the kids."

"Given a chance, I could be magnificent elsewhere, too."

I set my glass of water on the table, took her by the hand and stood. "I intend to give you that chance, *Aunt Marissa*."

THE DEFENSE

I was sitting in the coffee room, chatting with Julie when Ribs dragged in. "You look like a bus hit you," I said. "What the hell, I give you the night off and you look like shit."

"That's what happens, cuz. I got too much sleep."

"I can assure you it won't happen tonight. Those monsters kept me up half the night."

"That's what they're supposed to do," Ribs said. "Each one is geared to act like birth control. The problem is that Rosalee is a slow learner. It took seven of them, but I think she finally got the hint."

I laughed. "They're adorable. And Marissa had a ball."

"You don't have to tell me. That's all I've heard about. Hide and seek and Twister, stories…You name it. The kids had more fun than they should have; in fact, I heard that *Aunt Marissa* might be having some kids."

"Shut the hell up, Ribs. You know kids."

"I know kids make women want to have kids. Better watch out or you'll end up like me."

"I'll shoot myself first. Hurry up, we need to get going."

"Where are we going?"

"I thought we'd go to the court today. Cusper is supposed to start his case."

"You think they'll put Hemphill on the stand?"

"Not a chance," I said. "On second thought, there is a chance, but I wouldn't if I were his attorney."

We got done what we needed to, and still arrived at the courthouse by ten o'clock, plenty of time to catch what was going on.

Cusper was just beginning when we walked in. "The defense calls for its first witness, Mr. Kevin Hemphill."

"Holy shit," Ribs said. "He's putting him on the stand."

"I wonder why," I said. "It seems like he's created enough doubt already. Guess we'll have to see what happens."

Hemphill walked up, meticulously dressed in a dark-blue suit, light-blue shirt, and yellow tie. After being sworn in, which I always thought was a joke anyway—think about it—if you're on trial for murder, what's a little lie going to matter?

Anyway, after he swore to tell the truth, Hemphill waited for Cusper to start.

Cusper walked over to the jury box, greeted them all good morning then went back to Hemphill. I'm sure he just wanted to get their attention.

"Mr. Hemphill. It's already been established that Mr. Farnsworth purchased the gun, the very gun he was shot with. How do you think that happened?"

"Objection."

"Sustained," the judge said.

Cusper turned to the jury. "It seems like the court has no desire to hear the truth, so let's try another angle. We know that Mr. Farnsworth bought the gun—according to the testimony of Mr. Arnie Milford—but do you know *why* he bought it?"

"Objection. The witness can't know what the victim intended."

"Your Honor," Cusper said. "If you let the witness finish, he'll establish a connection."

"Overruled. The witness may continue."

Hemphill cleared his throat. "He bought the gun because that was part of an elaborate plot laid out by my wife."

"What? Please explain."

"My wife came up with an idea for a book and she wanted to test it out in real life. Finding a decoy, like Farnsworth, and pretending to go to Atlanta were part of the plot. The original plot called for Farnsworth to buy the gun. Susan intended to put blanks in the gun, then instead of going to Atlanta, I would stay here and the decoy would go."

"Sounds good. What went wrong?"

"A couple of hours before the flight was to leave, I called Susan and told her that I received a call from a client in Atlanta, so I would have to *really* make the trip; therefore the plan was off.

"I did it to so that she would *think* I was in Atlanta, making the plot more realistic. I was supposed to have gone home, used the gun— loaded with blanks—and shot her while she was sleeping. Then, I was to haul the body out, she would go to a hotel under a fake name. When I returned, I would alert the police, who would only know that she was missing. The sound of the gun fired was to have created enough noise so that the neighbors would call the police, swearing to have heard shots. But when the police arrived, there would be nothing. And of course, when they checked, I would have been in Atlanta."

Cusper whistled. "You're right. It *was* an elaborate plot. What went wrong?"

"I went home, as we planned originally, but when I went to do the fake shooting, she was already dead. I turned her over and saw it was Chlorinda, and I almost died, wondering how it happened."

"So, you went home and found her already dead? What did you do then? Where did you put the gun?"

"The gun? The gun was gone. When I found her dead, I got out of there. Ran."

"Where did you go?"

"I got in the boat and took it back to the cove. Then I got in my car and left."

"The boat? That brings up another question—there were two boats found on the lake, yours and one other. Who do you think that other boat belonged to?"

"Objection."

"Sustained. Move on counselor."

"That's fine, Your Honor. I think we made out point."

"One more thing, Mr. Hemphill. A big fuss was made about DNA evidence being found at the scene of the murder of Mr. Farnsworth. Were you at the scene?"

"Yes. I had gone there to see why Farnsworth was being such a pain in the neck. He threatened to blackmail me, saying he'd tell the police that I was really in Houston the night of the murder."

"And?"

"And I told him to go ahead. I had nothing to hide. He shoved me and I shoved him back. Perhaps that's how my hairs got on him. But when I left him, he was alive. Alive and hollering about what he intended to do."

"I said one more thing, but I do have another question. What about the gun? Did you throw it into the lake?"

"Not a chance. I hadn't even seen that gun. It was gone when I got home and found Chlorinda dead. Whoever killed her must have taken it with them."

"No further questions," Cusper said.

Sanchez walked to the stand, leaned against it, and made a very loud sigh. "Mr. Hemphill, you testified that you found Ms. Barker dead when you arrived at the house. Why didn't you call the police?"

"I panicked. I didn't know what to do. I wasn't supposed to be there."

"Wouldn't it have been better to have to tell the police why you were there at that time, than to run and have to explain it now?"

"In hindsight, yes. But as they say, hindsight is 20-20."

"So it is. So it is.

"Why don't you tell us about the necklace, Mr. Hemphill. You must have heard the manager from Donoho's testify about you being there with a woman other than your wife."

"I did. And he's correct. It was Chlorinda…Ms. Barker who was with me. My wife was writing that day and Chlorinda offered to go with me."

"How convenient? So, your lover, who happens to also be your wife's assistant, offers to go with you to the jewelers and pick out a present for your wife? Is that the story?"

"It's not a story."

"Really. Then perhaps you'd like to explain this picture to me." Sanchez walked to the table and picked up an eight-by-ten photograph. "In this photo, Ms. Barker is exiting Macy's, and she appears to be wearing the same necklace you purchased. Do you have an explanation for that?"

Hemphill shrugged. "No. I don't. I have no idea."

"This picture was taken by surveillance two days prior to her murder. As you can see, it clearly shows her wearing the same necklace you say you purchased for your wife."

"I can see that."

"Where is the necklace you purchased, Mr. Hemphill?"

"It was taken the night of the break-in."

"Did you report it to the insurance company along with your other missing jewelry?"

"No."

"Why not?"

"Because I hadn't given it to my wife yet. It was in a dresser drawer."

"So how is it that Ms. Barker wearing it two days prior to her being shot?"

"Perhaps she bought one for herself. She seemed to like it."

"She didn't, Mr. Hemphill. I checked with Donoho's, who, by the way, designed this themselves. It is not sold elsewhere."

"Then I don't know."

"Okay, we'll chalk that up to one of the many unanswered questions. Besides, you have—"

"Objection. Does Ms. Sanchez have a question?"

"Sustained. Ms. Sanchez."

"Fine, Your Honor."

She glanced at the jury, probably to make sure they were paying attention, then focused on Hemphill. "Is there a reason why you wanted Ms. Barker dead?"

Hemphill laughed. "I didn't want her dead."

"Weren't you having an affair with her?"

"I'm not proud of that, but yes. I was."

"And didn't she send you an email threatening to tell your wife about the affair, if you didn't tell her?"

"That didn't matter. I still had no reason to kill her, and I wouldn't have killed her."

"Then were you trying to kill your wife?"

"I didn't try to kill anybody. And I *didn't* kill anybody."

"Really? By your own admission, your wife put blanks in the gun. Who do you suppose put in the real bullets?"

Hemphill seemed to be getting frustrated. "I have no idea."

"Mr. Hemphill, wouldn't it mean a lot of money to you if you *did not* get divorced? And wouldn't it also mean a lot to you if your wife died?

"It seems like you would benefit no matter which woman ended up dead. You couldn't lose."

"That's not true."

"Not true? My investigative team uncovered a prenuptial agreement that you signed—"

"Objection."

"Overruled. I'll allow it."

"...A prenuptial agreement that you signed, which limited your benefits to a mere five thousand a month if you were found to be having an affair. And if convicted of a felony, payments drop to nothing. Isn't that right?"

Hemphill looked over to Cusper and raised his eyebrows. Cusper nodded.

Sanchez smiled. "I realize that the prenup is not a matter of public record, but we found it. It's like saying the gun was your personal property, but we found that, too."

"Yes, that's correct."

"What's correct, Mr. Hemphill, that we found the gun or that the prenup limits you to five thousand per month?"

"Both."

"I see. Just so the members of the jury will know in case they are not familiar with California alimony law, how much would you have received from a normal divorce?"

"About forty thousand."

Sanchez raised her eyes. "Per month?"

"Yes, per month."

"You figured that out pretty quickly, Mr. Hemphill. Or did you already know?"

"Objection."

"Disregard that question."

Sanchez straightened. "Mr. Hemphill, if my math is correct, the difference between what you would receive in alimony if you *weren't* cheating, and what you would receive if you *were*, is about thirty-five thousand dollars *per month*. Is that correct?"

Hemphill bit his lip, and appeared to clench his jaw, then he said, "Yes, I believe your math is correct."

"I thought so," Sanchez said, then, "No further questions."

STATISTICS

"For our next witness, the defense calls Mr. Robert Wilson."

An older gentleman, perhaps in his sixties, walked to the witness stand and sat.

"Mr. Wilson," Cusper said. "I'm about to tackle some pretty steep odds, and it's going to be a tough road. Are you ready?"

"I guess I am."

"Mr. Wilson, please tell the court what you do."

"I'm an author. I wrote a nationally acclaimed book titled, *Strange Occurrences and Unlikely Events.* It was on the *New York Times* bestseller list for twelve weeks, and the *USA Today* bestseller list for twenty-six weeks."

"That's quite an accomplishment, Mr. Wilson. What is the book about?"

"It's about out-of-the-ordinary things that happen to people. Things that you don't ordinarily see."

"And do you know the odds of these things happening?"

"Not all of them, but a lot. I had to do a lot of research while writing the book."

"Well, let's just take a couple of them. According to the *National Geographic Magazine*—and your book—the chance of being struck by lightning is approximately one in 700,000. Is that correct?"

He nodded, then said, "Yes, that's correct. That's one of the facts I remember."

"They are high odds, but a man named Roy Sullivan—a park ranger in Shenandoah National Park, in Virginia—was struck by lightning *seven* times during the course of his thirty-five year career."

Cusper stopped and spun toward the jury. "Seven times," he said, then focused again on Wilson. "Another man, Melvin Roberts of South Carolina, has been struck *ten* times. That's almost unbelievable. They sure were pushing their luck, weren't they?"

"Yes, indeed."

"As against the odds as these two examples are, the men survived. Now, what are the odds of *that*?"

"I don't know, but it's damn big odds. It's—"

"Objection."

"Sustained."

Cusper smiled. "Let's move on. Mr. Wilson, you may step down." Cusper hesitated. "Unless the prosecutor has any questions."

"No questions, Your Honor."

"I didn't think so," Cusper said. "

"For my next witness I call Mrs. Sandra Messer."

A middle-aged woman with lightly tinted glasses walked up to the stand. Cusper approached. "Mrs. Messer, please state your occupation for the court."

"I'm a strategist for the state of Texas lottery programs."

"And as a strategist, what is your job?"

"I calculate the odds of any combination of numbers winning money and calculate what the payoff will be."

"So you're familiar with the different programs and how easy or difficult it is to win money?"

"Yes."

"Objection, Your Honor."

"On what grounds?"

"Relevancy. Where is Mr. Cusper going with this? I'm as interested as the next person in the odds of hitting the lottery, but what bearing does that have on the case?"

"Quite a bit," Cusper said, and he approached the judge's bench. "Your Honor, I intend to show that the odds and probabilities that the prosecutor has been spitting out for the jury to chew on, are just so much fat. This woman will help with that."

The judge looked at Cusper with a skeptical glance. "If you don't connect the dots quickly, I'm yanking your privileges. Understand?"

"Completely, Your Honor."

Cusper went back to the stand and leaned his elbow on it. "Mrs. Messer, according to the great state of Texas, the odds of winning the Texas Lotto are one in 25,827,165, and yet, people do it every week—usually twice a week. So, two times every single week, someone beats the odds of 25,000,000 to one and hits the lotto. Imagine that. That happens almost one hundred and four times a year."

"Yes, sir."

"Twenty-five million to one seems like big odds, and when you add the fact that someone wins it about one hundred times a year, that makes it seem even more impossible. As a strategist, what do you think of that?"

"Odds aren't as complicated as they sound, and they are seldom as *impossible* as they sound. Take the—"

"Objection."

"Sustained. Move on, Mr. Cusper."

"No problem. Mrs. Messer, it appears as if the judge wants us to move to another topic. Let's look at this. Are you familiar with the name of Ms. Wendy Amrstrong, of Elizabeth, New Jersey?"

She smiled. "Most certainly am. I wouldn't be doing my job if I weren't."

"And why is that, Mrs. Messer? What is so important about Ms. Armstrong?"

"She hit the New Jersey lottery, which carries odds of about fourteen million to one, then one year later, she hit it again."

Cusper said, "Oh my God! Are you kidding me? She hit it twice?"

Messer grinned ear to ear. "That she did. And the best thing was that both times she only played one ticket."

Cusper shook his head. "What are the odds of that?" he said.

"Never mind, Mrs. Messer. You don't have to answer that, but if you would be good enough to tell me, do you know the odds of hitting the Mega Millions or the Powerball lotteries?"

She nodded. "Of course. The Mega is about two hundred and fifty million to one and the Powerball is about two hundred and ninety million to one."

"And yet, people hit them?"

"All the time," she said.

"Damn. Okay. That's all for me. Any questions, prosecutor?"

"No questions," Sanchez said.

On his way back to the defense table, Cusper turned and said to the jury, "After this trial, I might have to start playing the lottery."

CLOSING ARGUMENTS

Sanchez paced slowly in front of the jury box. She tapped a pencil on the knuckles of her left hand.

"I don't want to rehash all of the evidence we have in this case. I don't want to bring up the one thousand reasons why we know that Mr. Hemphill killed Ms. Barker and Mr. Farnsworth. I don't want to point to the obviously greedy motive he had for doing all of this."

"She walked back, took a sip of water, then returned and set her palms on the railing of the jury box. "I don't *want* to, but I *have* to.

"I have to because Mr. Hemphill's *very* expensive attorney, Mr. Cusper, did an excellent job of finding technical faults in our case—not *real* faults, but technical ones. And he did an excellent job of attempting to convince you that statistics and odds and probabilities can lie. Maybe they can lie. Maybe. But they didn't.

"Mr. Hemphill killed Ms. Barker—either because he wanted to ensure his money supply or even worse, because he thought he was killing his wife."

Sanchez walked back to juror number one and pointed her index finger. "Look at the facts. They speak for themselves. And they speak for Ms. Barker and Mr. Farnsworth. But these facts are so strong that they don't just speak, they scream. They scream for justice, and it's up to you twelve people to dispense that justice. No one else can do it."

Sanchez went and picked up a folder from her desk, walked back, and waved it in front of the jury. "Let's start at the beginning. We have an affidavit from Officer Muscelli, who is with the San Francisco Police Department and another one from Agent Jim Hutchison, who is with Homeland Security. Both of them swear to the fact that either Mr. Hemphill or Mrs. Hemphill visited a well-known café seeking information on how to murder someone professionally."

Sanchez nodded. "I know. Disgusting isn't it. But we know this because Homeland Security has that café under surveillance as a possible site for terrorists to meet. On the day in question, a monitored website was visited and the Hemphill's car was photographed leaving the scene. And we also have sworn testimony from Detective Cataldi that he and Detective Delgado greeted the Hemphills when they arrived in Houston and warned them that they were aware of the visit to the café."

Sanchez looked back and forth at the jury, shaking her head. "You'd think Mr. Hemphill would have waited after that. But he went right ahead with his plan. It was a diabolical plan. I'll grant you that. But he made plenty of mistakes."

Sanchez walked back to the table and exchanged folders. "Let's look at some of the mistakes he made. First, he shouldn't have bought so much life insurance, a dead giveaway for any policeman.

"Also, we can't ignore the fact that an empty bottle of spiked wine was found in the trash behind the Hemphill's house. I say spiked, but let me be more specific. It had been laced with clonazepam? Coincidentally that is one of the prescriptions that Mrs. Hemphill takes, and it just so happens to be one that the pharmacy in San Francisco conveniently *forgot* to give the proper number of pills for, although when I checked with them they swear it was impossible as they used a pill counter. Not surprisingly, Mr. Hemphill is the one who picked up these prescriptions. If he intended to drug his wife, he should have used something besides the same prescription pills that he stole from her pharmacy in San Francisco."

She started walking away, then stopped and turned. "Oh, and in case you didn't know, you might be interested in knowing that clonazepam, the prescription Mrs. Hemphill was taking, is very sedating when mixed with alcohol, that is, it puts you to sleep."

Sanchez frowned. "And getting back to the insurance a moment—really, if you make two million dollars a year do you need a life insurance policy? Wouldn't other investments be better?"

Sanchez waited for the jury chatter to settle down, then said, "Hemphill testified that he worked with his wife on planning a 'fake' murder to fool the police. He said that his wife had put blanks in the gun to make noise so that it sounded realistic. Suddenly, when he arrived home, someone had been shot, and not with blanks. Did the real bullets magically appear, or was Hemphill not really in Atlanta? And did he put the real bullets in the gun and use it on Ms. Barker thinking it was his wife?"

Sanchez paced a moment, then said, "At this point, you might be asking, 'Is that all?' My answer to that is, 'Not even close.' We also have an email from Chlorinda to Mr. Hemphill. In the email, she threatened to tell Mrs. Hemphill about their affair unless he told his wife himself. Barker said she wanted a marriage and a home. And who can blame her?"

Sanchez pointed at the jurors, one by one. "So, did Hemphill pull the trigger thinking he was getting rid of his wife, or, did he squeeze that trigger knowing it was his mistress who was trying to ruin his golden goose. And make no mistake about it, Mrs. Hemphill *was* a golden goose, laying almost two million dollars last year alone.

"But surely Hemphill would have gotten rid of the email, you say. One might think so, but he's not the smart one. That's his wife's job. Maybe he really thought it was his wife lying in bed, and he planned on killing her. In that case, the email would not necessarily have come to light. We've checked, and it was not obvious on Mr. Hemphill's computer or phone. He must have deleted all correspondence with Ms. Barker, and it only came to light when the forensics performed a recovery on his hard drive." The DA smiled. "It's very difficult to hide a digital document from the forensics team."

Sanchez reached into the folder and held up a photo of Barker wearing the necklace. "I might add that if you're bold enough—or dumb enough—to have an affair with your wife's assistant, don't buy her a twenty-thousand-dollar necklace, or at least not from the same store that you purchase your wife's jewelry."

Sanchez took another pause. "Let's not forget that Mr. Hemphill signed up for an online service that uses a software program to find lookalikes that match your image. Roger Farnsworth, the dead man in Huntsville, was one of the people that program found. And as the picture I'm about to give you shows, he was a dead ringer." The prosecutor smiled. "Pun intended."

She let the smile linger momentarily, then said, "He used Mr. Farnsworth as a part of a scheme to deceive the airlines. Farnsworth is the one who flew to Atlanta, pretending to be Hemphill, while Hemphill took Mr. Farnsworth's flight back to Dallas, where we believe he then drove home, shot his wife—or who he believed was his wife—and waited for Farnsworth to return to Houston after receiving a call from Detective Cataldi."

The prosecutor scoffed again. "And if you intend on using 'being in Atlanta' as an alibi, don't tell the police that you were there, then turn around and testify that you weren't. It doesn't look good. It makes people think, that if you lied about one thing, you probably lied about another."

She laughed. "I forgot to mention that it's on record that either

Hemphill or Farnsworth—depending on who you believe—purchased the murder weapon as well as the silencer. It's not illegal to purchase a suppressor, but it makes you wonder why a consultant would need one? And it makes you wonder a lot more when that very same gun turns out to be the murder weapon, according to our ballistics test."

Sanchez went and picked up the evidence bag containing the gun and dangled it in front of the jury. "And it makes you wonder that much more when you realize that the silencer wasn't used in the initial murder, but only in the second murder. Was it premeditated also? Did he intend to kill Mr. Farnsworth when he went to that motel?"

Sanchez shuffled through the papers in the folder. Near the end, she stopped and pulled one out. "Oh, and let's not forget the most important thing—DNA. I know that Mr. Cusper bedazzled you with his citations of dozens of errors using DNA, and he brought in witnesses to testify about the impossible odds that people have experienced, but the facts remain, the evidence was collected by the Walker County Medical Examiner's team, a crime scene unit that has never had a complaint lodged against them. They then delivered it to Harris County for comparison testing. This is *not* the same group of people who were involved with the previous scandals in the Houston Police Department. These employees—like Walker County—have never had a test questioned or had a complaint filed against them. Mr. Cusper would like you to believe that they are one and the same, but they're not."

The prosecutor closed the folder, walked back, and set it on her table, then returned to the jury. "I know that each and every one of you wants to do the right thing. And believe me when I say that I go to bed every night praying I never put a person in prison for a crime they did not commit. But during the course of this trial, I have slept like a baby. Never once doubting that what I was doing was right. I *know* I'm helping society by trying to lock up a murderer, and only you can help me. So dig deep, see through Mr. Cusper's strategy of lies and deceit.

Once you do that, you'll find the truth, and once you find the truth, you'll find the defendant guilty.

"The state rests, Your Honor."

Cusper moved slowly to the jury box. When he arrived, he took out a handkerchief and wiped his brow. "Whew! That was powerful. She almost had me convinced that my defendant was guilty. *Almost*. But I know better. I *know* he's innocent. He didn't kill Ms. Barker. He loved her. And he didn't kill Mr. Farnsworth. Why would he? For a few bucks?" Cusper laughed. "Come on. What's a few bucks to someone like Mr. Hemphill? According to the prosecutor, he spent twenty thousand dollars on a necklace."

Cusper paused while he stared at each member of the jury. "As for motive, I already mentioned that Mr. Hemphill loved Ms. Barker. Of course, we could infer that from the evidence that shows he spent twenty thousand dollars on her necklace, but if you listen to the prosecutor, she'd have you believe he killed her to protect his alimony, or that he thought he was killing his wife and killed Ms. Barker by mistake."

Cusper shook his head. "I don't know about you, but if I were married to someone for twenty-five years, I think I'd recognize her lying in bed. As to the reason for wanting to kill his wife—life insurance? Come on? She made almost that much in a single year. And if she divorced him, he'd get forty thousand dollars per *month*. That's per *month* mind you. Even if she claimed he was cheating on her—and if the judge agreed—he'd get five thousand per month, and that's in addition to the six-figure income he already made. Not too shabby if you ask me; in fact, that extra sixty thousand dollars per year is more than what some people earn in total."

Cusper looked at his notes. "Ah, yes, the drugged wine. *Anyone* could have drugged the wine. It could have even been done at the liquor store. It's not like tampering hasn't been done before. And clonazepam is not the only drug that becomes a sedative when mixed with alcohol; in fact, read the labels—almost all antidepressants and a high percentage of other drugs carry warnings against using with them with alcohol. Hell, even Tylenol has that as a warning and I give it to my children."

Cusper walked up and down the courtroom side of the jury railing. "Ladies and gentlemen, you heard me rebut every false motive, demonstrate that evidence was not really evidence, and raise doubt about supposedly irrefutable facts known as DNA. If you want, I could spend several more days doing it again, but I trust your memory, and I would hate to keep you here any longer. All I'm asking is that you think hard when you deliberate, and you think fair. If there is even one iota of doubt about whether the defendant committed these heinous crimes, then, by law, you must acquit him. He *must* be found not guilty. Remember, you hold a man's life in your hands. Treat him gently. But it's more important that you treat him fairly."

Cusper looked each juror in the eye, then said, "That's all."

VERDICT

I was disappointed when I didn't see Marissa's car in the driveway, but she pulled up before I even got into the house. It was getting to the point where I looked forward to having her there waiting. On those nights I ate alone, I hated it, wishing she were sitting beside me, laughing and sharing a bottle of wine.

"What's new with my favorite detective?" she called from behind me.

"Not much," I said. "Looking forward to a relaxing evening, and glad I won't be alone."

"You can probably forget about the relaxing part. I spent the day listening to closing arguments, and while Sanchez did a good job, I think Cusper did too."

"You think he'll get off?"

"I think they'll have a difficult time convicting him if they buy into the reasonable doubt theory."

"That bad, huh?"

She nodded and grabbed a bottle of wine from the counter. "That bad."

"How would you vote?" I asked.

She shifted weight to her left leg, leaned on the island, and said, "Not guilty."

"Not guilty? Are you shitting me?"

"I don't think he did it. At least not how they're saying he did."

"What do you mean?"

She unscrewed the cork, then poured the wine into a decanter to breathe. I shook my head every time she did that. I was more of the type to just open the bottle and pour a glass. Marissa thought every bottle had to breathe, and not just breathe, but do so in a decanter for a designated period of time.

"I've been giving this a lot of thought since the trial began, and I think the wife had a lot more to do with it. I'm not saying he's innocent, but I don't think he's guilty of all of it either."

"Shit!" I said. "Then I'm going to need to hear these theories. And I want Ribs here too. Because if you're right, we're going to have a lot more work to do."

I called Ribs and asked him to come over. "Bring Rosalee if you want. That is, if you can trust those gangsters you have for kids."

"Go to hell, cuz. I should bring them over just to teach you a lesson."

"Go ahead. I dare you. Remember, it's you who will have to drive with them screaming the whole way."

"Rosalee, you want to go to Gino's? Marissa is there."

"I'm getting dressed now," she hollered. "Tell Clarita she's in charge, and make sure the rest of them know it."

I was able to hear all of Rosalee's conversation through the phone, without the speaker. "Shit, Ribs. It's a wonder you can still hear."

"Tell me about it," he said. "We'll be there in half an hour. You need anything?"

"No. We're good."

"We're, huh?"

"Screw you," I whispered into the phone.

It didn't take the full half an hour that Ribs thought. He was at the house in twenty minutes.

Ribs popped the top on a cold beer and patted his lap, inviting Rosalee to sit on it.

"Gino said you have doubts about our murderer?"

Marissa kicked off her shoes and tucked her feet under her legs on the sofa. "Not doubts the way you probably think. I'm convinced he's guilty of something, but I don't know what."

"What do you mean?" I asked.

"Think about it. If he was smart enough to think this whole thing up, with the decoy and all, why would he ditch his gun in the most logical place? The place you'd be most likely to search."

I took a drink of wine and stuffed a cracker with cheese into my mouth. "Maybe a smart detective just used more logic?"

Marissa grinned. "I hate to say it, but it didn't take a stroke of genius to figure out where to look."

"Explain," Ribs said.

"He supposedly committed the murder in Huntsville, right? If he did, then the most logical place to get rid of the gun—assuming he would be going back to Bentwater—would be the spot in the lake where you found it. You even established that in court."

I nodded. She was right. That was *exactly* how we determined where to look.

"Now, give it some real thought, which is what someone who commits murder would do. I looked on the map. It's only fifteen minutes from Huntsville to Riverside and the Trinity River. He could have detoured on route Route 19, tossed the gun, and then gone home, and nobody would have been the wiser. Who would think to look in the Trinity River?" She looked at me with raised eyebrows. "Would you? Did you? Did it even cross your mind?"

"Not really," I said, and I saw Ribs shaking his head, too.

"And if the guy really wanted to get clever, he'd have driven all the way to Lake Livingston, a mere thirty minutes away. Sherlock Holmes wouldn't think to look there. Besides, who would pay for the search?"

"Which brings up another question. Why did his wife fund the search for the gun?"

"You're right," Ribs said. "We were dead in the water until she stepped up."

"So why did she do it?" Marissa asked.

Rosalee got off Ribs's lap, and he leaned forward and said, "She said she wanted to help him, regardless of what he'd done."

"Do you believe her?" Marissa asked. "Remember, she had already stated her plan to divorce him."

Ribs shrugged. "I don't know. Maybe you're right. Not many people I know would spend that kind of money on someone they planned on divorcing."

"Unless they *knew* that their search would produce the desired results."

"What do you mean by that?" I asked.

"I mean if she knew the gun was there, then she wouldn't be wasting her money. She'd know it would be found and used as evidence against him."

"And if convicted of a felony, he gets nothing, right?"

"Right," Marissa said. "Not to mention, she gets her revenge."

"And the only way she would know the gun was in that spot is if she put it there, tossed it over the bridge herself," Ribs said.

I thought about what Ribs said. "And the only way she'd have the gun to toss is if she was the one who shot Farnsworth."

"Exactly. And let's not forget that she was logged out of Bentwater even longer than her husband was." Marissa said.

"She has an alibi," Ribs said. "She was at the discount mall."

"Do you have witnesses for the entire time, or is there a gap?"

"I don't know," Ribs said. "I'll check."

"What else?" I asked. Marissa had my attention now.

"The boat. It's too much of a coincidence that there was a second boat adrift on the lake. I could buy it if it was a boat out there for a day or so and someone claimed it. But this one was there for more than a week, and *no one* claimed it."

Marissa looked to me, then Ribs. "Think about what you've already said. It was you who said Hemphill must have used a boat to get ashore because he wasn't logged in at the gate. So if he used the first boat, who used the other one?"

"The wife," I said.

"She has an alibi," Ribs said. "She was at the hotel."

"Or so she says. I'm betting we can bust that," I said.

"And I'm betting you'll have to," Marissa said. "If she did go to the house, I'm betting she either killed Barker or at the very least, took the jewelry. And assuming she was at the house means she wasn't at the hotel."

"This is exciting," Rosalee said. "Marissa, where did you learn all of this?"

Marissa blushed. "Here and there. Mostly by listening to Gino and Ribs talk." She thought for a minute and decided she may as well be honest. "And I wasn't always on the right side of the law, so I picked up a few pointers then."

Rosalee brushed her hand in the air, and said, "I'm going to call and check on the kids." Then she got up to go to the kitchen.

Marissa sat up straight. "And then there's the wine and drugs. Somebody gave her the drugs, but who did it? If it was Hemphill, then we admit that he had to know she would be there, and that he wanted to kill her. I don't buy it. I think he wanted to kill his wife, so either the wife 'accidentally' left Barker the wine, or she planned it all along, knowing Hemphill would be back to kill her."

"How the hell would she know that?" Ribs asked.

"Because you tipped your hand," Marissa said.

"How?" I asked.

"No way," Ribs said.

"When they first came to Houston, you met them at the airport and told them that Homeland Security had video that one of them had been at that café. All she had to do was realize that since it wasn't her, it must have been him. If it was him at the café, she must have figured that if an opportunity presented itself, he'd take advantage of it."

Ribs still looked confused.

"So she plotted the whole thing to look infallible, handed it to her husband on a silver platter and then pulled a switch on him. He never know what hit him."

"In other words, she *assumed* he'd try to kill her, so she switched with Barker?"

"Exactly," Marissa said.

"How did Mrs. Hemphill get Barker to stay there?"

"I don't know, but it probably wouldn't be too difficult. The lady worked for her. And the plan was perfect," Marissa said. "If the husband kills Barker, fine. All is well. If he doesn't, also fine. But the wife presumes he *will* try to kill her, so she drugs the wine, gets a room at the hotel, then sneaks back to get the jewelry."

"But she was at the hotel," Ribs said.

"So she says. You need to prove that she wasn't. At least at the time when she was at Bentwater."

"Why go to this trouble?" I said. "Why not just kill her if she wanted her dead?"

Ribs said, "I don't know."

Marissa laughed. "You two would never make it in the revenge business. Mrs. Hemphill felt betrayed, both by him and her. She was vindictive. Wanted revenge. Cutting off his money was not enough. Besides, he'd still get a healthy alimony, according to the prenup. There was no way she'd let that happen. She'd make him suffer. And what better way to make him suffer than to have him kill his mistress and then be convicted of it. Doing it that way, not only does he have to live his life in prison, but he has to do it knowing he killed the woman he loves."

I crushed the empty beer can that Ribs had set on the end table, then tossed it in the trash. "If the good wife thought this up, she's pretty inventive and pretty cruel."

"We know from her books that she can be inventive," Ribs said. "Some of them are downright complex."

"Add cruel to the mix and you have the ingredients for murder," Marissa said.

I munched on a few more crackers and drank a few more sips of wine. "What about the silencer?" I said. "That's been bugging the hell out of me. Why buy a silencer if you're not going to use it."

"I don't get what you're saying," Rosalee said, as she returned from the kitchen.

"About the gun?" Marissa said. "Let Gino explain it."

I faced Rosalee, but spoke to all of them. "We found the gun with a suppressor on it—a silencer. We know that Farnsworth was shot with a gun that used a silencer. He had to have been, or someone would have heard it. And we know the silencer was bought at the same time as the gun according to Milford, the gun dealer. So I'll ask again—why buy a silencer if you're not going to use it? I say not going to use it because Chlorinda was shot by a regular gun that did not use a silencer. Remember—the neighbors heard the shots?"

Ribs took a sip of beer. "I can think of one reason *not* to use a silencer —to purposefully make noise and establish an alibi for TOD. But if you're not going to use it, like you said, why buy it? Think about it. If Hemphill had used a silencer on Chlorinda, no one would have heard the shots. Knowing what we know now—that he already had the silencer—that means he *wanted* people to hear the shots."

"And who needed an alibi for time?" Marissa said. "Not Hemphill. The police thought he was in Atlanta."

Ribs looked at Marissa. "*Dios mío.* Mrs. Hemphill."

Marissa smiled. "You might make a detective yet, Ribs. An imaginary burglar wouldn't need an alibi, and Hemphill wouldn't—as we stated. The only one we know of who would need an alibi would be Mrs. Hemphill. She was supposed to be at the hotel at the time of the murder."

"I agree with that," Ribs said. "But still, why buy the silencer? That's bugging me."

"Maybe to buy it for the future," Marissa said.

"What do you mean?" Ribs asked.

"Maybe whoever did this had another reason to use it. Another murder planned."

"Farnsworth!" I said.

Marissa nodded. "I only have one problem with that. The gun was supposedly bought two weeks before the murder. If we assume that Farnsworth was blackmailing Hemphill, and that is what got him killed, then how did Hemphill know to buy the silencer so far in advance? And if it was really Farnsworth who bought the gun, he must have done so at the instructions of either Hemphill or his wife. If it was his wife, who did she plan on killing?"

"She would have had to plan on killing him from the beginning," I said.

"Exactly," Marissa said.

Rosalee said, "Ribs, baby. I'd love to stay and talk all night, but we need to get home. I don't like leaving the kids this long."

Ribs looked at his watch and nodded. "You're right. We better go."

"You better hurry too, or Little Marissa might murder them all."

Ribs laughed. "You take care of big Marissa, and I'll mind Little Marissa. Deal?"

I slapped his outstretched hand. "Deal," I said. "See you tomorrow. I'm guessing the verdict will be in by mid-afternoon."

"Morning," Ribs said. "Remember, they've had all night?"

"I've seen it take days to deliver a verdict."

Ribs opened the door and shook his head. "Not this time. It'll be guilty, and it'll be before noon."

"All right. See you tomorrow."

I said goodnight to Rosalee, closed the door, then sat on the couch next to Marissa. She rested her feet on my legs. "The jewelry still bothers me," she said. "Show me the list again and I'll tell you if she'd sell them or not. You have pictures?"

"Yeah, I've got pictures but you already looked at them."

"But that was when I was thinking it was the husband, not her. There's a difference."

"What's the difference?"

Marissa smiled. "That's what I mean. Men don't know. Were there any sentimental pieces in there? I mean jewelry her husband or father or someone had given her that couldn't be replaced with money."

I don't know," I said. "Why"

"Because if there were, she wouldn't have dumped them, or pawned them, regardless of the insurance. She'd have kept them. Somewhere."

BREAKING ALIBIS

In the morning, Ribs and I got to work on a new case—a drug dealer found lying in the gutter on Navigation. I wasn't excited by it, as he was probably killed by a rival dealer wanting to expand his turf.

If we were lucky, it wouldn't be another dealer and it would turn out to be a pissed off parent of someone he sold drugs to, but there was a slim chance of that.

"What did you and Marissa do after we left?"

"Discussed the case. Mostly talked about the missing jewelry. She's convinced that Hemphill's wife kept them."

"Kept them? What for?"

"She said it's a woman thing. And I didn't argue."

"That's the first smart thing you've done since Mary died."

"What do you think? You think Marissa's right? That Mrs. Hemphill kept the jewelry? And do you think she's right about the other stuff?"

I thought about what Ribs asked, and had to admit that I *did* agree with Marissa. I was now convinced that Mrs. Hemphill was as much a part of this plot as her husband. "I do, Ribs. I don't know exactly what she did, but I'm convinced she did something."

"Then it's about time we started breaking alibis, amigo."

"You're right. And we're going to need to start with the hotel."

We drove to the scene on Navigation. Ben was already there with his crew and a crowd of onlookers were close by. Officer Lopez was working the crowd, and after a few questions, we learned he had been the first officer on the scene.

"Lopez," Ribs said. "You want to fill us in?"

Lopez walked over, pen and pad in hand. "Looks like it's open and shut to me. We've got three witnesses who are willing to swear it was a rival drug dealer, a guy by the name of Ricardo Sufero. All three of them claim to have seen him do the shooting."

"You know where to find him?" Ribs asked.

"Already have him cuffed and on the way downtown," Lopez said. "He didn't admit to what he did, but he didn't deny it either. All he said was that he wanted a lawyer."

"Sounds good to me," I said. "Take it away. We've got other stuff to do."

I grabbed Ribs by the upper arm and said, "Let's go, partner. We've got a hotel to visit."

Forty minutes later, we pulled up to the Marriott. Ribs and I introduced ourselves to the manager and told him what we wanted—room access information and surveillance tapes of the front and back entrance. He told us that information was private and he couldn't provide it.

Marriott, the Woodlands on the waterway

We stepped away from the counter and called Coop. "Captain, if you know anyone who can help it would be appreciated. They're giving us the run-around on surveillance and access."

"Give me the guy's name," Coop said. "And give me the hotel number as well."

"You know somebody?"

"No, but I'm willing to bet that Cybil does."

Ten minutes later, we saw the manager take a call and step into his office. Shortly afterward, he came back and motioned us over. "Excuse me, Detectives. If you'll follow me, I'll get the information you wanted."

The access card information was easy. Hemphill checked in about 9:30 p.m. and entered the hotel room a few minutes afterward. Then, she re-entered at about 12.30, but she *was* seen in the restaurant earlier. There was a chance she slipped out, but things didn't look good for putting her at Bentwater. At least not yet.

When we examined the surveillance videos; however, we spotted a woman who looked similar to Mrs. Hemphill, and she was leaving the front door at about 9:45 p.m.

We took the video with us, and went downtown to have it analyzed and enhanced and have the image blown up. Once they were done enhancing it, there was no doubt about who was in the photo. It was Mrs. Hemphill.

"How the hell is she leaving if the room shows her inside?" Ribs asked.

"After checking, we discovered that the access system the hotel used only records a person's entrance. So a person could go in, then close the door and not return for six hours and as far as the access key knows, you're still in the room. It wouldn't show anything else until you entered the room again using the card."

"In other words, it ain't worth shit," Ribs said.

"If a crime is committed in the hotel room it is. It would tell you every time someone entered the room. What it wouldn't tell you is when someone leaves."

We took a copy of the video and one of the blown-up stills when we left. I wanted them to present to Mrs. Hemphill.

"Where to now, cuz?"

"I thought we'd start with the mall. See if we can bust that alibi."

We had never tried hard to bust her alibi at the discount mall, because it seemed as if she had been the victim, or at least the intended victim. Now, things were different.

"It would be nice to break this alibi," I said. "But I'm still curious about the boat and the jewelry."

"Wouldn't she need a dock to use?" Ribs asked. "There are no public ones close by and there aren't any other hidden coves close by. If we presume that she took a boat to her house, where did she take it from?"

"A dock would be nice, but she wouldn't need one; however, there's an older subdivision across the lake from her house," I said. "Maybe she knows somebody there?"

Ribs got on his cell. "Jules, this is Ribs. Listen, I need you to look up some tax records for me. There is an older subdivision across from the Hemphill's house on the lake. I don't know the name, but it shouldn't be difficult to find. Hell, ask Tip. He'll know. Anyway, I need a printout of all of the owners. Get it to me as soon as you can."

"What good will this list do?" I asked.

"We'll show it to Mr. Hemphill. He's bound to be willing to cooperate. If he recognizes any of the names, we've got her."

We spoke to Miranda, the cashier who remembered Mrs. Hemphill previously, and her story remained the same. Mrs. Hemphill had been in and purchased items at about noon. The second cashier claimed to have waited on her at about 2:30. But nobody recalls seeing her in between those times. It didn't mean she *wasn't* there, but it definitely negated shopping at the mall as an alibi. She could have easily gone to the Dressbarn, bought something, driven to Huntsville and shot Farnsworth, then returned to the mall and purchased something at the Nike store.

We drove to the Cracker Barrel to eat a breakfast lunch and while we waited for a table, the phone rang. "Hello?"

"Verdict is in," Coop said. "A goddamn hung jury."

"What?"

"You heard me. Now, get your asses busy because Sanchez said she's going for a retrial. And it won't be any easier the next time unless we have more evidence."

"Don't worry. We're on it."

"I've heard that before. Don't tell me about it, just do it."

"You got it, Coop. We're working on it now."

"I thought you were over on Navigation?"

"Nah. They didn't need us there. We're busy busting alibis."

"I don't even want to ask," she said, and hung up.

I told Ribs about the verdict and about Coop's response. "Shit!" he said. "I knew Sanchez didn't push hard enough."

The phone rang again, but this time it was Ribs's phone. "Yeah?"

"Ribs, it's Julie."

"You got what I need?"

"I've got it all. Do you want me to email it?"

"Yeah. Use the Delgado account. And thanks, Julie. You're a doll."

"Julie?" I asked.

"Yeah. She said it should be here in a few minutes. She's the best."

"She does good work," I said. "Despite her looks, she's good."

We were seated, ordered breakfast, and before it arrived, Ribs heard the alert meaning he had a new email. It was the one we were waiting on.

I scooted the chair over, and he opened the file, then we started going through the names.

"A lot of names here," I said. "We'll have to take them to Hemphill. I want to see his reaction as he reads them in case he's not as cooperative as he should be."

Ribs grinned. "No need," he said, and jabbed the phone with his index finger. "You see this name? Sheila Wingate. That's Hemphill's pseudonym. Ten dollars to a doughnut says that's the house we're looking for."

"The address puts that house almost directly across from the

Hemphill's, so I'm not taking that bet, but I think we should get a warrant. Call Coop."

We went and talked to Mr. Hemphill first, not wanting to tip our hand with her. They were living separately now, so I felt fairly certain that he wouldn't tell.

When we talked to him about the house, it was obvious he knew nothing of it. He didn't know she owned the house, and a further check into the tax records produced her pen name only. Nothing of his, or even her married name. The property was in the name of Sheila Wingate, and property taxes had been paid with checks using that same name.

"I think we should talk to her neighbors," Ribs said. "We have time."

"Are you sure? They might tell her."

Ribs laughed. "I doubt if they even know her name. In case you hadn't noticed, she's not the friendly type."

I turned the car around and headed back toward the lake. "You're probably right. Let's see what we can find out."

An hour later, we had finished talking to the fourth neighbor and had nothing to show for it. As Ribs had predicted, they didn't even know her name.

We knocked on another door, and a woman who appeared to be in her sixties or seventies answered. "May I help you?"

"I hope so," Ribs said. "We're looking at anything odd or unusual that happened here on the night of the murder over in Bentwater. In particular, with the house across the street," Ribs said, pointing to Hemphill's place.

"A couple of weeks ago, a strange car was parked in the driveway for a few hours. I wrote down the license plate because it wasn't one I recognized, and you can't be too careful these days. I'm all alone now that Richard is gone."

I was getting excited. Maybe we were going to catch a break. "Did you report it, ma'am?"

She shook her head. "I was goin' to, but then nothin' happened, so I let it be."

"Nothing happened?" I was appalled. She *had* to know about the murder. "Ma'am, there was a murder over in Bentwater just—"

"Bentwater? That's across the lake. I meant nothing happened here. On this side."

"Oh," I said, just realizing the significance of her statement. The "other side" of the lake was a different world to her. That side was rich, and the people lived in big houses. The murder might as well have never happened.

We ran the plate numbers and got a hit for Chlorinda Barker, the assistant who was murdered. "Mrs. Hemphill must have used the car the night of the murder, when she was supposedly at the hotel."

"Supposedly is the key word," Ribs said. "I think we're poking holes in her unbreakable alibi."

Much to my disappointment, Marissa wasn't at the house when I got home. Even worse, she didn't show up for dinner or drinks. I had come to look forward to those nightly conversations; they helped take the loneliness away.

The phone rang about seven o'clock. "Hello?"

"Gino. I'm sorry I didn't answer the phone. I was shopping with Connie and I had the volume on the ringer turned down. I must not have heard it when you called."

"Shopping with Connie? Where did you go?"

"Tip's girlfriend owns an upscale clothing store. She steered us to a few places where she knows the owners…and let me tell you, those places are fantastic."

"Did you have fun?"

"I had a ball. And you should see some of the stuff we got."

"I can't wait. You comin' over?"

"Yeah, but I'll be another hour. I have to drop Connie off."

"I'd wait all night. See you when you get here."

 judge issued the warrant the next morning, and Ribs and I went along with a few others to execute it. It only took about half an hour to locate the jewelry.

"Got something," Officer Sweeney said.

It wasn't difficult to find the jewelry; it was in a dresser drawer in the bedroom.

"Looks like the same jewelry," Ribs said. "I recognize a few of the pieces from the insurance pictures."

I grinned. "I'd like to see her try to wiggle out of this."

Try to wiggle out, she did. "I must have moved them there when I went to work one night. I forgot. I'll have to notify the insurance company."

"I'm going to nail you for this," I said. "You know that, so be prepared."

She huffed up. "Detective, I'm surprised at you. First, you're convinced that my husband did something and now me."

"You're right, Mrs. Hemphill. I am convinced you did something, and I'm still convinced that he did. And I intend to prove that both of you were involved."

"Good luck with that," she said.

We took the jewelry back to the station and handed the pieces over to Julie. "Document these and match them up against the photos of the jewelry taken in the alleged break-in. Make note of anything unusual or any jewelry that is missing. And please make it a priority?"

"No problem, Gino. I'll get right on it."

I called Ron on the way home, and we had a great talk. I filled him in on my relationship with Marissa, which he seemed happy about, and he then told me he had met a girl, too. "She's fantastic, Dad. I met her at a meeting."

"At a meeting? You mean…"

He sighed. "Yes, Dad. She's an alcoholic, or should I say used to be an alcoholic, but she's been clean for three years."

"How old is she?"

"She's twenty," Ron said. "And she has a good job, and she's going to night school, and no, she's not trying to sponge off me."

I laughed. He always could read my mind. "Great. I'm happy for you, Ron. When we come down, maybe we'll all go out to dinner."

"We? It must be getting serious."

I smiled. I hadn't realized I'd said "we," but I definitely meant it. "It is getting serious, Ron. And I *will* bring her with me. I think you'll like her."

"I'm sure I will, Dad. Look forward to it. You'll love Lisa, too. That's her name—Lisa."

"Okay, see you next week then."

I thought about my conversation all the way home. I saw Marissa's car in the driveway and breathed a sigh of relief, relaxing. It wasn't until then that I realized how tense I had been.

I opened the back door and walked in, eager to hear her voice.

"Hey, babe," she said. "What's up?

I pulled out the folder with the pictures of the jewelry and set it on the kitchen table. "We found the jewelry. That's what's up."

"So what's wrong?" she said. "I thought that would be a good thing."

"It would be a good thing if we could tie her to the murder, but as always, she had an excuse for everything. 'I must have moved them there when I went to work one night. There's nothing wrong with owning a second house, is there?' That's what she told us."

"She's got a point," Marissa said, while stirring the pot of sauce that was simmering on the stove. "Do you have pictures of the jewelry. I'd love to look at them."

"You're in luck, then. I just happen to have photos of them sitting right here."

She walked to the table, grinning. "Something tells me that's not all coincidence."

"Maybe. Maybe not."

Just then, Julie called. "I finished cataloguing, Gino. There are only two items missing—the necklace that Mr. Hemphill bought for Ms. Barker and a bracelet that Mrs. Hemphill's father had given her as a child. I'll send up the picture of the bracelet and the photo that Dono-ho's jewelers provided us for the necklace."

I didn't give the pictures Julie sent up to Marissa. I wanted to see what she'd say without them.

Marissa sat at the table and studied the pictures, then she jabbed with her finger. "This one," she said, pointing to the description of the bracelet from her father. It was inscribed,

> *To my special princess,*
> *love, Dad.*

"She'd never get rid of this one. It would have too much emotional value. I still have a 'lucky penny,' as my mom called it. It was nothing but a plain old penny that had been crushed by a train on the tracks, but it was special to me because she gave it to me."

Marissa reached into her pocket and pulled out a crushed penny with a barely visible image of Abraham Lincoln on the front. I still carry this with me, and she gave that to me thirty years ago."

I nodded and opened a beer. "I was hoping to find Barker's necklace," I said. "With that, we might have had enough to lock up her ass. Without it, the jury might buy a lame story like moving the jewelry to the other house."

"Just so that I know, what was Barker's necklace, and why was it so special? Is it the necklace the husband bought for the girlfriend?"

"Yeah. And damn expensive, too. I think about twenty thousand."

"It'll be someplace special then. She'd have put it with the bracelet from her father. I'd bet on it."

"And where would that be?"

"I don't know," Marissa said, "But it wouldn't be with the other jewelry. And neither would the bracelet. The bracelet is too emotional, and the necklace too incriminating."

"Incriminating is right. That photo we have from Macy's was taken two days before the murder and it clearly showed Barker wearing the necklace. If we find that necklace in Mrs. Hemphill's possession, there is only one logical explanation for how it got there—she killed her."

"Then all you have to do is find it," Marissa said. "I have faith in you. I'm confident that you will."

"I'm glad you have confidence," I said. "Because I'm not so sure. And you might have to take a raincheck on—"

"What?"

"Check! Holy shit, that's it." I started to get up from the table. "I've got to call Ribs."

"Whoa," Marissa said. "Whatever you're thinking of can wait till tomorrow. You have other things to do tonight."

"Like what?" I said.

Marissa placed her right hand on the back of my head and slowly pulled me toward her. Then she kissed me.

"Like this," she said.

A warm, wonderful feeling ran through me. I smiled, then kissed her back. "You're right. I guess everything else can wait."

BUST HER ASS

I called Ribs and told him to meet me at the station early. I got there before eight and waited. About ten minutes later, Ribs showed up.

"About time you got here," I said. "I was beginning to wonder."

"Wonder all you want, cuz. I've been here, drank my coffee, took a piss, and held three conversations while I waited for you."

I laughed. "You're so full of shit, Ribs. It's getting to the point where you're like Tip—you don't even know when you're lying."

"Then it's a good thing I have you to keep track," Ribs said. "What's up? What have you got planned for today?"

"I thought we'd gather everything we've got and go see the wife. But first, I've got an idea."

"That's dangerous. What's the idea?"

"I thought of it last night. Remember when we were looking at the tax records for her second house?"

"I remember."

"The files said she paid for her property taxes every year, *with a check.*"

"So what?"

"Whose name was the check in? I have Julie looking into it, but I'm willing to bet it was her pseudonym, same as the listed owner of the property."

"I still don't follow you," Ribs said.

"If she has a checking account under the name of her pseudonym, that means she has a bank account, and if she has a bank account, she might have a safe deposit box too."

"Son of a bitch," Ribs said. "And if she's got a safe deposit box, it might be where she's got the other jewelry."

Within an hour, Julie found the bank, a BBVA Compass bank in the Woodlands. We got Coop to get a warrant right away, and we drove up to the bank to have a look. The manager opened the box for us—after we presented the warrant—and inside we found Barker's necklace as well as Hemphill's bracelet. "Do you have video of the last time she accessed the box?" I asked.

"I'll have them get it for you," he said.

We took what he had and began the drive to see Mrs. Hemphill. As far as I was concerned, we had enough to go to court with. Considering what Sanchez had just been through, she might feel differently.

On the drive up to the Hemphill house, Ribs and I discussed the case. We tried to figure out logically what Mrs. Hemphill knew and what she didn't.

"How did she know her husband would shoot her?" Ribs asked. "Or in this case, shoot her assistant."

"I thought we already discussed this," I said. "Remember, when they first arrived in Houston, we told them that someone had picked up on their activity in San Francisco about one of them wanting to kill the other."

"Yeah? I remember, but let's go over it again."

"Think about it. If she knew it wasn't her that was at the café, then it had to be her husband. And if it was him who wanted her dead, this scenario would have been the perfect opportunity—she had basically plotted her own murder. But then, assuming she knew of the affair, she made plans to have the lover be in bed instead of her. Which would explain the spiked wine bottle we found. It had to be her that put in the drugs."

"Son of a bitch," Ribs said. "She's an evil one."

Ribs and I walked up to the door and knocked. Mrs. Hemphill answered right away. "Detectives, how nice to see you, though it is unexpected."

"I doubt if you'll think it's nice by the time we're done," Ribs said.

"You may want to call your attorney," I said. "We're here to arrest you."

"Arrest me? What on earth for?"

"For the murder of Roger Farnsworth and the conspiracy to commit the murder of Chlorinda Barker."

She laughed. "Detectives, you're a riot. I was at the hotel when Barker was killed and at the mall when Farnsworth was killed."

"I think you know you weren't, and we're going to prove it. May we come in?"

She stepped aside and gestured with a sweeping arm. "By all means. Come in and sit."

We sat at the kitchen table, while Mrs. Hemphill got us water to drink. "I think we should start chronologically," I said. "It will make things easier."

"Please do," she said.

"On the night of the murder, you claimed to have been at the Marriott hotel in The Woodlands."

"That's correct. You can check with the—"

"I know who you said we could check with, but the fact of the matter is, we have evidence that proves you were *not* at the hotel."

That's absurd. I have a receipt." She started to get up.

"Please sit, Mrs. Hemphill. I misspoke. I didn't mean to imply that you were were never at the hotel, just that you weren't there when the murder was committed."

"What proof?"

I held my hand out, and Ribs gave me a folder. "You said you checked in at about 9:30, and we verified that. The trouble is that your room shows you entering a few minutes afterward, then you were seen in the restaurant, then you didn't re-enter your room until approximately 12:30 a.m. Can you explain where you were during those three hours?"

"Something's wrong. I never left the hotel."

I held my hand out again and Ribs gave me a USB drive. "May I use your laptop, ma'am?"

She seemed confused, but nodded anyway. "Of course. Go ahead."

I slipped the USB into the slot and quickly opened the video. "This video is from surveillance tapes the night of the murder. As you can see, that is a picture of you leaving at approximately 9:45 p.m., and then returning at approximately 12:25 a.m. Considering your earlier statement where you said you never left the hotel, would you care to explain that?"

"I don't know what to say."

"I'm sure you don't. Perhaps you didn't know it but surveillance videos now have good resolution. As you can see, despite you attempting to cover your face, it *is* plainly noticeable."

"I could argue—"

"Yes, you could argue, but I think anyone would see right through that argument. The woman in the picture is you. No doubt. Moving on, there is the whole question about the second boat we found on the lake. I know you can explain that the same way that your husband did, but how do you explain Ms. Barker's car being parked in your other house in the subdivision across the lake?"

Hemphill looked around, first to Ribs, then the refrigerator, then back to me. "I don't know. Perhaps someone had their times mixed up. I recall going there at some point, but not then."

"Really? The neighbor I spoke with was fairly specific; in fact, she said that you pulled in at precisely 10:12 p.m., and didn't leave again until 11:40 p.m. She even copied the license plate number exactly."

"I don't know."

"And how about the visit to the mall on the day of Mr. Farnsworth's murder?"

"What about it?"

"It doesn't hold up," I said. "Yes, you were at the Dressbarn *prior* to the murder, and yes, you were at the Nike store *after* the murder, but no one can confirm you were anywhere while the murder was being committed."

"That certainly doesn't prove anything."

"You're right. It doesn't. But it will give the jury one more thing to think about."

"If that's all you have, Detective, you better go back to square one."

"We've got a lot more than that, Mrs. Hemphill. And what we have left is the key."

"What?"

"We have the jewelry," I said.

"What about it?"

"We found the jewelry. You remember, the items you swore had been stolen during the faked break-in."

"Great!" she said. "I was beginning to think they were gone. Where did you find them?"

"You know where they were," Ribs said.

"Oh, yes. I forgot you told me. I must have moved them to the other house. I'll notify the insurance company right away."

"That would probably be good," I said. "The last thing you want is to tack insurance fraud on to the other charges."

"What fraud? I said I was going to notify the insurance company."

"Were you planning on telling them about the bracelet also?"

She furrowed her brows. "What bracelet?"

"The one you put in the safe deposit box along with Ms. Barker's necklace," Ribs said. "While you're thinking up an answer, explain how you ended up with Ms. Barker's necklace. We have a picture of her wearing it earlier. And before you go too far with your lies, you need to know that we have video of you depositing the necklace and bracelet in the safe deposit box the day after the murder. And yes, it is date-and-time stamped."

Mrs. Hemphill leaned against the back of her chair and looked at Ribs, then at me. "I guess I should have gotten rid of that damn necklace."

"I guess so," I said. "But you'll have plenty of time to wonder why you didn't. Probably about twenty-five years."

Hemphill smiled. "Maybe I'll write a book," she said. "You never know. It may sell."

MIDNIGHT SWIM

We got Hemphill put in the system, then got her set up with the district attorney's office. Sanchez offered her a minor reduction in sentence if she agreed to testify against her husband, which she was more than willing to do.

She admitted to killing Farnsworth, but swore that Kevin had killed Chlorinda. She said she had been hiding behind some bushes and saw him do it.

I didn't know if he did or didn't but it made no difference to me. I was convinced the guy was guilty.

By the end of the day, Sanchez had made deals with both of them. He admitted he had killed Barker and she admitted to killing Farnsworth. Both got twenty to life.

They weren't happy with the deals, but Sanchez reminded them that Texas puts more people to death than any other state; in fact, it puts more people to death than the rest of the top ten states combined. And she assured them that if this went to trial, she would be seeking charges of first degree murder and asking for the death penalty.

After hearing the news, I went to tell Ribs. He was ecstatic and wanted to celebrate. "Let's go get a few beers, cuz. We'll see if Tip and Connie want to join us."

"Not for me, Ribs. Marissa is cooking dinner, and we're going to spend some time together."

"*Dios mío.* Whipped already."

"Go to hell, Ribs, or I'll tell Rosalee how you talk at work."

He laughed. "Have fun, amigo. See you tomorrow."

"See you then," I said.

When I got home, Marissa's car was in the driveway. I went inside, smelled meatballs—one of my favorites—and saw two bottles of Santa Cristina sitting on the counter, one of them open and already in the decanter breathing.

"What's going on?" I said.

Marissa poured a glass of wine, a healthy portion, handed it to me, and said, "The verdict came in. Guilty on all counts."

"I was confused. Who's guilty of what?"

"You're guilty of not paying attention to me. I'm beginning to not like this job. Maybe you should retire."

"Retire? I'm twenty years away from that."

"I've got enough money. We can live off the interest and still be better off."

I wrapped my arms around her waist and squeezed. "As attractive as that sounds, and as much as I'd love to do it, I can't. I like what I do. And I like coming home to you. If I were here all the time, I might get tired of you."

She pushed me back. "I knew I'd get to the bottom of it. I guess I'll just have to find a new cop."

"While you're looking, please pour me another glass of wine?"

She grabbed the bottle and poured about two sips into a glass. "For the please, you get this. If you want more, you have to beg."

I laughed. "You like to see me beg, don't you?"

"I do. I might start making you beg for *other things*."

I pulled her to me and we kissed again. "For *other things*, I'll beg all night."

She undid a couple of buttons on her blouse, pushed herself toward me, and said, "Start begging."

We ate dinner while we chatted. I told her about the outcome of the case and acknowledged her help and thanked her for it. After a few glasses of wine, we retired to the sofa to relax.

We spent the remainder of the night talking about the case, but switched to vacation spots near the end. "I want to go to Spain," she said. "I've never been there."

I thought about what she said, then responded. "Sounds good. Let's go."

"What! Are you serious?"

"I've never been either, and I'd love to see Barcelona and Madrid. Besides, I have some vacation time coming up. We could go then."

Marissa was already sitting up straight. She wrapped her arms around my neck, almost spilling the wine. "Oh my God, that's perfect, Gino. It's perfect."

I know that the smile on my face reflected how I felt. "Great."

Suddenly, Marissa grew very serious. "Gino. One thing. I don't want you to think I'm trying to take Mary's place. I'm not. All of this business—like shopping with Connie and going out with Rosalee—it's just to make you more comfortable. I—"

I leaned up and moved to her and kissed her like never before. "Marissa, I know why you do what you do, and I love you all the more for it. The bottom line is, I love you. And I'll never stop."

She smiled, and a tear formed in her eye. "Thanks, Gino. I love you, too."

She got off the couch, went to the kitchen and grabbed her purse. "But now, I have to go. I've got some bookwork to do, and it has to be done before the weekend. Besides, now I feel as if I can get some sleep."

"Don't leave," I said.

"I have to," Marissa said, "but why don't you come over to my place tomorrow night. Better yet, come over tonight for a midnight swim. The weather is perfect."

I thought about it a moment, but only for a moment. "Okay. I'll be there."

"Good. And don't forget to forget your bathing suit."

I said, "Don't you mean 'don't *forget* your bathing suit?'"

She smiled wickedly. "I meant *exactly* what I said." As she swung the door shut, she said, "See you tonight."

My heart raced. The way she smiled, and the way she said 'see you tonight' had me all but panting. I went upstairs to shower. I couldn't wait to see her again. Maybe life didn't end with Mary. Maybe the priests were right—maybe there is redemption for everyone.

ABOUT THE AUTHOR

Giacomo Giammatteo is the author of gritty crime dramas about murder, mystery, and family. He also writes non-fiction books including the No Mistakes Careers series.

When Giacomo isn't writing, he's helping his wife take care of the animals on their sanctuary. At last count they had 45 animals—11 dogs, a horse, 6 cats, and 26 pigs.

Oh, and one crazy—and very large—wild boar, who takes walks with Giacomo every day and happens to also be his best buddy.

giacomogiammatteo.com
gg@giacomog.com

ALSO BY GIACOMO GIAMMATTEO

You can see all of my books here.

And you can buy them on the platform of your choice here.

Nonfiction :

No Mistakes Resumes, Book I of No Mistakes Careers

No Mistakes Interviews, Book II of No Mistakes Careers

Misused Words, No Mistakes Grammar, Volume I

Misused Words for Business, No Mistakes Grammar, Volume II

More Misused Words, No Mistakes Grammar, Volume III

No Mistakes Writing, Volume I—Writing Shortcuts

How to Publish an eBook, No Mistakes Publishing, Volume I

How to Format an eBook, No Mistakes Publishing, Volume II

eBook Distribution, No Mistakes Publishing, Volume III

Uneducated

Fiction:

Friendship & Honor Series:

Murder Takes Time

Murder Has Consequences

Murder Takes Patience

Blood Flows South Series:

A Bullet For Carlos: A Connie Gianelli Mystery

Finding Family, a Novella

A Bullet From Dominic

Redemption Series:

Necessary Decisions: A Gino Cataldi Mystery

Old Wounds

Promises Kept, the Story of Number Two

Premeditated

~

OTHER BOOKS COMING SOON:

You can always see the current and coming-soon books on my website.

Fiction:

A Promise of Vengeance (Fantasy)

My first fantasy, and the first book in a four-book series—the Rules of Vengeance. (Three are already written and the fourth is being outlined.)

A Hard Life, the Story of Tip Denton

Memories for Sale (mystery/sf)

The Joshua Citadel (SF novella)

Nonfiction:

Whiskers and Bear—Volume I of the Life on the Farm Series (sent to editor)

Children's Books:

No Mistakes Grammar for Kids, Volume I—Much and Many (Sent to editor)

No Mistakes Grammar for Kids, Volume II—Lie and Lay (Sent to editor)

No Mistakes Grammar for Kids, Volume III—Then and Than (Sent to editor)

Shinobi Goes to School—Life on the Farm for kids. (working on illustrations)

Get on the mailing list and you'll be sure to be notified of release dates and sales.

Mailing list

And don't forget to leave a review!

By the way, if you're an author and you liked the formatting in this book, you might consider us for your next book. Information can be obtained here.

ACKNOWLEDGMENTS

As always, thanks to my amazingly supportive family. But I also want to thank the dedicated beta readers, including Jeanne Haskin, Cary Lory, JJ Toner, Missy, Rose, and Elizabeth. They found the problems I didn't.

www.ingramcontent.com/pod-product-compliance
Lightning Source LLC
Chambersburg PA
CBHW032159180726
48284CB00001B/107